The Grooms arrived C.O.D.

Groom #1—Tanner Jones

He's been looking for love in all the wrong places.
Now he's putting himself on the market—
satisfaction guaranteed!

Groom #2—Hunter Pryde

His marriage to Leah Hampton will be strictly
business. Only he's hoping she'll throw in
a few fringe benefits.

MAIL-
ORDER
GROOMS

When all else fails, U.S. Mail delivers!

Relive the romance...

Two complete novels
by your favorite authors!

VICKI LEWIS THOMPSON

began her writing career at the age of eleven with a short story in the *Auburn Illinois Weekly* and quickly became a byline junkie. Then she discovered she could write books—and she's written a lot of them! In the year 2000, Vicki will see her 50th book on the shelves. Vicki lives in Tucson, Arizona, and has two grown children and a husband who encourages her to write from the heart.

DAY LECLAIRE

and her family live in the middle of a maritime forest on a small island off the coast of North Carolina. Despite the yearly storms and the power outages that batter them, they find the beautiful climate, superb fishing and unbeatable seascape more than adequate compensation. One of their first acquisitions upon moving to Hatteras Island was a cat named Fuzzy. He has recently discovered that laps are wonderful places to curl up and nap—and that Day's son really was kidding when he named the hamster "Cat Food."

MAIL-ORDER GROOMS

VICKI LEWIS THOMPSON

DAY LECLAIRE

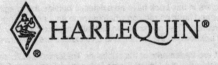

HARLEQUIN®

TORONTO • NEW YORK • LONDON
AMSTERDAM • PARIS • SYDNEY • HAMBURG
STOCKHOLM • ATHENS • TOKYO • MILAN • MADRID
PRAGUE • WARSAW • BUDAPEST • AUCKLAND

HARLEQUIN BOOKS

by Request—MAIL-ORDER GROOMS

Copyright © 2000 by Harlequin Books S.A.

ISBN 0-373-21711-0

The publisher acknowledges the copyright holders
of the individual works as follows:

HOLDING OUT FOR A HERO
Copyright © 1996 by Vicki Lewis Thompson
MAIL-ORDER BRIDEGROOM
Copyright © 1995 by Day Totten Smith

This edition published by arrangement with Harlequin Books S.A.

Visit us at www.eHarlequin.com

Printed in U.S.A.

CONTENTS

Sexy, single—and special delivery!

Holding Out for a Hero
Vicki Lewis Thompson

1

FOR THE HUNDREDTH TIME, Dori Fitzpatrick checked the wall clock. Twenty minutes to go. At exactly 9:00 p.m., Tanner Jones would walk through the door of the Double Nickel Truck Stop and Café with the power to change her life.

Nearly all Dori's customers knew about her date with Tanner and understood the significance of it. But nobody had brought up the subject, which only increased her nervousness. Maybe if she brought it up, her system would settle down a little.

"The best thing about Tanner is that he's not rich," she announced as she moved down the red Formica counter, topping off coffee cups. She'd known most of these truckers for years and they expected a bottomless cup when they sat at her counter. It didn't matter to them that she was about to have her life transformed on this Sunday evening in the West Texas town of Los Lobos.

Heck Tyrrell adjusted his Peterbilt gimme cap. "Just sayin' he ain't rich ain't sayin' much, Dori."

"It most certainly is." Dori emptied the pot and measured fragrant grounds into the basket for a fresh brew. "I wouldn't marry a rich man again if he made love like an angel and looked like Mel Gibson."

"Not everybody with money is like Jimmy Jr.," said the man sitting next to Heck. Travis Neff, a veteran trucker, had given Dori her first tip years ago when she'd started working at the café as a teenager.

Dori started the coffee trickling into the pot, then turned back to Heck and Travis. "Maybe not, but I don't care to take the chance. No rich man will run my life ever again."

Heck set down his cup. "But I sure think you're making a big mistake, taking up with some ol' boy who put his picture in a magazine just to attract women. What kinda person would do that?"

Dori opened her mouth to reply.

"Number five's up," called the cook as he shoved an order of pork chops, mashed potatoes and gravy onto the pass-through from the kitchen.

"That'd be mine," said Travis. He loved to eat and it showed. "For once I agree with Heck," he said. "I don't like the idea of you setting up a date with some stranger from East Texas."

"We've written several letters back and forth." Dori set the steaming plate in front of Travis along with side dishes of applesauce, coleslaw and a basket of rolls. "I don't think of him as a stranger."

"Letters," Travis said with a dismissive shrug as he picked up his fork. "Anybody can write letters. Isn't he from around Dallas somewhere? Those big-city boys are slick as hog fat, Dori. He could have a police record or be one of them left-wingers. He could be—" Travis paused and his round face turned pink "—one of them kinky types...you know what I mean."

Dori took a box from underneath the counter and started restocking sugar packets. "He's a construction worker, and his letters don't sound kinky at all. Besides, I've told y'all why I wrote in to the magazine. Nobody in this town will ask me out, let alone consider something more serious, and that's the plain fact of it, Travis."

"Bunch of lily-livered pansies," Travis muttered into his plate.

"Easy for you to say. You're married," Heck replied in a low voice, glancing around to see who might be listening. Almost every one of the men sitting on counter stools was intent on the conversation, not to mention several others gathered in the café's four booths. A good portion of them drove for Devaney Trucking, the town's chief industry.

"Aw, hell," Heck said in a more normal voice. "Might as well get it out in the open. There's lots of guys in this room who would take you out in a heartbeat, if they didn't think they'd suffer the consequences." He gave a half turn on his stool to survey the room. "Am I right?" The room was silent except for Waylon Jennings crooning from the jukebox.

Dori didn't need to look into the faces of the single men in the restaurant to see every man jack of them was embarrassed by the truth of what Heck had said. She cleared an empty plate from the counter and swept up crumbs with a damp rag as she talked. "Hey, I don't expect anybody to risk his job by crossing the Devaneys. I know good and well Jimmy Jr. has threatened to fire or blackball any driver who so much as buys me an ice-cream cone. I wouldn't *let* any of y'all take that chance. That's why I decided to try this magazine thing."

Travis put down his fork. "Let me take a look at that magazine one more time."

Dori rinsed her cleaning rag in the sink and dried her hands before reaching under the counter for her copy of *Texas Men*, which she'd folded back permanently to the picture of Tanner Jones, East Texas construction worker. Beneath his hard hat shone the bluest eyes she'd ever seen. Tanner Jones wouldn't be so tough to sit across from at the breakfast table every morning, she thought, her heartbeat quickening.

"Don't be getting any gravy on it," she warned as she handed it to Travis. "This picture may turn out to be an heirloom for my children and grandchildren."

The whole counter full of men snorted at that, but she faced them down. "Y'all know that nine is my lucky number. Tanner's bachelor number nine in the magazine. And as if that's not enough, that's the September issue, and I picked it up on September the ninth."

"And you asked him to meet you here at nine tonight." Travis sounded pleased with himself that he'd made the connection. "How come you didn't make it for October ninth?"

"I wanted to, but it didn't fall right, with my day off being Monday. I didn't want to have to come in to work the first day he's in town."

Heck shook his head. "You're way too superstitious, Dori Mae Fitzpatrick."

"Ha." She took a piece of pie out of a clear plastic display case and brought it to one of the truckers who'd signaled to her. She remembered his favorite was apple and he smiled when she brought the right flavor. "I happen to know, Heck Tyrrell, that you have a rabbit's foot dangling from the rearview mirror of your cab. Don't go telling me who's superstitious."

A trucker spoke up from the end of the counter. "I've got a lucky silver dollar from Vegas. I take that dang thing pretty near everywhere I go. Leave Dori alone about her lucky number, Heck. Everybody's got something like that."

"Yeah," Heck grumbled, "but Dori's fixing to spend her life with some ol' boy because he happened to be the ninth bachelor in a matchmaking magazine."

"I am not!" Dori moved around the counter as she added up a ticket for booth number three and placed it facedown on the table. "This first date is just a look-see," she continued, glancing at the clock again. Ten minutes to go. "Don't worry, I'll put Tanner Jones through his paces. And of course, he has to be good with kids, so I'm trying him out right away on Little Jim. Tomorrow the three of us are going into Abilene."

"How's that little cowpoke doing?" Travis asked, munching a roll.

"I just picked up some new pictures." Dori scanned her customers and made sure everyone had what they needed before she reached beneath the counter again and came up with a packet of snapshots. "Last Monday I took him to Abilene Lake. We got a little sun-burned, but it was great." She handed the packet to Travis and noticed the men from booth three coming up to the cash register. "Excuse me a minute, Travis."

Dori rang up the bill and delivered her standard, "Y'all come back," before returning to where Travis and Heck were going through her twenty-four snap-shots. "Isn't he the handsomest boy in the world?"

"Good-lookin' tadpole," Heck agreed. "Where'd all that red hair come from?"

"My side." Dori touched her brunette hair that was caught back in a net for work. "I have some red high-lights, but my grandmother was a flaming redhead. And Little Jim has the spirit to go with that hair!" Dori laughed. Just thinking about her son put her in a good mood. "He has a mind of his own, all right. Those kindergarten teachers better be ready for some surprises when he shows up next fall."

"He'll be in school already?" Travis handed the pictures back to her. "Seems like he was born just last month."

"That's how it is with kids," Dori said. "I'm sure your two were like that. Babies one day, all grown up the next. I just wish..." She didn't finish the sentence. Travis, Heck and many of the men at the counter knew what Dori wished. Jimmy Jr. had taken Dori to court soon after the divorce and obtained custody on the grounds that Dori had to work and put the toddler in day care.

If she'd insisted on a bigger settlement at the time of the divorce, she wouldn't have had to hire someone to watch Little Jim. Her pride had essentially robbed her of her beloved son. Friends had advised her that one reasonable way to get him back was to remarry and prove to the judge that a two-parent household was a healthier environment for Little Jim. Tanner Jones was due in six minutes.

"Say, Dori, sweetheart, what's the chance of getting a cup of coffee down at this end of the counter?"

Dori tensed at the sound of the familiar voice and looked down the length of the counter straight into Jimmy Jr.'s green eyes.

Jimmy lounged on a stool, his Stetson at a rakish angle. His blond good looks were the sort to turn women's heads, and they'd turned hers at the age of eighteen. But she'd outgrown Jimmy Jr. Her hands balled into fists. She should have guessed he'd show up tonight.

"Heard you had some East Texas stud coming in at nine," Jimmy said. "Thought I'd take a look at him."

AS HE CRUISED WEST on Interstate 20 past cotton fields and bobbing oil rigs, Tanner Jones caught the fragrance of the single rose he'd picked up in Abilene. The scent cut through a slight gas smell that told him the engine needed tuning. Considering the odometer read more than a hundred and fifty thousand miles, he was lucky the truck hadn't broken down between here and Dallas. He hadn't thought of that when he'd borrowed one of his employees' pickups to make this trip. There were a lot of things he probably hadn't thought of.

Clothes hadn't been a problem. He'd packed his most worn, comfortable jeans and Western shirts and left the custom-made suits in the closet. He preferred the old clothes, anyway. Sometimes he wondered if he'd be happier living the life of a construction worker. But then he'd have to work for someone else, and he'd never been very good at that.

His independence had paid off, and he'd become one of the richest home builders in East Texas. But recently, it seemed that every woman he'd dated was only attracted to his money. Now that he'd achieved financial security he longed for the basics his parents enjoyed—a cheerful home, a loving mate, children. Ironically, money seemed to be getting in his way.

So here he was driving an old truck to Los Lobos while his shiny new Dodge Ram sat in the garage. The man Dori Fitzpatrick would meet tonight was the real Tanner Jones, he told himself. There was nothing wrong with disguising his wealth to see if a woman could fall in love with him for himself alone. That had been his plan from the moment he'd agreed to appear in *Texas Men*. Nothing in the profile was untrue—just incomplete—and the picture could have been taken on any day he visited one of his construction sites.

But when creating his plan he hadn't figured on battling his honest streak, which ran through him a mile wide, apparently. He pacified his conscience by thinking about how thrilled Dori would be when she eventually found out he was rich. No doubt she'd forgive the white lie.

As the miles ticked off, Tanner looked for the Los Lobos exit. Dori had instructed him to drive through town to the far side until he saw the Double Nickel Truck Stop and Café. She said he could come in on the second exit and miss the town's main street, but she thought he should get a look at where she lived. He was willing to follow her lead, so he flipped on his turn signal at the first exit for Los Lobos, marked Business Loop.

The town limit sign recorded a population of 8,857. Just beyond that, Tanner noticed a huge sign at the fenced entryway to a large lot full of identically painted eighteen-wheeler cabs. The sign read Devaney Trucking. Must be a gold mine, he thought. Positioned on I-20 not far from the intersection of Highway 84, the company was well placed in Texas and nearly dead center between the Atlantic and Pacific coasts. Tanner bet the Devaneys pretty much ran the town of Los Lobos.

He drove past the Prairie Schooner Motel and RV Park where he had reservations for the next week, then on down the main street. The shopping basics were represented—hardware store, bank, post office, clothing store, hair salon—but Tanner figured most people drove to Abilene for major purchases. That's where he'd take Dori for a nice dinner one night, and maybe even some live theater. If nothing looked good to him in Abilene, he could always charter a plane and... Tanner blinked and cursed softly in the darkness. He had to stop thinking like a rich man. The first time he forgot and pulled out a gold card, the ruse would be over.

Then he began to wonder if he remembered how to court a woman without expensive dinners and extravagant gifts. Maybe this wouldn't be quite as easy as he'd imagined. He glanced at his watch and realized it looked far too expensive for the image he was trying to give. After checking the time he took it off and shoved it in the glove compartment.

Dori had agreed to meet him at nine—no sooner and no later. She'd been very specific about that and had even confessed she'd written to him in the first place because he was the ninth bachelor in the September issue of the magazine. He hoped she wasn't too hung up on superstition.

Hell, this whole thing was crazy. They'd probably hate each other on sight. Maybe she'd been entranced by the hard hat and wouldn't care for the way he looked in a worn black Stetson. And what would he talk about? He couldn't describe his work without getting into trouble, and work had been his whole life for the past ten years. He didn't know if he could make conversation about much else.

As for Dori, she might have all sorts of irritating habits. She might not look anything like her picture, and he was basing a lot on that photograph. Her beauty had captured his attention first, but he'd received lots of pictures of good-looking women in the past few weeks. He'd had no way of knowing if the photos were recent or even legitimate. One woman had sent in a magazine clipping of a rising movie star and had claimed to look "just like her."

But Dori's picture had seemed right to him. Especially her eyes, which were a vulnerable soft brown with a touch of sadness and a hint of smoky passion lurking in their depths.

Tanner chuckled and shook his head. What a romantic he was. The expression he'd read as a mixture of sorrow and passion was probably nearsightedness. And all those letters she'd written about loving sunsets more than diamonds, and moonlight more than pearls, might be something she'd copied from a book, not something she truly believed.

Neon glowed up ahead on the right side of the road, and he made out the words Double Nickel. Rows of canopied gas pumps dwarfed the small building housing the café. Several big rigs were parked nearby, along with a few cowboy Cadillacs—fancy pickups with plenty of chrome gleaming in the lights from the parking lot. Tanner's stomach clenched as he realized Dori was inside that cozy little building waiting for him. He could still turn around and forget the whole thing. But he flipped on the right-turn signal. He'd come this far. He might as well see it through.

DORI WEIGHED HER OPTIONS. Technically, she couldn't deny Jimmy Jr. service in the Double Nickel unless he became obnoxious. She removed a cup and saucer from a stack on the drain board, poured Jimmy's coffee and carried it to him, along with a handful of creamer containers. Jimmy would wail about needing more cream in his coffee if she didn't.

Jimmy pushed back his hat with his thumb and winked at her. "Thanks, darlin'."

She looked him in the eye. "If you make trouble with Tanner Jones, I'll call Deputy Holt. So help me, I will."

Jimmy shrugged and glanced down the counter to where Travis Neff still held the issue of *Texas Men*. "Whatcha got there, Travis?"

"This here belongs to Dori." Travis held it out to her.

Dori started down the counter to retrieve her magazine, but Jimmy caught her wrist. "I think I'll have me a piece of pie, too, Dori. Would you get that for me? You know the kind I like."

Dori trembled with fury. "Let go of me."

"Oh." Jimmy looked down at his fingers encircling her wrist. "Force of habit, darlin'." He didn't release her, and his thumb caressed her pulse. "While I'm eating my pie, I'll take a look at that magazine, Travis."

Dori glanced at Travis, who appeared ready to resist. And if he did, he'd no longer be working for Devaney Trucking come morning. Travis had a wife, and kids in college. It was just a magazine, Dori reasoned, not worth having a man lose his job over. She swallowed. "He's welcome to see it, Travis."

Travis looked unhappy but relieved. As he passed the magazine down the counter, Jimmy released Dori's wrist and reached for it. Dori turned toward the pie keeper and pulled out the last piece of lemon meringue. *Someday*, she vowed. But when she made her stand against Jimmy Jr., she wouldn't risk the welfare of innocent bystanders.

"So this is the ol' boy I've been hearing about for days." Jimmy held the magazine at arm's length and squinted at the picture of Tanner. "He don't look so tough to me."

Dori clenched her fists. "Jimmy, I'm warning you..."

"Hey, relax, baby." Jimmy set the magazine beside

his pie plate. "I ain't fixin' to do a single thing except look him over, just like everybody else packed in here. This is the most excitin' thing happening in town tonight."

Dori sighed. She had herself to blame for this mess. Meeting Tanner in such a public place and telling people about it was bound to stir up curiosity. But she'd done it for her own protection. Despite Tanner's wonderful letters, he could be some weirdo. Even the publishers of the magazine warned their women readers to use caution until they got to know the bachelor they'd decided to contact.

Pulling her order pad from her pocket, she wrote out Jimmy's ticket. She wanted to slap it on the counter, but she laid it down carefully and walked away. It was almost nine, and Alice had just come in the door to relieve her.

"Now see what I've done," Jimmy said. "I'm powerful sorry, Dori Mae. I spilled coffee all over your Romeo's face."

Dori had known it would happen the moment she'd given up the fight for the magazine. She could probably order another, if she wanted it as a keepsake. While she waited for Alice to put her purse away in the back and come out to take over, Dori pointedly ignored Jimmy as she finished cleaning up and pocketing her tips. An uneasy silence had fallen over the men sitting at the counter, but none of them made a move to leave.

"I'll find a way to get rid of him," Jimmy said, obviously trying to goad her into a response.

She glanced up at Jimmy and fought the urge to scream that she was never coming back to him, so he might as well get on with his life. But he wouldn't have believed her. He'd bragged to his friends, who had passed on the word to her, that eventually she'd come crawling back, love starved and desperate to be with her son again.

And the truth was that she *was* desperate—longing to greet her son every morning when he awoke and kiss him every night before he went to sleep. And sometimes she desperately craved the comfort—and yes, the excitement—of a man's strong arms. But Jimmy Jr. was not that man.

"I'll discourage him in no time. See if I don't," Jimmy said.

Dori lifted her chin. "Maybe he's the kind who won't discourage so easy."

Then a man walked through the door at exactly nine o'clock. Dori noticed that his eyes were even bluer than in his picture. Tanner Jones had arrived.

2

MINUS THE ROSE, which he'd lost the nerve to take with him into a café full of truckers, Tanner pushed open the door of the Double Nickel. Just inside the entrance he paused to get his bearings and saw Dori at once. After that, he could see no one else.

Her picture hadn't done her justice. Her skin was more translucent, her eyes more luminous, than a mere camera could reveal. She noticed him as quickly as he'd noticed her and she became absolutely still, mirroring his absorption. For a few seconds they just looked at each other. Tanner knew it was the sort of crystallized moment that would live forever in his memory, no matter how things turned out.

"As I live and breathe, if it ain't the famous Tanner Jones."

The comment snapped through Tanner's preoccupation like a whiplash. If someone in this cafe had already recognized him as the owner of Jones Construction, his plan was dead. He glanced warily at the cowboy standing about three feet from him, his hat tilted back and a mocking smile on his handsome face. All conversation in the café had stopped.

"You fooled me at first," the cowboy said into the strained silence. "I thought maybe you'd wear your hard hat and muscle shirt."

Tanner relaxed a little. The guy probably recognized

him from the article in *Texas Men*. And for some reason, he was threatened by Tanner's arrival. Tanner shifted his weight to the balls of his feet so he could sidestep a punch if one came. From the gleam in the guy's eyes, Tanner almost expected it might.

Instead, the cowboy stuck out his hand. "Let me be the first to welcome you to Los Lobos, Mr. Tanner Jones." His exaggerated courtesy reeked of sarcasm. "I'm Jimmy Devaney, Jr., Dori's husband."

Husband. Tanner had wondered what little glitch would pop up to spoil his fantasy of Dori as the perfect woman for him, but this sure as hell hadn't been one he'd expected. He could have sworn Dori had written that she was divorced. Not separated, or thinking of leaving her husband, but divorced.

Then Tanner registered the last name this cowboy had just given him. Devaney. As in Devaney Trucking, the biggest business in town. Wonderful. He shook Jimmy Devaney's hand. "Didn't know Dori was married," he said quietly.

"I'm not. We've been divorced for two years." Her voice had a lazy drawl that he liked, but there was a strong current of tension running beneath her words. She approached him with a small purse slung over her shoulder, bringing with her the scent of fresh flowers. Her cheeks were pink and the dreaminess he'd seen in her deep brown eyes when he'd first walked in had been replaced with anger.

She inserted herself between Tanner and Jimmy Devaney, with her back to Jimmy. Then she took an unsteady breath and managed a smile as she looked up at Tanner. "I'm Dori Fitzpatrick. I'm happy to meet you, Tanner."

Her smile made him forget all about her ex-husband.

It was the most uncomplicated, honest smile he'd seen on a woman in years. He touched the brim of his hat. "I'm happy to meet you, too, Dori."

She gestured toward an empty booth. "How about a cup of coffee?"

"Sounds great."

As he started to take her elbow to guide her in that direction, Devaney grabbed his arm. Tanner released Dori's elbow and shook off Devaney's grasp. Then he turned slowly to face him. "What's your problem, mister?"

Devaney glared at him. "I'd advise you to keep your hands off my wife."

"Dori tells me you're divorced." Tanner kept his voice even. "That makes her your ex-wife, cowboy."

"Dori's the mother of my kid. And I aim to see she don't disgrace him by acting like a little tramp."

Tanner's jaw tightened. "Now that's a real ugly thing to say about a lady, Devaney. I advise you to apologize."

"Apologize?" Devaney waved something in his left hand and Tanner recognized a coffee-stained copy of *Texas Men*. "When she goes and writes to a total stranger and asks him for a date? Where I come from, there's a name for a woman who'd do that!"

Tanner sighed. He was going to have to fight the guy now. "Okay, Devaney," he said, his voice echoing the weariness he felt at the prospect of a fistfight in the parking lot of the Double Nickel Truck Stop and Café. "You win. Let's go settle this outside."

Devaney's jaw worked and he clenched his hands, but he didn't move. "You'd like that, wouldn't you?"

"No, but I thought you could hardly wait."

Dori came up beside Tanner. "You're not going to fight him. I can't let you do that."

"How sweet." Devaney sneered as he glanced around the café. "She's worried about him. Anybody think I should dirty my hands on a drifter from East Texas? Hell, I could buy and sell you twenty times over, Jones."

"If you say so." Tanner now understood the glitch he'd been expecting. If he wanted Dori Fitzpatrick, he'd have to get past this moron, who was unfortunately connected to the most powerful family in town. Tanner figured anybody with a lick of sense would make his excuses and start the long drive back to Dallas. Hell, he was still getting responses from that article in *Texas Men*. Somebody else would turn up, somebody without a belligerent ex-husband in the wings.

"And I got important contacts," Devaney added.

"I'm sure you do." Tanner was sick of the prolonged exchange, but at least it confirmed what he'd suspected. Like most bullies, Devaney was a coward. There would be no fight in the parking lot, at least not until Devaney had rounded up a few of his friends to safeguard the outcome and make sure the attack caught Tanner unprepared. "Tell you what, let's table this discussion for now," Tanner said.

"Table it?" Devaney sneered. "What are you, some chairman of the board?"

Dammit. Tanner sucked in a breath. "Just an expression," he said quickly. "We're both tired. Let's discuss this later."

Devaney pulled his hat over his eyes. "Nothin' more to discuss, sucker. Here's the deal." He pointed a finger at Tanner. "Get too friendly with Dori and I'll make your life so miserable you'll wish you'd never set foot

in Los Lobos." He stormed out of the café without a
backward glance.

The truckers sitting in the café muttered under their
breaths. Then they gradually returned to their meals
and conversations.

Dori touched Tanner's arm. "Forget the coffee. I
should have known this wouldn't work."

Readying his excuses about why he needed to get
back to Dallas, Tanner faced her.

"I'm sorry I made you drive all this way for nothing," she said. The light had died in her brown eyes.
"I'll be happy to pay for your motel room and gas,
though."

The memory of how excited she'd looked when he'd
walked in the door came back to haunt him. He felt his
resolve to leave being replaced with a desire to bring
back that glow of anticipation. He fought that desire
with images of himself beaten to a bloody pulp by Devaney's friends. In a town run by Devaneys, nobody
would come to the aid of a stranger from East Texas.

"Look, I understand completely," Dori said.
"There's no point in taking on somebody like Jimmy Jr.
when there's no reason to."

Ah, but there was. He'd begun to fall in love, just a
little, while reading and rereading her letters and gazing at her picture. In person she was even more beautiful, with a sweetly curved body and dewy skin that
beckoned for his touch. He searched her expression.
"Do you want me to leave?"

A sad smile appeared. "That's not a fair question."

The sad smile did it. The last of his good sense evaporated in its gentle warmth. "Let's have coffee," he
said. Then he watched the glimmer of hope in her eyes

grow and discovered it gave him far too much pleasure. He was in big trouble.

"I guess I owe you at least a cup of coffee," she said, as if she dared not read too much into his suggestion.

"At least that much." Tanner settled across from her in the booth and watched in fascination as she removed the net from her hair. Red-brown tresses the color of polished walnut tumbled over her shoulders and caught the light. She raised a hand and signaled the waitress behind the counter with a grace that captivated him. No wonder Jimmy Devaney, Jr., wanted her back, Tanner thought. Her equal wouldn't exist within a five-hundred-mile radius of this tiny burg.

"Are you hungry?" Dori asked as the waitress approached. "I get a discount here, so order anything you want."

"Coffee's fine," he said.

She looked disappointed.

"Maybe a piece of pie," he added, ridiculously willing to please her. "Apple, if they have it."

Dori smiled at the waitress. "Two cups of coffee, Alice, and a piece of apple pie for Mr. Jones." She glanced at him. "Warm, with ice cream?"

"Sure." He loved the way Dori said "ice," as if it were spelled "ahce." Tanner had grown up in the Midwest, and although he'd lived in East Texas for fifteen years, he'd never picked up a Texas drawl.

Alice wrote the order on her ticket pad. "Cream in your coffee, Mr. Jones?" She studied him closely.

"Black, thanks."

"Good." Alice left with a satisfied expression on her face.

"What's good about black coffee?" Tanner asked Dori.

"Jimmy Jr. drinks it with a ton of cream."

"Oh." It wasn't much, but at least here was a little evidence that somebody wanted Dori to find a new love. He wasn't sure how Alice would stack up in a back-alley brawl, though. Then he remembered the rose sitting on the seat of his truck. Now might be just the right moment to get it. "Would you excuse me a minute?" he asked. "I left something in the truck."

She looked startled, then suspicious. "Uh, sure. I'll, ah, be here."

As he headed out the door, he realized she thought he was never coming back. Well, now was as good a time as any for her to learn that her ex-husband might be a coward, but Tanner Jones didn't operate that way.

DORI WATCHED HIM walk out and berated herself for being surprised. Of course he was leaving. He'd just been waiting for a convenient moment, and her intuition about his strength of character had only been wishful thinking. A soggy blanket of despair settled over her. Until his unimaginative exit just now, she'd liked everything about him, from his startling blue eyes to his scuffed Western boots. She'd liked the way he'd been willing to step outside with Jimmy, although she never would have allowed that to happen. He hadn't seemed like the kind to sneak out of a thorny situation, but that's exactly what he'd done with some lame excuse about getting something from his truck.

Damn, she just might cry. Grabbing a napkin from the metal holder, she pressed it against her eyes and lowered her head while she thought of the one subject that usually kept her spirits up. But even the mental image of Little Jim didn't help much tonight, because now she wondered if she'd ever live in the same house with her child again.

"It's a little wilted, but still pretty," explained a deep baritone near her shoulder.

She sniffed and glanced up into the concerned blue depths of Tanner's eyes. Then her gaze drifted to the deep red rose he held toward her. She looked away quickly and bit her trembling lip as tears quivered on her eyelashes.

"Hey, Dori," he murmured, easing in next to her on the seat and covering her hand with his.

His thigh rested next to hers and the hand holding the rose lay over the back of the booth. The scent of deep, piney woods enveloped her, and she had an almost uncontrollable urge to nestle into the curve of his arm, to soak up his solid strength.

"You thought I was leaving."

She nodded, still not trusting herself to look at him.

He rubbed his fingers across the hollows between her knuckles. "I knew you thought that. I could see it in your eyes when I told you I had to get something out of the truck. Even if I'd have reassured you, you wouldn't have believed me."

His easy caress was the most gentle, loving touch she'd experienced in months. She'd suspected how needy she was, but hadn't understood the depth of it. With almost no effort, he was transforming her wariness into a languorous anticipation for anything he suggested. As she reacted to his touch, she began to worry that her objectivity would disappear in no time, and she had to remain objective. So much was at stake.

She took a deep breath and pulled her hand from beneath his. Then she angled herself to face him, but moved to the far corner of the booth. He watched her with compelling intensity. A tightening of sensual awareness told her she would have to be very careful. She didn't plan to become physically involved with this man until she knew a great deal more about him, but restraining herself wouldn't be easy—not when he could churn her up so completely with just a look.

When he smiled and held out the rose, her breath caught in her throat. There was more tenderness in that one smile than Jimmy Jr. had shown her in the entire seven years of their marriage. And as she absorbed it, she realized she couldn't let this obviously nice guy stay and be subjected to whatever Jimmy might dish out.

She accepted the rose. "I will remember this night, and your gallantry, for the rest of my life," she said softly. She lowered her lashes and buried her nose in the fragrant petals for a long, heady moment before lifting her gaze to his once more. "But I want you to go. I wasn't honest about the situation here, and I've lured you into a trap because I needed..."

"A hero? A knight in shining armor?"

"Something like that. It was selfish to ask you to come in and slay these dragons for me. I'm sure you had dozens of answers to that article in *Texas Men.*"

"Nope. Just yours." His eyes twinkled.

"You folks ready for that pie and coffee now?"

Dori glanced up at Alice, who stood patiently balancing a tray holding two coffees and apple pie à la mode. Dori blushed with embarrassment. She'd forgotten all about the order, which Alice must have held in the kitchen while she waited for the most diplomatic moment to deliver it. The truckers had probably been watching the whole scene between Dori and her new beau with great interest, too.

"Certainly," Dori said, sitting up straighter and placing the rose out of sight on her lap. "Thanks, Alice."

"Sure thing, honey." Alice took elaborate care setting up Tanner's napkin and fork. She put down both cups of coffee and then positioned Tanner's pie squarely in front of him. "If that's not warm enough, or if the ice cream's too melted, just send it back and I'll fix you another one," she said.

"I'm sure it'll be fine."

Alice glanced from him to Dori. "I hope so. I truly do."

After Alice left, Tanner made no move to pick up his fork.

"Start eating," Dori suggested, "before the pie gets cold or the ice cream turns into soup. You can't put off enjoying pie à la mode."

He pushed the plate aside and concentrated the power of those incredible blue eyes on her. "I'm learning that life's like that, too. Which is as good an explanation as any for why I'm not leaving."

Her heartbeat quickened. "Look, I didn't realize how nasty Jimmy Jr. would get if somebody actually showed an interest in me. I guess I was hoping he was mostly hot air."

"Maybe he is. I think we should find out."

She shook her head. "No. Go back to Dallas and pick out somebody else from your bushel basket of letters. I know there must be a lot, with someone who looks like you."

The corner of his mouth tilted upward, which made him even more appealing. "I'll take that as a compliment."

Heat climbed into her cheeks again, but she braved it out. "I guess it was."

"And encouragement. Apparently, you find me reasonably acceptable so far."

That was the understatement of the year, Dori thought. From the way he filled out the shoulders of his Western shirt, she could imagine how he looked without it. The image was enough to make her faint with desire. "I...think you're very attractive." She made a grab for her coffee to hide her nervousness and promptly scalded her tongue.

"And I think you're the most beautiful woman I've seen in a long time." His quiet declaration brought her startled gaze back to his face. "You don't even know how beautiful you are, do you?"

"You're embarrassing me, Tanner."

"Why? You should be used to having people tell you you're beautiful. These truckers should mention it about every five minutes, if they have eyes in their heads."

"Well, they don't mention it. So there."

He regarded her thoughtfully. "They might be afraid Devaney would find out and have a fit. How about him? Did he ever compliment you on your looks?"

"He used to say I was 'passably pretty.'"

Tanner grimaced. "What a guy."

"Well, that's a fair description of me, after all. I wasn't even elected homecoming queen, just one of the attendants."

"You married Devaney right out of high school, didn't you?"

Dori nodded. "My folks tried to talk me out of it, but at eighteen I thought I knew everything. Jimmy Jr. was the catch of the town, three years older than me and the only son of James Devaney who owned the biggest business in Los Lobos. I had you drive past there on the way in."

"I wondered if that was on purpose."

"It was. I wanted you to see how important that name was in Los Lobos, because I thought it would help explain everything, when the time came."

Tanner leaned back against the booth. "I think I get the picture. Devaney snapped you up when you were still naive enough to believe he was a prince and you, being 'passably pretty,' were lucky to snag him. He probably thought he'd undermine your confidence enough to keep you shackled to him."

Dori had considered the very same thing, but hearing Tanner say it gave her self-confidence a big boost.

"But the thing he knew then," Tanner continued, "and what he understands even more now, is that you were the catch, Dori. If he had nothing else going for him, he had vision. He could imagine how you'd grow more beautiful every day. Only he didn't count on your spirit being stronger than his."

She drank in his words as if she were dying of thirst. "It's been so hard, Tanner. Especially after he took Little Jim away."

Tanner leaned forward. "And when am I going to meet your son?"

With a great effort, she brought herself back to reality. Not looking at him made the next statement easier. "You're not. I want you to head back tomorrow and forget all about me."

He regarded her quietly. "No can do."

She kept her face averted as she swallowed the lump that rose in her throat. "Of course you can. Just get up right now and walk out of here. Be smart, Tanner. Do it."

He cupped her chin and guided her face around until she was forced to look into his eyes. "I hate the idea of dealing with a jerk like Devaney, and I'd rather not have to. But when I walked into the Double Nickel tonight and saw you, I felt as if I'd won the lottery. I can't allow Jimmy Devaney, Jr., to spoil my chances with you."

She stared at him, her senses reeling from his touch and the magnetism of his gaze. *I felt as if I'd won the lottery,* he'd said. "What time is it?" she murmured.

Looking perplexed, he nevertheless released her chin to glance at his bare wrist. An untanned strip of skin revealed where he normally wore a watch, but for some reason it was gone. He frowned and looked up at the clock on the wall behind her. "Almost ten. Why?"

"No. Tell me exactly."

"Nine fifty-nine."

She smiled at him. "I thought so."

"I suppose that's significant because it has two nines in it?"

"It's a really lucky number for me, Tanner." A Mac Davis song provided a backdrop to the murmur of voices in the café as she gazed at him and dared to hope that he represented a change in her fortunes.

"A lucky number for me, too, I guess. From the look on your face, you've decided to let me stay."

She took a deep breath. "Yes."

"Then how about a little walk in the moonlight, Ms. Fitzpatrick?"

"I'd love it."

He reached for his billfold, pulled out some money

and tucked it under his saucer. "Let's go." He held out his hand to her.

Dori picked up her rose and scooted across the seat toward him. Before she took his hand, she glanced at the denomination on the folded bill he'd left for Alice, and she gasped. "Tanner, that's way too much."

"I don't care. It was worth every penny. Come on."

Dori snatched up the money and shoved it at him. "Take this back. I'll settle with Alice on Tuesday."

"No. I—"

"Tanner, are you trying to dazzle me by throwing money around? Because that doesn't impress me one bit. I told you that in my letters."

Tanner looked away and rubbed a hand over his face. When he turned back, he smiled and took the money she held out, but she could tell it wasn't an easy thing for him to do. "Thanks, Dori. Thanks a lot."

"Sure thing." As she left the booth and walked out of the café with her hand in his, Dori vowed to watch Tanner's spending habits carefully. She appreciated generous tippers as much as any waitress, but not if a person couldn't afford the extra. Tanner might be gorgeous, courageous and kind, but if he couldn't handle money she wanted to know it before she or her heart made any promises.

3

TANNER SCANNED THE AREA looking for any sign of Devaney when he and Dori walked out into the café parking lot. The air was surprisingly warm for the middle of October, and Dori's ex-husband was nowhere in sight.

Dori glanced up into the sky. "There is a moon tonight," she said. "I was hoping it could be full, but instead it looks sort of—"

"Like a guy with a beer belly," Tanner finished for her.

Dori laughed and he wondered how many jokes he could come up with so he could make her do that again. Her laughter contained a ripple of sensuality that suggested moments to come, experiences they didn't know each other well enough yet to share. A diesel pulled away from the gas pumps and its air brakes wheezed before it rumbled down the road toward the interstate. The fumes didn't add much to the ambience, and Dori's highly visible white uniform was making Tanner uneasy. He wasn't going to back away from a fight, but he'd rather not be ambushed now, before...before what? Before he'd even had a chance to kiss her? Maybe.

She glanced up at him shyly. "I'm out of practice with this sort of thing, but I remember when I was in high school, Jimmy Jr. and I used to drive out one of the back roads to be alone."

He gave her a quick look.

"Not that I'm suggesting we rush into anything physical," she added quickly. "In fact, I think that's a big mistake couples often make."

"Probably," he agreed with some reluctance.

"But we could take that moonlit walk you mentioned, and get to know each other."

"Are you sure you trust me enough to go out to a deserted back road with me?"

Her expression was adorably serious. "Nowadays that could work both ways. Maybe I'm planning to plunge a knife into your heart and steal you blind. Women do that sort of thing, too."

He realized that. Figuratively speaking, he'd suspected those were the motives of the past couple of women he'd dated, which was why he was here with Dori, who professed not to care about material wealth. That reminded him of his role as a hand-to-mouth construction worker. "But that would be a waste of time, trying to steal from somebody like me," he said. "You're the one who should be careful, considering you have the more valuable assets."

Dori gave him a wry smile. "I'm certainly not a virgin anymore, Tanner."

"I didn't expect you to be. Little Jim had to come from somewhere, didn't he?" He looked around the parking lot. "Where's your car? You can show me this lonely road where we can be alone."

She ushered him over to a somewhat battered white Pontiac Sunbird convertible. "I think it's warm enough to put the top down," she said once they'd climbed into the car and she'd laid the rose across the dashboard. They each unlatched their side and she lowered the canvas top. Then she reached across his knees, brushing them just enough to make him a little crazy, and opened the glove compartment.

The city women he'd known had always been concerned about their hair becoming disarranged, so her preparations for driving with the top down intrigued him. She took out an elasticized piece of fabric from the glove compartment and wound it around her hair at the nape of her neck. He would have loved to do it for her, but watching her efficient movements as she worked with the silky strands was almost as inspirational. Before this evening ended he hoped he'd be allowed to run his fingers through her glorious hair. Surely that wouldn't be pushing her self-imposed limits. After all, the whole purpose of *Texas Men* was to bring couples together, and not just for conversation.

She backed the car out of the parking space and headed toward town, but before she reached the main drag she swung left onto a two-lane road. A small subdivision on the right gave way to cotton fields anchored with square little structures, some with lights glowing from the windows.

He turned his head to watch strands of her hair work loose from their tie and whip around her cheeks. "Where do you live?" he asked.

"On the other side of town. I found a small house for rent not far from the Devaneys'. Little Jim's bedroom window is on the second floor, and I can see his light from my backyard."

Tanner's heart wrenched, imagining Dori standing in her yard staring at that shining square of light that represented her son's presence. "It sounds as if you came out of that divorce with nothing. How did that happen?"

"My own stupid fault. I was so sick of Jimmy Jr.'s using his money to get what he wanted that I asked for the minimum child support and no alimony. Jimmy Jr. thought I'd come running back after a few months of poverty. When I didn't, he got tired of waiting and sued for custody of Little Jim on the grounds that he could give him a better home. He won. That's it."

Partway through the explanation Tanner began regretting that Devaney hadn't instigated a fight in the parking lot. Tanner would have loved an opportunity to punch the guy right now.

"When I wrote to you, I didn't put all my cards on the table," Dori said.

Neither did I. Tanner's conscience pricked him. "For example?"

"What I said is true, as far as it goes. I am looking for male companionship."

Her statement sounded so formal, he couldn't resist teasing her. "You could get a little boy dog."

She blew out an exasperated sigh. "You know what I mean."

"Not really." He gave her an amused glance. "You have all those truckers to talk to nearly every day."

"All right! I miss being held, being kissed and...all that. Is that plain enough for you?"

"It's music to my ears, Dori." *And damn stimulating to the rest of me, too.*

"But don't you get the idea that I'm easy!"

"I would never get that idea."

"I mean it! Because my real reason for wanting to get married again has nothing to do with sex."

"That's too bad."

"I'm being perfectly honest with you, Tanner. Stop making fun of me."

"Sorry." But he was having trouble controlling his thoughts as they skimmed down the moonlit road and the houses became few and far between. The air streaming past his cheeks was cool, but not cold. It was a perfect night for lovers, and here was Dori talking about kissing and...all that.

"I've been getting advice from friends, and they think if I remarry and establish a two-parent household, I'll stand a better chance of getting Little Jim back. That's the real reason I wrote to you, Tanner. So if that makes you mad, I'll turn this car around and head straight for the Double Nickel."

Tanner knew he couldn't sound as disappointed as he felt or Dori really would cancel the whole thing. Her son was obviously the most important person in the world to her, and he couldn't blame her for wanting him back. Her solution was logical and practical, even if it took the romance right out of the situation they were in. He was simply the means to an end.

Hell, if she wanted a husband in a hurry, he could propose now and in no time enjoy those conjugal rights he'd been dreaming about ever since he first saw her. No time for courtship or falling in love, but a whale of a good time in bed, no doubt. Dori wouldn't welch on that part of the bargain, and she might even enjoy it.

He spoke carefully. "If all you really want is a husband, then why don't we fly up to Vegas and get married tonight? By tomorrow you can begin filing those papers to get custody of your little boy."

Her screeching stop and abrupt U-turn caught him by surprise and he whacked his shoulder against the car door. "Hey! Take it easy!"

"I won't," she said through clenched teeth. "And you can go straight to Dallas and be damned!" She peeled out in a spurt of gravel that sent the rose tumbling into his lap.

He was thrown back against the seat as she bore down on the gas. "What? What did I say? I was only trying to give you what you wanted!" He wondered if she always drove like a maniac.

"That is *not* what I want."

He glanced at the speedometer and decided it would help his peace of mind if he didn't look at it again as the wind created by her speed buffeted them. "But you said—"

"My goal is to provide a two-parent household for Little Jim. But I intend to do it *right*. What you have in mind is like throwing up a house with warped wood and rusty nails, hoping the whole thing will hold together after you slap some stucco over the crooked parts! My daddy's in construction, too, and he taught me that nothing's worth building unless it's built to last!"

Tanner forgot about the perils of taking a Texas farm road at ninety miles an hour as her statement hit him like a bowling ball aimed at his chest. He'd been waiting a lifetime to hear a woman say that. "Turn the car around."

"Not until you take back what you said."

"I take it back! I didn't like the idea, either, but I felt so sorry for you, wanting custody of your little boy, that I—"

"Sorry for me?" she cried, and stepped down harder on the gas. "That's worse!"

"Okay, not sorry! Forget sorry! Sympathetic! God,

Dori, I want to help! Stop this damned car so we won't be killed before I can explain!"

Fortunately, the road was deserted, because Dori burned rubber as she slammed on the brakes, throwing them both hard against the seat belts. She turned her head in his direction. Her dark eyes blazed and her jaw was set. "Okay, start explaining."

He took a steadying breath. "You drive fast."

"Only when I'm mad. And never when Little Jim's in the car. Now talk, and you'd better not make any more immoral suggestions, or so help me, I'm taking you straight back to the Double Nickel."

Unsnapping his seat belt was a calculated risk. If this didn't work and only increased her anger, he'd be socked around like a punching bag when she peeled out again. He took off his hat and set it, along with her rose, on the dashboard before facing her. "I'm sorry I suggested getting married before we could learn to know each other, learn to love each other." He closed the gap between them slowly, as if she were a wild animal whose confidence he must win. "You're right. That would be a mortal sin."

She watched him warily but with complete absorption. He touched her cheek, and she didn't flinch. Good.

"I won't insult you like that again, Dori." Her cheek was softer than the petals of the rose he'd brought her. Desire burned slow and steady in his groin, but his touch was light, his tone gentle. "Please give me a chance to show you I know how to build without rushing."

Her angry gaze mellowed and her lips parted ever so slightly.

He smoothed a strand of hair back behind her ear.

"If you'll let me, I'll put up a solid foundation, and only use the truest wood and the strongest nails." He drew closer, and sweet heaven, she didn't move away. "This is the most important task I'll ever have in this world," he murmured as her wildflower scent threatened his control. "Trust me, and I'll do everything in my power to get it right."

Then he kissed her, slowly and with a restraint that nearly killed him. Velvet and honey beckoned him to deepen the kiss. He almost gave in and took her fully. But a shred of sanity remained, and he lifted his head to gaze into dark eyes that spoke of surrender. He wanted to shout with joy, but he swallowed his triumph and reminded himself that he'd only mortared the first brick in place. Heart pounding, he settled back in his seat and buckled his seat belt. Then he replaced his hat and tugged on the brim, as if for emphasis.

She sat looking at him for a full minute. Then, with a small smile, she swung the convertible in a lazy turn and headed away from civilization once more. He closed his eyes in gratitude. Maybe this argument would be the rockiest part of their relationship, he thought. Then he remembered Devaney. But after that kiss he'd vastly increased his estimate of what he'd tolerate just to be near Dori Fitzpatrick.

DORI GRIPPED THE WHEEL tight to keep from trembling. No man had ever talked to her like that, echoing her belief in the sanctity of marriage, a belief she carried like a precious jewel deep in her soul despite her disillusionment with Jimmy. A first kiss had never felt like that, either—so rich, yet so brief. She wanted more, although after all her speeches she couldn't let Tanner know that. At least not yet.

Maybe everything had to do with her lucky number. She'd never put it to such a critical test, but Tanner seemed to be the one she'd been destined for all her life. Still, before she became too dizzy to think clearly, she'd better find out more about this apparent dream man.

"I've—" She paused and cleared her throat. Talking wasn't so easy after a kiss like Tanner's. "I've explained why I wrote in to the magazine," she said. "But I've wondered ever since I saw your picture why in the world you were in it."

He hesitated a few seconds before answering. "I guess the simple truth is I was lonely."

"Lonely? Was there a plague that killed off all the women in Dallas?"

He chuckled.

"Come on, Tanner. I may be a small-town girl, but I'm not stupid. If you were lonely, all you'd have had to do was stroll into one of those singles' bars I've heard about and find yourself somebody. I guarantee women would be hanging all over you, with a body like yours." Dori realized what she'd said and winced. So much for playing it cool. "What I meant to say is—"

"Don't change a thing, Dori." He was laughing now. "I liked the statement the way it was."

"Don't be getting a big head, Mr. Jones. Handsome is as handsome does. So, did you have dates or not?"

"I had dates," he admitted.

"Ha. I knew it. You'll have to come up with a better reason than loneliness for putting your picture in that magazine."

"Nope. That's it. I had dates, but they always seemed to be with the wrong kind of women for me. I couldn't imagine taking any of them home to my mom and dad and introducing them as my wife."

My wife. The phrase, coming from Tanner, sounded warm and intimate, the exact opposite of the belligerent, possessive way Jimmy had always said it. "That's important to you, what your folks think of your wife?"

"Yep, sure is."

"And what wouldn't your parents have liked about these women you've been dating?"

"They seemed to be focused on material things."

Dori smiled, relieved to have something make sense at last. "Well, I can tell you why. Flashing twenty-dollar bills around the way you did in the café is a surefire way to attract women who like spending money." She sent him a look of triumph.

"You may have a point."

"Of course I do. Now, I don't think much of a stingy man, either, but you can't give a woman the impression you plan to buy her any little thing her heart desires. Greedy women will be on you like flies on horse poop."

"What if I told you I want to buy you any little thing your heart desires?"

She turned down a dirt road and slowed so as not to stir up too much dust. "In the first place, I wouldn't believe a word of it. Unless you planned to run up a huge debt. Don't forget, I've lived around construction workers all my life. My daddy and momma had to leave Los Lobos and move to San Antonio because that's where the work was. Just about killed them to leave me and Little Jim, especially when I had to go through all that trouble. They tried to loan me money to hire a good lawyer, but I couldn't take it. They don't have any to spare. I'm sure you don't, either. Throwing money around makes me think a man is either stupid or trying to make up for some sort of sexual inadequacy."

Tanner seemed to be caught in a coughing fit.

Concerned, Dori pulled to the shoulder of the road and shut off the ignition. "What's wrong? Are you allergic to dust or something?"

"No," he choked out.

She realized he was laughing. That had been the cause of his coughing fit. "What's so funny now?"

"Which—" He gasped and shook his head. "Which do you think I am?"

"Which what?"

"Stupid or sexually inadequate?"

"Oh." She remembered his potent kiss and doubted he was lacking in that area. Neither did he seem particularly stupid. "Well, I'll make an allowance for this being an unusual situation. But if you kept doing that, I'd be worried."

"With luck I'd get the stupid label."

Her body warmed at his implication that soon she'd have discovered he wasn't inadequate. "People in our circumstances have to be careful with money, Tanner. I don't put a great deal of importance on it, but on the other hand, we need a certain amount to live on, and there's always our old age to be considered."

He was quiet for a moment. "I got the strangest tingle down my spine when you said *our old age.*" He turned to her. "What do you think, Dori? Is there a chance we'll grow old together? Can you picture rocking chairs on the porch and visits from the grandkids?"

Her heart thudded in her chest. "I don't know."

He opened his door and unlatched his seat belt. "Come on. Let's take that walk in the moonlight."

When she joined him at the front of the car he slipped his fingers through hers and they started down the dirt road as if they'd been taking walks together for years. Water ran in an irrigation ditch nearby, filling the air with the scent of rain. Dori tried to remember a single time she'd ever taken a walk with Jimmy Jr. They'd driven out to the back roads when they were dating, of course. But Jimmy hadn't wanted to leave the car, or more specifically, the back seat.

Dori paused and lifted her chin skyward. "Look up," she said. "And take off your hat."

He lifted off his hat by the crown and held it against his thigh as he gazed into the night sky. "My God. I've never seen so many stars. They go all the way to the horizon."

"Because there's nothing to block them. No mountains, almost no trees. You should see a sunset out here, Tanner. The whole sky's on fire."

He stood quietly for a while. "It's not just Little Jim holding you in Los Lobos, is it?"

"No. I was raised here, and I got used to having all that empty space around me. When I go where there are lots of trees, or mountains cutting out the view, I get claustrophobia." She also suspected why he'd asked the question. His home was East Texas. "There's talk of construction work picking up in the area," she said. "My daddy's keeping track of it, because he and Momma would love to move back."

When he didn't respond right away, she glanced at him. He was staring off into the distance, seemingly lost in thought.

"I know it seems stark at first, but give yourself a chance to get used to the openness," she said. "How long have you lived in East Texas?"

He brought his attention back to her. "About fifteen years." He squeezed her hand and replaced his hat as they started down the road again. Crickets chirped in the dry grass beside the road. "It's not the terrain that I'm in love with, although some of it's real pretty, Dori. I'd like you to see it. Lakes so blue you'd swear somebody dropped food coloring in them. But the... business opportunities are better there."

"You need to talk to my daddy. What's your trade?"

"I've done a little of everything. I have both a carpenter's and an electrician's license. I can frame when necessary and drywall in a pinch."

"Goodness, Tanner. You could find a job around here, I'll bet." She paused, becoming unsure of herself. "If you wanted to," she said more softly. "We shouldn't get ahead of ourselves, should we? I mean, you haven't even met Little Jim yet."

"Tomorrow, right?"

"It's my day with him. He wants to go see the Power Rangers movie again, and it's finally come back to the budget movie house in Abilene. That may not seem too exciting, but—"

"Dori, you have something to learn." He pulled her to a stop and caught her other hand to bring her around in front of him. "Just being with you at last is exciting to me. And I think something low-key like going to the movies is a perfect way to start out with Little Jim. Besides, I don't know who the Power Rangers are. Sounds as if I'd better learn if I expect to have anything in common with him."

"That's for sure." She smiled with relief that he approved of her plans. "I thought that would be a low-cost thing we could all do together, and he loves McDonald's, so we don't have to spend a lot of money entertaining him. He's not used to that from me, anyway. Just from Jimmy Jr."

"I think I can manage a budget movie house and McDonald's," Tanner said with a trace of sarcasm. "Maybe I can even squeeze out enough for an icecream cone on the way home."

"Now, don't take that tone! Remember what I said about throwing money around."

He chuckled. "I doubt I'll ever forget. Every time I reach for my wallet I'll wonder if I'm displaying my sexual inadequacies."

She gazed at him standing before her in the moonlight, his face cast in shadow from the brim of his hat. In his yoked Western shirt and snug-fitting jeans he projected the epitome of all her sexual fantasies. Her pulse quickened and she couldn't look away.

"You'd better stop that," he said.

"Stop what?" she murmured.

"Looking at me like that."

"Why?"

"Because it makes me want to kiss the living daylights out of you."

The blood sang in her ears. "Maybe that's exactly what I want you to do."

4

TANNER HADN'T HEARD such a tempting invitation in a long while. The first kiss had been an experiment and could have become a disaster, but this time Dori had asked.

She stood before him, her uniform carving an alabaster silhouette against the night sky. Stars twinkled around her shoulders and tangled in the windblown tresses of her hair. Her gaze lifted to his with the innocence of a child, but the seductive curve of her mouth suggested the passion of a woman. Tanner was too entranced to move.

She smiled and guided his hands around her waist. "You're not going to turn shy on me now, are you?"

"Not shy, just dazzled." His fingers encountered the warm cotton of her uniform. He discovered he could span her waist with his hands as he drew her close and savored the first soft contact with her breasts.

"My goodness." Her breathing became shallow as she gazed up at him. "I don't recall ever dazzling a man before."

"I'm sure you have." His glance traveled over her face, memorizing the graceful arch of her eyebrows, the fathomless depths of her eyes, the beckoning fullness of her mouth. "You just didn't know it."

"You'd better not be overcome by it." She reached for his hat and dangled it from the brim behind his back as she wound her arms around his neck. "You haven't kissed me yet."

Her taunt almost destroyed his control, but he took a deep breath and maintained his equilibrium. She might be used to a grab-and-grope kind of guy, but he wanted to separate himself from that type of low-life lover. Smiling, he slid his fingers through her luxuriant hair and found the elastic fabric holding it captive. "When I was a kid I was always the slowest at eating an ice-cream cone, too. I figured when something was that good, you should make it last." He eased the circle of material from her hair and tucked it into his back pocket. "And this," he continued, burying his fingers in her hair once again, "is going to be very good."

"Oh." The word came out almost as a sigh.

"And very slow." He lightly massaged her scalp and combed his hands through her hair, reveling in the silken richness that slid through his fingers.

Her eyes drifted closed in pleasure.

"You are a rare and beautiful woman, Dori."

Her eyelids fluttered open and she gazed at him.

"One who deserves to be treated with tenderness and care." He bunched her hair in his fist and inhaled its sweet aroma before releasing it, letting it tumble down the slope of her breast. "One who deserves a lover who takes his time."

"You're a sweet-talkin' man, Tanner," she said. "I've been warned about men like you."

"Have you?" He cupped her cameo-perfect face in both hands and brushed his thumbs across her elegant cheekbones. Every touch bought a jolt of pleasure that settled deep within him and fed the fire. "And what have you been warned about?"

"Momma always said a sweet-talkin' man could break your heart."

"So can an ugly-talking one," he said gently.

A flash of sorrow in her eyes made his heart ache. "True," she whispered.

"I don't intend to break your heart." He dropped a light kiss on her brow, and when she closed her eyes once more in surrender, he moved his lips to each quivering eyelid. "I intend to make it sing."

She took a long, shuddering breath as he feathered kisses at her temple, her earlobe, the curve of her jaw. As he dipped to the hollow of her throat, he savored the creamy texture of skin that heated beneath his lazy ministrations. When his lips returned to her cheek and found the corner of her mouth, she moaned softly. He moved with deliberate care to the other corner. She murmured his name.

"I'm here." He hovered close and drank in the warmth of her breath on his face. "Right here." When at last he brought his mouth down to hers, the pleasure was so intense he felt as if he might explode in her arms.

He abandoned himself to the ripe bounty, growing dizzy on the riches she offered. He'd had no idea, he thought fleetingly. No idea at all. He felt himself drowning in her eagerness as she parted her lips and invited him inside. He shifted the angle of his mouth to go deeper and she welcomed him with a little whimper that roused him to a frenzy of wanting—wanting that made him crush her closer and increase the pressure on those sweet lips. Wanting that had to be overruled. Somehow.

With a groan he wrenched his mouth from hers.

Chest heaving, he relaxed his grip and stepped back, but the look in her eyes still held him prisoner.

She struggled with her breathing, too. "I...think you...did," she managed to whisper.

He fought for air and cleared his throat. "Did what?"

"Kissed...the living daylights out of me."

Laughter helped, but he was still trembling with need. "Unfortunately, that's not all I want to do right now."

Her gaze drifted downward to the aching bulge in his jeans. "That's not unfortunate," she murmured. "Just premature."

"Would you think I'm crude if I asked by how much?"

Her dark eyes sparkled. "Are you asking for a construction timetable?"

"Yes...no. No." He pushed aside the urge to haul her against him for another round. "But if we're going to postpone making love to each other, you'll have to help me out."

"I will, Tanner." Her smile was mysterious and knowing. "If you hadn't stopped just now, I would have stopped you."

"If you say so," he said cautiously, not quite sure he believed it. She was still too close for comfort, and he started to back away from the temptation she presented.

She grabbed his arm. "Careful where you step. I dropped your hat while you were kissing me."

"Did you now?" He gave her a long look.

"Well, yes. I got a little carried away, but I still could have stopped you. I was in command of myself enough for that."

"I see."

"Don't be difficult. Certainly you agree that we need to get acquainted on many levels before we satisfy ourselves sexually?"

"Of course," he said. The concept of satisfying themselves, especially with the delightful drawl she gave the word *satisfy*, sounded pretty darned appealing at the moment.

Her eyebrows lifted as if she expected a more complete answer.

"I'm sure it's a very good idea to become friends before we become lovers." He tried to say it with conviction.

"I've read a lot on the subject," she said. "You see, if we're friends first, and the lovemaking isn't perfect, we'll be able to work through that."

He couldn't help laughing. "After that kiss, you doubt whether we'll be good together? Get real, Dori. Physically, we're a perfect match. You know it and I know it."

A pulse beat in her throat, and she swallowed before replying. "Okay, let's say we are physically compatible, and we make love tonight."

His heart thudded in his chest. He'd give several years of his life for that chance.

Her voice quivered just a little, betraying her banked passion, but she soldiered on with a determination he found endearing. "If we made love tonight," she said, "we could be blinded by sexual excitement and miss the signs that we weren't compatible otherwise."

He grinned and stuck out his hand. "Meet Tanner Jones, who's already a blind man."

She batted his hand away. "That's ridiculous. One

little kiss. Surely you can still be objective about our relationship."

"Speak for yourself."

She sighed mightily. "Then apparently I have to do the job for both of us. Momma always said men think with their...male equipment."

Tanner chuckled and turned around to retrieve his hat. As he dusted it off, he glanced at her. "And what were you thinking with when you dropped my hat in the dirt?"

"I...I was—"

"Dori, we're no different. Both of us are crazy to make love, but if you want to wait, we'll wait. It won't be easy, but I guess when we finally do give in, the whole experience will be better." He paused and gazed at her. "If that's even remotely possible."

Dori clasped her hands in front of her and gave him a long, approving glance.

He pointed a finger at her. "And stop that. I'm only human, and that look is what got us started in the first place."

"I'm just so pleased with you, Tanner. That's all."

"Pleased with me?" He didn't think any woman had said those words to him before. He kind of liked it, but he wasn't sure he understood what she meant. "Why?"

"For respecting my wishes."

He thought about that while he adjusted his hat. It didn't take much imagination to picture Devaney riding roughshod over any idea she had, so he guessed it would be a big deal to her if a man paid attention to what she said. He shrugged. "I've gone out with women who didn't really mean it when they told me no. Unfortunately for them, I always stop when a woman asks me to. I don't enjoy playing those guessing games."

"I don't play games."

"I'm counting on that." He longed to touch her again but didn't dare. He braced his hands on his hips to keep himself from reaching for her. "Better take me back, Dori."

"Right." She started down the road, and he fell into step beside her. "You did make reservations at the Prairie Schooner Motel and RV Park, like I suggested?"

"I did." And secretly he'd hoped he could cancel that reservation, but it didn't look as if Dori would invite him home with her tonight. His more noble self argued that she was absolutely right in delaying their lovemaking. But his baser self was frustrated as hell.

AFTER LEAVING TANNER at the Double Nickel, Dori drove home to her two-bedroom tract home. Although most of her neighbors were low-income families struggling to get by, they kept up their yards and applied paint to the wooden trim of the stucco homes when necessary. Cardboard pumpkins and witches were taped to many front windows in anticipation of Halloween two weeks away. It was the sort of street she could feel safe taking little Jim trick-or-treating on—if she'd be allowed to do that this year. Halloween fell on a Thursday, which wasn't her day. Her jaw clenched at the reminder of all Jimmy Jr. had stolen from her.

She wasn't surprised to see Jimmy's big truck backed up into her driveway, blocking her way into her garage. She half expected him to turn on the spotlights mounted on the cab roof in an effort to frighten her into a dazed panic the way he trapped deer when he went hunting at night.

She pulled up at the curb so he'd have a way out when he left. And he was definitely leaving.

As she got out of the car he materialized from the shadows and sauntered toward her. "Where you been, Dori Mae? It's after eleven, and accordin' to Travis Neff, you left the Double Nickel at nine-thirty."

"You should be ashamed of yourself, making Travis spy on me like that."

"It just came up in conversation when I dropped in there about ten. After all, you and that ol' boy from Dallas were making quite a spectacle of yourselves. Can't expect people not to talk."

"Go home, Jimmy." She could smell beer on his breath, but he wasn't drunk. His speech was too precise, his gaze too clear, for him to be impaired by alcohol. She started past him.

He stepped in front of her again. "What do you think you're doin', bringing that ol' boy to town? Trying to make me jealous, Dori Mae?"

"No." She hated the thought that he'd create a scene in her front yard. Some of the neighbors had been a little suspicious of her moving in. Not only was she the only divorcée on the block, she'd defied the powerful Devaneys to gain that status, which labeled her a troublemaker. But in the two years she'd lived in the neighborhood, she'd proven to everyone that she could live as respectable a life as the traditional families surrounding her. Screaming fights on the front lawn weren't part of that picture.

"Then maybe you're getting a little lonely. Is that it, darlin'?"

She had an uneasy feeling where this was headed.

"Because if you want a little action, you know right

where to come," he drawled. "We had us some good times in bed, sugar."

She remembered that he'd had some good times. At first she'd been happy to make him feel good and figured eventually he'd want the same thing for her. Then she'd begun to realize that he was as selfish in lovemaking as he was in everything else. "That's over with, Jimmy."

"I'll be damned if it is." He made a grab for her, but she pushed him away. "Don't be like that, sweetheart," he whined, but he stayed put. A few months after the divorce he'd tried to force himself on her and she'd kneed him in the crotch. A friend had suggested she might require some self-defense to handle Jimmy, and she'd practiced with a dummy she'd made from an old pair of jeans stuffed with rags. Jimmy hadn't tried anything similar since.

"Look, I'm only trying to get on with my life," she said. "And I wish you'd do the same."

"But that's the problem. You belong in my life, but you're too danged stubborn to see it. Little Jim misses you something fierce."

Dori's heart twisted at the mention of her son. "Then let him live with me," she said, although she knew she was wasting her breath.

"Here?" Jimmy swept an arm back toward her little house. "Is that how you want him to grow up? You don't even have a computer, Dori Mae. In fact, you don't have a damn thing to offer that boy."

Except all my love. But she didn't say it. "Let me by, Jimmy. It's late, and we both have things to do tomorrow."

"Don't think I don't remember tomorrow's Monday. That ol' boy from Dallas better be gone tomorrow. I don't want him within ten miles of Little Jim. You got that?"

"Good night, Jimmy." She shoved past him and started toward her front door, opening her purse on the way. She kept pepper spray on her key chain.

He didn't follow her, but he didn't leave, either. "You could lose those Mondays, you know," he said, raising his voice. "If the judge was to hear that you'd been behaving like a common streetwalker in front of the boy, he'd probably want to take those Monday visitations away."

She winced at how that would sound to any neighbors with their windows open on this warm night. She put the key in the lock with trembling fingers. Jimmy's threat was ridiculous, of course. But she'd thought his threat about getting custody of Little Jim had been ridiculous, too.

"It's just your pride making you act this way, Dori Mae. You can't admit you made a mistake walkin' out on me. That's okay. I won't ask you to apologize, like some guys might. Just come back, and everything will be fine."

Dori was afraid any response would only escalate the conflict. She opened the door.

"You'll come back," Jimmy called out as she stepped inside. "I guarantee you'll come back!"

Dori closed the door and latched the dead bolt. Shaking, she leaned against the doorjamb. She'd never hated anyone in her life until Jimmy took away her son. But she'd never loved anyone as much as she did Little Jim. If Tanner Jones wouldn't marry her and give her a chance to get Little Jim back, then she'd do whatever she had to do in order to be with her son every day. Even if that meant crawling on her hands and knees back to Jimmy Devaney, Jr.

DORI WOKE BEFORE the alarm buzzed, as she did every Monday morning these days. And as she did every morning, especially on Mondays, she said hello to Little Jim. Unfortunately, it was a picture of him and not the real thing that grinned back at her when she wished him a good morning. The picture was her current favorite and sat in a small frame on her bedside table. In the snapshot he stood in her backyard, his right arm cocked as if to throw the football she'd given him for his last birthday.

But he was only pretending, because he would never have risked throwing the ball at her and perhaps hurting her or breaking the camera. The camera was their lifeline. Every Monday she took a roll of Little Jim for herself. Then she let him take a roll of her so he'd have a whole new batch of pictures every week. She didn't know what he did with his pictures of her, but she'd covered the walls of her bedroom with snapshots of her son. For now, it was all she could think to do.

She threw back the covers and got out of bed as nervous excitement churned in her stomach. She glanced out the bedroom window at a sky that reminded her of a blue pillow slept on by a white cat. The wispy clouds didn't look as if they held rain. She was glad of that. Plenty of things could go wrong today, and it was nice to know the weather wouldn't be one of them.

She lived neatly, but her little house was cleaner than usual this morning. If all went well, Tanner would visit her here before the week was over. Therefore, she'd rearranged her sparse secondhand furniture and vacuumed the corners of every room. She'd washed

the bright curtains she'd sewn for the windows and set
out vases of yellow and white chrysanthemums from
her yard. Padding barefoot from room to room, she
studied the effect. Tanner would like it, she decided.
He'd stated clearly in his letters that he didn't care for
pretension. With her income and legal debts, she didn't
have to worry about offending him on that score.

She dressed in jeans and a Power Rangers T-shirt
that matched the one Little Jim would no doubt wear
today. She'd found the T-shirts on sale and they'd become a Monday uniform for mother and son, a subtle
show of solidarity. Then she plaited her hair into a long
braid down her back in anticipation that Little Jim
would want to ride to Abilene with the convertible top
down.

Standing at the sink with one eye on the clock, she
forced herself to eat a piece of toast and drink a glass of
orange juice. She didn't want to be starving by the time
lunch came, considering that Tanner would probably
insist on picking up the tab. Judging from his clothes
and his truck, he didn't have a lot of money to spare.

Finally, she grabbed her sunglasses and her purse
and headed out the door. Even after months of doing
it, she hadn't become used to driving to the Devaney
mansion to pick up her son. She felt more like a hired
nanny than a mother as she spoke into the intercom at
the iron gate and drove down the winding road toward the house. The curving entrance was pure pretension. When the Devaneys bought the property it
had been flat and treeless, like most of the terrain
around Los Lobos. They'd laid out the winding road
up to the house and planted fast-growing cottonwoods
along it, as if the trees had dictated the route and not
the other way around. Dori had always figured the

long route up to the house was supposed to create anticipation for what lay at the end.

In Dori's opinion, travelers up the driveway were in
for a disappointment. The house squatted at the end of
the road like a huge building block. No porches softened the austere lines of its two-story bulk, no bay windows added a graceful curve to the exterior and no bal-
conies hinted at romanticism or whimsy on the part of
the owners. The sole nod to architectural interest was a
flurry of white shutters framing square windows cut
into the redbrick facade. Dori accepted the uninspired
lines of her little house because she couldn't afford better. But these people could.

She parked in the circular driveway near the front
door. At least the flowers in their rectangular beds
were beautiful, but then again, Dori didn't think there
was such a thing as an ugly flower. If there had been,
the Devaneys would have demanded the gardener
plant some, she thought with a wicked smile. She gave
the doorbell a firm push.

Jimmy Jr.'s mother answered the door. Dori had discovered long ago that Crystal Devaney channeled all
her time and energy into keeping her job as James P.
Devaney's wife. To that end she'd endured a face-lift,
the rigors of a personal trainer, hunger pangs and bore-
dom.

Then Little Jim had come into her life, and in her first
and only grandchild she'd finally found a distraction
that met with James P. Devaney's complete approval.
In fact, the child had brought a new spark to their relationship. Dori had always known she was fighting
more than Jimmy in trying to regain custody of her
son. Little Jim's grandparents needed him desperately.

"Oh, hello, Dori." Crystal always sounded astonished to see Dori every Monday morning, although Dori had been appearing at precisely eight-thirty each Monday for six months. "You're welcome to come in, but I don't think Little Jim feels up to going with you today."

DORI FOUGHT DOWN the panic that rose within her at Crystal's statement. Not living with Little Jim when he was healthy was hard enough. Thankfully, he hadn't been sick in the time they'd been apart, but she'd dreaded the time when he'd catch some flu bug.

Cold sweat trickled down her back as she stepped inside and started for the stairs. "What's wrong with him? Does he have a fever?"

"He's not sick."

Dori turned back toward Crystal. In her casually elegant turquoise jumpsuit she could easily pass for forty instead of her true age of fifty-three. She reminded Dori of a woman posing for a hormone replacement therapy advertisement. "I thought you said he didn't feel well enough to go out today."

"I said I didn't think he'd feel up to it."

Dori tensed. "And why is that?"

"He's afraid you're taking this construction worker from Dallas along today."

A chill ran through Dori as she gazed into Crystal's eyes, the same green as Jimmy Jr.'s. "And who told him that?"

Crystal shrugged. "He could have heard it anywhere. The whole town's talking about you contacting this man through a matchmaking magazine. I kept hoping the whole thing would go away. It's quite embarrassing, really. I thought you had more class than that, Dori Mae."

"I doubt a five-year-old spends much time listening to town gossip. Someone in this house has prejudiced him against Tanner before he had a chance to form his own opinion. I suppose I should have expected that, but for some reason I didn't."

Crystal crossed her arms and stared at the Oriental hall runner beneath her feet for a moment. When she looked up again her expression had softened. "Dori, honey, I really wish you'd give Jimmy Jr. another chance. I can understand that you're lonely, but some stranger from Dallas isn't the answer. Not when you have a fine man like my Jimmy who wants to give you the world. He's just devastated about this misunderstanding you two have had. Send this construction worker home. James has offered to grant Jimmy Jr. time off so the two of you can take a second honeymoon. How does a trip to the Bahamas sound?"

Dori closed her eyes. She couldn't be upset with Crystal for offering bribes—the whole family operated that way. And of course Crystal saw nothing but good in her only son and couldn't figure out why Dori didn't want him. Dori understood that fierce mother love more than ever now that she had Little Jim. "I'm sorry, Crystal. I wish Jimmy and I were more compatible, but we're not. We never will be."

"Then at least think of the child." Crystal's voice was thick with unshed tears. "He doesn't understand why his momma and daddy don't live together anymore."

Dori gazed at her in speechless agony. There was nothing to say to that. Little Jim didn't deserve to pay the price for his parents' mistakes, but he would pay them, anyway.

"Momma?" In jeans and his Power Rangers T-shirt, Little Jim stood at the top of the stairs, not running down to her for the first time in his life.

The tears pooling in Dori's eyes blurred his image. "Hi, sweetheart."

"Daddy said some ol' boy from Dallas might come with us today, Momma," Little Jim said in a fair imitation of his father's drawl.

Dori grimaced, wondering how much else of Jimmy Jr. was rubbing off on her son. "There's a very nice man named Tanner Jones I'd like you to meet," she said. "If you really don't like him, he doesn't have to go with us."

Little Jim grabbed the banister for support and swung his leg back and forth. "Daddy says this ol' boy doesn't like kids."

"Your daddy—" Dori caught herself before she criticized Jimmy Jr. Every book she'd ever read on divorce advised against running down the ex-spouse to the child. "Your daddy might have misunderstood," she said. "Tanner likes kids a lot." Actually, Dori didn't know that for a fact, but if he didn't, he'd be history, anyway.

Crystal stepped forward. "You don't have to go today if you don't want to, L.J."

Dori hated the nickname, which made her son sound like some sort of oil baron, but she'd never told Crystal that. Little Jim didn't seem to mind, and considering all the other negative influences Dori worried about in the Devaney household, including prejudice against women, the nickname wasn't important enough to challenge.

"If you want to stay here, we could bake those M&M cookies you like," Crystal added.

The suggestion seemed out of place coming from somebody dressed in turquoise silk, but Dori knew Crystal meant it. She'd do anything for her grandson, including tying on an apron and risking her manicure in the name of baking Little Jim's favorite cookies. Part of Dori appreciated that kind of devotion; part of her was terrified by its intensity.

Little Jim swung his leg harder, nearly upsetting his balance. "I guess I wanna see the movie," he said. "But I don't know about that ol' boy."

"Just meet him," Dori said. "If you don't want him to go after you meet him, he won't go. I promise."

"Okay."

As quickly as that, the crisis was over and Little Jim skipped down the stairs. Dori crouched down and held out her arms for their traditional hug. Little Jim squeezed her hard around the neck, and she choked back a fresh wave of tears as she breathed in his familiar boy scent that always reminded her of fresh-mown grass. She hugged him back, careful not to give in to the urge to crush him against her. She'd never allowed him to see the depth of her grief at losing him, and she never would.

"I'll go get everything ready for baking the cookies," Crystal said.

Dori glanced up at her in surprise.

"In case L.J. comes back," she added.

Dori watched her former mother-in-law walk regally back to the kitchen and felt an unexpected stab of pity.

ABOUT TEN MINUTES before nine, Tanner walked to the front parking area of the Prairie Schooner Motel and RV Park and searched for a spot to wait where he'd have an unobstructed view of the road. He chose to lean against a pole where he was shaded by a small but authentic-looking covered wagon that perched twenty-five feet over his head.

He smiled to himself. Here he was waiting for nine o'clock to roll around again and facing a whole new set of challenges. Yet he felt more prepared than he had twelve hours ago, more convinced that his plan was a good one.

He'd actually enjoyed spending the night in the clean but Spartan motel room and had opened his window to listen to crickets and the rumble of trucks on the access road. The lack of bellboys and room service was a refreshing change from his usual business trips. He'd never learned to appreciate the prestige of executive suite elevators and mints on his pillow at night. Being able to open his door and step into the fresh air appealed to him far more than a penthouse view of city lights and twenty-four-hour room service.

The motel owner, an old guy named Elmer, had seemed to know who Tanner was when he checked in, but Tanner had stopped being edgy about that. In the Dallas area he was known as the president of Jones Construction and a community leader, but here he was famous for only one thing. He was the man Dori had chosen out of *Texas Men*. After last night's kiss—the second one—he was damn grateful she had.

A sedan with three little kids in the back seat pulled up to the front office. The father got out of the car to return the room key, and the sound of bickering surged from the back seat. The mother turned and shouted to the children, and Tanner winced as the children shouted back.

He couldn't picture Dori screaming at her son that

way, but he didn't know her well enough to be sure. She'd certainly reacted with fury when he'd suggested the quickie marriage in Vegas. Tanner smiled to himself. And good for her, he thought. She'd been suitably outraged by an outrageous proposal. In fact, that might have been the moment he truly began to believe in a future with Dori Fitzpatrick.

But he was still on trial. He needed to get along with Little Jim today or the whole show was over. Tanner wished he'd had more opportunity to be around little kids recently, but his younger sister was too busy becoming a trial lawyer to settle down with babies, and his social life had been spent in the company of adults for the past ten years. He felt as if he were about to take a final exam for a class he'd never attended. But he was sure of one thing—with kids, you didn't dare fake it.

To Tanner's left, a block away, the white Sunbird appeared, top down. He straightened and took a deep breath. Jimmy Jr. might turn out to be an obstacle to winning Dori, but he was a manageable one. Little Jim could make or break the relationship. Tanner didn't intend to forget that.

Dori pulled up beside him, and Tanner got his first look at her son. Tufts of copper-colored hair poked out from around his Dallas Cowboys cap, and his face and arms were sprinkled with freckles. His mouth, nose and chin reminded Tanner of Dori, but his eyes were the same shade of green as his father's. Tanner vowed not to let an accident of birth prejudice him against that green-eyed stare.

Little Jim seemed just as intent on getting his first look at Tanner. Dori remained behind the wheel instead of leaping out of the car to introduce them. She turned off the motor, pushed her sunglasses to the top of her head and gave Tanner a tentative smile. It seemed as if she didn't want to trivialize this moment with meaningless social customs.

Taking his cue from Dori, Tanner stood quietly without speaking or pasting on an ingratiating smile, and let himself be studied like a specimen under a microscope. The thoroughness of the boy's inspection indicated he understood all too well the change Tanner represented in his young life. As the son of a couple happily married for forty years, Tanner could only guess at the mental gymnastics required of this little guy.

Finally, Little Jim finished his survey and gazed straight into Tanner's eyes. "I bet you don't know who the White Ranger is," he challenged.

"You're right, I don't."

Little Jim stuck out his chest and pointed. "That's him." He glanced at Dori. "Momma's wearing him, too. We always wear these shirts on Mondays. Even if they're still in the dirty clothes hamper. We fish them out and wear them, anyway. Right, Momma?"

Tanner's amused glance flicked over to catch Dori's reaction.

She blushed at this revelation, but she supported her son's statement. "Yep. Just fish them right out and put them right on," she said.

Tanner laughed, and to his surprise, so did Little Jim. Green eyes twinkling, he covered his mouth and looked up at Tanner. Some of the tension eased in Tanner's solar plexus. Apparently, he'd just passed the first test by understanding the importance of shirts that must be worn, regardless of their condition.

Dori cleared her throat and spoke to her son. "This cowboy wanted to hitch a ride into Abilene with us.

He's never seen the Power Rangers movie and he realizes that's a big gap in his education. What do you think? Should we let him go along?"

Tanner was taken aback that Dori was leaving the decision up to her son. Maybe she had her reasons for giving him that kind of power over this day they'd planned to spend together, but he suddenly realized that if Little Jim's response was thumbs-down, he'd be left standing in the parking lot. He hadn't considered that as an option.

Tanner met Little Jim's assessing glance with an outward calm that he'd perfected for dealing with belligerent subcontractors and excitable clients. But inside, his gut was churning. Usually he could figure out what adults were thinking, but a five-year-old's mind was unknown territory, unless he reached back to his own childhood for enlightenment. When he remembered what an independent little cuss he'd been at that age, he wasn't comforted.

"I guess it's okay if he comes," Little Jim said. There was no arrogance in the statement, only an underlying uneasiness.

If Tanner had anticipated dealing with a preschooler on a power trip, he needn't have worried. Little Jim wasn't interested in challenging anybody's authority. He was just plain scared. And Tanner didn't blame him, poor kid. His first five years in this world hadn't been a model of stability. Tanner began to understand Dori's single-mindedness where this tyke was concerned.

"Thank you," Tanner said to Little Jim. "I know this day with your momma is very special."

Little Jim nodded, his devotion to his mother shining in his eyes. Then he gazed up at Tanner as if he'd come to another decision. "Wanna ride in front with Momma?"

The concession, given so soon, took his breath away. "That's the most generous thing anyone's done for me in a long time," he said.

Dori chuckled as her son unbuckled his seat belt and scrambled between the bucket seats to the back. "Don't be getting a big head, Tanner. Little Jim loves riding in the back seat when the top's down. There's more wind back there. He'd do it all the time, except I refuse to look like his chauffeur, so I make him ride up front with me when it's just the two of us."

"I see." Tanner opened the passenger door and climbed in. Then he turned around and glanced at Little Jim, who was grinning at him. "You'd rather sit back there than up here with this beautiful lady?"

Little Jim's grin widened as he nodded. "Riding in the back seat is like flying."

"The funny thing is, the front seat can be like that, too." Tanner winked at Dori.

"No, it can't," Little Jim said. "The front seat is *boring*."

"Not always." Tanner caught the quick look of awareness in Dori's eyes before she pulled her sunglasses down and presented her profile to him. Pink tinged her creamy cheeks.

"Buckle up, you two," she said. "I'm starting the engine."

Tanner settled in his seat and snapped the belt over his lap before glancing over at Dori. She'd pressed her lips together in an unsuccessful attempt to hide the tiny smile creating a dimple at the corner of her mouth. Tanner hadn't felt this good in ages.

THE GOOD FEELING LASTED until sometime around four in the afternoon. Tanner was congratulating himself on how well everything had turned out as the three of them left the ice-cream shop located in an Abilene indoor shopping mall. They'd had lunch at McDonald's and sat in a nearly empty theater to see the Power Rangers movie. Dori's placement of Little Jim in the middle seat had been a wise move. The darkened theater was a tempting place with someone like Dori around, but Tanner didn't think displaying affection in front of Little Jim was a good idea yet. Just having the kid accept him as part of the excursion to Abilene was enough for now.

They'd taken endless pictures during the day, and Tanner had felt flattered to be included in a few. Now they strolled the mall in easy camaraderie while they worked off the ice-cream sundaes they'd just eaten. As they walked, Little Jim relived aloud his favorite moments from the movie.

"Momma, look!" He ran over to the window of a large toy store and stood transfixed at the display of deluxe Power Ranger figures and all their assorted gear.

Dori's small sigh of frustration was subtle, but Tanner caught it.

"Can we go in and see how much?" Little Jim asked.

"You know we can't buy any of that now," Dori said. "It doesn't matter how much it is. You'll just make yourself feel bad because you can't have it."

Little Jim turned an imploring gaze up at her. "Maybe it's on *sale*. A really big sale. Can we just see? Please, Momma?"

Tanner looked at Dori in surprise. "He doesn't have any of this stuff?"

"Not anything so fancy." She gave Tanner a look that warned him to drop the subject.

"*Please,* Momma? I don't care if I can't buy it now. I just want to look at it. Can I?"

"All right," Dori said. "You can show me one thing you want Santa to bring this year. That way I can help you spell it when you write your letter to him."

"That's easy." Little Jim marched into the store with Dori and Tanner trailing behind. "I want the White Ranger."

For Tanner, the store was a bewildering array of stuffed animals, colorful plastic toys and games he'd never heard of. He really was out of the loop when it came to this age group, he conceded silently. Little Jim seemed to know exactly where he was going, however, and led them directly to the Power Rangers shelf. Once there he became totally absorbed, handling the figures with reverence.

Tanner stepped back from the display and pulled Dori with him. "I still can't believe he doesn't at least have that White Ranger. It's his favorite character," he said, keeping his voice low.

"I can't afford it," she murmured. "The custody fight put me in a financial hole."

"I understand that, but what about his father and grandparents? I thought they were wealthy."

"And very dictatorial. They don't like the Power Ranger craze, maybe partly because I took Little Jim to the movie as a special treat last year, when I still had custody. They refuse to buy him anything to do with the Power Rangers."

"That's insane." Anger boiled up within Tanner as he watched Little Jim caress the figure of the White Ranger and put him gently back on the shelf. "He's just a little kid, for God's sake. Who do these people think they are?"

Dori gave him a sad smile. "The Devaneys."

"Well, they don't have dominion over me." Tanner stepped forward and crouched down next to Little Jim. "Pick out whatever you want on this shelf. I'll buy it for you." He had a moment to see the shock and joy register on Little Jim's face before Dori yanked him upright.

"No," she said, her dark gaze adamant. "Thank you, but no."

Tanner frowned at her display of pride. "He loves those characters. I can remember loving G.I. Joe the same way. I still have that stuff packed away somewhere. That's how we preserve a piece of our childhood, Dori. I can't believe you'd deny him that." He turned back to the boy. "Anything on the shelf. Pick it out."

Dori grabbed Tanner's arm. Her voice was low and intense. "Forget it, Tanner. He'll want it all. Do you know how much money that would be?"

"Less than dinner for two at a five-star restaurant," Tanner snapped, and immediately regretted it.

Dori's eyes widened. "And how would you know that?"

He stood mutely before her and wondered if he'd have to confess everything right now, before they'd had twenty-four hours together. He'd blown it, and all because he'd suddenly remembered the rush of joy when he'd become the proud owner of his first G.I. Joe figure. And if anybody needed that kind of joy in his confusing life, it was Little Jim.

"You've taken a date to a five-star restaurant, haven't you, Tanner?" Dori's expression was stormy.

"Yes." He waited for her to guess the rest of it. They hadn't built enough friendship between them, let alone love, for her to forgive his deception. Everything was ruined.

She braced her hands on her hips. "I can certainly see what your problem is. I suppose your credit cards are maxed out, aren't they?"

"Actually, I—"

"Never mind." She held up a hand. "We'll talk about it later. It's time to start home, anyway. Come on, Little Jim."

Her son looked ready to burst into tears. "I can't have anything?"

"Not today, sweetheart. But Christmas isn't so far away."

Tanner felt like a jerk. In his attempt to do something nice for the kid, he'd brought more stress into his young life. And although Dori hadn't guessed that Tanner was rich, she'd decided he was in debt. He didn't like that conclusion any better. He put a hand on Dori's arm. "Wait."

"Let's just get beyond this, okay?" she said gently. "We'll discuss it later."

"I'm not in debt. I—"

"I find that hard to believe."

"Please believe it. And let me buy at least one thing for Little Jim. I promise you it won't break the bank. And it means so much to him." Tanner was amazed that during the exchange Little Jim just stared up at them without saying a word. From Tanner's small store of knowledge about kids, he would have expected the boy to beg his mother for the toy. His silence was a tribute to Dori's careful teaching.

Dori glanced at her son. Then she crouched down so

she was at eye level with him. "If I let Tanner buy you a present, don't expect that every time you see him you'll get something else. Tanner's in construction, like Grandpa Fitzpatrick, and he doesn't have the kind of money your daddy and your Grandma and Grandpa Devaney do. So this is a very, very special occasion. Can you remember that?"

As Little Jim nodded vigorously, Tanner felt worse and worse. What he'd thought to be an innocent subterfuge was turning into a gigantic misrepresentation. He'd once thought it would be easy to tell Dori the truth when the time came. Now he wasn't so sure. Ironically, everthing Dori had said was true. Tanner didn't have the kind of money the Devaneys had. He had much more.

Picking Out and Shooting

6

TANNER OFFERED TO DRIVE home, and Dori took him up on it. She didn't trust herself to concentrate on the road, considering the disturbing thoughts chasing themselves around in her mind.

While Little Jim played happily with the White Ranger in the back seat and Tanner dealt with the heavier traffic that usually hit the stretch between Abilene and Los Lobos at five o'clock, Dori sorted through her limited options. She couldn't let herself become involved with a spendthrift. She'd seen that mentality a thousand times in people with sporadic paychecks. When the money came in, they spent lavishly until it was gone, giving no thought to budgeting for the lean times. Her mother and father had taught her how to avoid that trap. When she'd married Jimmy Jr., she'd thought that particular survival skill wouldn't be necessary anymore. Now it was her lifeline.

If she married again and began another campaign to get custody of Little Jim, she'd need every penny to pay her lawyer. A man who allowed money to dribble through his fingers would be more of a liability than an asset. Not that she didn't understand the impulse that had driven Tanner to suggest buying out the toy store. She'd had the same impulse many times in her desire to make up for her son's suffering. Tanner was a soft-hearted guy who was new to the situation and perhaps overspending should be forgiven.

Yet it seemed that extravagance was a pattern with him. Twice, he'd demonstrated in her presence that he wasn't careful with money, and he'd admitted taking a date to a restaurant way beyond his means. Dori kept trying to think about that, when all she wanted to think about was his kiss, his strong arms holding her close, his body becoming aroused....

The night before she'd vowed not to be blinded by sexual attraction. And she wouldn't be. Before she got in any deeper, she'd ask Tanner to leave. She simply couldn't take the chance of making another gigantic mistake.

"Momma!" Little Jim shook her shoulder.

Dori snapped out of her trance with a guilty start and turned toward the back seat. "What, sweetheart?"

"I was calling you and calling you, but you didn't hear me."

"Sorry. I was thinking." She noticed the movement as Tanner glanced at her. He knew she was worried about that scene in the store.

"You're always thinking," Little Jim complained.

"I suppose I am." She managed a smile. His Dallas Cowboys cap was crammed down tight on his head to keep it from blowing off in the wind, and he had to peer up at her from under the bill of the cap. He clutched the White Ranger in a death grip. Dori suspected he'd sleep with the action figure and hoped none of the Devaneys would give him a hard time about the new toy. "What did you want to say?" she asked.

"Can you make me a White Ranger costume for Halloween?"

"Hold him up and let me look."

Little Jim raised the figure cautiously from his lap. "Just don't want him to blow out," he explained.

Dori studied the Power Ranger's outfit and estimated how much fabric it would take, and how much skill. Thank goodness for her mother's old sewing machine. "I think I can manage that," she said.

"*Okay!* Wait'll Jerry and Melissa and Stanley see me!"

Dori felt the familiar tug of regret. He didn't spend much time with his neighborhood playmates anymore and she knew he missed them. "I...I'm not sure you'll be going trick-or-treating with them this year, sweetheart."

"Why not?"

"Halloween's on a Thursday."

Little Jim seemed to absorb that news. "I have to go there. We don't have any houses around Grandpa and Grandma Devaney's."

"We'll see. I'll talk to them about it."

"Will Tanner be here on Halloween?"

"Oh, I don't think so, honey," Dori answered. "He has to get back to Dallas soon."

"Will he be here next Monday?"

"No, he won't, sweetheart." She glanced at Tanner. He'd suggested spending approximately a week in Los Lobos, although they'd both known the time could be shortened if the relationship didn't seem to be working.

He took his eyes from traffic long enough to meet her gaze. "I plan to still be here next Monday," he said as he returned his attention to the road.

Dori worked to get her racing heart under control. In one brief glance, Tanner had managed to convey an intensity of desire that swept away her latest resolution and left thudding passion in its wake. Suddenly the money issue seemed unimportant, even petty, compared to the searing force of that look. Dori struggled to remain rational, but she was at war with a body that demanded the very thing Tanner had silently promised to give. Still, she had to send him away, no matter how much she wanted him.

Tanner spoke over his shoulder to Little Jim. "Any objection if I hang around until Monday?"

"I guess not," Little Jim said.

"Thanks."

Dori evaluated Tanner's grim smile and concluded he wasn't satisfied with her son's lukewarm answer. Maybe he thought buying the White Ranger should have made them friends for life. If so, he was in for a rude awakening. Little Jim's affections couldn't be bought, and neither could his mother. Not even with potent kisses and melting looks.

A few minutes later Tanner flicked on the turn signal for the exit to Los Lobos. Dori had two more hours before she was scheduled to take Little Jim home, and she wanted to spend them alone with her son. She directed Tanner to the motel, and he drove there without comment.

In front of the motel, she got out and climbed into the driver's seat of the convertible as Tanner held the door.

He closed it firmly and rested both hands on the doorframe as he gazed down at her. "We need to talk."

"Yes, we do. I'll drop my son off at eight. I can come by after that, if it's not too late."

"Not at all." He straightened. "Oh, it's room nine."

She lifted a startled gaze to his. "You're kidding."

"Nope."

"Nine is Momma's lucky number," Little Jim chimed in from the back seat.

"So I hear."

Dori still couldn't believe it. "Out of twenty-seven rooms in this motel, you're in number nine. That's incredible."

"Isn't it?"

"Well, we'd better get going." She turned toward the back seat. "Come on, son." As he made his way between the bucket seats and plopped down, she touched his shoulder. "Thank Tanner for your gift."

"Thank you, Tanner," Little Jim said. "I really like him."

"That's good. I'll see you next Monday, buddy."

"Okay."

Dori waved and pulled out of the parking lot. Room number nine. She really couldn't believe it. Maybe she was tempting fate to doubt that this was the right man for her. Maybe she should give him just a little longer to prove it one way or the other.

WHEN THE CONVERTIBLE was out of sight, Tanner headed straight for the motel office. Elmer wasn't there. Behind the front desk stood a white-haired, matronly woman whose name tag read Beatrice. Tanner guessed she might be Elmer's wife.

Apparently, she knew all about Tanner, because she smiled when he walked in. "Mr. Jones, isn't it?"

"That's right."

"Elmer told me you were here. You're in room sixteen, aren't you? I trust you had a pleasant night?"

AFTER DORI DROVE BACK to her house, she fixed Little Jim his favorite dinner of toasted cheese sandwiches and they played slapjack until it was time for him to go back to the Devaneys. Those last few minutes as they rushed around gathering Little Jim's belongings were usually the hardest for Dori. She always saved the packet of the previous week's pictures to tuck into his knapsack just before they walked out the door of the house they used to share. Little Jim hoarded them for when he was alone in his room, so he'd still have his mother's face to look at.

Normally on the short drive to the Devaney mansion, Little Jim was subdued, but tonight he had questions. "Do you like Tanner, Momma?"

She hesitated, thinking about Tanner's habit of tossing money around. Although it was a big worry, it was the only negative she'd found. Otherwise he'd shown himself to be courageous, gallant, sensitive...and sexy. "Yes, I like him," she said.

"Better than Daddy?"

Absolutely, she thought, but she couldn't say that. "Your daddy has some fine qualities," she forced herself to say. "But we just don't see things the same."

"Do you see things the same as Tanner?"

Dori took a deep breath. "I don't know yet. That's what I'm trying to find out."

"Why?"

She couldn't tell Little Jim her long-range plan. He was too young to understand the plotting she'd done in an attempt to get him back. "Well, someday I'd like to get married again," she said. "But I want to make sure the man is somebody I like a lot, and somebody you like a lot, too."

"Daddy says you're gonna marry him again."

Dori silently cursed Jimmy Jr. for confiding his fantasies to their son. "When did he say that?"

"Oh, he says it all the time. He says then we can all be together again."

She clenched her jaw. Jimmy was shameless. "I'm afraid that's not going to happen, sweetheart."

"Couldn't you *try* to like Daddy?"

Dori turned down the winding road to the mansion, her stomach in knots. "Sometimes all the trying in the world won't work. Remember when I read that article about tofu?"

"Yeah, I sure do!"

"But I kept thinking if I cooked it a different way, or with different food, we'd learn to like it. We really tried, didn't we?"

"I hated that yucky tofu."

Dori braked the car. No lights shone from the front windows, so everyone must be in the back of the house, she thought. Even at night the house didn't look welcoming. "But some people like tofu fine," she continued. "I just gave up trying."

"Daddy's like tofu?"

"Yep. For me he is."

Little Jim sat quite still as he seemed to turn the concept over in his mind. Then he looked up at her. "If Daddy's tofu, what's Tanner?"

A hot fudge sundae. "I'm not sure yet. We have to get better acquainted." Finally, she asked the most important question, knowing she'd been putting it off until the last moment. "What do you think of him?"

Little Jim stared out the windshield into the darkness. "He's okay. But—"

"But?"

"But I sure wish Daddy wasn't tofu," he said softly.

Dori reached an arm around him and gave him a squeeze. "So do I."

She walked him up the steps and rang the bell. If she was lucky Crystal would answer the door again. She wasn't lucky. Jimmy Jr. opened the door and gazed out at them.

Little Jim did what most five-year-olds would have, and held up his new toy. "See, Daddy? The White Ranger!"

Jimmy frowned. "Your momma must be feelin' flush if she's buying you stuff."

"Tanner bought it," Little Jim said. Then he glanced into his father's face and cringed.

"You went with that ol' boy to Abilene?" Jimmy demanded. "After I told you not to?"

"But Momma said—"

"Your momma has taken leave of her senses. Give me that stupid toy."

Dori stepped in front of Little Jim to shield him. "You're not depriving him of that toy, Jimmy. If he can't keep it here, then I'll take it home with me, to have for him when he comes over."

"Don't be telling me what I can and can't do with my own son! Your time's up, Dori Mae. What happens with him is my business now."

"What's going on here?" James Devaney strode into the hallway, the light from the back of the house surrounding him. A good two inches taller than his son, with a lean, tanned face and a full head of silver hair, he had the sort of manner that made people step back in deference.

His son was no exception. As Jimmy moved away from the door, he motioned to Dori and Little Jim. "She had a date with that construction worker today and dragged my son along."

James lifted an eyebrow in obvious disapproval as

he glanced at Jimmy Jr. "So you make things worse by causing a commotion out here on the front porch, like some poor white trash. And in front of the boy, too. You should both be ashamed of yourselves."

Behind her back, Dori motioned for Little Jim to give her the White Ranger. It wasn't safe in this house, and they both knew it now. Little Jim put the White Ranger into her hand slowly, keeping his own grip on it as long as possible.

"I'll be running along," Dori said, keeping the figure behind her as she backed toward the steps. "See you next Monday, Little Jim."

"Bye, Momma." He tried manfully not to cry, but his lower lip quivered.

Dori trembled with fury. She could guess what it cost him to give up his beloved White Ranger, but she figured it would land in the trash compactor if she hadn't taken it. That would be worse.

"Come on, L.J.," James said, putting his hand on Little Jim's shoulder. "I think Grandma has some cookies for you." As he guided the child away, he glanced back at Jimmy. "Cut it short. This is not the time or place."

Jimmy glared back at his father but didn't reply. Dori knew he was too aware of his own interests to risk crossing the man who wrote out his paycheck. Unlike his older sister, who'd finally had enough and had fled to California, Jimmy seemed willing to bide his time until he could be in charge. At which time, Dori had no doubt, he'd behave exactly as his father did. In the meantime, he'd expected to have Dori to boss around. She'd cheated him of that opportunity, and he didn't like it.

"I warned you to get that ol' boy out of town," Jimmy said in a low voice.

Dori eased down the steps, careful not to let him see the toy in her hand. "Good night, Jimmy."

"I warned you," he said again.

She reached the car and got in quickly. As she drove away, the White Ranger in her lap, she checked her rear-view mirror. She kept checking all the way to the Prairie Schooner Motel. But even if Jimmy didn't follow her there, he'd eventually find out where she'd gone. People in Los Lobos kept track of each other by noticing where vehicles were parked. Everybody in town knew her white Sunbird convertible. Too bad she hadn't chosen a more ordinary car, but it couldn't be helped now. She'd promised to have a talk with Tanner. She wouldn't stay long.

WHEN THE SOFT KNOCK CAME at the door, Tanner switched off the television and leapt from the bed where he'd been sprawling, the pillows shoved behind his head. His heart pounded in anticipation of whether this would be her kiss-off speech. He sure as hell hoped not, but she'd been angry about his offer to buy all those Power Ranger things, and he'd been a fool to suggest it.

Telling her he was in room nine had been an inspiration. And his luck had held, because nine hadn't been rented out yet and he was able to convince Beatrice to let him switch by making up some story about the television not working right. Before he'd moved out of sixteen he'd screwed up the controls enough to give Elmer something to do when he went to check out the set later. Elmer had reported to him that nothing was wrong with the set except that somebody had messed with the settings, but by that time Tanner had taken possession of room nine.

He opened the door and restrained himself from gathering her immediately into his arms. Instead, he stepped back and allowed her to walk past him into the room. Then he noticed that she held the White Ranger in one hand. His stomach clenched. She was about to deliver the kiss-off speech, complete with the return of his gift to her son.

He closed the door and turned to her. Desperation made him reckless.

"Tanner, I—"

"Don't." He closed the gap between them and pulled her into his arms. He'd told himself not to use Neanderthal tactics, but the specter of losing her canceled his good intentions. In the middle of her startled exclamation of surprise he brought his mouth down on hers. If she fought him, he'd let her go.

She didn't fight. She caught fire. Her shoulder purse slid to the floor and the White Ranger's leg pressed into his shoulder as she wound her arms around his neck. He didn't care. Nothing mattered except the urgency of her mouth inviting him to delve inside and possess her. His thrusting tongue presented a blatant suggestion of the more complete union he sought. Cupping her bottom, he brought her tight against his arousal, wanting her to know exactly how she was affecting him. His pulse raced as she wiggled even closer, and he groaned at the perfect way they fit together.

He pulled the hem of her T-shirt from her jeans and reached beneath it to unfasten her bra. Before he could accomplish it, she shoved him away.

"Not yet," she gasped.

His voice was husky with need. "Why not? We're both ready for it, Dori."

She waited until her breathing slowed before answering. "Physically, perhaps. Not mentally. I hope you didn't think, because I offered to come to your room, that I was giving you permission to sleep with me."

"No, I didn't think that." He couldn't keep the impatience from his voice. "But after the way you responded when I kissed you just now, I thought the time had arrived."

"You caught me by surprise, is all. I wasn't expecting you to grab me like that, and it was..." She glanced up at him through her lashes. "Exciting." Her endearing habit of drawing out the letter *i* gave a whole new emphasis to the word.

He swallowed. "No kidding."

"But I really came here to talk."

"And return Little Jim's gift?"

She glanced down at the figure in her hand as if she'd forgotten she was holding it. "Oh! No, I just brought this in because the top's still down on the car and somebody might take it. I could have used the glove compartment or the trunk, I suppose, but bringing it in was the easiest thing to do." She laid the figure on the bed and reached behind her to tuck in her T-shirt where he'd pulled it out.

If the gesture was meant to discourage Tanner from trying to kiss her again, it did. "How come Little Jim doesn't have his toy?"

Her eyes darkened. "I was afraid somebody in that house would destroy it."

"Destroy a kid's toy?" The idea left a bitter taste in his mouth. "What kind of people are they?"

"They'd make it look like an accident, but I could see by the expression on Jimmy's face, and even his father's, that they'd get rid of it. I told you they didn't want him playing with Power Ranger stuff. He gets the toys they want him to have. Some of them are very expensive, but he doesn't have any choice in the matter. They control his life completely."

"That's sick."

"That's why I want him back."

He looked into her eyes. It could all be so easy, so quick. He could tell her about his thriving business and ask her to marry him. His lawyers would make mincemeat of the Devaneys, and Little Jim would be reunited with his mother. But Tanner couldn't forget her speech about carelessly throwing up a house and hoping the structure was solid instead of taking the time to do it right. She'd already put Little Jim through one divorce. He knew she didn't want to risk a second one. They'd have to do this her way.

"I should warn you about Jimmy Jr.," she said. "He came to the door and wasn't pleased about you going along to Abilene with me and Little Jim. He might try something."

"And he might be all talk."

"He might. I doubt he'd ever take you on man-to-man."

"No. He's a certified bully."

Dori shoved her hands in the front pockets of her jeans and stared down at her running shoes. "That's what worries me. He won't challenge you to a fair fight, but he might talk some of his buddies into waylaying you sometime when you're alone." She glanced up, her expression troubled. "I don't want you to get hurt, Tanner. Maybe it would be best if you gave up on me."

"We've already had this discussion. You're wasting your time trying to convince me to leave, unless you want me to go for your own reasons. But I refuse to run away from Jimmy's threats."

Admiration shone from her eyes. "You're almost perfect, you know that?"

There. That was what he'd been searching for all these years, a woman who looked at him, not at what he represented in material perks, and was impressed. "I'm far from perfect, but I'm glad you think I'm even close."

"The one bad thing is the way you spend money, Tanner. I couldn't tolerate that in a husband."

"I can change."

She smiled. "I'm glad you said that, because I've thought of a way to help you. Here's my plan. For the next week, if you agree, you'll be on a budget."

"A what?"

She looked a trifle smug, but on Dori the expression was cute. "I figured you weren't closely acquainted with that concept. Here's how it would work. Whatever we do together all week has to cost less than the total I've come up with."

He already knew he'd hate this. "And what is that total, pray tell?"

She walked over to the desk and picked up the pad and pen left there for guests. She wrote a figure on the pad, ripped off the page and handed it to him.

He stared at the small amount, less than it would cost him to dry-clean one of his custom suits. "No way."

"It can be done. You just have to use your imagination instead of your wallet. That's my condition, Tanner. Unless I truly believe you can be more careful with money, we have no future together. We should end it now before we both get hurt."

He looked at the amount and considered once more spilling the beans. Then he gazed at her standing in the circle of light created by the desk lamp. Her braid had loosened during the day, giving her a wonderfully disheveled look that he longed to improve upon. He recalled the promise in her kiss, the press of her ripe body, and could think of one thing they could do that would cost nothing at all.

"It's a deal," he said.

"Good." She took the paper back and drew a crude map on the back. "Here's how you get to my house." She handed him the paper before picking up her purse and the White Ranger. "You can come by for me at nine tomorrow morning. I don't have to be at work until one. Good night, Tanner."

He watched her head for the door. He wanted to call her back, yet knew she wouldn't stay the night, which was what he really wanted. "Thanks for giving me a second chance," he said.

She opened the door and stopped, turning to look back at him. "I thought about calling everything off, but when you told me you were in room nine, I figured that was a sign we should hang on a while longer."

After she left, Tanner shook his head. Talk about close calls.

TANNER WASN'T SLEEPING as well as usual since he arrived in Los Lobos. Sexual frustration could do that to a person, he'd discovered. He'd finally drifted off about one in the morning when the sound of yelling and people running brought him wide-awake. He pulled on his jeans and boots and opened his door, expecting to see flames leaping from one of the motel rooms.

The sidewalk in front of the long row of rooms was crowded with guests in various stages of undress, so that Tanner had a hard time figuring out where the problem originated. He moved out into the parking lot for a better perspective, which was when the breeze blew the stench in his direction. He coughed and held his breath as he studied the row of open doors and noticed wispy smoke drifting from room sixteen.

A cowboy ambled over to him, buttoning his shirt as he walked. "Smells like somebody threw a stink bomb in that room," he commented to Tanner. "Probably high school kids."

"Could be." Tanner breathed through his mouth as the smell became worse. He didn't think for a minute it was high school kids, despite the juvenile nature of the vandalism.

"Aren't you that ol' boy from East Texas that's here to see Dori?"

Tanner gazed at him, not feeling particularly friendly at the moment. "Who wants to know?"

The man stuck out his hand. "Heck Tyrrell, a friend of Dori's. I stop in at the Double Nickel whenever I'm in town."

Tanner shook his hand. "Tanner Jones."

"I know. I was there Sunday night. I made a run to Amarillo yesterday, but now my rig's in the shop until tomorrow afternoon, so I'm bunking here."

Tanner grew wary. "So you work for Devaney Trucking?"

"Yeah." Tyrrell rubbed his neck and looked uncomfortable. "A man's gotta have a job, and Devaney pays good."

"I understand."

Tyrrell hesitated, then spoke again. "Listen, Dori's something special. We don't want to see her get hurt."

"Seems like she's already been hurt."

Tyrrell looked down the road, where a wailing siren and flashing red lights indicated a fire truck was on the way. "Somebody shoulda punched Jimmy Jr. a long time ago," he said quietly.

"Probably."

"Treat her right, Jones."

"I intend to."

As the fire truck pulled in, Tanner excused himself from Tyrrell and headed back to his room. Room number nine. Dori's lucky number had saved him from some inconvenient nastiness.

THE NEXT MORNING Dori dressed in jeans and a San Antonio Spurs T-shirt her parents had sent her. With the budget she'd put Tanner on, he wouldn't be taking her anywhere fancy. She smiled as she remembered the look of disbelief that had crossed his handsome face when she'd set a limit on the amount he could spend on her in the next week. She'd half expected him to refuse to abide by her budget and was very glad he'd decided to go along. Apparently, he understood the importance of proving he could be thrifty.

And someday she might tell him how tough it had been for her to walk out of his motel room after the way he'd kissed her. Keeping him at arm's length while she evaluated his suitability as a husband and father was the most difficult thing she'd ever had to do. But she would continue with that course of action for Little Jim's sake.

After some inner debate, she left her freshly washed hair loose. She didn't wear it that way often because she was either working at the café or puttering around her house, and unbound hair got in the way. Besides, Dori had always thought when a woman let her hair flow loose around her shoulders, she was signaling an interest in romance. Dori hadn't wanted to give off those signals. Until now.

Her doorbell rang at precisely nine, and she marked down punctuality on her mental list of Tanner's good qualities. The list was growing. If he could just learn to budget...

She pulled open the door and forgot all about the spending habits of the man standing on her tiny front porch. Dressed in a soft blue work shirt and snug jeans, Tanner looked even better than he had in the *Texas Men* magazine photo, and that was saying a lot. Or maybe her perception of him was beginning to shift as memories of passionate kisses colored her view.

From behind his back, he produced a Hershey chocolate bar and a single white carnation. "Bargain candy, bargain flower in virginal white, signifying my pure intentions," he said with a wink. "Do I have to save my receipts, or will you keep this all in your head?"

She laughed and accepted the candy bar and carnation. "After two years of watching every penny, I'll know when you've crossed the line. Thank you. This is very nice." She stepped back and ushered him inside.

"Let me have the flower back," he said as she closed the door.

"What, you're going to recycle it for tomorrow? That may be going a bit far, Tanner."

"You'll get it back in a minute." He slipped the carnation from her fingers and snapped off a good part of the stem.

"Hey! That's my present you're mutilating."

"I just found out where it goes." He moved closer and tucked the carnation in her hair. The delicate scent of the flower mingled in a heady combination with his woodsy after-shave, and his breath fell softly on her face as he concentrated on getting the flower anchored behind her ear. "There." His tone had undergone a subtle change, from bantering to husky, and his hand lingered on her cheek.

She looked up into his eyes and could read intentions that were far from pure. Her pulse raced.

With a rueful smile he backed away. "Sorry. Almost forgot myself for a minute."

She was impressed with his self-control. And perhaps a little disappointed. Which was very unfair of her, she realized.

He glanced down at her hand. "You're going to melt the candy bar, holding it like that."

Immediately, she relaxed her death grip on the Hershey bar.

"Gonna give me a tour of your house?"

"Sure. Let's go back to the kitchen first. I'll put the candy in the fridge." Her legs a bit rubbery, she led him to the kitchen, a long, narrow room with her refinished round oak table at one end, a closet for her secondhand washer and dryer at the other. The kitchen window looked out on the backyard, where Little Jim's swing set and a picnic table took up most of the area. A red oak, an unusual tree for the area, shaded the picnic table. The leaves had begun to turn and a few had fluttered down to make bright scarlet patches on the grass. The tree had captured Little Jim's imagination and Dori had rented the house because her son loved that tree.

Tanner braced his hands on the sink and peered out the window at the view over the cedar fence that surrounded the yard. He stared at the large two-story house about a mile away, where an upstairs window was visible in a break between the branches of the large cottonwoods that surrounded the house like sentinels. Tanner glanced over his shoulder at Dori. "Little Jim's room?"

"That's right. If those trees grow any more, I won't be able to see it."

Tanner looked back at the house. "Let's hope you don't have to worry about that."

Longing filled her heart as she imagined having this broad-shouldered man beside her, helping her fight what seemed like an impossible battle. A sigh must have escaped unnoticed, because he turned around, concern in his eyes.

"Let's drop that depressing subject," he said. "You spend enough time worrying, as it is." He winked. "Let's go see the rest of the house. I want to find out if you've put a velvet rope across the door to your bedroom."

"You really think I'm prissy, don't you?"

"No, I think you're sexy as hell, and if I don't crack jokes I'm liable to grab you and try to seduce you, which would spoil everything, right?"

She found breathing difficult. "Right," she whispered.

"Then let's get on with the tour."

"Right," she said again, and walked ahead of him out of the kitchen. This plan had seemed so logical when she'd written to Tanner suggesting he come to Los Lobos for a week so they could get acquainted. But the sexual tug she felt every time she looked at him had nothing to do with logic.

She led him back through the living room toward the hall.

"You've been very creative with your decorating, by the way," he said as they passed through the living room.

"You have to be creative when you're on a budget."

"So I'm learning."

She walked down the hall and paused before Little Jim's room, which looked pretty much as he'd left it six months ago. His yard-sale toy box sat in one corner and his twin bed held the assortment of stuffed animals he'd collected since he was a baby. "My son's room, obviously," she said. "Jimmy Jr. thought Little Jim was too big for stuffed animals, so he left them all here. He left most of his other toys, too." She didn't admit that sometimes, when the ache for her son was too much to bear, she slept here surrounded by his cherished bears, squirrels and bunnies. Little Jim's scent clung to the soft toys, and breathing it in helped her sleep.

Tanner glanced into the room but made no comment.

"I suppose he is too old for stuffed animals," Dori said.

"Nobody ever gets that old, Dori. The way your ex-husband treats Little Jim chills my blood."

She glanced into his eyes and drew strength from the anger there. "Jimmy always told me I didn't know anything about raising boys."

"That's ridiculous. I've seen what you've done with that boy, and you know everything you need to know. He's a great kid."

A smile trembled on her lips. "Thanks, Tanner. Hearing that helps a lot. You know, I think if Little Jim had been a girl, the judge would have ruled differently, thinking girls need their mothers more. God help me, I've sometimes wished Little Jim had been a girl so I wouldn't have lost my child."

His gaze grew more intense as she talked. "Dammit, why don't we just—" Abruptly he stopped speaking and turned away with a muted curse.

"What?"

He faced her again, his expression more placid. "Never mind. Let's continue the tour."

"Okay." She could guess what he'd been thinking. The talk about Little Jim had brought him back to the idea of a quickie marriage in Las Vegas. Fortunately, he'd thought better of bringing up the subject again. "This is my room." She gestured toward the door. "Bathroom's across the hall."

She stood back and let Tanner look in. He did a double take at the pictures of her son that covered all four walls.

"I had a lot of pictures, because Little Jim is the only grandchild on both sides. When he...went to live with the Devaneys, I hauled them all out and tacked them up. Then we take pictures every week, as you saw yesterday. Rolls of film are one extravagance I allow myself."

Tanner stood silently examining the walls full of pictures. Finally, he turned back to her, a grim set to his jaw. "Let's go," he said, his voice strained. "We have a house to build."

He wouldn't tell her where they were headed when he guided her out the door and into his truck, but she saw what appeared to be a picnic basket in the back.

"You won't get us lost, will you?" she asked as they took off down a back road.

He grinned at her. "Worried about being stranded with me in some lonely spot?"

The idea filled her with more excitement than she dared tell him. "I just meant you don't know the area very well."

"No, but Elmer does. I spent some time talking to him this morning before I picked you up."

He seemed so proud of himself, taking her out for an inexpensive picnic, that she hated to rain directly on his parade, so she chose a more oblique approach. "I'm surprised Hanson's Department Store was open this morning."

"Hanson's?" He glanced at her. "What do you mean?"

She angled her head back toward the truck bed. "Isn't that where you bought the picnic basket?"

"Oh." He nodded. "A picnic basket would blow the budget right off, wouldn't it?"

"I'm afraid so, Tanner. But still, it's a great idea. You have a handicap, being from out of town and all. You don't have a lot of the things you might otherwise."

"I hate to tell you, but even if we were in East Texas, I'd be out of luck. I don't own a picnic basket."

"Well, now you do."

"No, I don't."

"But—"

"I borrowed it from Elmer's wife, Beatrice."

Dori chuckled at his self-righteous expression. "That's great, Tanner."

"I'll be darned if she didn't have the whole works— tablecloth, silverware, plastic plates and glasses. The only thing I paid for was the food, and she helped me make the sandwiches in her kitchen."

"I'm impressed." She was also touched. Tanner had taken her so seriously that he'd befriended the motel owners and asked for their help. She suspected Tanner wasn't used to asking people for special favors. "So you've made friends with Beatrice, then?"

He drove with one hand on the steering wheel, the other resting on the floor shift. "I think you're the reason she was so helpful."

"Me?" She found herself staring at his shift hand only a few inches from her knee. The Texas sun had burnished his skin, and there was a small scratch near his thumb that had nearly healed. His fingers curved lazily over the shift knob, and she could see that his nails were short and clean. It was a working hand, probably scratched by a rough piece of board or a wayward screwdriver. And she wanted to feel the caress of that capable hand on her skin.

"I get the idea that a lot of people in Los Lobos would like to see you break free of Jimmy Jr.'s domination," he said. "They just can't be too vocal about it."

Dori sighed, as much to release sexual tension as anything. "I know. I've had some great support from a couple of old high school friends. They're the ones who advised me to get married again. They were all set to help me find somebody, but then I saw the magazine and decided to try that, first."

Quietly, smoothly, Tanner moved his hand from the gearshift and laced his fingers through hers. "I'm glad."

Desire jolted through her at the subtle pressure of those strong fingers. She took a deep breath. "You know, we have to remember something."

The corner of his mouth lifted. "Tell me and I'll add it to the list."

"We might not get Little Jim back. We could get married, and pay the lawyer a lot of money, and still not get him."

"We would get him."

He spoke with such complete confidence that she wanted to take his word for it, but that was being naive. "You don't know the power the Devaneys have down here. The judge who heard the case last time had known James Devaney for thirty years. Like I said, we might not get him."

Tanner was silent for a moment. "And what would you do then?"

She honestly hadn't thought that far.

"Because if you'd divorce me and go back to Jimmy, just so you could be with Little Jim, you'd better tell me now."

"That would be horrible!"

"I agree. Would you do it?"

She thought about it, knowing that whatever her answer, it would have to be the final one. As recently as Sunday night she'd contemplated going back to Jimmy as a last resort. But now, with Tanner's hand holding hers, that seemed like a sin against herself that she could not commit, not even to be with her son.

"No," she said. "No, I wouldn't divorce you and go back to Jimmy."

His grip on her hand relaxed a fraction. "That's good to know," he said mildly, but there was a note of underlying tension.

"I'd want to keep trying to get Little Jim, though," she said.

"Of course. We'd never give up."

A lump lodged in her throat. That was what she'd needed to know. She remained silent until she trusted herself to speak again. "Tell me about your family," she said at last.

As he complied, she worked to keep details in mind, when what she really wanted was to hold him close and thank him for being the kind of man she'd dreamed about all her life. She managed to retain information about a younger sister struggling with the rigors of law school and parents who lived a comfortable but unpretentious life in Illinois.

Most important of all, Dori sensed the love that had surrounded Tanner as he grew up. Perhaps his devoted parents had indulged him a few times too often, which would explain his readiness to spend money without considering the consequences. But she'd rather deal with that problem than a lack of love, which tended to warp people in a way that was hard to straighten.

"Does your family know you came down here to meet me?" she asked.

"Yeah." Tanner laughed. "My mother couldn't understand why I needed to advertise for a wife, considering that I'm such a wonderful catch."

"You are, Tanner."

He took his attention from the road to glance at her in amusement. "As long as I learn some financial restraint, right?"

She nodded.

He returned his gaze to the road and rubbed his thumb across the back of her hand. "Financial restraint won't be the tough part."

As Dori's body warmed in response, she had to agree.

Tanner took a left turn on a dirt road. Driving slow enough that he kept the dust from billowing around them, he headed for a stand of cottonwoods. Dori had forgotten about this little oasis in the mostly treeless flatland around Los Lobos, although she'd come here a few times as a child. A rare underground spring fed the spot, creating a small pond that encouraged the cottonwoods to grow. This time of year, they shone yellow as ripe corn in the sunlight.

Dori smiled. "Trust you to seek out the only trees around for miles."

"I know how you like the open sky, but picnics and trees seem to go together. Elmer told me about Abilene Lake, but it would have taken longer to get there and we wouldn't have been alone."

Dori's heart pounded. "Which might have been a good thing."

Leaves crunched under the tires as Tanner guided the truck off the roadway and found a shady place to park. He switched off the engine and turned to her. "I said my intentions were pure. I never promised not to kiss you. And I prefer kissing in private."

Her heart pounded faster. "Just kissing?"

He regarded her with a twinkle in his eyes. "You sound disappointed."

"No! I just...wanted us to be clear."

His gaze became more serious. "We're clear." Then he opened his door. "Come on. We have to start back in less than two hours."

Dori helped him spread the red gingham tablecloth over a bed of fallen leaves and unpack the lunch. In the cottonwood tree above them a pair of canyon wrens sent their shimmering call down through the gold leaves. Little Jim would have loved this outing, she thought. Then she experienced a flash of guilt because she was secretly glad her son wasn't with them today. With a start she realized that being with Tanner eased the grief of not having Little Jim with her. That was important, considering there were no guarantees about making this group a threesome in the future.

"You do know about poison ivy, don't you?" she asked as Tanner set the basket in the middle of the cloth and opened it.

He glanced toward a scarlet-leaved plant about twenty feet away. "Like that?"

"Like that. Years ago one of my cousins visiting from Arizona brought me a bouquet of fall leaves. He was especially proud of the bright red ones. He had a miserable visit after that."

Tanner laughed. "Poor guy. Did you have him on a budget, too?"

"For your information, I am not in the habit of putting people on budgets. In fact, I've never done it before."

He sat back on his heels and gazed at her. "I guess that puts me in a special category."

"I guess it does."

He grinned. "Shoot, anything to stand out from the crowd, I always say. Let's eat."

Tanner's choice for lunch was ham sandwiches, chips, lemonade and a package of chocolate cupcakes. They sat on either side of the picnic basket, plates balanced on their laps and their lemonade glasses sitting on the closed lid of the basket as they ate.

"The sandwiches are delicious," Dori said after enjoying her first bite.

"Thanks. I haven't made sandwiches in a long time, but I guess it's not the sort of thing you forget how to do."

"You eat out a lot, don't you?"

"Yep." He bit a big chunk from his sandwich.

"That's wasteful, Tanner."

He finished chewing and swallowed before glancing sideways at her. "Maybe I was compensating for not having someone like you sitting across from me."

"There you go again, with that sweet talk."

"Want me to stop?"

"No. I'm truly beginning to enjoy it." She watched an orange dragonfly dip toward the small pond, take on water and buzz skyward again like a miniature biplane dusting crops. "You know, I haven't shared a picnic lunch with a man since..." She paused and reached into her memory. "Since high school, I guess. And back then my dates were technically boys, not men. So I guess I've never had a picnic with a man unless you count my daddy."

"Did you ever come out here?"

She finished a bite of sandwich. "Not on dates. We always went to Abilene Lake. But my momma and daddy brought me out here when I was younger than Little Jim." She glanced at the pond, not much bigger than her backyard. "They teased me about that picnic for years afterward. It seems that when I saw the water, I asked Daddy if this was the ocean."

Tanner chuckled.

"I hadn't traveled much. In fact, when I married Jimmy Jr., I still hadn't been very many places. We went to Hawaii on our honeymoon and I just stared at that amazing water. All the different colors just knocked me out."

"It's spectacular, all right."

"You've been there?" She gazed at him and shook her head. "I'm really worried about you. Champagne tastes on a beer budget, as they say. You have to live within your means if you're not rich like the Devaneys."

He set aside his plate. "Reform me."

Her pulse quickened at the look in his eyes. "I'm trying. But Hawaii, Tanner! You're going to be a hard case."

"Maybe I didn't have anything better to do." He lifted the picnic basket, careful not to spill the lemonade, and settled it at the far edge of the tablecloth. Then he took her plate from her unresisting hands and set it on the top of the basket. "Going to Hawaii was the most exciting thing I could think of."

Her breathing grew shallow as he leaned toward her, the promise of a kiss in his intense gaze. Balanced on one outstretched hand, she met him halfway.

"Didn't anyone ever tell you that the best things in life are free?" she whispered.

"I didn't really believe it." He paused a fraction away from the kiss. "Until I met you."

Only their lips touched, withdrew and touched again, almost as if they'd choreographed the delicate movement required. Too much pressure by either of them would send one of them toppling. Too little would mute the satisfaction of tasting each other. His tongue questioned, hers answered. Then, as she began to tremble and lose her balance, he caught her shoulders and guided her down, his mouth never leaving hers.

Beneath them the leaves crunched. Dori accepted Tanner's weight with a sigh of delight and wound her arms around him, bringing him closer. She'd forgotten the delicious feeling of a man lying against her breasts, exerting just enough pressure to knead their fullness with his movements.

He lifted his head to gaze down at her, but kept her lightly pinned to the gingham cloth with his upper body. Slowly he combed her hair with his fingers, his eyes alight with pleasure. "You wore your hair down. Was that for me?"

"Yes."

His glance roamed over her face. "You were made for this season of the year. The red in your hair..." He buried his fingers in it before leaning in close again. "The little gold flecks in your eyes when the sun's just right." He ran the tip of his finger over her parted lips. "And your mouth is the color of ripe apples."

"Sweet talker." She cupped the back of his head. "Kiss me again, Tanner. Kiss me real good."

His mouth came down again, hungrier now, but so

was she. This time when he pulled her T-shirt from the waistband of her jeans and reached for the back catch of her bra, she arched her back to allow him to do it. And at last those workman's hands she'd fantasized about were cupping her breasts, stroking her nipples, making her whimper with desire.

It was heaven on earth, but she couldn't let him go on and think her a tease. She grasped his hands, holding on tight, and his movements stilled. He raised his head and gazed down at her. Silently, she looked into his eyes and watched the resignation settle in their blue depths. Slowly, he helped her up and refastened her bra. She noted his expertise and decided Tanner Jones was far more experienced than she, but then, most people were. Jimmy Jr. was her whole point of reference.

"Tell me again why we're waiting," Tanner said.

"So we can get to know each other first."

"Couldn't we sort of work on both things at once?"

She took his face in her hands. She longed to crush his mouth against hers once more, but she remembered her ultimate goal and resisted the urge. "You put your picture in *Texas Men* because you weren't happy with the relationships you'd had so far. Is that right?"

He sighed, as if knowing he'd lost the battle. "Yes, that's right."

"Besides throwing your money around, you probably rushed into intimacy with a woman, didn't you?"

"Maybe. But that was different, because—"

She laid her finger against his lips. "Not so different, perhaps. I won't let you ruin this. Not by spending too much money and not by making love before your heart's in it."

He leaned his forehead against hers and closed his

eyes. "What if I told you my heart's in it now, right this minute, and the rest of me is dying to follow?"

"I'd say you're a sweet-talkin' man who's used to getting what he wants immediately. But you're here now, not in East Texas." She took a long, steadying breath. "And thanks to me you're going to learn the art of anticipation."

8

DORI DIDN'T THINK anything could affect her positive mood as she started her shift that afternoon at the Double Nickel. She smiled at Heck Tyrrell when she saw him sitting at the counter enjoying an order of liver and onions. "Didn't expect to see you again so soon, Heck."

"My rig's in the shop until three," he said after swallowing a bite of food. "Had to put up at the Prairie Schooner last night."

Dori thought about that while she took a couple of orders from people sitting in the booths and clipped them to the stainless-steel ticket carousel. Heck had more to say on the subject of staying at the Prairie Schooner. She could feel it. Well, she had nothing to hide or be ashamed of.

She picked up the coffeepot and moved down the counter, deliberately serving Heck last. "I stopped by the Prairie Schooner myself last night," she said casually.

"I know. Saw your car."

"I didn't stay long." Darn it, she sounded defensive when she had no reason to be.

Heck blew across the surface of his coffee and glanced up at her. "That's your business, how long you stayed."

Dori felt heat climb into her cheeks. "Heck—"

"Easy, Dori Mae. I'm not fixing to judge you. It ain't

my place. Besides, I talked to that ol' boy later on. He ain't so bad considerin' he's from East Texas."

"You talked to him?" Dori wondered why Tanner had failed to mention that. "When?"

"When we had all the commotion out there. You didn't hear about it?"

"No. What—" She paused as the cook set an order on the pass-through and another customer took a seat at the counter. "Don't you move from that spot, Heck Tyrrell. I want to hear all about this commotion."

"I ain't goin' anywheres until three." Heck pushed away his empty plate and reached in his breast pocket for a toothpick.

A rush of business kept Dori busy for another fifteen minutes, but Heck sat patiently drinking coffee. Finally, she made it back to him, stuck her order pad and pencil in the pocket of her uniform and braced her elbows on the counter. "Now tell me about this commotion."

Heck took his toothpick from the corner of his mouth. "I figured you'd know about it by now. Some high school kids threw a stink bomb in one of the rooms. The parking lot smelled like a pig farm for quite a while. I guess the poor folks in the room had to borrow some clothes from Elmer and Beatrice while they washed every stitch they had."

"So that's when you talked to Tanner?"

"Yeah, everybody came out of their rooms to see what the ruckus was about. I recognized your new beau, so I decided to go over and say howdy. Check him out."

Dori noticed two truckers at the cash register, ready to pay. "Stay there," she instructed Heck. "I'll be right back."

A thought niggled at her as she finished the transaction for the truckers. She smiled at them as she closed the cash register. "Y'all come back now," she said automatically, but her thoughts were on the vandalism at the Prairie Schooner. It could be coincidence that the motel was hit soon after Tanner arrived there, but she didn't think so. Besides, Tanner hadn't mentioned the incident, maybe because he didn't want to worry her. That would be like Tanner, trying to protect her.

Finally, she poured coffee for everyone at the counter and topped off Heck's cup. "Are you sure it was high school kids?" she asked.

"Nothin' else makes sense. Those folks were from New Mexico, and they'd just stopped for one night. They didn't have time to get somebody riled enough to throw a stink bomb in their room in the middle of the night."

Dori lowered her voice. "Maybe it was meant for Tanner. Did you think of that?"

Heck glanced down the counter and leaned closer to Dori before he spoke. "Jimmy's information would've been better. He would've hit the right room."

"I suppose."

Soon after that Heck left and customers kept Dori busy for the next two hours. Yet she couldn't forget about the incident at the Prairie Schooner. The act was so like one Jimmy had pulled when he was a senior at Los Lobos High. The geometry teacher, Mr. Confer, had flunked him. He'd slit the screen of an open window of Mr. Confer's house and pitched a stink bomb inside. He hadn't been caught, but he couldn't resist bragging about it to Dori after they were married.

This time he'd probably have bribed a maid to find out Tanner's room number and then sent somebody else to throw the bomb. Jimmy wouldn't have risked being tied to the episode. And the only reason Tanner hadn't ended up with a stink bomb perfuming all his belongings was that Jimmy's hired punk had bombed the wrong room.

Or had he?

The Double Nickel had telephones in each of the booths for any truckers who wanted to call home. Dori looked up the number for the Prairie Schooner in the phone book the café kept behind the cash register. Then during a lull in business she slid into an empty booth and called the motel.

Elmer answered. "Dori! Did you and that ol' boy have a good time today?"

"We sure did, Elmer. Please thank Beatrice for the loan of her picnic basket. That was right generous of her."

"She thinks the world of you, Dori Mae, and we both feel bad about what you've been through. Your East Texan seems okay. Doesn't even act much like he's from the city."

"Well, he says you and Beatrice have been taking real good care of him, changing his room for him and all."

"Good thing we did, too! Some kids threw a stink bomb in the room he was in before."

Dori closed her eyes. So he hadn't been in room nine all along. He'd deliberately lied to her. It wasn't a big lie. Some would say it wasn't even worth bothering about. But she was putting her life, not to mention Little Jim's, on the line. With stakes like that, there was no such thing as a small lie.

TANNER HAD DECIDED to take Dori dancing after she got off work. Given his budget, he'd had to settle for the Golden Spur, a small bar on the outskirts of town. Elmer had told him to expect reasonable drink prices, a jukebox and a postage-stamp-sized dance floor. Elmer hadn't thought it would be very crowded on a Tuesday night.

When Tanner had picked Dori up at her house he'd been looking forward to the pleasures of a honky-tonk sort of evening, the kind he'd enjoyed years ago before he'd graduated to expensive nightclubs. He'd viewed Dori's choice of clothing with appreciation—a scoop-necked white blouse tucked into a colorful broomstick skirt. She'd looked feminine, sexy...and madder than a wet hen.

They'd ridden to the Golden Spur in silence, and now they sat across from each other at a small table right next to the tiny, deserted dance floor. A couple of cowboys sat at the bar a distance away from them, but otherwise the place was empty. Two draft beers sat sweating on two small napkins in front of Tanner and Dori. She hadn't touched hers.

Whatever was bothering her, she wasn't having much success broaching the subject. Tanner really hated to ask, because it seemed to be the equivalent of poking in a hollow tree with a stick to find out what the buzzing sound was all about. But finally he couldn't stand the tension any longer.

"Will you tell me about it?"

To his surprise her eyes filled with tears. She swiped at them with angry motions of both hands.

"Dori, for goodness' sake, what's wrong?"

She shoved away his hand as he reached for her. "I suppose you think it's real funny that somebody uses a lucky number to guide their actions."

"No, no I don't. I might not believe in it myself, but I respect—"

"The hell you do." Her voice was low and tight. "You used the information to hornswoggle me, though." She glared at him, unsuccessfully trying to hide her hurt behind a facade of anger. "Room nine. What a coincidence. And all the time you were laughing at me."

The bottom seemed to drop out of his stomach. The truth was his only defense. "I wasn't laughing. I thought I was going to lose you."

"So you made a mockery of my little superstition. How charming."

"No, I grabbed at the first thing I could think of to keep you around. Desperation makes people do all sorts of things." He captured her gaze with his and willed her to understand.

"Like lie?"

"I would have told you the truth about the room eventually. Sure, I manipulated the situation to my advantage, and I'd do it again, just to spend a morning like we shared, just to hold you in my arms one more time. I'll never forget the pleasure of touching you, Dori."

She glanced away, and color rose in her cheeks. "You're getting away from the subject."

"Am I? You told me yourself that you'd thought of sending me back to Dallas before you found out what room I had at the motel. I bought myself more time with you. I bought us more time."

Her eyes were large and shining with the vulnerability that had tugged at him when he'd first seen her picture. "And I suppose that makes it all right."

"For me it does. You'll have to answer for yourself."

She stared at him wordlessly, looking like a waxen image except for the gentle motion of her throat as she swallowed.

"Think about it for a minute," he said softly. "I'll be right back." He walked over to the silent jukebox and put coins in the slot. Then he picked out every damn song next to a number with a nine in it. He didn't even look at the selections. Maybe it was time to trust this mystical connection she had with a number. After all, it had gotten him this far. Maybe it would pull him out of this hole he was in.

He walked back to the table just as the opening chords of an Alan Jackson song surged from the juke-box. He gazed down at her. "Care to dance?"

She looked up at him, her heart in her eyes. Then slowly she stood and moved into his arms. He gathered her close with an unspoken prayer of gratitude. She wouldn't disappear from his life yet. Maybe in a few moments, when the song ended, she'd collect herself and order him to leave. But for now she wound one arm around his neck and laid her head on his shoulder. He held her hand cupped against his chest as they swayed, barely moving their feet.

Tanner rested his cheek against her silky hair and breathed in the fragrance as if he needed her scent to live. And maybe he did. Alan Jackson crooned about lovers being able to walk through fire without blink-ing, and Tanner understood completely. For the first time since he'd met Dori, his primary concern wasn't how soon he'd be able to make love to her. She could probably change his focus with a kiss, but for the mo-ment he cherished the simple act of holding her. A de-sire for her body had been replaced by a desire for her trust.

He thought of all she didn't know about him and decided the time had come to tell her about his financial situation. Dori wasn't a gold digger. It wasn't in her nature to be greedy. But she valued the truth, and she deserved to have it. After this dance.

Gradually, she relaxed against him, and as the song ended she was snuggled so close, he hated to move and break the mood. The next song slipped into place on the jukebox, and it was another love ballad, this time by George Strait.

With a sigh Dori lifted her head and looked into Tanner's eyes as she swayed to the gentle rhythm. "I like your taste in songs."

"I didn't pick them."

"Of course you did. I watched you do it."

"I put in the money. Then I let your lucky number do the picking."

Her eyes narrowed. "Are you making fun of me again?"

"I never was making fun of you." He held her close and moved to the music. This subject wouldn't come between them again if he could help it. "And as you well know, changing to room nine saved me from that stink bomb. Without your belief in number nine, you wouldn't have bought the September issue of *Texas Men* or picked me out as the ninth bachelor. I owe that number a lot, so I decided to find out what happened if I abandoned myself to its power."

"You *are* making fun of me."

"Absolutely not." Her body was so warm, so supple, against his. "I'm more convinced than ever that you're on to something. You just said you liked the songs."

The suspicion gradually disappeared, leaving her eyes soft as a doe's. "They're so...romantic."

He caressed the small of her back. "And exactly what we needed."

"Promise to tell me the truth from now on, Tanner."

"I will," he vowed. *Right after this dance.* Sure, he could have led her back immediately to the table and resolutely presented the news of his healthy investment portfolio. Maybe there was a man somewhere with the strength to resist the petal-soft feel of her cheek against his, her gentle fragrance wafting from the tender spot behind her ear where women dabbed their cologne, her ripe woman's body undulating in time to the music. Tanner wasn't that man.

Somebody tapped him on the shoulder. He edged slowly out of his daze and turned, wondering if one of the idiots who'd been sitting at the bar really expected to cut in.

A young buck in a formfitting T-shirt that showed off his pecs stood behind Tanner. He adjusted his black Stetson. "You the ol' boy who owns that Chevy pickup out front?" he asked.

Technically, it belonged to one of his electricians. "Why?"

"Excuse me, ma'am." The cowboy tipped his hat toward Dori before facing Tanner again. "Your bucket of bolts just rolled into my truck, that's why, sucker. Don't they know about emergency brakes in East Texas?"

Tanner knew the guy was lying about the accident, if there even was one. He could be part of an insurance scam or he could be connected to Jimmy Jr. The East Texas crack indicated he knew who Tanner was, so Devaney could be behind it. Tanner would rather have it be about insurance. That would only take money to fix.

He released Dori. "Why don't you go have some of that draft we ordered while I take care of this?"

She started to protest.

"Please."

She looked doubtful but made her way back to the table, where she glanced back at him, a worried expression on her face.

"Let's go take a look," Tanner said to the muscleman, whose sculpted body was probably more the result of constant contact with a weight machine than hours spent in honest labor.

The guy headed toward the front door of the bar. "Just got my truck painted, a primo job, too. I don't appreciate having some screwup like you ruin it just because he can't pull a damn handle."

Tanner remembered leaving the truck in gear, setting the emergency and locking both doors. But there was no alarm system, no security club for the wheel. Anybody with a slim-jim bar could have opened it, put it in neutral and released the brake.

Outside, the parking lot lights illuminated his electrician's old truck, the tailgate wedged against the dented passenger door of a cherry red pickup. It looked like a setup, but that wasn't what worried him. Three more bulked-up cowboys stood around the wreck, beer cans in hand, voices loud as they discussed the accident. When Tanner walked out they all looked up with a decidedly predatory expression.

"This the one?" asked a guy with a droopy mustache.

"Yeah," said the cowboy who had come into the bar. He swung back to Tanner. "See what you did to my truck? Somebody's gonna pay for that, and it sure as hell ain't gonna be me."

Tanner evaluated his chances against the four men. Not good. "I distinctly remember putting the car in gear and setting the brake," he said. "Besides that, I locked it."

"Did you now?" The truck owner sneered at him. "I don't think so, sucker. My friends here saw it all happen. We pulled in, figuring to grab us a beer at the Golden Spur, and just as we cruised by, your truck started roll-in'. Couldn't get out of the way."

"You're lying, mister," Tanner said easily.

The truck owner glanced back at his pals. "You hear that? This ol' boy from East Texas called me a liar."

"Don't be lettin' him get away with that, Billy Joe."

There was an inevitable quality about the exchange. Tanner had pretty much known what to expect from the minute he walked out the door of the bar and saw the other guys. "We'll see what the insurance adjusters have to say about it," he said, reaching for his wallet to give the guy a card he didn't expect him to accept. This wasn't about vehicle repair.

"That usually takes a long time, don't it?" the truck owner said.

Tanner met his mocking gaze. "Depends on whether you have a legitimate claim."

"I don't think I want to wait for no insurance adjuster. I want satisfaction now."

"Too bad." Tanner watched the other three move closer. He flexed his shoulders and shifted his weight to the balls of his feet. "I don't carry much cash."

"Then I guess I'll have to take it out of your hide."

Tanner's knuckles smashed against the truck owner's jaw. It was the only punch he was able to throw before the others closed in.

DORI SIPPED HER BEER, but she kept a constant watch on the front door of the bar. Tanner's selections kept playing on the jukebox, and she loved all of them. She'd be sure and tell him as soon as he got back, which should be any minute. He and the cowboy would exchange insurance information and be done with it. She hoped Tanner carried good insurance. The way he was about money, he might have skimped on his coverage.

Interspersed with her thoughts was a remembered sound. She kept hearing the sound in her mind and wondered why. Finally, she identified it—the rasp of an emergency brake. She'd been preoccupied by her feelings of betrayal when they'd turned into the parking lot, and if the cowboy had asked her, she wouldn't have been able to swear whether Tanner had pulled on the brake. Except that he had. As she replayed their arrival in her mind, she heard him shut off the engine and set the brake.

She bolted from her chair and ran for the door. As she flung it open a red truck peeled out of the lot. Tanner lay crumpled on the ground.

With a cry she ran over and dropped to her knees beside him. His right eye was already swelling shut and he was bleeding from his nose. He looked blearily up at her with his one good eye. "Coulda taken him, 'cept for his three friends," he mumbled through a mouth cut and bleeding. Then he passed out.

9

THE NEXT COUPLE of hours were a scrambled nightmare for Dori. She instructed the bartender to call 9-1-1, which brought Deputy Holt in a squad car and Los Lobos's single licensed paramedic, Ned Fickett, in the volunteer fire department's truck. Tanner regained consciousness just as they arrived and protested all the attention for what he insisted were minor injuries. Nevertheless, the paramedic applied first aid and the deputy took a report. Dori wasn't able to identify the man who had entered the bar, and neither she nor Tanner could remember the license number of the truck.

On Ned Fickett's advice, Dori drove Tanner to the small emergency clinic for a more thorough examination. He was diagnosed with two cracked ribs, which were taped, a broken nose, which was splinted, and numerous gashes, which were bandaged. He wanted to drive when they left the clinic, but Dori refused to give him the keys to the truck.

When he allowed her to keep them, she knew how whipped he really was. She drove straight to her house, parked the truck defiantly in her driveway and helped him inside. She'd love Jimmy Jr. to make a big deal out of it. At this moment she felt that if he showed up she could do at least as much damage to him as his hired punks had done to Tanner. Every time Tanner winced, or she looked at the bruise darkening around his swollen eye, her rage grew.

With a supportive arm around his waist, she guided him down the hall toward her bedroom.

"Bad idea, coming here," he mumbled through swollen lips. "I can't promise I won't—"

"I can. You're a mess. And you're too big and too injured to cram yourself on the couch or Little Jim's bed. I'll sleep in my son's room tonight."

"Okay." He stumbled. "Sorry. Guess I'm a bit dizzy."

"No kidding." She pulled back the covers, sat him on the bed and started unbuttoning his shirt.

He allowed her to take that off, but when she reached for his belt buckle he caught her hand. "Don't test me," he muttered.

"You can do it?"

"You might be surprised what I can do." His smile ended in a groan as his split lip began bleeding again. "Got a washcloth?"

"Coming up." She hurried into the bathroom, dampened a red washcloth and brought it back. She dabbed at his lip.

"Can't see the blood," he said.

She glanced down at the washcloth. She'd automatically grabbed the one she used to clean up Little Jim's scratches. "On purpose. It keeps people from getting scared by seeing their own blood all over the place."

"Good idea." He sounded incredibly weary.

"The bleeding's stopped." She set the washcloth on the night table and helped him to his feet. "Let's get you into bed."

"Nicest offer I've had all night."

But she could tell, despite his lighthearted comments, that he felt as bad as he looked. "Are you sure you can get your jeans off by yourself?"

He nodded.

She stayed in the room just to make sure he didn't fall and hurt himself even worse. At least, she told herself that was the reason. He'd just been beaten up, for heaven's sake, so now wasn't an appropriate time to admire his strong-looking thighs or the substantial bulk contained in the crotch of his white briefs.

"You don't have to sleep in Little Jim's bed."

She glanced into his face with a guilty start. "Yes, I do. Goodness, Tanner, you have two cracked ribs. How can you even be thinking—"

"Weren't you?"

"I—" She could feel the blush spreading. "Never mind. Get under the covers. And I'll bet you could use a glass of water. And a fresh ice pack for your eye. I'll get them." She started toward the door.

"Sleep with me, Dori."

She paused, her back to him.

"We don't have to make love."

She shook her head.

"You don't trust me?"

"I trust you just fine. It's me I don't trust."

"Oh." Even through his weariness and pain, male satisfaction was obvious in that single syllable.

Dori left the room quickly.

By the time she returned with a soft-gel ice pack and a glass of water, Tanner had climbed into her bed and thrown a sheet over himself. His eyes were closed, and she thought he might have already gone to sleep. She crept to his bedside, set the glass of water down carefully and switched off the bedside lamp. Then she started to walk away.

"Don't go."

She turned back to him. "I thought you were asleep. Do you want the ice pack for your eye?"

"I'd rather have you lie down beside me."

"Tanner—"

"Outside the covers, if you want." He sighed. "I don't have any devious plans, unfortunately. I think the adrenaline rush is about gone, and I feel like hell."

"You need another pain pill." She reached for the bottle on the bedside table.

"I hate those damn things. They make me disoriented. Please, Dori. Just lie beside me. That's better than any painkiller they could prescribe."

"Okay." She walked around to the other side of the bed, took off her shoes and eased down on top of the bedspread, not wanting to jiggle him and cause him more discomfort. She laid her head on the pillow and gazed up at the shadowy ceiling above them.

In the darkness, his hand found hers and held it loosely as they lay together, their breathing the only sound in the room. Dori gradually relaxed as a floating, peaceful feeling traveled from their joined hands and spread throughout her tense body.

"The worst part of it was feeling so helpless," he said.

The peaceful feeling evaporated, and she didn't trust herself to speak. Thinking about him being beaten up by four men made her stomach churn.

"I haven't felt that much loss of control since I had my tonsils out when I was fifteen, and they put me under the anesthetic. I tried to fight back, but those guys operated like a trained machine."

She finally voiced a thought she'd had some time

ago. "You knew it could turn out like that when you left the bar, didn't you?"

"I knew I'd set the brake. I was hoping it was all about insurance. Then I saw the three other guys and figured it wasn't."

Her jaw clenched. "Then why in heaven's name didn't you turn around and come back inside?"

"Because he just would have tried again later, with a new set of bullies. I decided to get this part over with."

"Oh, did you? And what's the next part, allowing him to have you killed?"

"He won't go that far."

She laughed in disbelief.

"No, seriously. This is just an old-fashioned brand of intimidation. Once he finds out that I'm still here, even after his boys beat me up, he'll search for a new tactic. I'm not sure what it'll be, but I think the physical part is over."

As Dori listened to him breathe, she thought of how every inhalation must hurt his cracked ribs. Yes, the physical intimidation was indeed over. She'd make sure of it. Beneath her rage at Jimmy and her impatience at Tanner's willingness to take such punishment lay a reservoir of guilt, boiling hot enough to scald her conscience. She'd brought Tanner into this situation. If she hadn't written to him, he wouldn't have a black eye, broken nose and cracked ribs. He'd be dating some other woman who had admired his picture in *Texas Men*. Some safe woman with a cozy apartment, and a cat, and no complications in her life.

Dori had to convince him to go back to Dallas, even if that meant giving up her idea of creating a two-parent household for Little Jim. Even if it meant giving up Tanner before she knew if they'd make wonderful lovers and best friends. No matter how much she wanted that, she wouldn't sacrifice another human being, let alone a dear man like Tanner, in her efforts to get it.

Maybe Jimmy Jr. wouldn't send another bunch of punks to use Tanner as a human punching bag, but then again maybe he would. It would be simple, really, to get Tanner out of town. She'd just tell him that she couldn't imagine a future together and he might as well go home and answer somebody else's letter. He couldn't argue with her if she told him she didn't want him.

She took a deep breath and shoved her own dreams and plans aside. Might as well get it over with. "Tanner?"

There was no response except for the sound of his breathing. She disengaged herself from his loose grip and propped herself up so she could study his face. He was asleep.

She tried to ignore a feeling of relief as she crept out of the bed and left the room. They'd still have to have their final conversation, of course. But not quite yet. She closed the door softly behind her and headed for her kitchen phone. It was nearly one in the morning, but she didn't give a damn. She had a call to make and the idea of waking up the Devaney household didn't faze her.

After five rings, James Devaney answered with a curt and impatient "Yes?"

"Let me speak to Jimmy."

"Dori, Jimmy Jr. is asleep." He sounded furious, but then he often sounded furious. "So is everyone else in this house, or, at least, we were. Are you drunk?"

"I am stone-cold sober, James." She'd seldom had

the nerve to use his given name when she'd lived there. There was great satisfaction in using it tonight. "And I want to talk to your son. Now."

He raised his voice, one of his favorite tricks for subduing subordinates. "I'm hanging up this phone, Dori Mae. And don't you *ever* try to give me orders again."

"Did Jimmy tell you about throwing the stink bomb in Mr. Confer's window when he was a senior in high school?"

"What?"

"He told me. I imagine Deputy Holt would like to know about that little prank. The sheriff's department keeps records on things like that. He might be able to compare the type of bomb used with the type somebody tossed into a room at the Prairie Schooner Monday night."

"You *are* drunk, young lady. I—"

She heard the sound of him muffling the receiver.

Then the muffling disappeared. "Make it quick," James said from a distance. "I don't appreciate getting calls at one in the morning."

Jimmy Jr. came on the line. "Miss me, sweetheart? Want Jimmy to come over and make you feel good?"

"You arrogant, mean son of a bitch."

"Dori, honey, you know our women don't swear like that. It's so unbecomin' on somebody as pretty as you."

Her fingers tightened around the receiver. "You sent those punks to beat him up, didn't you?"

"I don't have the first clue what you're talkin' about, baby. Beat who up?"

"You did it, all right, just like you arranged to have the stink bomb thrown into his motel room. I know you, Jimmy. I'm telling Deputy Holt about the bomb you put in Mr. Confer's house. He was around then,

probably remembers it real well. Maybe he can tie the
two bombings together."

"I guess you got ahold of some locoweed, sweetheart. I didn't do any such thing as throw a stink bomb,
either into old man Confer's house or the Prairie
Schooner."

"You did! You told me exactly how!"

"But that'd be your word against mine, now
wouldn't it? And everybody knows you're tryin' to get
me in trouble, on account of Little Jim and all."

She ground her back teeth together. She'd thought
that confession of his would give her some leverage,
but he was right. It was his word against hers. She'd
never mentioned the incident to any of her friends after
Jimmy told her about it, not even after the divorce, because she'd imagined she owed Jimmy some loyalty
considering she'd been the one who'd left the marriage. She should have taken out an ad in the *Los Lobos
Weekly Tribune* listing all Jimmy Jr.'s transgressions.

"Little Jim asked me again when you were coming
home, Dori Mae."

"You know something, Jimmy? Last Sunday I
thought I might be able to put up with you if that was
my last resort for getting to be with Little Jim every
day. But the way you've acted with Tanner, I know I
couldn't humiliate myself that much, even for Little
Jim. Get this straight. I'm never coming back. Never."
She slammed down the phone—a small victory and
cold comfort, considering that she wasn't in a very
wonderful position right now. But the gesture felt
good, nonetheless.

It was very late, and she'd been through a lot today,
she thought, yawning. She made sure the house was
secure, flipped out the lights in the kitchen and living

room and went to check on Tanner. He slept, looking vulnerable with his splint on his nose and his taped chest visible where the sheet had pulled back. She placed a kiss on the tips of her fingers and touched his cheek lightly. He moaned and shifted to his side, but didn't awaken.

"Sleep well, my hero," she whispered. "You've been wonderful, and far more than I deserve."

Then she went into Little Jim's room. Her night things were back in her bedroom, so she decided to sleep in her panties and her white blouse rather than risk disturbing Tanner. Pulling back the spread, she slipped into his narrow twin bed, made even narrower by all the stuffed animals grouped on it.

She lay in the darkness, expecting sleep. But only grief arrived. She'd tried so hard to remedy the mistake she'd made when she'd said "I do" to Jimmy Jr. Nothing seemed to be working, and she'd brought misery to a good man in the process of searching for a solution. She pulled Little Jim's favorite bear close and its soft fur absorbed her tears.

WHEN TANNER FIRST TRIED to open his eyes, he thought he must have the hangover of the decade. Then gradually he remembered the night before and the four weight lifters dressed like cowboys. He'd be willing to bet they'd been imported from Amarillo, or even as far away as El Paso. The cherry red truck was probably in some chop-shop by now, being dismantled for parts so no evidence would remain.

And he was in Dori's bed, surrounded by a million pictures of her son. She'd left him sometime during the night, probably to snuggle in with Little Jim's collection of furry friends. He raised himself up slowly, and discovered his head wasn't spinning the way it had last night. Sure, he hurt, but at least he was awake. Last night he'd been spaced out on the damn painkillers, and God knows what he'd said. Probably acted like a complete idiot.

He pulled on his jeans, took the bottle of pills from the bedside table on his way to the bathroom and flushed them away. Enough of that nonsense. He took a quick look at himself in the mirror and almost wished he hadn't. Now there was a face to inspire love in a fair damsel. Maybe if she was into the legend of Beauty and the Beast, he'd have a better than even chance.

Debating the issue for only a moment, he used the spare toothbrush she'd put out for him and the razor she kept in the shower for her legs. A guy who looked like the Phantom of the Opera needed all the help he could get.

The house was quiet as he walked barefoot down the hall. Sure enough, she was in Little Jim's twin bed, at least four stuffed animals gathered into her arms as she slept. In his estimation she needed something more substantial to hold, something with a pulse. And this morning, thanks to the healing powers of sleep, he had one.

Her kitchen was easy to figure out. She'd put things where he would have if he'd been deciding. That was probably a good sign, and he should remember to tell her about it later. Breakfast was the only meal of the day he normally fixed for himself, and he set about brewing coffee and pouring juice with a practiced hand. With each step he marveled that she had the exact supplies he would have required in his own place.

Today he'd tell her about his high-rise luxury apartment unit in Dallas, his Jaguar in the apartment's underground garage, his small cabin in the lake country and his yacht moored in Galveston Harbor. He'd explain how he'd caught the boom in the bedroom community of Bravo, east of Dallas, where homes sold for millions and builders with vision could name their price. He'd been that sort of builder.

He soft-boiled a couple of eggs, toasted some whole-wheat bread and was ready to bring her breakfast on a tray. It seemed like the perfect gesture after she'd cared for him so capably the night before. Apparently, she'd driven the truck without a flicker of doubt, and brought him home with her rather than dump him at an impersonal motel. That was also a good sign. He'd build on that.

A selection of trays sat on top of the refrigerator, and he found one in wicker that held everything he'd created. On an impulse, he went out the front door to pick a chrysanthemum for the tray. There in the driveway sat his electrician's truck, the side spray-painted in white with the message Go Home, City Boy. Sweet. His electrician, Jay, would end up with a paint job on his truck as well as a tailgate and rear bumper replacement.

If this was Jimmy Jr.'s next move, it lacked originality. Tanner could live with a little spray paint. He picked his chrysanthemum, a striking orange one, and stuck it in the bud vase he'd found in a cabinet over the stove. Closing the front door, he latched the dead bolt and picked up the tray, complete with flower. Time for his lady fair to awaken.

He set the tray on the brightly painted child's dresser against the wall near the bed. The tray shared the surface with the White Ranger. Then he crouched down so his face was even with Dori's. For a moment he watched her sleep, her rosy lips slightly parted, her wondrous eyes shuttered, her luxuriant eyelashes resting against her cheeks. His heart contracted. This view could be his every morning. The possibility made his throat ache with longing.

Leaning closer, he angled his mouth and brushed a kiss against her sleep-softened lips. He barely noticed the slight sting of discomfort from his split lip, because he was so entranced by her response. She turned her face upward, as if seeking the source of pleasure as she struggled toward wakefulness. Needing no more encouragement, he placed his mouth over hers again and stroked his tongue inside. Yes. He wanted this every morning.

She wound her arms around his neck and drew him down. He pushed the stuffed animals out of the way, threw back the light cover and eased over her. He would have loved to have more room, but if she was inviting him to bed he wouldn't be choosy about the details. As he settled against her breasts he winced at the pain from his taped ribs, but he was more impatient with the tape than the pain. It kept him from a total experience of skin touching skin.

Because that would happen now. She would let him love her. She was too warm, too willing, for there to be any other outcome.

As he continued to plunder her lips, he reached between them to pull the end of the tie that gathered her blouse into a modest scooped neck. Once the tie was released, the neckline became much less modest, giving him easy access to her breasts. Filling one hand with her bounty, he released her mouth and raised his head. He wanted to see her eyes.

Slowly, they fluttered open. The passion filling their brown depths made his heart pound.

"Good morning," he murmured as he caressed her, his thumb brushing over her nipple. "I brought you breakfast in bed."

Her voice was husky from sleep and desire. "Is this it?"

"Chef's special."

"I was going to ask you to leave town this morning."

"Oh?" He cupped her other breast and continued to build the heat in her gaze.

She arched against his hand with a soft moan. "You're not safe here."

He grazed her nipple with his thumb until it matched the pert attention of its mate. "And what made you think I'd agree to go?"

"I was..." She paused, caught her lower lip between her teeth and closed her eyes. "Oh, Tanner," she whispered. "That feels so good."

"Want me to leave town?"

"No. Yes." She opened her eyes again, rich laughter mixing with the desire in her glance. "But you're ruining the line I'd planned to use."

"Which was?"

"That I didn't want you."

He smiled down at her. "I wouldn't have believed you, anyway." He released her breast and worked the blouse off her shoulders. "You may not like the way I spend money, but you've always been crazy about the way I kiss you."

Her voice was low and sexy. "Conceited man."

"Lucky man." He kissed the pulse throbbing in her throat and breathed in the scent of wildflowers and arousal. "You're going to let me make love to you this morning."

"Am I?"

"Yes." He lifted his head to look into her eyes.

"No," she murmured, a sensuous smile curving her mouth.

"You're kidding." He ached all over from wanting her. A woman who could deny a man at this stage...

"I'm not kidding. You're not going to make love to me. You're injured."

"I don't give a good goddamn! I want—"

"So I'll make love to you."

He stared down at her.

"In a bigger bed. So we have room to enjoy this. Come on, Tanner. Move it."

10

TANNER HAD EXPECTED Dori to be alluring, voluptuous and deeply satisfying. He hadn't expected her to be an artist. He'd known that her mouth tempted him beyond reason. He'd hadn't known her mouth could carry him to levels of excitement he'd never experienced.

He lay trembling beneath the sweet assault, which began with his lips. Her kiss was so openly provocative he could hardly believe this was the same Dori Mae who had primly tucked her shirt back in her jeans at the motel on Monday night. She used her tongue to outline his lips, to explore the roof of his mouth, to stroke the inside of his cheeks. Then she drew his tongue into her mouth and sucked gently, giving him his first preview of what she had in mind. Her kiss alone brought him to a fever pitch of need, but she'd only begun.

She caught his earlobe between her teeth and raked gently. He'd never known he was so sensitive there, but that was nothing compared to the sensation she created by dipping her tongue into his ear. As she licked the curve of his jaw and the hollow of his throat, the warm, damp caress ignited nerve endings he hadn't known existed.

Then her sweet breath touched his shoulder, and she nibbled her way down his inner arm to the inside of his elbow. He'd been told women liked to be kissed there. Now he knew why.

Her journey continued to the palm of his hand, where she ran her tongue into the crevices between his fingers before taking each finger in turn into her mouth. He was a wild man, desperate for release yet never wanting the experience to end. She toyed with his nipples until he was panting, but she never put any weight on his taped ribs. When her tongue found his navel, he moaned in anticipation, but she had more sweet torture in mind before giving him her final gift.

She treated his toes to the same attention she had his fingers, and gently bent his legs to kiss the backs of his knees. The warmth of her mouth on his inner thighs nearly destroyed him. She licked higher, and he held his breath. The woman had a real sense of drama.

When she finally enclosed him with her clever mouth, he let out a shameless groan of pleasure. In moments, she had him deliriously close to losing control, which he'd promised himself not to do. He'd always prided himself on being able to hold a climax at bay, but this... Finally, in desperation, he asked her to stop.

She did, moving upward to gaze into his eyes. "You didn't like it?"

"I loved every incredible moment. Too much. I'm not leaving you behind."

Her smile was the first shy thing he'd seen about her since they entered her bedroom. "I wouldn't mind. You really are injured, and I—"

"I would mind." He reached up to cup her cheek. "This is about mutual pleasure, and I'm not so crippled that I can't do my part."

Her expression was hopeful, but hesitant. "Tanner, I'm not very...I have trouble..."

He almost swore, but he swallowed the first word that came to him. It didn't belong in a room where such incredible lovemaking was going on. That ass Devaney had taught her how to please, but not how to be pleased. He pulled her down for a long, slow kiss. Then he rolled to his side, bringing her with him. The pain didn't matter. She deserved this.

"Leave everything to me," he murmured, reaching behind him for the packet he'd tossed on the bedside table. He didn't want to stop in the middle of loving her to put on a condom. A woman as nervous about her response as Dori could lose everything he'd worked to build in the seconds it took him to sheath himself.

When he finished the job she was gazing at him. "I don't want you to worry about me," she said. "I know men can't always control when they...I mean, they're so much faster, and I...I'll...be fine, Tanner. Truly."

He gave her a lopsided smile. "Yes, ma'am, you'll be mighty fine."

"I—"

"Hush." Then he guaranteed that she'd drop the subject by leaning over her and kissing her until her breath grew fast and shallow. That quickened breath made kissing her breasts all the more exciting as she quivered beneath him. He took his time. She needed to be at the brink, perhaps beyond. It might require mere days to undo the damage her selfish ex-husband had done; it might take years. He hoped with all his heart he'd be hired for the job.

He allowed instinct to guide him. He kept his mouth at her breast as he caressed her flat belly and slid his hand down, combing his fingers through her silken curls. His first touch was light, questing. She tensed, as if expecting rougher treatment to follow. He silently cursed his predecessor one more time and teased her gently once again, and again, until she began to relax.

Her ascent was gradual but steady as he coaxed her along and slowly increased the pressure of his stroking fingers. He wanted to shout with joy when she began to lead, opening her thighs and lifting her hips for his caress. Her panting became inarticulate cries of passion. Close now. He lifted his mouth from her breast and shifted his position while he maintained a constant rhythm, bringing her closer still.

He continued stroking her as he moved between her thighs. He was nearly bursting himself, but he had to hold back, no matter how much he wanted to lose himself in her. Gradually, he replaced the touch of his hand with the slow slide of his penis. She gasped and brought her hips up to meet him.

He looked deep into her eyes as he pushed forward, withdrew and pushed forward again.

Her eyes widened and she clutched his shoulders. "Tanner," she whispered.

"Let go." He felt her first tremor and increased the rhythm. "That's it."

"I...oh!" Her lips parted as she drank in air, and then her world exploded.

The violent contractions destroyed his resolution to let her enjoy herself without his pleasure interfering. The torrent rushed from him with such force he cried out, submerged in an intensity that left him breathless and disoriented. Gradually, through the whirling in his head, came the sound of her voice murmuring. He listened, and realized she was reciting his name, over and over. He'd never heard it said quite that way, with a combination of awe and possessive delight. At that moment he knew he would give everything he owned to hear her say his name like that for the rest of his life.

DORI INSISTED ON EATING the cold eggs and toast, although she allowed Tanner to make a fresh cup of coffee. "Wasting food is another bad habit," she chided him, although her heart wasn't in it. They sat at her oak kitchen table, she in her housecoat and Tanner in his jeans. It had happened, the thing she'd most feared. She was too entranced with Tanner's lovemaking to give a fig about whether he was financially responsible or not.

She reached out her foot and caressed his bare toes under the table. "Well, you may be a little loose with money," she said, "but at least you're not rich." She was surprised at his reaction, almost as if she'd slapped him. "What did I say?"

He took a sip of his coffee before glancing up at her again. "I've just never had a woman mention it was great that I didn't have any money. I thought women always preferred a guy with a good income."

"A good income is okay. A good income would be very nice, as a matter of fact. I was talking about filthy rich, like the Devaneys. And in their case, *filthy* is the right word."

"I'm no lover of the Devaneys, especially the sleaze-ball Devaney you were married to, but I don't think their behavior has anything to do with money. I think they'd be rotten rich or poor."

"Maybe." Dori got up to get the coffee carafe and refill their cups.

"I could have done that," he said with a gentle smile.

"Habit," she said, topping off his cup. "You can take

the waitress out of the café but you can't take the café out of the waitress."

Tanner leaned back in his chair to study her. "Are you happy with your job?"

"Everything except the pay," she said with a chuckle. Then she replaced the carafe and shut off the heat, buying herself some thinking time before she returned to the table. His question set off a warning in her brain. "To be honest, I don't mind waitressing. It's good, honest work, and I'm performing a service those truckers desperately need."

"Feeding them and pouring coffee?"

Her uneasiness grew. "That, of course, but mostly the conversation." She sat at the table and curved her hand around her coffee mug. "People that move around as much as truck drivers need some things to be predictable. They seem to appreciate coming into the Double Nickel and knowing they'll be able to talk to me, same as they did last time they stopped in. It makes them feel more secure, somehow."

Tanner nodded. "That makes sense."

She decided to turn the question back on him. "How about you? Would you rather be doing something else besides construction?"

"Not really. I love watching a house take shape, knowing that people will have a solid, beautiful place to come home to, a refuge from the rat race."

Dori laughed. "Then you must have some trouble when you're working on an office building."

"Actually, I don't work on them anymore. Just houses."

"Because you like them better?"

"Yep."

She took a sip of her coffee. So, he was picky about

the jobs he accepted. Not a good sign. "In this economy I wouldn't think you could afford to be that choosy."

"Dori, I'm better off financially than you think. In fact, I—"

"Wait." She held up one hand. "I've been afraid where this discussion was leading to the moment you asked if I was happy with my job. We've had a lovely morning, Tanner. Please don't spoil it by telling me that you wouldn't want me to work if we get married. Because I always plan to work. Partly because I like it, and partly to maintain a balance of power."

He sat forward, a look of astonishment on his face. "Excuse me?"

"Money is power. I learned that the hard way with Jimmy Jr. Keeping my job seemed silly after we got married. And even if I had, my piddly little income wouldn't have been enough to balance against all the money Jimmy had."

Tanner leaned toward her. "But if two people love each other, then who has the money shouldn't matter."

"Ha. That's what I thought at eighteen. At twenty-seven I know better. It's the Golden Rule. The one who has the gold makes the rules." She waved a hand out the window. "Look around you. It works in business, and it works in marriage, too. I would never marry a rich man again, or quit work and depend entirely on my husband's income. It's not worth a hundred trips to Hawaii to have someone lord it over me financially."

"But—"

"That's it, Tanner. I want economic equality in my next marriage. End of discussion."

Tanner gazed at her, a thoughtful expression on his face. "I see."

"You *were* going to ask me about giving up my job, weren't you?"

His tone was guarded. "Not exactly. But I'm glad you told me how you feel. I'm not sure I agree with you about the money-and-power thing, but it's good to know up front what you're thinking is on the subject."

Dori didn't care for his answer. Although he didn't come right out and say so, he could very well have some ideas about women that clashed with hers. "Tanner, are you one of those men who deep down believes a woman's place is in the home?"

"I—no. No, I don't. My sister is studying law, after all."

"But your mother didn't work outside the home, did she?"

He hesitated. "No."

"Who makes the financial decisions in that marriage?"

He looked uncomfortable. "My father."

"You see, this is why I didn't want to make love too soon. We should have had this discussion before we—"

"No, you don't." He was out of his chair and pulling her from hers before she knew what was happening. "Don't be putting guilt on either of us for this morning. You didn't want me to spoil it by asking you to be a stay-at-home wife." He wrapped his arms around her and brought her in close. "Don't you spoil it by saying it was a mistake we'll both regret."

"But my goal was not to let sexual attraction muddle my thinking." She felt his arousal through the terry cloth of her housecoat, and immediately she responded with a rush of moisture.

He rubbed his hands over her bottom in a sensuous kneading motion. "And is that happening?"

"Yes, that's happening, and I don't think—"

"Then I must be doing something right." Capturing her mouth, he slid both hands inside her housecoat.

She was helpless once he did that. The memory of the pleasure he'd given her earlier fueled what was already strong chemistry. Yesterday she'd wanted him without knowing what making love to him could mean. Now she knew, and the thought of repeating the experience drove her crazy with anticipation.

When he backed her down the hall to her bedroom, his hands and mouth already preparing her for what was to come, she didn't protest. By the time they got through the door she had opened the front of his jeans to run her hands over the instrument of her satisfaction. In seconds they'd shed their clothes and he'd rolled a condom over his erection.

But when he lay on his back and started to guide her on top of him, she felt a wave of disappointment.

He caught her face in her hands. "What is it?"

"Nothing." She leaned down and kissed him. "Nothing at all."

He held her slightly away from him. "Dori, I saw that look in your eyes, as if somebody had snatched away your favorite Christmas present and thrown it into the fireplace."

Heat seared her face. "Last time was so...lovely. But if we make love this way, I..." She didn't have the courage to go on.

"Yes, you will," he promised, looking into her eyes. "I haven't let you down yet."

"No, you sure haven't, Tanner."

He bracketed her hips with his hands. "Come here, sexy lady."

She straddled his hips, and he guided her slowly, sensuously down over his waiting shaft.

He sucked in a breath. "You are so fine, Dori." He cradled her breasts. "Lean down and let me taste you."

She braced her hands on either side of his head and lowered her breasts to his mouth. As he suckled, the tightening began again deep within her, the tightening that had led to such wonder not long ago. Almost instinctively she initiated a gentle rhythm that allowed his mouth to continue to tantalize her nipple. She began to throb with a remembered pulse. Ahh.

The tension built, and he let her guide their progress. She moaned softly, reaching for that tumbling free-fall that was like no other feeling on earth. As if sensing her eagerness, he slipped his hand up her thigh and pressed his thumb deep to the wellspring of her response. Her own movement provided the delicious friction that drove her closer to the precipice. The speed was in her control, and it was a dizzying experience.

Instead of racing headlong to her satisfaction, she felt it coming and held back. She savored it, then moved closer, and again retreated to prolong the inevitable. Tanner never coaxed, never projected his own needs. When she'd toyed with ecstasy beyond endurance, she gave herself the final reward, shuddering with a cataclysmic, joyful feeling of release.

Only then did his mouth leave her breast as he grasped her hips and urged her to a new motion. "Now, Dori," he murmured. "Now, sweetheart. Ahh, yes. Ahh, so good. There. Like that." His moan of surrender as he surged upward, lost in the moment, filled her with joy.

She rested her head in the curve of his shoulder while her breathing gradually slowed. She'd never known anything like the excitement they could generate together. It left her dazed with its potency and greedy for more. Their personal philosophies might be different, she thought as they lay sated and slicked with moisture, but only a foolish woman would turn away from a man who could love like this.

DORI SUGGESTED that Tanner check out of the Prairie Schooner and move his things to her house. He was willing to keep the room if she was worried about appearances, but she seemed more interested in the time they could spend in each other's company than appearances. That was a gigantic step in a community as tight as Los Lobos, and Tanner didn't minimize the extent of her commitment when she suggested the move.

She'd become furious when she looked out the front door for the first time and noticed the spray-painted truck. Tanner had shrugged it off to keep her from flying off the handle and doing something that could jeopardize her or her son. Once she was safely on her way to work, Tanner fired up the truck's engine and headed toward Devaney Trucking.

The outer office of the low building housing the trucking company was neat but unimposing. Imitation pine-paneled wallboard, gray indoor-outdoor carpeting and steel office furniture indicated an interest in utility rather than decor. A young blonde who looked like a recent prom queen sat at the desk that had the "receptionist" nameplate positioned at its front edge.

She blinked in apparent concern when Tanner

walked in. "Goodness, have you been in an accident?" she asked, obviously forgetting the standard "Can I help you" drill.

"You might say that." He glanced down a hallway that began about five feet behind her desk. That was his destination. "I'd like to see Jimmy Devaney, Jr."

"If it's about a job, you'll have to fill out an application first." She rose and turned toward the bank of file cabinets, revealing a very short skirt and spectacular legs.

"I don't want a job."

"Oh." She turned back to him. "Do you have an appointment?"

"No. Is he here?"

Her sympathy for his battered face was replaced with a professional mask. "I'm afraid I'll need more information. May I have your name and the purpose of your visit?"

Tanner figured if he gave his name and she buzzed the Devaney heir with the information, the cowardly son of a bitch would take a back way out of the building and Tanner would be left standing in the outer office like a jilted bridegroom. The image didn't please him.

"It's a surprise," he said with the most engaging grin he could manage considering his split lip and black eye. "I'll just go and find that ol' boy."

The blonde moved as if to stop him. "I don't think that's a good idea, Mr.—"

"Trust me." He strode past her with the bluffing technique that had seen him through several financial crises on his way to the top. "It's a fine idea."

She trailed behind him as he walked down the hall. He expected that Jimmy Jr. would have the first office and his father the one in the back, with more potential for space and prestige. He was right. The door immediately on his left had Jimmy's name stenciled on it. Tanner seized the knob, turned it and walked in. He shut the door in the receptionist's face and twisted the lock.

"What the hell?" Devaney looked up from the magazine he was reading. It looked like an issue of *Playboy*.

Tanner moved while the element of surprise was still in his favor. He rounded the desk and pulled Devaney up by his shirtfront. The man looked scared spitless, which was exactly how Tanner wanted him.

"Didn't expect to see me again, did you?" he rasped as Devaney gulped like a beached trout. "Get this straight, punk. You make a move against me again and I'll wait for you. You'll never know when it'll come, but it'll come, and I won't need three other guys to put you away." He shoved Devaney back in the chair.

As he walked toward the door, Devaney found his voice. "You can't talk to me like that!"

Tanner flipped open the lock on the door and turned back to Dori's ex-husband. "I just did." Then he left the office and smiled at the pretty receptionist on the way out.

11

TANNER DROVE from Devaney Trucking to the Prairie Schooner Motel to pick up his clothes and settle his bill.

"No charge," Elmer said when Tanner walked into the motel office and dug out his wallet.

Tanner stopped in mid-motion and looked at the gray-haired man in surprise. "I can pay," he said. "I know the truck looks old, but I—"

"Doesn't matter if you're King Midas hisself." Elmer peered at Tanner through thick bifocals. "Beatrice would have my hide if I was to charge you anything, considerin' all you've been through since you hit town."

Tanner nodded. "It's been interesting, all right." He paused. "You know you've got a security leak at the motel. That stink bomb was meant for me."

"I know it. We can't pay the maids much, y'know, and I'm pretty sure which one of them took the money to tell what room you was in. I'm watchin' her real close."

"Did that couple from New Mexico ever get the smell out of their clothes?"

"Yeah, with some help from Beatrice. Refunded their room rent, o' course. Lucky for us they didn't decide to sue."

"It hasn't been a very profitable few days, has it?"

Elmer shrugged. "You know how it is. We all manage to get by somehow."

"Well, thank you for the nice gesture." Tanner reached across the counter and offered his hand to Elmer. "I'm sure Dori appreciates it, too." Tanner knew better than to insist on paying, but he felt guilty all the same. He could afford the rent a lot more than Elmer and Beatrice could afford to lose it.

"You tell Dori Mae we're rootin' for y'all," Elmer said. "And I'll give you a tip, son. Marry the girl as quick as you can. People in these parts don't cotton to others livin' together without being joined in holy matrimony."

"Good," Tanner said. "Maybe that will hurry the lady along to a decision." He touched the brim of his Stetson, picked up his duffel bag and left the motel office.

On the drive to Dori's house he couldn't help wondering if Elmer would have been so friendly if he'd known Tanner could buy and sell him. Probably not. But Elmer wasn't the person Tanner was most concerned about. Dori's statement played over and over in his mind. *I would never marry a rich man again.*

Maybe it served him right. He'd been so determined to find a woman who wasn't lured by wealth that he'd found one who was repelled by it. And the joke was on him, because this was the woman he had to have. He craved everything about her—her unbreakable spirit, her devotion to her child, her generosity and her largely untapped passion. He'd fallen irrevocably, completely and happily in love.

He stopped by the local Piggly Wiggly on his way back to Dori's house and picked up a few things for a late-evening snack, keeping her budget for him in mind. He'd decided to postpone any announcement of his financial status for the time being. Their connection was too new and fragile to withstand that sort of information, given her deep-rooted prejudice.

And prejudice it was, though an understandable one. His willingness to let her lead in bed after she'd proclaimed her need for independence had been a subtle message. He'd deliver more of them before he told her the complete truth about himself. Funny, but his goal hadn't really changed. He still had to convince a woman to love him for himself and ignore what he possessed.

He reached her house and let himself in with the spare key she'd given him. Then he set about organizing romance on a shoestring. When she came home he wanted her to be transported to a world where there were no jealous ex-husbands, no difficult customers, no disappointing tips.

He carried her small oak table into the living room and located a white tablecloth tucked in the linen closet. The single candle had been on sale, but he hadn't thought what to put it in. Then he remembered the six-pack of long-necks he'd bought, thinking he'd like to have some beer around for the rest of the week. He'd just drink one and use the bottle for a candle holder.

Pulling the bottle from Dori's little refrigerator, he uncapped it and took a drink. He couldn't believe how much fun he was having planning a cheap evening at home. He'd become accustomed to dropping big sums of money when he entertained women, and he'd unconsciously fallen into the trap of thinking you could measure the kind of time you had by how much you spent.

He leaned one hip against her sink and glanced out the kitchen window toward the Devaney mansion. Tanner would describe it as the Devaney monstrosity. Whoever had designed that gigantic block of rooms should be shot. Dori's little house had more charm, because it was an honest, utilitarian dwelling that didn't pretend to be something it wasn't.

His shirt chafed against the tape around his ribs, and he unbuttoned it, leaving it hanging open as he turned away from the uninspiring view out the kitchen window. He and Dori would get Little Jim out of that stifling atmosphere, no matter how much time and money it took.

When the doorbell chimed, Tanner feared a delegation of churchgoers had arrived to protest his and Dori's living arrangements. He wouldn't have been terribly surprised. The people around here took their morals very seriously, as evidenced by Elmer's remark. He set the beer on the counter and walked to the front door.

He opened it to find Little Jim gazing up at him in total shock. Tanner remembered his bandaged nose and black eye. Little Jim was holding the hand of a very attractive blonde who looked barely forty and obviously understood dressing to attract male admiration. Her beige dress dipped softly and subtly to reveal cleavage and wrapped her hips to accentuate her womanly curves. The whole thing looked as if it would come off with the removal of one strategically placed decorative pin.

"Tanner, what *happened*?" Little Jim asked.

"Just clumsy," Tanner said. "Ran into a door."

"You look terrible."

Tanner smiled. "Thanks."

The woman stepped forward. "I'm Crystal Devaney, Little Jim's grandmother," she said. "May we come in?"

He knew modern grandmothers didn't look like the Norman Rockwell version anymore, but still he was taken aback. He revised his estimate of her age upward by about ten years. "Sure. Come in." He stepped back and let them pass.

"L.J., go play in your room while Mr. Jones and I talk," she ordered.

Little Jim's glance was hopeful as he directed it toward Tanner. "Is the White Ranger in my room?"

"Last time I checked."

"Oh, boy!" He tore off in search of his treasure.

Tanner watched him go. Then he turned back to Crystal and found her staring at his bandaged chest. "Uh, sorry, ma'am." He started buttoning his shirt.

She fingered the clasp on her elegantly miniaturized shoulder purse. "You've been in some terrible sort of fight, haven't you?"

He gave her a level look. "You could say that."

"I have a dreadful feeling it had something to do with my son. He dotes on that girl, you know."

"Mmm."

She glanced around the room. "Could we...sit down or something?"

He supposed he should be at least marginally polite, although he doubted Dori would want him to roll out the red carpet. Still, he was very curious as to what had prompted Crystal Devaney to show up in her powder blue Cadillac coupe. He waved her toward the couch. "By all means. I was having a beer. Would you like one?"

"That would be very nice."

When Tanner returned with his half-empty bottle and Crystal's beer in a glass he'd unearthed, he could hear the sound of an imaginary space battle going on in Little Jim's room. Probably the White Ranger against an invasion of aliens disguised as teddy bears. He handed Crystal the glass and a napkin before sitting on the opposite end of the couch. She set her purse next to her and crossed her legs. The skirt of her dress inched up, probably on purpose, to reveal excellently toned calves and thighs. This was a woman used to using her appearance to get what she wanted, he thought. Good thing she had no idea she was dealing with a corporate executive who'd seen all those moves before.

"Thank you kindly." She took a dainty sip. "Elmer told me you'd checked out today, and although he didn't say where you were, I guessed you might be here. So I took the liberty of calling on you."

"You probably knew it was the right place when you saw the spray painting on the side of my truck."

Her green eyes, the genetic predecessor of Jimmy Jr.'s and Little Jim's, clouded in apparent distress. "I hate all this ugliness. I truly do. I'd like to put a stop to it."

"That would be terrific."

"But I need your help, Mr. Jones."

Uh-oh. Here it comes. "Is that right?"

She lowered her voice and leaned forward, as if to make them coconspirators. Her cleavage became more visible. "It's for L.J. that I'm askin', Mr. Jones. That little boy needs his momma and daddy livin' in the same house again. They've had a lovers' spat, that's all. Nothing that a second honeymoon in the Caribbean wouldn't cure."

Something deep in Tanner rebelled. He'd already

become possessive enough not to want Dori in any other man's arms, but the specific idea of her sharing a marriage bed again with Jimmy Devaney, Jr., made him a little crazy. "If I understand Dori correctly, and I think I'm in a position to do that, she'd rather roll a walnut with her nose five miles down the main street of Los Lobos, immediately following the Los Lobos sheriff's mounted posse, than have anything more to do with your son."

Crystal's hoot of laughter surprised him. "I didn't expect you to be so clever." She batted her eyelashes. "I'm beginning to see why Dori is so distracted by you."

"She's not distracted, Mrs. Devaney. She knows exactly what she wants."

"Please call me Crystal. Everyone does."

"Grandma, can I come out now?" Little Jim stood in the hallway clutching his White Ranger.

"Except this little devil," Crystal amended. "Come here, L.J."

Little Jim walked over to the couch and stood by her knee.

"What's the one thing you want more than anything in the world?" she asked him.

"All the Power Ranger stuff."

Crystal rolled her eyes. "No. What do you *really* want?"

Little Jim took a deep breath, as if about to recite. "Momma and Daddy back together." It was almost a chant.

Crystal glanced at Tanner, her eyebrows raised as if to say, "See there?"

Tanner was sickened. Encouraging the kid to believe in a happily-ever-after for his parents, who'd never belonged together in the first place, was just plain cruel. "Hey, Jim," he said. "I think there's some orange soda in the refrigerator. And that swing set out back looks as if nobody's played on it in a long time. Why don't you get the soda and show the White Ranger all your secret places in the backyard?"

The boy's eyes widened. "How did you know I had secret places?"

Tanner smiled at him. "Good guess."

Little Jim gave him an admiring glance before he headed into the kitchen.

Once Tanner heard the back door close, he turned to Crystal. "Face reality, Crystal. Dori doesn't want to be married to your son. Accept that and stop making life more miserable for that little boy by pretending there will be a reconciliation. There won't."

"You can't know that!"

He held her gaze. "Oh, yes, I can."

"You're the problem." She stared into her glass of beer. Her lower lip had begun to quiver as her composure slipped. "I know they won't get together as long as you're around. She imagines you as some white knight dashing into town to make everything all right. What a foolish thought."

"Only if you don't believe in white knights."

Her gaze lifted to his. "Well, I don't, Mr. Jones. And I can tell I'm wasting my time appealing to your finer nature, so I'll come right to the point." She laid a manicured hand on her leather purse. "I have ten thousand dollars in cash. Leave this afternoon and you can take it with you."

He glanced at the purse. "I'm afraid that's not enough."

"Then tell me what is enough." Her voice crackled

with eagerness. "I'll find a way to get it. Just say you'll leave."

He looked into her eyes. "Sorry. You couldn't pay me enough to abandon Dori to a pack of jackals like you, your husband and son. Not to mention my concern for Little Jim. Some authorities might construe what you're doing, using him as a tool to reinstate the marriage, as child abuse."

She almost spilled her beer all over her expensive beige dress. "I love that boy!"

"If that's true, which I seriously doubt, you'll help him adjust to the confusing world of divorce, instead of giving him false hope that the divorce will go away."

Tears spilled from her eyes and coursed through the artful makeup on her cheeks. She clutched her beer glass like a votive candle holder, and tears splashed into the amber liquid. "You don't understand. I need that little boy. James and I need him. When Dori had him, when he didn't live with us, I...I didn't feel like livin' anymore."

Tanner felt some sympathy, but not much. "Then I guess you can imagine how Dori feels. She's his mother, and she never gets to read him bedtime stories, or kiss him before he goes to sleep, or fix him his favorite breakfast, or watch Saturday-morning cartoons with him. You've stolen six months of Little Jim's childhood from her."

"But if she'd just come back..." Crystal choked back a sob.

Tanner took a wild guess. "Not every woman's willing to settle for a hellish marriage."

Crystal sniffed and set her beer on the end table beside her. She used the napkin to dab under her eyes. "It's not hellish."

"No?"

"There were times..." She looked away from him. "But ever since Little Jim was born, James has been a whole new person. Having that child around has made everything wonderful."

"Well, you have him back now. Why are you trying to get Dori, too?"

She glanced at him. "Jimmy Jr. wants her. He can't stand the idea that she threw him over. No girl ever did that. And L.J.—well, he really misses her. Sometimes I come up to his room, and he's got all the pictures of her spread out on his bed, and he just looks so pitiful."

"I'm sure he does."

She twisted the napkin between her fingers. "I just don't know what to do."

"Yes, you do. You just don't want to do it."

Abruptly, she stood. "I'm going to fetch him. We have to get back. James will be home any minute, and he likes to see L.J. first thing when he gets home from the office."

Tanner rose when she did. She picked up her glass of beer and carried it with her to the kitchen. She put it on the counter before she walked to the back door, opened it and called for Little Jim. The simple act of picking up after herself revealed to Tanner that she hadn't always had money. She'd obviously allowed herself to like it far too much, which made her a slave to the wishes of James Devaney, Sr. And he was Tanner's true adversary. Not Jimmy Jr., who was a coward, and not Crystal, who could still be moved to tears over the fate of her grandson. But James Devaney claimed ownership of Little Jim to satisfy his own ego without any thought to the child's welfare. Tanner realized he'd walked into the wrong office that afternoon, after all.

ALL DURING HER SHIFT Dori expected Jimmy Jr. to show up and make a scene, but finally nine o'clock arrived and he hadn't made an appearance. She could go home to Tanner. Her body quickened with anticipation as she drove the familiar route to her house. Along the way, she pulled the net from her hair and tossed it on the seat beside her.

A part of her still feared that Tanner would disappear when she wasn't looking, but his battered truck sat in her driveway. He was inside, waiting. Coming home to Tanner every night would be very special indeed. If she could come home to Tanner and Little Jim, life would be perfect.

He opened the door before she got her key in the lock and drew her into a fairyland of dancing candle flame and muted love songs on the tape player. Nudging the door closed with his foot, he gathered her close and kissed her gently. "Welcome home," he murmured. The next kiss was deeper, filled with a longing that heated her blood and sent it singing through her veins. He pushed her hair aside and nuzzled the curve of her neck. "I thought you'd never get here."

She molded her body to his. "It was the longest shift of my life."

"Then you missed me?" He leaned away from her to look into her eyes.

"Desperately."

He cupped her bottom and pressed his hips gently against her. "Is that what you missed?"

"Yes." She laced her fingers behind his neck and leaned back, keeping her pelvis locked tight with his. "But that's not all. I missed your smile, and the way you make me believe that no matter how hopeless the situation seems, it will turn out okay. I missed the way you listen to me, as if what I say really matters. I missed the sound of your voice, which has a bit of a caress in it whenever you talk to me."

He gazed at her. "That's dangerous talk, lady."

"I know," she murmured, her heart full of the emotion she didn't quite have the courage to name. Not yet.

"I hope you know where it could lead."

"I think I do."

"How about joining me at this intimate café I know, and we'll talk about it?"

"I'd love to."

He led her to the table he'd placed in the center of the living room. On it sat a beer bottle holding a candle, an uncorked bottle of wine, two unmatched stem glasses from her cupboard and a tray of crackers, cheese and fruit.

"Tanner, this is so creative."

He held her chair for her. "You have to be creative when you're on a budget."

"Are you mocking me again?"

"Absolutely not." As he scooted her forward he leaned down and kissed the side of her neck. "You've taught me what's important. I had more fun putting this together than I did going to those five-star restaurants."

"Those?" She turned her face up to his. "You've been to more than one?"

He caught her chin between his thumb and forefinger. "Yes, but I'm a changed man, Dori. Anybody can make reservations."

She smiled up at him. "No one has ever gone to this much trouble to give me a romantic evening, Tanner."

"It's only the beginning, my love."

Her heart lurched as she looked into his eyes.

He met her gaze. The endearment hadn't been carelessly tossed out. He dropped a lingering kiss on her lips before going to his chair opposite hers and sliding into it. He reached for the bottle on the table. "Wine?"

"Please." Her country-western tapes played softly in the background.

He poured a glass for each of them. Then he picked up his glass. "I remember something couples used to do when they toasted each other. I don't know if anybody ever does it anymore. They'd—"

"Link arms," Dori finished, leaning forward. "Yes. Let's."

"You wouldn't think that was overdoing it?"

"Tanner, I want to overdo it."

"Me, too."

She positioned her arm on the table, glass raised, and he leaned forward to wrap his forearm around hers.

"To us," he said.

"To us." She moved close, keeping her gaze on his as they sipped from their glasses.

He lowered his glass but didn't move away. "Give me your other hand."

She placed her left hand in his.

He twined his fingers through hers, and his gaze burned hotter than the candle flame. Her heart thumped in response.

"I want to tell you something," he said gently. "And I wish it could be the first time I'd ever said it, because then I could offer it to you brand-new and untarnished."

Her fingers tightened in his.

"Maybe you'll think it's too soon, but when something's right, time doesn't matter anymore."

She swallowed the lump in her throat. She didn't want to cry. He might not understand.

"I love you, Dori Mae Fitzpatrick."

Tears slipped down her cheeks no matter how hard she tried to hold them back and she couldn't say a word.

His gaze grew troubled. "I guess you weren't ready to hear that."

"Oh, Tanner." She choked back a sob. "I've been waiting a lifetime to hear that."

She wasn't quite sure how he managed it, but somehow her wineglass disappeared. Then he scooped her from her chair and carried her down the hall before she had a chance to protest that a man with cracked ribs shouldn't be lifting people. His lovemaking was the most exquisite experience she'd ever had as he repeated his love in a hundred ways, both spoken and unspoken.

As he entered her, she cupped his face in her hands. He paused.

"And I love you, Tanner Jones," she said.

With a groan of triumph he buried himself deep within her.

12

DORI SLEPT LIGHTLY, waking often during the night to wonder anew at her good fortune. She'd found herself a hero.

When dawn breathed the first suggestion of light into the eastern sky, she slipped out of bed carefully. The day before he'd made breakfast for her, and she would take great pleasure in returning the favor. How sweet to labor for someone you loved, she thought as she quietly took her housecoat from the bedroom closet and belted it around her. She'd forgotten the joy of giving to a man in the bitterness of Jimmy's neglect. Now her generous nature swelled with delight at the prospect of lavishing Tanner with loving care for the rest of his life.

For that's what it would be. Although marriage had not been proposed last night, Dori expected Tanner to ask her this morning. And she would accept. She paused at the doorway to Little Jim's room and gazed fondly around. Together she and Tanner would bring her son home where he belonged. He'd be able to play with his beloved Power Rangers to his heart's content. He'd— Dori's thoughts came to a halt as she realized the White Ranger wasn't on the dresser where she'd left it.

Walking into the room, she checked around and began to doubt herself. *Had* she put it on the dresser? She searched the closet, the drawers, the toy chest and under the bed. The more she looked, the more confused she became.

"Is something wrong?" Tanner asked from the doorway.

On her knees by the bed, she glanced up and her heart lurched with happiness at the thought that this wonderful man loved her. His left eye was healing nicely, and he looked tousled and rakish as he stood there wearing only his jeans.

"I woke you with all this banging around, didn't I?" she apologized.

"I've been awake since you left the bed, but you seemed to be up to something, so I played possum."

She sat back on her heels and gave him a wry smile. "I meant to bring you breakfast in bed, but I glanced in here on my way to the kitchen and now I can't find Little Jim's White Ranger. I can't imagine where it is."

Tanner frowned. "Maybe he took it outside, although I can't imagine him leaving it out there."

"That's not possible. I brought it back here after I dropped him off on Monday."

"No, I'm talking about yesterday afternoon. Your ex-mother-in-law came over and brought Little Jim with her."

"She did?" Dori pushed herself to her feet and stared at him. "Why didn't you tell me?"

"I'd planned to, but the evening was so perfect, and I figured it could wait until this morning. Nothing came of it, anyway, except that maybe Little Jim spirited his White Ranger away without my noticing."

"What did Crystal want?"

"She offered me money to leave town."

Dori gasped. "No!"

"I gathered that Little Jim is the glue holding her marriage together."

Dori sank to the bed. "She told you that?"

"Not exactly, but I could read between the lines. She needs Little Jim, but she realizes Little Jim needs you, so the obvious solution is for you and your ex to reconcile."

Dori gazed at him and marveled that she'd even considered such a thing. Slowly, she shook her head.

His eyes reflected his joy at her response. "These people are playing for keeps," he warned. "I hope you're prepared. I'm going to do everything I can, but—"

"Then it will be okay." Rising from the bed, she walked over to wrap her arms around his taped chest. She looked up into his face. "Because with a man like you, everything is a lot."

He framed her face with his hands. "We'll get him back."

"I know we will."

His mouth curved into a soft smile. "I haven't wished you good morning."

"It's not too late," she murmured, lifting her mouth for his kiss.

"Good morning, my love." He touched her lips gently at first, then proceeded with more purpose as his hands slid down her shoulders. He splayed his hand across the small of her back and molded his body to hers.

With a long sigh of pleasure she nestled close and anticipated the magic of Tanner's caress. The jangle of the telephone filled her with regret and she longed to let it ring. But it could be her parents, or even something to do with Little Jim. Slowly, she extricated herself. "Don't lose your place," she whispered before she headed for the kitchen wall phone. "It's probably somebody wanting to clean the carpet."

"I'll start the coffee," he said, following her.

She glanced at him over her shoulder before she picked up the receiver. "You're right handy to have around."

"That's the idea."

There was a smile in her voice as she answered the phone, but it quickly faded.

"Momma," came Little Jim's choked whisper, "Daddy took away my White Ranger."

Anger burned white-hot through Dori. "Don't you worry, sweetheart. We'll get him back."

"I shoulda left him with you."

"It's okay, darlin'." A warm arm curved around her shoulder and she glanced up into Tanner's concerned blue gaze. "I'll come right over. Just give me time to get dressed. I'll talk to your daddy." Would she ever.

"No!" His protest was low and urgent. "I'm not supposed to call! I'll get in trouble."

Dori reached for Tanner's hand and gripped it hard. "Your daddy's the one who will be in trouble. I—"

"Momma, you can't! They'll be really mad. Just tell Tanner I didn't lose my White Ranger. But don't come. Promise."

Helpless rage engulfed her. "But, sweetheart—"

"Please, Momma. You'll get me in trouble."

His plea tore at her heart. "Little Jim—"

"Promise!"

"Okay, but let me—" The dial tone buzzed in her ear. She replaced the receiver and faced Tanner. "Jimmy took his White Ranger."

Tanner's look of disbelief was gradually replaced

with angry determination. He squeezed her shoulder. "Let's get dressed and find Devaney."

"We can't. Little Jim is petrified he'll be in trouble for calling me."

"We'll protect him, but we can't let Devaney get away with this. Come on." He started toward the bedroom.

"No."

Tanner spun around, his expression incredulous.

"I promised Little Jim we wouldn't come riding in like the cavalry. And we don't know what they might pull, when you get right down to it."

Tanner braced his hands on his hips. "So we do nothing?"

"For now." Dori met his obvious frustration with a level stare. "Look, I don't like it any more than you do."

"You've got to call a bully on his behavior or he'll just get worse."

"I promised my son I wouldn't do it. That's the end of it."

"You didn't promise I wouldn't go down and beat the stuffing out of Devaney, though, did you?"

"Tanner, stop it. It's just a battle, not the whole war. And I don't want to heap more misery on my son than I have to."

"I don't like standing around letting some son of a bitch pick on a little kid."

"Neither do I."

His defiant gaze gradually gentled. He walked back and took hold of both of her hands and drew in a deep breath. "It's time for us to present that united front we talked about. Marry me."

She looked into his eyes and found more love and

compassion than she'd ever had sense enough to want in a man. "I'd be a fool not to."

Slowly, he released his breath and a grin spread across his face. "Then I passed the test?"

She smiled back. "With flying colors. And I've never known anybody who could be so creative on such a small budget."

His face became more serious and he tugged her toward the couch in the living room. "Dori, we have to talk about that."

"Why, did you cheat?" She chuckled as he led her into the living room. "What'd you do, buy expensive wine and pour it into bargain bottles?"

"No." He sat and pulled her down next to him. "But you need to know something about—"

The doorbell chimed.

She looked at him and frowned. "My house is never this busy in the morning."

"Want me to disappear?"

"Absolutely not. We have nothing to hide." She did, however, pull her housecoat more closely around her and tighten the sash before she went to the door. Through the peephole she saw Deputy Holt in uniform.

Panic took hold of her as she flung open the door and noticed his black-and-white squad car sitting at her curb. "What's happened?" she demanded of the middle-aged officer. "Is Little Jim okay?"

Deputy Holt hitched up his belt and glanced away from Dori. "He's fine, far as I know." He didn't look grief-stricken or filled with doom, just embarrassed. "I just need to talk to you for a bit."

Dori relaxed some, but she was still confused by having the deputy show up at her door first thing in the morning. "Come on in. We were about to have some coffee." It bordered on the truth. Actually, she'd decided coffee could wait until they'd celebrated their recent engagement with more earthy delights.

Deputy Holt walked into the living room, but he clearly didn't want to be there. His gaze skittered over Tanner, who had stood when the visitor entered the room. "No coffee for me, Dori," the deputy said as he pulled a notebook from his back pocket. "Thanks, anyway."

Dori crossed her arms in front of her, feeling slightly indecent despite the thickness of her housecoat. "Well, have a seat, anyway."

He remained standing. "I won't be but a minute." He glanced at Tanner again.

"Would you like me to leave the room?" Tanner asked mildly.

"Uh, no. It's on account of you that I'm here." Deputy Holt gripped a stubby pencil in his big hand as he stared down at his open notebook. "Gotta make a report."

Dori and Tanner exchanged a puzzled look. Dori faced the deputy. "A report about what?"

"Cohabitation," the deputy mumbled, not looking up.

Dori blinked. "Pardon?"

The deputy waved his pencil at Tanner. "He's been spending the night here, right?"

A chill skittered down her spine. "I—"

"Don't answer that," Tanner cut in. He stepped closer to the deputy. "That's no business of yours, officer. You're invading our privacy."

Deputy Holt glanced up at him. "Not accordin' to

our county ordinance against a man and woman living together without benefit of clergy."

Dori's mouth dropped open. "You've got to be kidding."

"Wish I was. There really is an ordinance, a real old one, but it's still on the books. I looked it up."

Tanner's eyes narrowed. "Sounds like this is one of those archaic laws nobody bothers to enforce anymore."

The deputy scratched the back of his head. "Guess you could call it that. Don't ever recall anybody turning in a report like this since I've been with the sheriff's department. But nobody's voted to change it, either."

Dori felt sick to her stomach. She knew exactly who'd dug up the old ordinance and where the complaint had come from. And where it was leading. Tanner had warned her the Devaneys were playing for keeps, and nobody had ever accused them of being a stupid family.

Deputy Holt gazed at Dori, his pencil poised. "How many nights has he spent in this house?"

"You already know that." Dori lifted her chin. "I'm sure you have a report about the truck being parked in my driveway."

His gaze shifted away. "If you'll just answer the questions, Dori Mae, this will go easier."

Tanner cleared his throat. "I've spent two nights here because I wasn't feeling well after being attacked Tuesday night and I have no friends in Los Lobos besides Dori. But she and I have not shared a bed or had any sexual relations. That's what you really want to know, isn't it?"

Tanner's willingness to tell an officer of the law such

a blatant lie for her sake was stunning. She dared not look at him for fear her shocked gratitude would show.

"That's the gist of it," the deputy said. He sent Tanner a piercing look. "You'd be willing to swear to that under oath?"

Tanner made an impatient noise and turned away.

"Is that the truth of it, Dori Mae?" Deputy Holt asked her.

She swallowed. "Yes."

He flipped his notebook closed. "Now that you're up and about, Jones, I'd suggest you get yourself back to the motel."

Tanner didn't reply.

Dori forced herself to be polite as she walked Deputy Holt to the door and opened it for him. After she closed the door she leaned against it and stared at Tanner, her eyes filling with tears. "You'll have to move back to the motel."

"The hell I will. I'm calling my lawyer."

"*Your* lawyer? Now you're sounding like one of the Devaneys!" She squeezed her eyes shut.

"It's time to fight fire with fire."

"We don't have any fire!" She opened her eyes. "Which is just fine with me. I hate the way money makes people act. They buy the sheriff! They buy the judge! Money corrupts people, Tanner. We're lucky not to have it."

He regarded her steadily. "It's not the money. It's the way they use it. Money's not bad in itself."

"Yes, it is! Have you ever watched the difference between people with money and people without it? The ones with money act as if they can have anything they want. Nope. I don't want a thing to do with a person who has lots of money. Give me plain, honest, hard-working people any day."

He rubbed the back of his neck and glanced at her. Then he sighed deeply. "So you want me to move back to the motel?"

"Just for now, Tanner. I can see the Devaneys are trying to build a case for my being an unfit mother, and I don't want to give them any more ammunition than they already have."

"Getting married would solve the problem."

"I know, but that will take time to plan." She saw the impatience in his eyes. "I know we could go to Vegas, like you said before, but my parents would be crushed. I want to do this right, Tanner. No rusty nails or warped boards."

"All right." He started toward the bedroom and turned back. "When will I see you again?"

"If you'll pick me up after work tonight, we could go out for a bite and start making our plans."

"At the café or here?"

She hesitated. "Here, I guess. Then I'll have a chance to change clothes."

He nodded, still watching her. Then, with a muttered oath, he strode over and kissed her until she was breathless.

"Goodness, Tanner," she said, gasping as her body pounded with desire. "How am I supposed to send you away after that?"

His smile was devilish as he fondled her breast. "You're not. But don't worry about it. I'm leaving. I just want to make sure you miss me after I go."

TANNER HATED THE IDEA of abandoning Dori and moving back into the motel, but in some ways it was a good move. He needed some thinking room, and he didn't get much of that when he was tempted by Dori's charms.

She was hopelessly prejudiced about wealth, and he'd have to approach the subject of his money very carefully. Before the untimely arrival of Deputy Holt he'd thought the mood was exactly right to broach the subject. But once Dori had been reminded of the evils that could be perpetrated by money, she was in no frame of mind to hear about his considerable holdings.

As he'd learned in business, timing was everything. Once she'd had a chance to be apart from him for several hours and miss the closeness they'd discovered to be so essential to both of them, once he'd made love to her again, in the bed of the old truck if necessary, he'd tell her. Then maybe, just maybe, her prejudice would be softened enough by love to allow him to convince her he wouldn't rule her life the way Jimmy Jr. had done.

In the meantime, he had some business to conduct. Elmer had been pleased, though confused, when Tanner presented himself and asked if number nine was still available. Dumb luck had been at work and the room was empty.

From the privacy of his room, he contacted his lawyers. Fortunately, he hadn't slipped and let on to Dori that he had more than one. He wanted his legal team up and ready when the time came, so he discussed the custody case with them and asked them to research similar cases and find all the established precedents.

"Finally going to marry somebody, Tanner?" asked Franklin, the senior partner in the firm.

"If she'll have me."

"With your net worth?" Franklin chuckled. "I can't

picture a woman turning that down. In addition to obtaining the bonus of your winning personality, of course."

"Would you believe she doesn't want anything to do with a rich guy?"

"Then marry the lady, Tanner. She sounds like a perfect candidate for that prenuptial agreement we have gathering dust in the files."

"Right." Tanner felt an unexplainable twinge at the thought of asking Dori to sign the agreement. But he'd sworn never to marry anyone unless they agreed to leave his business alone in the event of a divorce. Romance was one thing. Business was another. He wouldn't try to control Dori with the power of his wealth, but he certainly didn't want to be vulnerable to having his business chopped in half if everything went sour. After all, this was the nineties. People started out with great hopes, but in the end, one in three marriages ended in divorce.

Yet somehow the thought of that prenuptial agreement depressed the hell out of him. It was insurance, and he definitely wanted it. Any man in his position would expect that sort of cooperation from the woman he intended to marry. Dori didn't want money, anyway, so she'd probably gladly sign away her rights to his fortune. Gladly sign away, if she agreed to marry him in the first place, once she found out his financial status.

Tanner thought about the love in Dori's eyes when he'd caressed her the night before and was sure they could overcome this little problem between them. Then he considered the disdain in her expression when she talked about the evils of money, and his confidence evaporated.

13

IN ALL HER YEARS of working at the Double Nickel, Dori had never known Crystal Devaney to set foot in the place. Yet in the middle of the afternoon, Crystal's blue Caddy pulled up in front of the café. The car didn't look any more comfortable in a lot full of pickups than Crystal did in her green linen suit as she pushed through the door of the Double Nickel and stood looking around at truckers in Western shirts and baseball caps. Men such as these provided Crystal with her designer clothes and late-model luxury cars, but she'd stayed as removed from their labor as a princess ignoring the duties of her stable boys.

As Dori watched, coffee carafe in hand, Crystal hesitated and finally made her way to a stool at the far end of the counter. Dori concluded that Crystal had made this pilgrimage to talk to her, a possibility Dori met with mixed emotions. She saw a woman struggling to build a life in the face of training that had doomed her to heartbreak, yet Crystal had worked harder than anyone to deprive Dori of her son once the divorce had become official.

And Crystal continued to connive to get what she wanted. Just the day before she'd tried to bribe Tanner. Dori tempered her natural compassion with that reminder as she set the carafe on a burner and approached Crystal, an order pad in her hand.

"May I help you with something, Crystal?"

"I came to talk to you."

Dori cast an eye over her customers. Nobody seemed desperately in need of attention, so she drew closer to her ex-mother-in-law. "It's no good, you know. I just can't see myself going back to Jimmy."

Crystal picked up a sugar packet and tore the corner off. She poured the sugar in a neat pyramid on the counter. "You're a stubborn girl, Dori Mae." She glanced up from the pile of sugar. "But you're in over your head. When I failed with your boyfriend, I turned the matter over to James."

Dori should have expected it. Crystal always resorted to her husband's power when the going got tough. "So that's when he dug out that old ordinance and set the sheriff's department on us."

Crystal trained her green-eyed gaze on Dori. "James can use the information he has to make a case for immoral conduct. He will if he has to, and he'll eliminate your visitation rights completely."

"Even you and James wouldn't do that to Little Jim." Dori prayed it was true.

"It would be very sad, but how long can L.J. live torn between two worlds? James says maybe it's better to cut it off clean."

Dori felt very cold. "Is that what you think, Crystal? You're a mother. You still sneak money to your daughter. James wanted to cut that off clean after she left for L.A., but you couldn't do it, any more than I could have. You continue to care for Libby, even if James doesn't."

"James cares." Crystal flattened the sugar pyramid with deliberate motions of her forefinger. "But he's practical, too." She glanced up. "If you're not afraid of losing visitation with Little Jim, think of your boy-friend."

"He's already been beaten up. What's left? Surely James wouldn't stoop to murder."

"Economic murder," Crystal said quietly. "I heard him talking to Jimmy Jr. He's already started contacting people around the state. He could have your young man blackballed so he won't be able to get a construction job in the entire state of Texas. I could still stop that from happening, but you'd have to agree to send him out of town today. Within the hour."

Dori's insides turned to jelly. Blackballed. What an ugly concept.

"And a man with a bad record in Texas might have a tough time getting a job wherever he goes. Reputations follow people around, you know," Crystal added for good measure.

The fight went out of Dori. It seemed that whenever she tried to fix the mistake she'd made in marrying Jimmy, someone she loved ended up getting hurt. Little Jim was petrified of reprisals, and Tanner wasn't afraid, but he darn well should be. He'd been very brave until now, but he hadn't been faced with unemployment. That should change his tune.

"Tell him to leave by five this afternoon," Crystal said. "James won't put out the word if he's gone by five."

"Did James send you to tell me that?"

"I offered to go. James said it would do no good, that the two of you were bent on self-destruction, but I thought differently. I wanted you both to have a chance to change your minds before James rolled over you."

Dori looked into her eyes. "I'll tell him to leave. I don't know if he will."

"Why can't you just give in and come back?" Crystal asked, clearly perplexed by Dori's behavior.

"Because I don't want to end up like you," Dori said. Then she carefully wiped up the spilled sugar.

DORI TRIED TANNER several times at the Prairie Schooner and was told by Elmer that the line was busy. The concept of Tanner tying up the phone lines gave Dori pause. She wondered if he was calling family members to get support for his position or to ask advice. He'd presented himself as such a lone wolf that the idea of him gathering wisdom from friends and relatives altered her concept of Tanner Jones.

Finally at four-thirty she managed to get through. "James Devaney is prepared to blackball you if you don't leave town by five tonight," she said. "I believe he can do it. You'll never work construction in Texas again."

To her amazement he laughed. "That's what he thinks," Tanner said. "Bring him on."

"You're being completely foolish." She heard the note of hysteria in her voice but there wasn't much she could do about it. The man she'd come to love in the past few days was about to commit financial suicide, and she couldn't bear to watch. "If you can't earn a living, we won't have enough money to fight for custody of Little Jim," she reminded him. Desperation drove her to cruelty. "I don't want a man who can't hold up his end."

"I'll hold it up, Dori."

"You don't know what you're facing. If you love me,

you'll leave town right now. Do it for me, if you won't do it for yourself."

There was a long silence on the other end.

"Tanner, are you there?" she asked at last.

"Dori, I'm not leaving town before our date tonight. When we have a chance to talk, you'll understand."

"But by that time you'll be dead in the water!"

"The White Ranger doesn't give up that easily," he said softly.

"What?" She felt a sob lodge in her throat. "Listen, you crazy guy. Cartoons are not real life. You've proved that you're a hero. Now ride out of here, okay?"

"See you at the end of your shift, Dori."

"Tanner—" She replaced the receiver when she realized he was no longer at the other end.

By eight that night the café was buzzing and Dori raced from booths to counter, taking care of the crowd as country tunes blasted from the jukebox.

The cook shoved an order across the pass-through. "When you deliver that, somebody's waiting by the back door for you," he said. "Better hurry."

A wave of misery engulfed her as she took the plate and carried it to a booth. Tanner had decided to leave, after all, but he'd waited too long. James Devaney's spies would have informed him that Tanner had missed the five o'clock deadline. After delivering the order, she hurried through the kitchen and out the back door of the café, expecting to see Tanner's truck parked there.

Instead, she discovered James Devaney leaning against the fender of his black Cadillac. She recoiled as if she'd caught sight of a rattlesnake. The stench of garbage from a nearby Dumpster was highly appropriate, she thought.

"Hello, Dori Mae." He sounded almost friendly.

"What are you doing here?"

James folded his arms across his chest. He looked extremely pleased with himself. "I just received a piece of information that I thought you might be interested in hearing."

"I suppose all the big construction companies in the state have agreed never to hire Tanner Jones again." She shook her head. "You have a funny way of trying to win me over, James."

"Crystal tells me you have a strange aversion to men with money."

Dori clenched her fists at her sides. "You and Jimmy have taught me that rich men are into power. I have this thing about keeping my independence."

"So you're looking for someone poor, then?"

Dori's laugh was bitter. "I know what comes next. You've made certain Tanner will be extremely poor, haven't you? Well, let me tell you something. Tanner will survive. You may have messed him up temporarily, but you haven't broken his spirit. He's twice the man you'll ever be, and he'll be fine."

James stroked his chin as he gazed at her. "I imagine he will survive. As the owner of one of the most successful construction companies in East Texas, he should continue to do very well."

AT NINE-THIRTY that night Tanner pulled into Dori's driveway. He'd borrowed Elmer and Beatrice's picnic basket and stocked it with wine, cold cuts and cheese for a picnic out on some star-spangled country road. He figured they'd eat in the back of the pickup, and the blanket he'd brought along could serve for the other activity he had in mind for tonight.

The simple and inexpensive meal was only one way he planned to demonstrate how little he cared for the trappings of a monied existence. Yet he had to convince Dori that wealth could be used for a good cause, namely to restore Little Jim to her. But first he wanted to make love to her and reestablish the bond between them.

He parked the truck, but before he could climb out, Dori came out the front door and walked quickly toward the truck. He was gratified that she'd been watching for him and was apparently eager to spend the rest of the evening in his company, but he was surprised that she hadn't changed out of her waitressing uniform. Leaping from the cab, he came around to open the passenger door for her.

His smile of welcome faded at the expression on her face. "What's wrong?"

She flung him a look of utter loathing. "The only reason I'm getting into this truck with you is because I might start shouting, and I don't want to disturb the neighbors."

"Dori, what—"

"Get in and drive, Tanner. Go out somewhere in the fields, where nobody can hear us."

He closed her door and came around to the driver's seat. Only one thing could have created this level of rage in her. Dammit to hell. "You found out, didn't you?" he asked as he closed his door.

"I don't want to talk about it here."

She had found out. He was certain of it. This was the risk he'd taken by not telling her earlier, but he'd been so close to the right moment. So damn close. He drove the rattletrap old truck out of her subdivision and headed for open cotton fields while she sat fuming beside him. A couple of times he glanced at her rigid profile and cursed softly to himself.

Finally, he swung the truck onto a dirt road that ran off to the left from the two-lane blacktop. He cut the motor and cracked the window, letting in the scent of freshly turned earth and the chirp of crickets. He turned to her.

She, however, did not turn toward him. Instead, she stared out the bug-spattered windshield. "The thing I can't figure out is why you pretended to be poor in the first place. You had no way of knowing that was so important to me."

"I'd planned to tell you all that tonight."

She faced him then, her eyes shining with tears. "Oh, were you? Why should I believe that?" Her voice rose a notch. "Why should I believe anything you say, come to think of it?"

"Because I love you." It was one of two aces he held.

"Don't, Tanner." Tears spilled down her cheeks. "Love is about honesty, not lies!"

He reached for her, but she pulled away. That hurt more than anything. If he couldn't hold her close while he explained this, she wouldn't buy it. She'd trumped one of his aces.

"Whose truck is this, anyway?" she asked, swiping the tears from her cheeks.

"It belongs to one of my employees."

"This was all a deliberate plan, wasn't it? To pretend to be a hand-to-mouth construction worker?"

"Yes." He thought how much she looked like the picture she'd sent him, her brown eyes wide and vulnerable, her full lips slightly parted. He'd never wanted her more than at this moment. Yet he didn't dare touch her.

"Why did you pretend all that?" she asked.

He sighed. "Because I wanted to make sure the woman I married wanted me and not my money."

"Oh, Tanner." She buried her face in her hands. "I can't believe everything has turned out this way."

Frustration roughened his voice. "You wouldn't have given me the time of day if I'd been honest!"

"No, and we both would have saved a lot of effort!" She sent him a withering glance. "Lying never works out, Tanner."

"I didn't like the lying part, either, and I would have told you sooner, but you kept raving about the evils of money."

"It *is* evil."

"No, it's not. Just because you've had one bad experience—"

"Which made me look around, and see how the world works. Money separates people, putting them on different levels. Now I understand why you asked me about being a waitress. That would hardly be appropriate for your wife, would it?"

"Dori, if you wanted to work as an elephant trainer after we're married, I wouldn't stop you."

"But you see, we won't be getting married."

He'd tried to prepare himself for her rejection during the drive out here, but it still hit him like an iron girder in the gut. "Please don't say that. At least listen to what—"

"Save your breath, Tanner. I won't put myself in that position again, where the man has all the power and I have none."

He wanted to grab her and kiss her until she listened

to reason, but he gripped the steering wheel instead. "That's bull. I won't tell you what to do any more than a poor man would. Just because you had that experience with Jimmy, don't lump all rich men in together. That's not fair."

Her brown gaze softened a fraction. "I know you're not like Jimmy. You wouldn't mean to throw your weight around, but it would happen, just the same. If you're bringing all that money into the family, then your doings would automatically become more important than mine. When I was married to Jimmy we had visitors at the Devaneys, couples in the same income bracket as Crystal and James, and it was always the same. The women were coddled, patted on the head and dismissed like children."

He hit the steering wheel with the flat of his hand. "I wouldn't do that, dammit!"

"Oh, wouldn't you?"

"No."

"If we got married, where would we live?"

"Somewhere near Dallas. I mean, that's where my business..." He paused as he realized what he was saying. She didn't even have to point it out. She'd talked about how much she loved the Texas plains, and yet he'd ignored her needs because it would be very inconvenient to live in Los Lobos and try to conduct business in Dallas.

"That's only the beginning, Tanner. You'll just assume those decisions are yours to make, because after all, you own this big successful company. I don't even blame you for feeling that way. I just don't want to be the little wife tucked away at home."

Which is exactly what he wanted, if he were completely honest with himself. The thought made him very uncomfortable. Desperate to turn events in his favor, he hauled out his other ace. "I could use my money to get Little Jim back."

She took a long, shaky breath. "Don't think I haven't thought of that."

"I thought that was your original goal."

"It was."

"Then what's the problem? I have lawyers who can make mincemeat of the Devaneys. Marry me and they'll be at your disposal."

She gazed down at her hands that were clenched tightly in her lap. "Oh, but you do tempt me, Mr. Jones."

Hope flared and he covered her hands with one of his. "Be tempted, Dori. I promise to make you the happiest woman in the world."

When she looked up the sadness in her eyes took his breath away. "I thought you didn't want a woman who married you for your money," she said.

He stared at her.

"That's what I'd be doing, Tanner. And believe me, I've considered it. Missing Little Jim like I do, I'll admit that sometimes I've thought about going back to Jimmy just to get my son back. And now I could marry you for the same reason. I wish I could do that. But I can't."

The pain in his heart was so great he wondered how he'd stand it. He squeezed her hand, which was cold beneath his. "Dori—"

"I would become just like Crystal. I understand now that she sacrificed herself to keep her family together, but you see, it backfired. She's given her children a weak role model. Her daughter's out in California trying to build some self-respect after years of having none, and Jimmy's growing up to treat women just like his father always has." Her chin lifted and resolution flashed in her eyes. "My son will have a different role model for a mother."

Tanner ground his teeth together. "How can I convince you that I won't use my money to control you?"

Her gaze was filled with tragic certainty. "You can't. Now please take me home."

His throat hurt. "You said you loved me."

"I loved Tanner Jones, the construction worker. I don't know who you are."

He searched her face for the slightest sign that would encourage him to gather her into his arms. There was none. Dazed by loss, he started the truck and headed back toward Los Lobos.

They drove in silence toward her house. When they were two blocks away he sat up straighter at the sight of a black-and-white cruiser and a black Caddy parked in front of Dori's house.

"Oh, my God," Dori whispered.

Tanner pressed down on the gas and in seconds screeched to a stop in front of the house. Dori leapt from the cab before he'd turned off the motor. She ran to the lawn where James, Jimmy and Crystal Devaney stood with Deputy Holt.

Tanner loped over toward them, his gut clenched. "What's happened?"

James Devaney turned to him. His hair was wildly out of place and his shirt was only half-tucked into his pants. His voice came out a hoarse croak. "L.J.'s missing."

14

TANNER'S ATTENTION FLEW to Dori, who looked as if she might pass out. He stepped close to her and put a bracing arm around her waist. "When did you discover he was gone?"

"About an hour ago." Crystal's voice was choked with tears, and without makeup and the clever cut of designer clothes she looked her age. "For some reason I decided to check on him, and he wasn't in his room. James and I tore all through the house, but he wasn't there. Then we thought he might be with Jimmy, but Jimmy came home and hadn't seen him. That's when we called Deputy Holt."

During Crystal's explanation, Dori had slid her hand down to clutch Tanner's. He gave her hand a reassuring squeeze. "We'll find him," he murmured close to her ear.

"Does he have a key to your house?" the deputy asked Dori.

"No." She swallowed. "But let's go look inside, anyway. Maybe he found a way to get in. Maybe he's asleep in his bed."

Tanner hoped so. Unfortunately, the Devaneys had enough money to make kidnapping for ransom a very real possibility. He figured Dori had already thought of that, too. Another reason for her to hate those with money.

Dori fumbled with the lock but eventually opened the door. Everyone spread out to search the house and call out for the boy. There was no answer.

"Let's try the yard," Dori said, heading for the back door.

Once again everyone searched and called, but the backyard was silent except for a breeze through the large oak tree in the corner of the yard.

"I'm going out to the cruiser and radio for backup," Deputy Holt said. "I'll need one of you to go back to the Devaney house in case he shows up there, and somebody should stay here, for the same reason. The rest of you can start driving around the area. We'll find him."

"Crystal will stay at our house," James said. "Jimmy and I will go out and search."

"Good." Deputy Holt's glance flicked to Tanner and Dori.

Tanner stepped forward. "I'll search."

"No. I want to search," said Dori.

He looked back at her. He didn't know what evil was out there, and he could be putting her in danger, but a newborn instinct guided him to agree. "Okay, I'll stay here." Her expression of gratitude told him he'd made the right decision.

Deputy Holt seemed skeptical, but he didn't comment on Dori's decision to join the search party. "I'll check back at the Devaney house every ten minutes," he said, heading for the door. "If anybody finds him, call there."

"I'll get my keys," Dori said.

Within seconds Tanner was alone in the house, and as he paced from room to room, he realized why Dori had been so determined to search. The passive role he'd agreed to take on didn't sit well. Tanner recalled how James had arbitrarily claimed the active role for himself and his son and Crystal hadn't even blinked. After years of training, she wouldn't. But Tanner chafed under the restriction of being the one waiting at home.

If he smoked, he'd do it now, but he'd given that up years ago. He didn't want to have a beer and risk blurring his reaction time by even a fraction of a second. Finally, he decided to roam the backyard for a while. He'd circled the perimeter of the block wall and had paused to lean against Little Jim's swing set when he thought he heard a noise. He listened more carefully and decided he was imagining things.

On his way back inside he heard it again, a faint rustling in the branches of the oak tree. Probably a squirrel, he thought, but he crossed the yard, anyway. He stood under the tree and peered up into the shadowy branches. Gradually, his vision sharpened. Little Jim was huddled there.

"Taking orders from Mighty Morphin?" Tanner asked gently.

"Hi, Tanner."

"Everybody's out looking for you."

"I know. I thought Momma would stay here, but then you did."

"And what would you have done if your momma had stayed instead of me?"

The leaves rustled again as Little Jim shifted his position. "I woulda come down and told her we had to run away."

"And why's that?"

After a long silence Little Jim replied. "I heard

Daddy and Grandpa say they're gonna fix it so Momma can't have Mondays anymore."

Tanner's heart ached as he imagined the desperation Little Jim must have felt when he overheard that conversation. And he'd shown great courage in making his way through the dark night to warn his mother. He'd obviously learned that courage from Dori. "We won't let them take you away from your momma," he said.

"You can stop them?" Little Jim sounded as if he wanted to believe, but he'd probably been disappointed too many times in his young life to accept whatever Tanner told him.

"Yes."

"How?"

"By hiring the best lawyers in the country."

"Oh." His sigh of defeat filtered down through the leaves. "But Momma and me, we don't have much money."

"I do."

Little Jim's gasp of surprise nearly made him topple from the tree. "You do?"

"Yes, and I'm going to help your momma fight this."

"You sure don't act rich."

Tanner smiled grimly. "Thanks. Say, Jim, I'm getting a stiff neck from looking up into this tree. Any chance you're ready to climb down?"

"Yeah. I hafta go to the bathroom, anyway."

Tanner helped the boy down from the tree and they walked together into the house. "I need to call your grandma and tell her you're okay," Tanner said as Little Jim scampered down the hall toward the bathroom.

Little Jim skidded to a halt and looked back at Tanner. "You promise they won't do that to Momma?"

"I promise." Tanner didn't know if Dori would ever marry him, but if she were faced with losing all contact with her son, she'd probably accept the loan of his lawyers. He'd make sure they gave her a reduced fee, because she'd probably want to pay the entire cost even if it took her the rest of her life.

"Then you can tell Grandma I'm here."

Tanner made the call. Once Crystal understood that her grandson was safe she began to sob, but Tanner was unmoved. "He decided to run away because he overheard your husband and son talking about denying Dori visitation privileges," he said.

"Oh, God."

"I suggest the three of you rethink your position with regard to that little boy."

She choked back another sob. "James gets so determined."

"And how about you? Is there any backbone left after thirty years of subjugation?"

The silence was filled with her sniffling. "I don't know," she said at last.

RED AND BLUE LIGHTS whirled in Dori's rearview mirror. She pulled off the road, shot out of the car and ran back toward the cruiser. "Any news?"

The young deputy who'd only been in uniform about six months looked proud to deliver the message. "Found him, Dori Mae. He's at your house, safe and sound."

Dori put out a hand to steady herself against the roof of the car and closed her eyes as the world began to spin. Thank God. Oh, thank God.

"You okay?"

His words galvanized her. "I'm fine," she said,

opening her eyes again. "Thank you. Thank you very much."

"Want a police escort to your house?"

"Absolutely."

She raced for her car and nearly flooded the engine in her eagerness to get moving. Gravel spurted from beneath her tires as she charged back onto the road and the cruiser had to put on a burst of speed to get ahead of her. She rode his bumper and beeped her horn for him to go faster, despite the fact they were exceeding the speed limit by at least twenty miles an hour.

"Come on," she muttered, landing on the horn again. "Come on."

She arrived just ahead of the black Caddy that brought Crystal, James and Jimmy. She beat them into the house and Little Jim ran into her arms. She noticed through a blur of tears that he was wearing his Power Rangers T-shirt.

"Momma, Tanner's gonna help us!" Little Jim said as he pulled away and looked into her face. "He's rich!"

Dori glanced up from where she'd crouched down to hug Little Jim.

Tanner stood just beyond her son, his gaze intense. "I guess some people don't have a problem with that."

"Neither did I when I was five years old," she said. "But I'm all grown up now."

"L.J.?" Crystal called from the open front door. "Where are you, honey?"

"Right here, Grandma." Little Jim tightened his grip around Dori's neck.

He was really too big to pick up, but Dori did it, anyway, holding him tight as she stood and faced Crystal, James and Jimmy. She glared at the three of them.

James stepped forward as if to take Little Jim from her, but Tanner moved to block his path.

"I'd keep my hands off that boy if I were you," Tanner said.

"Out of my way, Jones," the older man said. "Jimmy, let's take your son home."

"My lawyers have filed a suit in Dori's name against the two of you for conspiring to deprive this boy of his mother," Tanner said. "I'd tread lightly from here on out, or you may prejudice the case even more. Little Jim ran away from home because he was unhappy. He wants to stay here tonight. I've talked to a judge who says that's just fine. He'll be glad to issue a restraining order against all three of you if that becomes necessary."

James swung back to the door where Deputy Holt stood. "What's going on here, Holt?"

"I'm sorry, Mr. Devaney, but it's just like he said," the deputy replied. "I checked on it. You'd better leave Little Jim here for the time being."

"The hell I will. Jimmy, get L.J. and we'll be on our way. It's late."

Dori clutched her son, who buried his face against her neck. Tanner flexed his shoulders and Deputy Holt looked very worried.

"James, leave L.J. be." Crystal's voice was soft but laced with a determination Dori had never heard from her former mother-in-law.

James Devaney turned slowly, slack jawed with disbelief as he stared at his wife.

She met his incredulity with a steady gaze. Her voice gained power as she spoke. "We've allowed our selfishness to make that little boy's life miserable, and it's going to stop now."

James cleared his throat. "Crystal, honey, you've been under a strain. I'll handle this."

"I haven't been under a strain. I've been under your thumb."

"Oh, for crying out loud, Crystal."

She squared her shoulders and drew in a breath. "I thought it would be hard to buck you, but it's not that hard, after all. I love our grandson, and I won't stand by and watch you and Jimmy frighten him with stories about taking him away from his momma. I'll go to the mat with you on this, James."

James's eyes narrowed. "Is that a threat?"

"Take it however you want. Besides, Dori has a champion now." Crystal waved a hand in Tanner's direction. "From what I hear about him, he could drag you through the courts until all your money is gone. You may be stubborn, James, but you're not stupid enough to risk your entire fortune. It's time to throw in the towel and give Dori custody of L.J."

Veins pulsed at his temples and his face reddened. "Over my dead body!"

Crystal stared him down. "With your high blood pressure, you'd better calm down, or that's exactly how it will happen. Now let's go home. As you said, it's late."

James glanced to his son for support, but Jimmy Jr. only shrugged. Dori wasn't surprised. Jimmy followed whoever was leading, and right now that person was Crystal.

James turned back to Dori and shook a finger in her face. "Don't think this is the end of it, Dori Mae."

Dori didn't respond, but her heart sang with relief because it was the end of it. James Devaney's reign of terror was over. Just like that, Crystal had called his bluff and found that she held more control than she'd ever imagined. It also didn't hurt that she had Tanner Jones to hold over her husband's head.

Deputy Holt followed the Devaneys out, and Dori heard him apologizing the length of the walkway. Something about Mr. Jones having friends in high places leading all the way up to the governor's office, and the sheriff's hands being tied.

Tanner closed the door and Dori finally relaxed enough to ease Little Jim to the floor.

Her son gazed up at her. "I can stay here tonight?"

Dori gave him a shaky smile. She was almost afraid to believe it. "I think you'll be able to stay here every night."

"Really?"

Dori nodded and fought tears.

Little Jim hugged her hard. "That's good, Momma."

"Yes, it's good." She smoothed his red curls with trembling fingers. Then she looked at Tanner standing across the room by the door. "Thank you," she said around a lump in her throat.

"Crystal's the one you should thank," he said.

"I will, but I don't know if she would have stood up to James if you hadn't put the pressure on her in the first place."

"Momma?" Little Jim looked up at her, an impish gleam in his eyes. "Can I stay up and watch TV and eat popcorn because it's a special night?"

Dori gazed on her precious, freckle-faced son and was so filled with love she could scarcely speak. But he counted on her to be his mother, and she took the job very seriously. She tugged on his earlobe. "A special night? You scared the wits out of a lot of people who love you. You're lucky you aren't grounded, buddy."

"Then I can't stay up late?"

"You're already up late. Now go in and get your pajamas on and brush your teeth. Call when you're ready and I'll tuck you in." Her voice quivered on the last part of that statement. Tonight she would have the privilege of tucking Little Jim in his bed. She would never take that privilege for granted again.

"*Okay.*" Little Jim dragged himself down the hallway.

"If you're a very good boy tomorrow, we can see about some TV and popcorn tomorrow night," she called after him.

"Okay!" He skipped the rest of the way into his bedroom.

Dori faced Tanner. The faint scent of his woodsy after-shave drifted toward her, beckoning her closer. She held her ground. "I don't know what to say. You've been wonderful, more than wonderful."

His blue eyes filled with resignation. "But it doesn't change anything, does it?"

She shook her head.

"You realize you're an impossibly pigheaded, prejudiced woman? What do you want me to do, give it all away?"

"Of course not." She called on her last reserves of strength and somehow found the words she had to say. "I want you to go back to that bushel basket of letters you got from the article in *Texas Men* and find a woman who's delighted to be the little wife of a very rich man. I'm sure there's someone out there like that." She didn't allow herself to think of Tanner with another woman. The picture of him holding someone else might make her start screaming.

"I'm sure there are women out there like that. And I

happened to run into the one woman in the entire world who thinks *money* is a dirty word!" He braced his hands on his hips and stared at a point over her shoulder. Finally, his gaze moved back to her face. His voice was husky. "I love you. Doesn't that count for anything?"

Her throat tightened. "That's what makes this the most difficult decision I've made in my life. But I will not live like a kept woman, Tanner."

"Dammit, you would not be a kept woman!"

"When a waitress marries a CEO, that's the way it turns out, in my experience. I don't believe in the Cinderella story anymore. I'm sorry." She took a deep breath. "More sorry than I can say."

He stood looking at her, his throat working. "That's it, then." He reached in his back pocket and pulled out a card. "If the Devaneys don't cooperate in the custody case, get in touch with me."

She took the embossed card, careful not to touch his fingers. "I will."

"Dori—"

"Go, Tanner." She hurt all over. "Before we both break down and Little Jim comes in to find out what's wrong. He's had enough trauma for one night."

He turned and walked quietly out the door.

15

Two days later, while Dori and Little Jim were watching the Power Rangers on Saturday-morning cartoons, a parcel arrived in the overnight mail for Little Jim. Dori saw the return address and her stomach clenched. Most of the time she'd been able to keep thoughts of Tanner at bay by concentrating on her son, but seeing his handwriting on the package brought an image of his hand holding the pen, the same hand that had touched her so lovingly.

"Who's it from, Momma?" Little Jim hopped up and down in his excitement over the unexpected delivery.

"From Tanner." She handed him the box. "For you."

Little Jim sat down right where he was and started fumbling with the box. "I can't open it, Momma."

"I'll get the scissors." She helped him open the box and stepped back to let him enjoy unveiling the contents all by himself. She wasn't surprised when he pulled out a new White Ranger.

He let out a whoop of joy and hugged the toy to his chest. "I've got my White Ranger back, Momma! Tanner got him back. And he cleaned him up, too!" His green eyes shone with happiness.

Dori decided not to point out that this was a different White Ranger. She'd learned from Crystal that Jimmy Jr. had destroyed the original one. Crystal had offered to replace it, but Dori had asked her to hold off.

It would be just like Tanner to send a new one, Dori thought, and she didn't want Little Jim to become confused by getting two. And sure enough, Tanner had come through. Dori pressed a hand to her heart as if that could ease the aching there.

"Let's clean up the mess," she said, stooping to pick up the box. A note fell out. Little Jim's name was on the outside. "Looks like Tanner sent you a message," she said.

"Can you read it to me?"

Of course Tanner would have known that Little Jim hadn't learned to read and she'd have to help out with the note. He wanted her to read his message and think of him. Doggone his cleverness. She opened the note with shaking fingers and started to read out loud.

Dear Jim,
The White Ranger insisted on staying with you because he says you're the kind of guy he'd like to have on his team. He thinks you're very brave, and so do I. I think your mother's very brave, too. Tell her hello for me.

Love, Tanner

Little Jim clutched his toy close as he gazed up at his mother. "When's Tanner coming back, Momma?"

Dori pressed her lips together and swallowed hard. "He won't be coming back, sweetheart."

"Momma, you're crying!"

"No. I just got something in my eye." She grabbed a tissue from the pocket of her jeans and blew her nose. Then she turned toward the television. "Hey, we're missing our show!"

IN THE NEXT TWO WEEKS Crystal amazed Dori with her efficient handling of the custody matter. She'd explained to Dori that James wasn't much good at backing down, so he'd washed his hands of the whole thing. Crystal worked with a lawyer and had a new agreement written.

One Saturday morning early in November, Crystal appeared at Dori's house with a copy of the tentative agreement. Dori offered her a cup of coffee and she accepted. They sat at Dori's kitchen table, and while Dori scanned the agreement, Crystal enjoyed a view of Little Jim and his friends playing on the swing set in the backyard. As she watched him play and commented fondly on his good coordination and cheerful nature, Dori realized with surprise that Crystal had become a friend. The week before she'd invited Crystal to go trick-or-treating with her and Little Jim and Crystal had shown up for the event in a fairy godmother costume.

"Do these terms sound fair to you?" Crystal asked. She looked apprehensive as she waved her hand at the agreement her lawyer had drawn up.

"I think they sound very fair." The agreement gave her custody of Little Jim, and the Devaneys had visitation rights every other weekend.

"After what's happened, you're very generous to allow us this much."

"I would never want Little Jim to lose contact with his daddy and his grandparents."

Crystal looked very relieved. "Then I guess we're ready to set up a hearing."

"Fine. I'd like to get it settled." Dori got up and went over to the counter where she picked up a packet of snapshots. "I had a set of Halloween pictures made for you."

"Oh! Let me see!" Crystal reached for them eagerly and lingered over each shot, chuckling at Little Jim in his White Ranger outfit standing next to her in her fairy godmother costume. "These are terrific. They're going right up on the refrigerator."

"I thought they were good, too."

"I hope we can get the hearing over with by Thanksgiving, so it doesn't muddy up the holidays. I can't believe it's the ninth of November already."

"Is it? What do you know." Dori hadn't taken note of the date. But she wasn't likely to have anything particularly unusual happen to her today. The baby-sitter would arrive at twelve-thirty and she'd go to work. Then she'd come home and she and Little Jim would have popcorn and watch television, a privilege she still treasured, but which wasn't out of the ordinary now.

Crystal tucked the pictures into the envelope and put them in the purse she'd hung over the back of her chair. "Those snapshots are wonderful. I think it was seeing those walls of pictures in your bedroom the night Little Jim disappeared that made up my mind for me. That was heart-wrenching."

Dori slid the agreement across the table. "It was all I could think to do to keep him close."

Crystal cradled her coffee mug in both hands. "You're a good person, Dori Mae." She sipped her coffee. "I've learned a lot from you."

"How's Jimmy Jr. taking all this?"

"Oh, he's been surly, but lately he's started dating a nineteen-year-old. He can pull the wool over her eyes, I guess, and I understand now that's what he needs to bolster his ego. If he marries her, I'll probably have to check her mouth for bubble gum before the ceremony."

Dori laughed. "I hope he finds somebody he can be happy with."

"First he has to be happy with himself. His father's never given him much credit for being capable, and Jimmy always thinks he has to prove himself." She ran a manicured fingernail around the rim of her coffee mug. "I'd always hoped you could help him grow up." She smiled. "Instead, you helped me do that."

Dori reached across to squeeze Crystal's hand. "I have a lot to thank you for. All this business with the lawyers. Tell me the cost and I'll pay half."

Crystal shook her head. "No. Let James pay. He owes you at least that much, although he'll never acknowledge it." She gazed at Dori. "You probably wonder why I stay with him."

"Crystal, that's your business. I—"

"I've asked myself the same thing. The truth is, I'm lazy. I don't want to go through the hassle of divorce and I'd be lonesome living by myself. If I were your age, I might consider starting over, but not at fifty-three."

"I understand. I truly do."

"I'm sure you do. You're a perceptive young woman. And you know—"

The doorbell sounded, and Dori excused herself to answer it. Another package had arrived in the overnight mail from Dallas, and this time it was addressed to her. This package was slimmer than the one Little Jim had received two weeks before. Heart pounding, Dori carried it back to the kitchen.

Crystal glanced up, obviously curious, but she didn't ask any questions.

"Um, it's something from Tanner." Dori laid it on the counter, unopened.

"And you want some privacy before you open it." Crystal pushed back her chair and stood.

"You don't have to leave yet," Dori protested, although Crystal had hit the nail on the head. She was dying to open the package but didn't know how she'd react to whatever was inside. She did want privacy.

"I need to get going, anyway." Crystal picked up the custody agreement. "Thanks for the coffee and the pictures. I'll let you know when the hearing is scheduled." She hesitated and glanced out the window at the children on the swing set.

"Did you want to say goodbye? I can call him in."

"No, actually I..." Crystal made an impatient gesture. "Never mind. It's too soon."

"Too soon for what?"

"I was thinking of asking if Little Jim could spend the night, but you probably don't want to do that yet. I wouldn't trust us, if I were in your shoes."

Dori felt a nervous clutching of her stomach at the thought of Little Jim being away from her for the night.

"I'd bring him back first thing in the morning," Crystal said. She looked pathetically eager. "I—I miss him something terrible."

Dori looked into Crystal's eyes and saw only goodwill there. She had to start trusting the Devaneys at some point, because the new agreement would give them the right to have Little Jim every other weekend. She might as well start now. "Sure," she said. "I imagine he'd love to go. Especially if you bake cookies with him."

"That was my plan." Crystal came over and hugged her. When she backed away there were tears in her eyes. "Thank you. Thank you so much. If you want time to get him ready, I'll come back whenever you say."

Dori figured the longer she had to think about it, the more nervous she'd become. "If you don't mind taking him a little dusty, he can go now."

"Bless you."

"Let's go get him."

AS DORI HAD SUSPECTED, Little Jim was happy to go spend a night with his grandmother, who had become an important person in his life. She'd stood up for his rights, and he trusted her as he might never trust his father and grandfather. Dori was just as glad that her son maintained some suspicion toward those two men. They were unlikely to change much.

Ten minutes later Crystal drove away with Little Jim ensconced in the passenger seat of her blue Cadillac, and Dori went back to the kitchen. She called to cancel the baby-sitter and picked up her package from Tanner.

She stood there holding it for a moment and tried to imagine what he could be sending her. Perhaps it had something to do with the custody case. She'd wondered if his lawyers had kept in touch with the Devaney lawyers and if part of Crystal's efficiency had been prompted by Tanner's lawyers breathing down her neck. Crystal wanted to do the right thing, no doubt, but Dori knew she wouldn't want costly lawsuits any more than James would. Crystal liked her life-style.

So Tanner was probably sending her an update. Something impersonal. Still, her heart raced as she pulled the tab and took out an official-looking document. So she'd been right. A note in Tanner's handwriting was paper-clipped to the first page.

Dear Dori,
This is the best I can do.

Love, Tanner

Kind of an odd thing to say, she thought as she glanced at the first page. Then her eyes widened and she groped for a chair as her knees grew weak. She started reading, stumbling over all the whereas and wherefore clauses, but getting the central meaning of the document in front of her. She put her head in her hands and tried to steady her breathing.

The papers, when signed, would make her a full partner in Jones Construction.

TANNER HAD PARKED his red Dodge Ram a block away from Dori's house where he could see the overnight mail truck arrive. He noticed Crystal's Cadillac was in the driveway. According to reports from his lawyers, Crystal was hurrying the custody case along, both for Little Jim's sake and for her own. She understood, even if her husband did not, that the Devaneys would be sued within an inch of their lives if they didn't move quickly. But he still gave Crystal credit for standing up to her husband on Little Jim's behalf.

After the mail truck left, Tanner wondered if Dori was reading the document he'd sent, or if she'd put it aside because Crystal was still there. A short while later, Crystal came out with her grandson and they both climbed into the Cadillac. Good. Tanner had asked Crystal to spirit Little Jim away if possible, but he hadn't been sure Dori would agree to it. Having

Dori all to himself, even for a short while, would improve his chances a thousand percent. There were some methods of persuasion he wouldn't be able to employ with her son around.

He glanced at his watch and decided to give her fifteen minutes to read the document. Franklin had stammered like a schoolboy when Tanner had announced what he wanted in the way of a partnership contract. When Franklin had recovered from his shock, he'd mentioned that this was a damned far cry from the prenuptial agreement Tanner had asked him to prepare for any prospective bride. Franklin had repeated all Tanner's lectures about why he didn't want to have partners, let alone a wife who could ruin his business with one nasty divorce. And now Tanner wanted to make this woman a full partner, give her fifty percent of all he owned, before she'd even agreed to marry him? Franklin had suggested that perhaps Tanner needed a checkup. He seemed to be having a breakdown of some sort.

Franklin had been more right than he knew, Tanner thought as he watched the front of Dori's house. He was having a breakdown, and Dori Mae Fitzgerald was the only one who could put the pieces back together. He'd gone into this venture wanting exactly what she'd accused him of wanting, a little wife—somebody who wouldn't threaten his precious business or interfere too much in his schedule, somebody who would adore him and tell him how wonderful he was without making demands of her own.

And then he'd met Dori, who insisted on being a whole person and not an adjunct to some important man. She wanted equal footing, and this was the only way, short of bankrupting himself, that he could think of giving it to her. It was no paper title; the document specified that she'd have definite duties as his partner, including attending meetings and making recommendations on all projects. She'd have a lot to learn, but a woman of her intelligence would have no problem adjusting. She probably knew more than she realized. After all, she'd grown up around a father who was in construction.

Yet he could imagine her turning him down flat. He could imagine it in painful detail. That's why he wouldn't give her too much time before he moved in.

After fourteen minutes he started up the truck. As he pulled into her driveway, he couldn't remember being this nervous in his entire life. But then, nothing had ever been as important as her answer. He strode to the front door with more confidence than he felt and pressed the bell.

DORI WAS STILL STARING at the contract when the doorbell rang. She glanced up at the calendar again. Definitely the ninth of the month. And Tanner had been known to use her magic number to his advantage. Her heart thudding, she left the contract lying on the table and walked to the door.

Although she'd expected to see Tanner on the other side of it, the breath still whooshed out of her when she saw that he was really, truly there. All signs of his injuries were gone, and his eyes shone clear and blue, and filled with love for her. It took all her resolve not to fling herself into his arms. But she still had to decide what to do, and the decision was so very important.

"May I come in?" he asked gently.

"Of course." She stepped aside and he came through the door, bringing with him a remembered scent, a remembered way of moving that turned her insides to jelly. Before she closed the door she got a glimpse of the truck he'd driven this time. It was a far cry from the battered heap he'd arrived in several weeks ago.

But Tanner looked the same. His jeans still hugged his hips and reflected many washings, and his Western shirt was as faded as the one he'd worn when she'd first glimpsed him in the Double Nickel Café.

She licked her dry lips and gestured toward the couch. "Would you like to sit down?"

"Sure." He ambled over to the couch, but she noticed the tense line of his shoulders and decided he wasn't as nonchalant as he looked.

"Coffee?"

"No, thanks." He lifted off his black Stetson and laid it on the arm of the couch.

Dori took the easy chair opposite him, so that the coffee table separated them. Her gaze lingered on his face as she mentally retraced the sweep of his cheekbones, the curve of his jaw, the laugh lines bracketing his mouth and the faint horizontal lines across his forehead where he'd wrinkled his brow with worry. She'd probably given him a fair share of that worry lately. "Little Jim really loves having his White Ranger back. He thinks you found the original one. I didn't have the heart to tell him his daddy destroyed it."

Tanner nodded. "I figured that had happened. That's why I took all the tags off the new one." He smiled, and Dori's heart swelled with longing. "The thank-you note he dictated to you was great. And the drawing."

"I want him to learn good manners. A gift deserves a thank-you."

He leaned forward. "Just to clear the record, what I sent you today wasn't a gift."

Her breathing grew shallow at the fierce light in his eyes. "Then what was it?"

"A business deal. I've discovered I can't run my company without you."

She gripped the arms of the easy chair. "That's ridiculous."

"Ask anybody who works for me. I can't concentrate. I waffle on decisions and let details slip through my fingers. I need somebody with a clear head to help me run things."

"You could hire an assistant."

"I don't want an assistant." His gaze was as direct as a laser beam. "I want an equal. Somebody who will tell me to take a long walk off a short pier when necessary. Somebody tough and independent, with a good head on her shoulders. Somebody exactly like you."

"To help you run your business?"

"For starters. If you'll agree to that, I want you to be my wife."

"People buy into businesses, Tanner. They don't just become partners with a stroke of the pen. I wouldn't have any equity in Jones Construction."

"You already own the heart of the man trying to run it now," he said quietly. "How much is that worth?"

"Oh, Tanner..."

"I've listened to all you've said, and you were right. But I've changed. I want what you want. I have plans to create a community near Abilene that takes advantage of the sweep of the plains the way my houses near Dallas make use of the woods and the lakes. You'll help me, because you have a better feel for this land than I do. Your father can help me. Build a life with me, Dori."

Her head was spinning. She didn't want to be lured into the wrong decision, but he was so appealing, sitting there with his earnest expression. She groped for her objections to his plan. "I don't know how to be rich. I tried to fit in with the way the Devaneys did things, and I couldn't. I'm not comfortable with fancy cars and hotel suites where your clothes are laid out for you every day, and—"

"Neither am I. But money can buy other things. A deserted island in the middle of a turquoise sea of warm water." His voice became a caress. "A little hut, with enough provisions flown in to last a week. Soft sand you can sink your bare toes into as you walk in the sunlight, or the moonlight. A place where no one else will bother you." His voice dropped to a murmur. "And no one lays out your clothes, because you don't have to wear any."

Desire stirred, hot and furious, within her. "That sounds sinful."

"There's nothing sinful about it if you're on your honeymoon."

"A deserted island?" She couldn't help it. She pictured them there, playing at being Adam and Eve in the Garden of Eden. "Are you making this up?"

"I flew there last week to scout it out. The temperature is perfect, Dori. We can pick fruit from the trees, cook on an outdoor grill, make love under the stars. The world will disappear and there will only be the two of us. I reserved the island for a week beginning the ninth of December."

"Tanner! That was taking a big chance."

"No, it wasn't." He rose from the couch and came

over to kneel by her chair. "Sending you the contract was taking a big chance. I was afraid you might throw it in my face."

"I couldn't throw anything into such a dear face." She smoothed her palm over his cheek, and he caught her hand and turned his head to kiss it.

He closed his eyes and took a shaky breath. "Marry me, Dori." He looked up into her eyes. "My life isn't worth a plugged nickel without you in it."

"You planned this, on the ninth of the month," she murmured, cradling his head between her hands. "That was very devious of you, Tanner."

"I wanted every advantage I could get. I thought of coming into the café at nine o'clock tonight, which would be a nice touch, but I couldn't wait that long."

"Speaking of that, I have to go to work soon."

He stood and drew her to her feet. "Alice said she'd fill in."

"You talked to Alice?" Then a suspicion entered her mind. "And Crystal?"

"The whole town knows I'm here." He brought her in tight against his aroused body. "And they're all on my side."

"You're a sweet-talkin' man, Tanner Jones."

"Am I sweet enough?"

"Yes," she whispered just before she kissed him with all the love in her heart.

_____ Epilogue _____

WARM WAVES SWISHED like lace ruffles on the hem of a turquoise negligee. A few feet up the sloping beach, two towels lay spread on sand the color and consistency of light brown sugar. For the first time in her life Dori had an all-over tan.

She lay on her stomach, a briefcase beside her and corporate reports spread across the top of the towel. Tanner reached over and ran a finger down her spine. She brushed him away. "You know I can't concentrate when you do that."

"Depends on what you're trying to concentrate on."

She pulled her sunglasses down her nose and glanced at him over the top of them. "If I'm half owner of this business, I want to understand everything about it."

Tanner put his sunglasses aside and moved over to her towel. "I built the business. I think your best strategy would be to study me."

"I just bet you do." She laughed as he swept the documents out of the way and took her into his arms. His skin was warm from the sun and he was scented with coconut suntan lotion.

"I should never have let you bring that briefcase." He took off her sunglasses and nuzzled her neck before placing an exploratory hand between her thighs.

"You said I could bring reading material." But she'd

already lost interest in the reports. The tropical sun kept her skin and blood permanently heated to the temperature of lovemaking. All Tanner had to do was touch her and she became as pliable as a mound of sand.

"I should have been more specific." He fondled her breast with lazy strokes of his palm. "I thought women brought sexy novels to the beach."

"There you go, generalizing again."

"I really have to learn not to do that." He licked the space between her breasts. "You taste like coconut."

"So do you."

"Having a good time?"

"Tanner, this is better than winning the lottery."

"I should hope so. I—"

"That's it!" She sat up, toppling him off the towel.

"I don't think so, Dori. I'm good, but not that good. I barely touched you, and I don't think you're so responsive that you—"

"No, I mean, that's how I'll pay you for my share of the business!"

"You've lost me."

She laughed as she leaned down to give him a resounding kiss. "I nearly forgot, with all that's been going on. But you see, I'll win the lottery in 1999. I have it all worked out. I'll buy the ticket at nine in the morning, on September ninth." She threw her hands into the air. "And I'll be rich! I can pay you for my share in only three years!"

Tanner chuckled and drew her gently back down to the towel. "Thank goodness for that. I was worried about it."

"Well, worry no longer. I will soon be a full partner in all ways."

"I have no doubt." Tanner moved over her. "But right now, there's only one aspect of this partnership I'm concerned about, Mrs. Jones." And with that he solidified their contract in the way Dori had found was the most gratifying of all.

Husband Wanted:
No experience required

Mail-Order Bridegroom
Day Leclaire

PROLOGUE

HUSBAND WANTED!

Woman rancher in immediate and desperate need of a man! Interested applicants should:

1. Be 25-45 years of age and looking for a permanent relationship—a kind and gentle personality is a plus!
2. Have extensive ranching background—be able to sit a horse, deal fairly with employees, herd cattle, etc.
3. Have solid business know-how—particularly the type necessary to please a bullheaded banker.

I am a twenty-six-year-old woman and can offer you a comfortable home, three square meals and some of the most beautiful scenery in Texas Hill Country. (Details of a more personal nature are open to negotiation.) Interested parties should send a letter of introduction, a resumé and references to 'Miss Bluebonnet', Box 42, Crossroads, Texas.

HUNTER PRYDE picked up the newspaper ad and re-read it, a remorseless smile edging his mouth. So Leah was in 'desperate need' of a husband. How interesting. How very, very interesting...

CHAPTER ONE

'THIS will be a real marriage, right?' the applicant interrupted. 'I cain't take over the place 'lessen it's a real marriage.'

Leah glanced up from the resumé of one Titus T. Culpepper and regarded the man in question with a cool gaze. 'Could you by any chance be referring to your conjugal rights, Mr Culpepper?'

'If that means us sleepin' together, then that's what I'm referring to. Hell, yes, I mean conjugal rights.' He rocked his chair back on to two legs, her grandmother's precious Chippendale groaning beneath his bulky frame. 'You're a fine-looking woman, Miz Hampton. Always was partial to blue-eyed blondes.'

She stiffened, struggling to hide her distaste. 'I'm…flattered, but—'

'Like a bit of sweet-talk, do you?' He offered a toothy grin. 'So long as it'll get me what I want, I don't mind. Because as far as I'm concerned there's not much point in gettin' hitched if we ain't gonna share a bed.'

'I think any discussion about rights—conjugal or otherwise—is a trifle premature at this point,' she informed him shortly. Especially when she intended to find a nice, tame husband, willing to agree to a safe, platonic relationship. One brief, youthful brush with the more volatile type of emotions had been quite sufficient. 'About your resumé, Mr Culpepper—'

'Titus T.'

'Pardon me?'

'Most folks call me Titus T. If'n we're to be wed, you might as well get used to calling me by my proper name.' He winked.

'I see.' Leah glanced at the papers before her with a jaundiced eye. This interview was definitely not turning out as she'd hoped. Unfortunately she'd already eliminated all the other applicants, except Titus T. and one other—H.P. Smith, her final interview of the day. She didn't have any choice but to give Mr Culpepper a fair and thorough hearing. 'It says here that you have extensive ranching experience.'

'Fact is, it was a farm I ran. But ranch...farm.' He shrugged. 'Same difference. So long's I can tell which end of a cow to stick the bucket under it don't matter, right?'

She stared, appalled. 'Actually, it does.'

'Not to my way of thinking.' Before she had a chance to argue the point he leaned forward, studying her intently. 'Your ad also says you need a businessman. Why's that?'

He'd hit on the main reason for her ad. While she could run a ranch with no problem, she needed a husband well-skilled in business to handle her financial obligations. Leah hesitated, reluctant to explain the precariousness of her monetary situation, but knowing she didn't have much choice.

'The ranch is experiencing financial difficulties,' she admitted. 'In all honesty, we face bankruptcy if I can't obtain a loan. Our banker suggested that if I were married to an experienced rancher who had a strong business background they'd be willing to make that loan. That's why I placed the ad.'

Titus T. nodded, a thoughtful frown creasing his brow. 'I can understand a sweet thing like you having trouble with ciphering, so I'd be more than happy to keep track of the money for you.' An expansive smile slid across his face. 'Matter of fact, it might be a good idea to put all the accounts and such in my name for safekeeping. Then I'll talk the bank into giving us a nice fat loan. Don't you worry your head none about that.'

Leah fought to conceal her horror. There wasn't any point in continuing the interview. She knew a con-man when she met one. How had she managed to get herself into this predicament? She should have found some excuse the minute he opened his mouth. If she hadn't been so desperate, she would have. Determined to tread warily, she inclined her head, as though she found his every word to be perfectly acceptable.

'Of course. I don't see any problem with that,' she lied without a qualm, and stood, brushing her waist-length braid back over her shoulder. 'But I'm afraid our time is up. My next appointment is due any minute.' She could only pray that the final applicant would prove more suitable. The alternatives were unthinkable.

'Now, Miz Hampton...'

'I appreciate your coming,' she said, not giving him an opportunity to debate the issue. Loath as she was to come out from behind the protection of her father's huge oak desk, she wanted Titus T. Culpepper out of her study and on his way. Heading for the door, she kept a wary eye on him, hoping it wouldn't be necessary to call for Patrick, her foreman. 'I'll be making my decision in the next few days and will let you know.'

A trifle reluctantly he gained his feet and approached. 'You best think about one more thing afore you make that decision.'

She never saw it coming. Moving with amazing speed for a man of his size, he closed the distance separating them and snatched her into his arms. She turned her head just in time, his clumsy attempt at a kiss landing on her cheek instead of her mouth.

'Come on, sweetpea,' he growled, tightening his hold. 'How're you gonna know what sort of husband I'd be without a smooch or two?'

'Let go of me!'

Thoroughly disgusted and more than a little frightened, she fought his hold with a desperation that must have taken him by surprise, for his grip slackened just enough for her to wriggle out of his embrace. Taking instant advantage, Leah bolted across the room to the gun-rack. Snatching free her rifle, she rammed several slugs into the magazine and confronted Titus T.

'Time to leave, Mr Culpepper. And I do mean now,' she announced in a furious voice, giving him a brisk poke in the gut with the barrel of the rifle.

To her relief, he didn't require any further encouragement. His hands shot into the air and he took a hasty step backward. 'Now, Miz Hampton,' he protested. 'No need to get yourself in an uproar. It were jez a kiss. If we're to be wed—'

'I think you can forget that idea,' she cut in with conviction. Wisps of silver-blonde hair drifted into her eyes, but she didn't dare release her grip on the rifle long enough to push them back.

He glared in outrage. 'You sayin' no because of a little bitty kiss? Unless you marry a mouse, any man worthy of the name's gonna want a hell of a lot more from you than that.'

She refused to debate the point...especially when she'd lose the argument. It was the one detail in this whole crazy scheme that she preferred not to dwell on. 'It's not your problem, Mr Culpepper, since you won't be that man.'

'Damned tootin'.' He reached out and snatched a battered hat from off the rack by the study door. 'Don't know why you put an ad in the paper, if'n you didn't want a real husband. False advertising, that's what I call it.'

He stomped from the room and Leah followed, still carrying the rifle. No point in taking unnecessary risks. If nothing else, it would give Titus T. pause should he decide to turn amorous again. She needn't have worried. Without another word, he marched across the front porch and down the steps. Climbing into his battered flatbed truck, he slammed the rusty door closed. A minute later he disappeared down the drive.

Watching him leave, Leah's shoulders sagged. 'I must have been crazy to believe this would work,' she muttered, rubbing a weary hand across her brow. 'What am I doing?'

But she knew the answer to that. She was doing exactly what her father would have wanted her to do when faced with a buy-out attempt from one of the largest and most ruthless companies in the state: protecting the ranch and her grandmother by marrying. While every last ranch in the area had caved in to Lyon Enterprises' ruthless tactics and sold their property, Hampton Homestead remained firm. Even completely surrounded by the 'enemy', they refused to sell, no matter what.

Of course, there had been no other choice but to defy Lyon. For, as much as the ranch meant to Leah, it meant even more to Grandmother Rose. And Leah would do anything for her grandmother. Anything. Even stand up to a huge, ruthless company against overwhelming odds. Even offer herself in marriage in order to get the money necessary to win their fight.

'We're not selling the place; I don't care what dirty tricks they pull,' the elderly woman had announced just that morning, after the latest offer from Lyon Enterprises had arrived. 'The only way they'll get me out of here is in a pine box! My grandfather died fighting for this land. So did my father. And so will I, if that's what it comes to.'

Then she'd crossed her skinny arms across her non-existent bosom, stuck her chin in the air and squeezed her eyes closed, as though waiting for the undertaker to arrive.

But Leah had believed her. If the ranch went bankrupt and they were forced off the land, it would kill her grandmother. It was that simple. Keeping the ranch in the family was essential, which meant finding a solution to their current predicament. The problem was, unless she found a way to pry some money from the local bank, losing the ranch would soon be inevitable.

It had taken three long years of arguing to realize that the bank wouldn't loan money to a single woman in her mid-twenties. They'd proven especially reluctant when they'd discovered that she alone shouldered the financial burden of an elderly grandmother and a ranch full of human and animal 'lame ducks'. Learning of this year's running battle to prevent a take-over bid from one of the most powerful companies in the state gave them the best excuse of all to refuse any aid.

On the other hand, she'd recently been told that lending money to a family whose male head consisted in equal parts of a businessman and a rancher was a different proposition altogether. And, though she didn't fully understand why that should matter, it provided the loophole for which she'd been so desperately searching.

She took instant advantage. She immediately set out to find herself just such a husband, even if it meant putting an ad in the paper and offering herself to the highest bidder. She frowned, thinking of Titus T. Unfortunately, she wouldn't be offering herself to any of the applicants she'd interviewed to date.

What she really needed was a knight in shining armor to come riding up her drive, ready and able to slay all her dragons. A foolish wish, she knew. But still... Some silly, romantic part of her couldn't help dreaming for the impossible.

Leah glanced at her watch. Her final interview should arrive any time. She could only hope that he'd prove more acceptable than the others—docile enough to agree to all her demands and yet skilled enough in business matters to satisfy the bank. As though in response to her silent wish, a solitary rider appeared over a low ridge, shadowed black against the burnt-orange glow of a low-hanging sun. She shaded her eyes and studied him with keen curiosity. Could this be H.P. Smith, her final applicant?

He rode easily, at home in the saddle, swaying with

a natural, effortless rhythm. Even from a distance she could tell that his horse was a beauty—the pale tan coat without a blemish, the ebony mane and tail gleaming beneath the golden rays of a setting sun. The animal was also a handful. But a handful he mastered without difficulty.

She frowned, something about him bothering her. If only she could figure out what. Then it hit her. She knew the man. On some basic, intuitive level she recognized the way he sat his horse, the simple, decisive manner with which he controlled the animal, the square, authoritative set of his shoulders. Even the angle of his hat was faintly familiar.

But who the hell was he?

She waited and watched, intent on the stranger's every movement. He rode into the yard as though he owned the place…as though he were lord here and her purpose in life was to cater to his every pleasure. From beneath the brim of his hat Leah caught a glimpse of jet-black hair and deep-set, watchful eyes, his shadowed features taut and angled, as though hewn from granite. Then he dismounted, tying his buckskin to the hitching post. Not giving the vaguest acknowledgement, he turned to cross the yard toward her.

He stripped his gloves from his hands as he came, tucking them into his belt, and she found herself staring at those hands, at the strength and power conveyed by his loosely held fists. She knew those hands… But where? A flash of memory hit her—the gentle sweep of callused fingers against her breasts, tender and yet forceful, pain mixed with ecstasy—and she gasped.

And that was when he looked up.

Full sunlight cast the shadow from his face and revealed to her the threat—and the promise—in his cold black eyes. In that instant she realized who he was, and why he'd come.

'This just isn't my day,' she muttered and, acting on blind instinct, shouldered her rifle and fired.

The first blast cratered the ground a foot in front of him. He didn't flinch. He didn't even break stride. He came at her, his steady gaze fixed firmly on her face. She jacked out the shell and pumped another into the chamber. The second blast landed square between his boots, showering the black leather with dirt and debris. Still he kept coming, faster now, hard-packed muscle moving with cat-like speed. She wasn't given the opportunity to get off another round.

He hit the porch steps two at a time. Not hesitating a moment, he grabbed the barrel of the rifle and yanked it from her grasp, tossing it aside. His hands landed heavily on her shoulder, catapulting her straight into his arms. With a muffled shriek, she grabbed a fistful of shirt to keep from falling.

'You never were much of a shot,' he said, his voice low and rough. And then he kissed her.

His kiss was everything she remembered and more. He'd always combined strength with tenderness, but now there was also a ruthless demand to his kiss, a fierce assault on both mind and body that held her stunned and unmoving. His mouth shifted over hers, subduing any hint of resistance, taking with a relentless thirst, but also giving a wealth of passion in return. One hand settled low on her back, arching her into the tight cradle of his thighs. His other hand slid up her spine, beneath the heavy fall of her braid, his fingers thrusting through the silken strands of her hair and cupping her head.

Unable to help herself, she felt her arms tighten around him, discovering again the breadth of his shoulders and the lean, compact muscles sculpting his ribs and chest. With trembling fingers she searched out the tiny mole that hid in the hollow at the base of his throat, knowing that she should fight him, that she should end this farce. But somehow she couldn't. He'd been her first lover...her only lover. There was a connection between them that could never be severed, much as she might wish it otherwise.

He deepened the kiss between them, his thumb sliding along her jaw to the corner of her mouth and teasing the sensitive spot until her lips parted beneath his. To her shame, she kissed him back, kissed him with eight lonely years' worth of pent-up yearning. She needed this moment out of time, and part of her rejoiced in the exquisite memories his touch resurrected. She came alive in his arms, became the woman she'd once been. But another part of her, the part that had suffered at his hands, knew the danger, knew the price she'd pay for allowing him to sweep away the barriers she'd fought so hard to build. She couldn't afford to feel again. She'd almost been destroyed once by this man; she wouldn't offer him the opportunity to complete the job.

He kissed her at length, the conqueror staking his claim, and a small growl of satisfaction rumbled deep in his chest. It was that tiny sound which finally brought her to her senses. She fought her way free of his embrace and retreated several steps across the porch. Raising trembling fingers to her mouth, she stared at him...stared in stunned disbelief at Hunter Pryde—the one man she'd hoped never to see again.

He returned her look, his expression one of cool amusement. 'Hello, Leah,' he said. 'It's been a long time.'

His careless words brought a world of hurt. She struggled to conceal her devastation, to hide the pain his kiss had resurrected. After all that had gone before, after all they had once meant to each other, how could he be so casual, so heartless? Hadn't he caused enough anguish by walking out on her without...this?

'It hasn't been long enough, as far as I'm concerned. Why are you here, Hunter?' she demanded in a raw voice. 'What do you want?'

He smiled briefly, a flash of white teeth in a bronzed face. 'You know what I want. The same thing I've always wanted.'

She shook her head in desperation. 'No. Not the ranch.'

'The ranch? Try again, Leah.' He reached into his shirt pocket and retrieved a newspaper clipping. 'I've come in response to your ad.'

A small gasp escaped. 'You can't be serious,' she protested.

'I'm very serious.'

His voice held an implicit warning and she took another unthinking step away from him. 'You...you can't do this. You don't even have an appointment!' She used the first ridiculous excuse that occurred to her, but she was grasping at straws and they both knew it.

'Would you have given me one?' he asked, seemingly content to play the game her way. For now.

'Not a chance.'

'No. I didn't think so. Which is why I answered your ad under the name H.P. Smith.'

Briefly, she shut her eyes. After her experience with Titus T. Culpepper, she'd pinned ridiculously high hopes on the unknown H.P. Smith. So much for dreaming of a knight in shining armor. Hunter Pryde was no knight—a former lover, a one-time wrangler on her father's ranch, and a thief who'd stolen her heart before vanishing like the morning mist—but no knight. More likely he'd prove to be one more battle she'd have to fight...and win.

He tucked her ad back into his shirt pocket and cupped her elbow. 'Inside, Leah. We have a lot to discuss.'

'No!' she protested, yanking free of his grasp. 'I have nothing to discuss with you.'

He bent down, picked up her rifle and emptied the chamber of shells. He stared first at the slugs in his hand, then at her. 'I suggest you reconsider,' he told her.

It took every ounce of self-possession not to apologize for shooting at him. She faced him, hands planted on her hips. 'You're not wanted here.' She gestured toward the rifle, adding drily, 'You should have taken the hint.'

'Last chance, Leah. You don't want to fight me on this.'

The words were arctic-cold, the threat inexorable. He gazed down at her, and the expression in his eyes almost stopped her breath. Why did he look at her like that—as though all the sins in the world could be laid at her doorstep and he'd come to exact retribution? She'd done nothing to him, except love him. And he'd repaid that love with desertion. His fierce gaze continued to hold her, and with a sudden, gut-wrenching certainty she realized that somehow she'd wronged him and he'd come to even the score. She fought a mind-numbing panic. If she succumbed to panic she didn't stand a chance against him.

Instinct urged her to throw him off her property and be done with it. But she didn't have that luxury. Knowing him, he wouldn't go until he'd had his say. Instead, she'd handle this in a calm, intelligent manner. She'd hear him out—not that she had much choice in the matter. Then she'd throw him off her property.

'Leah,' Hunter prompted in a surprisingly gentle voice.

She didn't allow his mildness to mislead her. The softer he spoke, the more dangerous he became. Right now, he was deadly serious. 'All right, Hunter.' She forced out the words. 'We'll play it your way...for the time being.'

He rattled the rifle-slugs fisted in his hand, the sound more sinister than any made by a diamond-back snake. Settling his hat more firmly on his head, he snagged her elbow, his grip firm and purposeful. 'Let's go.'

She didn't flinch. Instead, she allowed herself to be drawn into the house. Peeking up at his rigid features, she released a silent sigh. With no rescue in sight, it looked as if she'd fight this battle alone. And she could, too.

So long as he didn't touch her again.

Once inside the study, Hunter closed the door and crossed to the far wall, where the family photos hung. He paused, assessing them, one in particular seeming

to capture his attention. It had been taken around the
time he'd known her; she'd been just eighteen.

In the picture she sat on a fence-rail, faded jeans
clinging to her coltish legs, a sleeveless checked shirt
revealing slim, sun-browned arms. She stared off into
the distance, a half-smile curving her mouth, her gaze
unfocused as though her thoughts were far, far away.
Just as the picture had been snapped she'd raised a
hand to her cheek, brushing a stray curl from her face.

'I expected your hair to have darkened.' He
glanced from the photo to Leah. 'It hasn't. It's still
almost silver. As I recall, it used to flow through my
fingers like silk. I wonder if it still would.'

'Stop it, Hunter,' she ordered tightly.

He glanced back at the photo. 'It doesn't do you
justice, you know.'

'What, the picture?' She shrugged uneasily. 'If you
say so. I think it looks just like I used to.'

'Not quite.' His mouth curled to one side. 'It
doesn't show the passion...nor the ruthlessness. Even
at that age you had a surplus of both.' He turned to
study her. 'Do you still?'

Her mouth tightened. 'I've changed a lot since
then. You figure out how.'

Turning away, she took a stance behind the huge
oak desk, hoping it would put her in a stronger, more
authoritative position. She hoped in vain. Hunter removed his hat, dropped it in the middle of the desk
and edged his hip on to the corner nearest her.

'You knew the ad in the paper was mine, didn't
you?' she began, determined to get their confrontation
over as quickly as possible. 'How?'

'The nickname you used. Miss Bluebonnet.'

She nodded in acknowledgement. 'Dad used to call

me that because of my eyes.' Then, with a sigh, she asked, 'Why are you really here, Hunter? Because I don't believe for one minute that it's in response to that ad.'

'You know why I'm here,' he said.

'I can guess.' Pierced by eyes that were panther-black and jungle-watchful, she'd never felt so intimidated in her life. And it took every ounce of resolve not to let it show.

Hunter Pryde had changed, attained a sophistication she'd never have believed possible. Eight years ago he'd been in his mid-twenties and wild, both in appearance and in attitude. In those days his black hair had brushed his shoulders, held back by a leather thong, his eyes reflecting a savage determination to succeed in a world just as determined to see him fail. But what had attracted her most had been his face—the high, sculpted cheekbones, the hawk-like nose, and the tough, bronzed features that reflected an unmistakable strength and vitality.

His long-limbed arms and legs, his broad chest and lean, sinewy build spoke of a mix of conquistadors and native American Indian, of a proud and noble heritage. When he'd taken her into his arms she'd sensed that no one else would ever make her come alive the way she did with him, that she'd never love anyone quite as much.

And she'd been right.

'You've come to see the Hamptons broken, is that it?' Leah asked with a directness she knew he'd appreciate.

A cynical smile touched his mouth. 'Swayed, never broken. Wasn't that your father's motto? No. I've come to discover why, if things are so bad, you haven't sold out. Are you really so destitute that you need to resort to this?' Removing the ad once more from his shirt pocket, he balled it in his fist and flicked the crumpled newspaper toward the trash can. It arched over the rim and hit the bottom with a faint metallic thud.

He couldn't have made his disapproval any clearer. She found it mortifying that he, of all people, had happened across that ad. But she wasn't a shy, easily coerced teenager any more. And she wouldn't be bullied. Not by anyone. Certainly not by Hunter.

'This isn't any of your business,' she informed him. 'I don't owe you a thing, least of all an explanation for my actions.'

'I'm making it my business,' he corrected in a hard, resolute voice. 'And, one way or another, I will have an explanation.'

She struggled to curb her anger. It wasn't easy. He had an uncanny knack for driving her into an uncontrollable fury. 'Are you really interested,' she snapped, 'or have you come to gloat?'

He folded his arms across his chest. 'I wouldn't be here if I wasn't interested.'

'Fine.' She'd try taking him at his word and see where it led. Though she suspected she wouldn't like it when they got there. 'I didn't have any choice but to place that ad.'

He dismissed her excuse with a contemptuous gesture. 'Don't give me that. We always have choices. You just have a knack for picking the wrong ones.'

'You may not agree with my decisions, but that doesn't make them wrong,' she retorted, stung. 'The last few years haven't been easy. Dad…Dad died a year after you left.' Hunter's leaving at a time she needed him most still hurt, even after all these years. Until he'd ridden up today, she hadn't realized how much of that pain lingered.

'Yes, I know.'

She flinched. 'You knew?' Knew and never bothered to return? Never bothered to see how she was, see if she required any help or support? She straightened her shoulders. No, not support. She'd support herself. And her grandmother. And the ranch. And all those she'd gathered beneath her wing. No matter what it cost.

'I read his obit in the papers.' He leaned closer, and she caught her breath, drawing in the rich, spicy scent of his aftershave. 'I understand the ranch has gone downhill ever since. You may be just as ruthless and single-minded as your old man, but you're sure as hell not the rancher he was.'

She jerked as though slapped, and for a moment the defiant, protective mask she'd kept rigidly in place slipped, leaving her vulnerable and exposed. How could she ever have been seduced by this man? Even at eighteen she should have had the sense to see the cold, heartless soul that ruled his keen intellect, no matter how attractive the outer packing.

'I won't defend myself to you. Why should I? Nor will I be judged by your yardstick,' she insisted fiercely. 'So spit out what you came to say and get the hell off my land.'

She saw the familiar spark of anger flicker to life in his eyes and wondered if she'd pushed him too far. Not that she cared. With her back against the wall, both literally and figuratively, she'd fight free any way she could and damn the consequences.

With an abrupt sweep of his arm he snagged her

waist, and forced her between his legs. 'Don't you know why I'm here?' He cupped her shoulders to curb her instinctive opposition, rough amusement edging his words.

As much as she wanted to tell him to go to hell, she knew he wouldn't release her until she'd answered. Glaring at him, she said, 'You came in response to the ad.'

'More than that, Leah. Much, much more,' he corrected, a bitter smile twisting his mouth. 'I came for the ranch.' His eyes grew black and pitiless, searing her with a burning determination. 'And…I came for you.'

CHAPTER TWO

Shock held Leah immobile for a split-second. Recovering swiftly, she lifted her chin. 'That's a real shame, Hunter,' she retorted, continuing to fight his hold. 'Because you aren't getting either one.'

His grip tightened. 'We'll see.'

She stopped struggling. Resistance was fruitless. Instead, she used the only other weapon she possessed. Words. 'Did you really believe that after all these years you could just come strolling back up my drive? Your arrogance is incredible. After what you did to me, I wouldn't give you so much as the time of day!'

'A little melodramatic, don't you think?'

Fury ripped through her and she gave in to it, needing the satisfaction losing her temper would provide. 'Melodramatic? Not by a long shot. You stole my innocence, you bastard. And you did it solely to get your hands on this ranch.' Bitterness spilled over, pouring out after years of suppression. Her pain, her agony, stripped of any protective cover, lay bare for him to see. 'I was eighteen and crazy in love. And you used me. *You used me!*'

'The hell I did. I just took what you offered.'

His cruelty cut her to the quick and it required all her willpower not to hit him. But she remembered his lightning-fast speed of old. Her blow would never land and his retaliation would be swift and unpleasant. She looked him straight in the eye. 'You can't get out of your responsibilities that easily. You took exactly what you wanted, no matter who suffered in the process.'

His mouth settled into a grim line. 'You never knew what I wanted. You still don't.'

'Oh, no?' Did he really consider her so blind, so ignorant of man's baser motivations? Perhaps eight years ago she'd been guilty of such an oversight, but no longer. He'd cured her of that. 'It's the same then as now. You want my land. Well, get in line.'

'There is no line,' he bit out. 'Nor will there be. You'd better face that fact right here and now.'

He tugged her closer, as though to obstruct any chance of flight. Slowly, relentlessly, he gathered her in, trapping her in a grasp as binding and inescapable as a mist-net around a struggling sparrow. She pressed her hands against his chest, striving to keep some small distance between them. But instead she found that touching him only resurrected long-forgotten emotions, reminding her of all that had gone before. Tears threatened, but she ruthlessly forced them back. Tears wouldn't accomplish a thing. Not with this man.

'Why are you doing this?' she asked. 'Why now, after all this time?'

'Because it will give me what I want most.'

She laughed quietly, the sound one of pain and disillusionment rather than amusement. 'When you said that eight years ago, I foolishly thought you meant me. But now I realize you meant the ranch.'

His expression closed over. 'Did I?'

'Yes! Is that why you bedded me? Because it

would give you your dream? It didn't work out that way, did it?'

'Bedded you? A rather quaint description for what we did together. Something a bit more elemental and a lot cruder would be closer to the truth. And, as I recall, we never did get around to using a bed.'

She refused to feel shame for an act that had been the most beautiful experience of her life. 'No, we didn't. Because you left before we ever had the chance. Of course, you didn't hit the road until Dad threatened to disinherit me. He offered me a choice. You or the ranch.'

'And we both know which you chose.'

She caught his shirt in her fists. 'How would you know that?' she demanded passionately, her distress breaking free of her control. 'You didn't stick around long enough to find out. But I can guarantee choosing you was a mistake I've lived to regret. It never occurred to me that, without the ranch, I wasn't much of a bargain.' Her pride had suffered from that knowledge. But her pride had handled the battering. Her heart hadn't been nearly so sturdy. 'So you took what you could and walked.'

A hard smile tilted his mouth to one side and his hands closed over hers, prying them free of his shirt. 'Let's be accurate. I didn't walk. I was dragged.'

'Don't give me that. I waited in the line-shack for hours. Does that amuse you?' Her breathing grew shallow and rapid, the dark recollections ones she rarely dredged from her memory. 'The afternoon was sweltering, but I waited inside the cabin for you anyway. I was so afraid one of the wranglers would stop by...that there'd be some unexpected strays to round up or fence to string and he'd decide to spend the night out there and I'd get caught. But I didn't leave. I kept telling myself you'd come. The hours became an eternity, as though the world had moved on and I'd somehow been left behind. Even after the sun set, I found excuse after excuse to explain your absence.'

'Stop it, Leah.'

But she couldn't. Once started, the memories continued to unravel, like a wind-up music-box grinding out its song until the music played down. 'It was a full moon that night. I sat on the floor and watched as it drifted from window to window, inching a path across the sky.'

He stared at her, impassive and remote. 'It rained.'

Surfacing from the remembered nightmare, she focused on his face. 'Not until two that morning,' she corrected, her voice dull and lifeless. 'The storm rolled in from the south and blotted out the stars as though an angry hand had wiped them from the sky. The roof leaked like a sieve but, fool that I was, I stayed.' She bowed her head, her emotions nearly spent. 'I stayed and stayed and stayed.'

'Why? Why did you stay?' he asked insistently. 'Look at me, Leah. Look me in the eye and tell me the rest of your lies. Because that's all they are.'

'How could you possibly know what's fact and what's fiction,' she whispered, 'when you weren't there to see?'

'Tell me!'

Forced by the relentless command, she lifted her head. He swept a wisp of ash-blonde hair from her face, and though he touched her with a tender hand his expression was anything but.

'I stayed because I was waiting for you to ride up and take me away like you promised,' she admitted, her voice breaking. 'At daybreak I finally realized you weren't coming. And I vowed that I'd never trust a man again. I'd never give him that sort of power over me or leave myself open and vulnerable to that much misery. So tell me, Hunter. Tell me the truth. What happened? What was so vital that it *dragged* you away and you couldn't be bothered to come back?'

'Sheriff Lomax happened.'

It took a long minute for his words to sink in. 'What do you mean?' she asked, dread balling in her stomach.

He laughed, the jarring sound slicing across her nerves like a finely honed blade. 'Cut the bull, Leah. All that nonsense about waiting for me at the line-shack and sweltering in the heat and watching the moon. It didn't happen. I know it. And you know it. Though I did enjoy the part about the roof leaking. Very pathetic.'

'What's the sheriff got to do with this?' she demanded, more urgently.

'I went to the line-shack, as agreed. You weren't there.' He paused significantly. 'The sheriff was. Along with a few of his men.'

'No. I don't believe you.'

'It took six of them to pull me out of there. You forgot to mention, in your heartbreaking tale of woe, about the smashed furniture or the broken window. Or the unhinged door. They might have taken me, but I didn't go easy.'

'I don't know...' She struggled to remember. Had the window and furniture been broken? 'Things were a bit of a mess, but—'

He didn't give her a chance to finish. 'I guess you were so busy staring at the stars you didn't notice.'

Catching hold of her long, silver braid, he wound it around his hand, pulling her close. His mouth hovered a hair's-breadth above hers. 'Or maybe you didn't notice because every word you've uttered is a lie. Admit it. You were never at that line-shack.'

'I was there!'

'Not a chance. Only two people knew about our meeting. You…and me. I didn't tell a soul. But, since the sheriff came in your place, there's only one explanation. You changed your mind. And, afraid of how I'd react, you spilled your guts to Daddy and begged him to get you out of a sticky situation.'

'No! It didn't happen that way.'

'Didn't it? Tell me this. If we had met that afternoon, would you have come away with me? Well…?' He pinned her with a hard, savage gaze. 'Would you?'

She'd never lied to him in the past and she wouldn't start now. No matter how it might look to him, no matter how he might react, she'd tell him the truth. 'No. I wouldn't have gone with you.'

For an instant his grip tightened and she waited for him to master his anger, unafraid, knowing with an absolute certainty that he'd never physically harm her. 'I didn't think so,' he said. He released her and stood, and she sensed that he'd set himself apart, distancing himself from her.

Her explanation wouldn't change anything, but she had to try. For the first time she deliberately touched him, placing a hand on his upper arm, feeling the rock-like muscles clench in reaction. 'There's a reason I wouldn't have gone away with you—'

'Enough, Leah.' He turned flat, cold eyes in her direction. 'I've heard enough. It's water under the bridge. And, to be honest, your excuses don't interest me.'

There was no point in trying to force him to listen. Not now. Maybe not ever. 'Then why are you here?' she asked. 'Why cause more grief—grief neither of us needs?'

'Because what's important is today. Here and now. Your ranch and that ad.'

'I won't let you get your hands on this ranch...or on me,' she informed him fiercely. 'You might as well give up and move on, because I won't marry you.'

He laughed, the sound harsh and mocking. 'I don't recall asking, sweetheart.'

A tide of color washed into her face at his biting response. 'I assumed that was why you'd come. You had the ad and you implied—'

He lifted an eyebrow. 'Implied what?'

'That you were interested in marrying me,' she maintained stubbornly. 'You came in response to my notice, didn't you?'

'Not to offer marriage, that's for damned sure. I came because you wouldn't have placed that ad if you weren't desperate, which makes it a powerful bargaining chip. So let's bargain. I want the ranch, Leah, and I mean to get it.'

They stared at each other for an endless moment. Before she could respond, a car horn sounded out front, and Hunter glanced towards the windows. 'Someone's here. Another applicant, perhaps?'

Slipping past him, Leah crossed to the window, recognizing the pick-up parked in front. The occupant leaned on the horn again and her mouth tightened in response. 'It would appear this is my day for surprises,' she murmured. 'Unpleasant surprises, that is.'

She crossed to the picture wall where Hunter had left her rifle and snatched it up.

'What's going on, Leah?' Hunter demanded, picking up his hat. 'Who's your company?'

Intent on reloading, she spared him a brief glance. 'His name is Bull Jones. He's the foreman of the Circle P.'

Hunter's eyes narrowed. 'The Circle P?'

'A new outfit. Actually, they're now the *only* outfit in these parts, except for us. They're owned by a big conglomerate, Lyon Enterprises, and they're not particularly friendly. So do me a favor and stay out of this, okay? It doesn't concern you.'

He looked as if he might debate the issue. Then, with an abrupt nod, he followed her out to the porch. Propping his shoulder against a pillar, he tipped his hat low on his brow, his face thrown into shadow. Satisfied by Hunter's apparent compliance, Leah turned her attention to the more immediate and far more menacing problem confronting her.

Bull Jones leaned negligently against the door of his pick-up—a pick-up parked directly in the middle of the tiny strip of flowerbed Grandmother Rose had painstakingly labored over these past three weeks. 'Afternoon, Miz Hampton,' he said, grinning around the stub of a thick cigar.

She ignored his greeting, taking a stand at the top of the porch steps. 'Get off my property, you thieving rattlesnake,' she ordered coldly, 'before I call the sheriff.'

'In one of your feisty moods, are you?' She didn't bother responding and he sighed. 'Call the sheriff if it'll make you feel any better. But you know and I know he won't be coming. He's tired of all your phone-calls.'

She couldn't argue with the truth. Instead, she brought the rifle to her shoulder and aimed the hurting end exactly six inches below Bull's massive silver belt buckle. 'Spit out why you came and get the hell off my land before I send you home with a few vital parts missing,' she said.

He didn't seem the least intimidated. In fact he laughed in genuine amusement. 'You do have a way with words.' He jerked his head toward Hunter. 'This *hombre* one of your prospective suitors? Doesn't have much to say for himself.'

Hunter smiled without amusement. 'Give it time, friend.'

Leah couldn't conceal her surprise. If Bull considered Hunter a potential suitor, then he knew about her advertisement. But how had he found out? Before the two men could exchange further words, she hastened to ask, 'Is that it, Jones? That's what you came about? My ad?'

'One of the reasons,' Bull acknowledged. 'I even considered offering myself up as a possible candidate. But I didn't think you'd go for it.'

'You thought right.'

'As to the other matter....' He paused to savor his cigar, puffing contentedly for a long minute. She knew it was a deliberate maneuver on his part—an attempt to drive her crazy. Unfortunately it was working.

'Out with it, Jones.'

'My, my. You are in a hurry.' He shrugged, a quick grin sliding across his face. 'You want it straight?

Okay. I'll give it to you straight. I came to offer a friendly little warning.'

'*Friendly*?'

'I'm a friendly sort of guy.' He took a step in her direction. 'You give me half the chance, you'd find just how friendly I can be.'

She didn't know whether it was the sound of her pumping home the shell in her rifle or the fact that Hunter suddenly straightened from his lounging position that stopped Bull in his tracks. Whichever it was, he froze. Then she glanced at Hunter and knew what had checked the foreman's movements.

She'd always found Hunter's eyes fascinating. One minute the blackness appeared, cold and remote, the next minute glittering with fire and passion. For the first time she saw his eyes burn with an implacable threat and for the first time she realized how intimidating it could be.

He leveled that look on Bull. 'If you have something more to say,' he informed the foreman softly, 'I suggest you say it. Fast.'

Bull Jones shot Hunter a look of fury, but Leah noticed he obeyed. 'Seems Lyon Enterprises is getting tired of playing games over this place.' His gaze shifted to Leah. 'Thought you should know they've decided to call in the big guns.'

'I'm shaking in my boots,' she said.

He removed his cigar from between his teeth and threw it to the ground. It landed amongst a clump of crushed pink begonias, wisps of smoke drifting up from the smoldering tip. 'You will be. From what I hear, this new guy's tough. You don't stand a chance.'

His words terrified her. But she refused to crack.

She wouldn't allow her fear to show. Not to this bastard. 'You've been saying that for a full year now,' she said calmly enough. 'And I've managed just fine.'

'That was kid-glove treatment.'

Anger stirred. The temptation to pull the trigger and be done with it was all too inviting. 'You call fouling wells and cutting fence-line and stampeding my herd kid-glove treatment?'

He shrugged. 'We were having a little fun, is all. But now the gloves are off. Don't say I didn't warn you.'

With that, he stomped through what remained of Grandmother Rose's flowerbed and climbed into his pick-up. The engine started with a noisy roar and he gunned it, a rooster-tail of dirt and grass spraying up from beneath his rear wheels. They watched in silence as he disappeared down the dirt drive. A minute later all that remained of Bull's passing was a tiny whirlwind of dust, spinning lazily in the distance. Leah eyed it with a thoughtful frown.

Hunter slipped the rifle from her grasp and leaned it against the porch rail. 'Something you forgot to tell me?' he murmured sardonically.

She lifted her chin. 'There might be one or two minor details we didn't get around to discussing. Not that it's any concern of yours.'

'I don't agree. I suggest we go back inside and discuss those minor details.'

'No!' She rounded on him. First Titus T., then Bull and now Hunter. This definitely wasn't her day. 'You know full well that there's nothing left to talk over. You want the ranch and I won't let you have it. Even if you were interested in responding to my ad—interested in marriage—I won't choose you for the position. How could you think I would?'

He raised an eyebrow. 'Position? I thought you wanted a husband.'

'That's right, I do. But since you aren't interested...' Fighting to keep the distress from her voice, she said, 'You've had your fun. So why don't you leave?'

He shook his head. 'We're not through with our conversation, and I'm not leaving until we are. If that means applying for your...position, then consider me applied.'

'Forget it. You don't qualify,' she insisted. 'That ends the conversation as far as I'm concerned.'

'I qualify, all right. On every point.'

She didn't want to continue with this charade but, aside from picking up her rifle and trying to force him off her property at gunpoint, she didn't see any other option available to her. Especially considering how far she'd gotten the last time she'd turned her rifle on him. 'Fine. You think you qualify? Then prove it,' she demanded.

'A challenge? Not a wise move, Leah, because once I've proven myself we'll finish that discussion.' He tilted his head to one side, his brow furrowed in thought. 'Let's see if I can get this right... Number one. You want a man between the ages of twenty-five and forty-five. No problem there.'

'You should have read the ad more carefully, Hunter! It says a *kind and gentle* man. You are neither kind nor gentle.'

His gaze, black and merciless, met hers. 'You'd do well to remember that.'

Tempted as she was, she didn't back down. 'I

haven't forgotten. The ad also says applicants should be looking for a permanent type of relationship.' She shot him a skeptical glance. 'Don't tell me you're finally ready to settle down?'

'That isn't my first choice, no. But I'd consider it if the right offer came along. Number two. As I recall that concerns ranching experience.' He folded his arms across his chest. 'You planning to debate my qualifications there?'

She shook her head. After all, there was nothing to debate. 'I'll concede your ranching abilities,' she agreed.

A grim smile touched his mouth. 'You'll concede a hell of a lot more before we're finished. Number three. He should also have solid business skills—particularly those skills necessary to please a bullheaded banker.' He settled his hat lower on his forehead. 'You've tipped your hand with that one.'

'Have I?' Something about his attitude worried her. He acted as though this were all a game, as though she'd already lost the match but didn't yet know it. What she couldn't figure was…how? How could she lose a game that she wasn't even playing?

His smile turned predatory. 'You're having financial difficulties and the bank won't help without a man backing you. Close enough?'

She gritted her teeth. 'Close enough,' she forced herself to confess. 'But you aren't that man. End of discussion.'

'Far from it. There isn't a bank in the world who wouldn't back me.'

That gave her pause. 'Since when?'

He closed the distance between them, crowding her against the porch rail. 'It's been eight years since our last meeting. A lot has happened in that time. I'm not the poor ranch-hand you once knew. You need me, Leah. And soon—very soon—I'm going to prove it to you.'

'I don't need you!' she denied passionately. 'I'll *never* need you.'

'Yes, you will.' His voice dropped, the timbre soft and caressing, but his words were as hard and chipped as stone. 'Because you won't get any cooperation from the bank without me. I guarantee it. And by tomorrow you'll know it, too.'

She caught her breath. 'You can prove that?'

'I'll give you all the proof you need. Count on it.' He lowered his head, his mouth inches from hers. 'Seems I've qualified after all.'

She glared, slipping from between him and the rail. 'I disagree. You've already admitted that you aren't kind or gentle. And since that *is* one of the qualifications...' She shrugged. "Fraid I'll have to pass.'

'And I'm afraid I'll have to insist. In the business world all negotiations are subject to compromise. You'll have to compromise on "kind and gentle".'

'And what will you compromise about?' she shot back.

'If I can get away with it...nothing.' He edged his hip on to the rail and glanced at her. 'Tell me something, Leah. Why haven't you sold the ranch?'

She shifted impatiently. 'I think you can guess. Hampton Homestead has been in our family for—'

'Generations. Yes, your father made that point quite clear. Along with the point that he wouldn't allow his ranch or his daughter to fall into the hands of some penniless mongrel whose bloodlines couldn't be traced past the orphanage where he'd been dumped.'

She stared at him, genuinely shocked. 'He said that to you?'

'He said it. But that's not the point. You're out of options, Leah. Soon you won't have any other alternative. My sources tell me that either you sell or you go bankrupt. At least if you sell you'll walk away with enough money to live in comfort.'

She lifted her chin. 'There is another alternative.'

His mouth twisted. 'The ad.'

'Don't look at me like that! It's not as foolish a decision as you might think. The banks will loan me the money I need to stay afloat if I have a husband who's both a businessman and a rancher.'

He stilled. 'They've guaranteed you the money?'

She shook her head. 'Not in writing, if that's what you mean. But Conrad Michaels is the senior loan officer and an old family friend. And, though he hasn't been in a position to help us in the past, he feels our business reversals are correctable, with some work. He's a bit...old-fashioned. It was his idea that I find an appropriate husband. He hasn't been able to get the loan committee to approve financing so far, but he's positive he can if I marry.'

She'd never seen Hunter look so furious. 'Are you telling me that this Michaels instructed you to advertise in the paper for a husband and you went along with his hare-brained notion?'

'It's not a hare-brained notion,' she protested. 'It's very practical. Conrad simply suggested I find a husband with the necessary qualifications as quickly as possible. Once I'd done that, he'd get the loan package put through.'

'He suggested that, did he? In his position as your banker?' Hunter didn't bother to conceal his contempt. 'Did it ever occur to you he could have trouble living up to that promise? He has a board of directors to answer to who might not agree with him any more now than before. And then where would you be? Bankrupt and married to some cowpoke who'll take whatever he can lay hands on and toss you over when the going gets tough.'

'You should know,' she shot back. 'You're a past master of that fine art.'

'Don't start something you can't finish, Leah,' he warned softly. 'I'm telling you—marry the next man who responds to your ad and you'll sacrifice everything and receive nothing but trouble.'

'You're wrong,' she said with absolute confidence. 'I have faith in Conrad. He'll put the loan through.'

She could tell Hunter didn't agree, but he kept his opinion to himself. 'What about the ad?' he asked.

'The ad was my idea. I needed results and I needed them fast.' She folded her arms across her chest in perfect imitation of his stance. 'And I got them.'

He laughed without amusement. 'If you got "kind and gentle" I'm less than impressed.'

'It's not you who has to be impressed,' she retorted defensively. 'It's Conrad whose approval I need.'

'I don't doubt your banker friend will make sure your prospective husband is qualified as a rancher and a businessman,' he stated with marked disapproval. 'But what about as a husband and lover? Who's going to make sure he qualifies in that area?' Hunter's voice dropped, the sound rough and seductive. '"Kind and gentle" couldn't satisfy you in bed in a million years.'

She silently cursed the color surging into her cheeks. 'That's the least of my concerns.'

'You're right. It will be.' He regarded her with derision. 'Is that how you see married life? A sterile partnership with a husband who hasn't a clue how to please his wife?'

Images leapt to her mind, images of the two of them entwined beneath an endless blue sky, their clothes scattered haphazardly around them, their nudity cloaked by thick, knee-high grass. She resisted the seductive pull of the memory. She couldn't afford to remember those times, couldn't afford to risk her emotions on something so fleeting and uncertain…nor so painful. Not if she intended to save the ranch.

'That's not important,' she stated coldly. 'Conrad has promised that if I marry someone the bank considers a sound businessman and rancher, I'll get my loan. And that's what I intend to do. Period. End of discussion. I'm keeping this ranch even if it means accepting the first qualified man who walks through my door. And nothing you say or do will change that.'

'I've got news for you. I *am* the first qualified man to walk through your door. The first and the last.' He reached into his pocket and retrieved a business card. 'Perhaps you'd better know who you're up against.'

'No, let me tell you who *you're* up against,' she retorted, almost at the end of her rope. 'That huge company I mentioned—Lyon Enterprises—is after this ranch. And they'll use any means necessary to acquire it. You've met Bull Jones. He's encouraged almost all my workers to leave with exorbitant bribes. Nor was I kidding when I accused him of cutting my fences and stampeding my herd and fouling the wells. The man I marry will have to contend with that.' She planted her hands on her hips. 'Well, Hunter? Maybe now that you have all the facts in your possession you'll decide to get out of my life. Just be sure that when you do, you make it for good.'

His eyes narrowed and, in a move so swift she didn't see it coming, he caught her by the elbows and swung her into his arms. She slammed into him, the breath knocked from her lungs. 'Don't threaten me, Leah. You won't like the results,' he warned curtly. 'Give it to me straight. Are you really being harassed, or is this another of your imaginative little fantasies?'

This time she didn't even try to fight his hold. She'd learned the hard way how pointless it would be. 'It's no fantasy! You saw a prime example today. Or ask my foreman. Patrick will tell you. He's one of the few they haven't managed to run off.'

His eyes glittered with barely suppressed wrath and a frown slashed deep furrows across his brow. Without releasing her, he tucked his business card back into his pocket. 'You're serious, aren't you?'

She nodded. 'Dead serious.'

'You're also serious about marrying, even if it means losing the ranch?'

'I am.'

'In that case you're down to one option.'

She sighed, weary of their argument. 'I told you. I'm not selling.'

'No, you're not. You're going to marry me.'

If he hadn't been holding her, she would have fallen. 'What?' she whispered, unable to hide her shock.

'You heard me. We'll marry and I'll see to it that you get your loan.'

She stared at him in bewilderment, the fierce determination she read there filling her with a sense of unease. 'You said... I thought you didn't want to marry me.'

'It wasn't my first choice, no,' he agreed. 'But the more I consider the idea, the greater the appeal.'

She caught her breath. 'That's the most insulting offer I've ever heard.'

'Count on it,' he said with a grim smile. 'I can get much more insulting than that.'

'I wouldn't advise it,' she snapped back. 'Not if you'd like me to accept.'

He inclined his head, but whether in acknowledgement or concurrence she wasn't quite clear. An endless moment stretched between them, a moment where they fought a silent battle of wills. It wasn't an even match. Slowly, Leah lowered her eyes. 'You agree,' Hunter stated in satisfaction.

'I didn't say that.' She stalled for time—not that it would help. Exhaustion dogged her heels, making it impossible to think straight. She needed time alone, time to consider, time to put all he'd told her into perspective. But she strongly suspected she wouldn't be given that time. 'What about the bank? Can you guarantee I'll get the loan?'

His expression hardened. 'I have some small influence. I'm not the poor, mixed-breed cur I was eight years ago.'

'I never saw you that way,' she reacted instantly, despising the crude comparison. 'And if my father did, he was wrong.'

He shrugged off her rejoinder. 'What's your decision, Leah?'

This time she did try and free herself. Not that she succeeded. 'What's your rush?' she asked. His touch grew gentle, soothing rather than restraining, at striking odds with his clipped tone. Had he decided an illusion of tenderness might better influence her? If so, he'd soon discover his mistake.

'I don't want anyone else coming along messing up my deal. You have twenty-four hours to make up your mind. Sell the ranch to me or marry me; I don't give a damn which. Because I know it all, Leah,' he informed her tautly. 'I've had your financial situation investigated. You're broke. Without a loan you'll go bankrupt. And without me you won't get that loan.'

She caught her breath in disbelief. 'I don't believe you!'

'You will. You will when the banks tell you that I'm your only choice other than bankruptcy.'

She shook her head, desperate to deny his words. 'How can you possibly do that?'

'You'd be surprised at what I can do.'

'What's happened to you?' she whispered. 'Mercy used to be a part of your nature.'

He gazed at her impassively. 'Not any more. You saw to that. It's your decision. And to help you decide…'

She knew what he intended; she recognized the passion in his expression, saw the resolve in his eyes. To her eternal disgust she lifted her face to meet his kiss. Curiosity, that was all it was, she told herself. But she lied. Her curiosity had been appeased earlier. She knew from that first kiss that her reaction to his touch hadn't changed, not even after eight years.

No, she returned his kiss because she wanted to experience the wonder of it again. To come alive beneath his mouth and hands. To relive, if only for a moment, the mind-splintering rapture only he could arouse. He took his time, drinking his fill, sharing the passion that blazed with such incredible urgency.

But it was all an illusion. She knew that. He wanted the ranch and would use any means available to get it. Even seducing her. Even marrying her. And she'd be a fool to forget that.

Lifting his head, he gazed down at her. 'What we once had isn't finished, Leah,' he informed her in a rough, husky voice. 'There's still something between us. Something that needs to be settled, once and for all.'

She eased back. 'And you think our marriage will settle it?'

'One way or another,' he confirmed.

'You don't leave me much choice.'

'I've left you one choice. And I'm it.'

He set her from him, his expression once more cool and distant. In that instant she hated him. Hated him for making her want again. Hated him for resurrecting all that she'd struggled so hard to forget. But she especially hated him for being able to turn off his emotions with so little effort. Because she knew her emotions weren't as easily mastered.

'Twenty-four hours, Leah. After that, you're history.' And, without another word, he left her.

Long after he'd ridden away she stood on the front porch, unable to move, unable to think. Finally, with a muffled sob, she buried her head in her hands and allowed the tears to come.

CHAPTER THREE

HUNTER walked into his office and set his briefcase on his desk. A brief knock sounded on the door behind him and his assistant, Kevin Anderson, poked his head in the door.

'Oh, you're back. How did it go? Did she agree to sell the ranch?'

Opening his briefcase, Hunter removed a bulky file and tossed it to one side. 'Not yet. But I'll have it soon…one way or another.' He turned and faced his assistant, allowing his displeasure to show. 'Why didn't you tell me about Bull Jones and what he's been up to?'

'The foreman?' Kevin hesitated, then shrugged. 'I didn't think it was important.'

Anger made Hunter speak more sharply than he would have otherwise. 'Well, it damned well is important. You don't make those decisions. I do.'

'Sorry, boss. It won't happen again,' came Kevin's swift apology. Then he asked cautiously, 'I assume you've made the foreman's acquaintance?'

'In a manner of speaking.'

'Did he recognize you?'

Hunter didn't answer immediately. Instead, he crossed to the window and stared out at the Houston skyline. The intense humidity from the Gulf of Mexico rippled the air on the far side of the thick, tinted glass, signaling the start of another South Texas heatwave. 'No,' he finally said. 'He didn't recognize me. But then I didn't go out of my way to introduce myself.'

'That's probably smart. What do you want done about him?'

'Nothing for now.' Hunter turned back and faced his assistant. 'But I may need to take action in the future.'

'Whatever you say. You're the boss.'

Hunter inclined his head. 'One last thing before you go.'

'Sure. Anything.'

'You keep me informed from now on. No matter how minor or insignificant. I won't be caught off-guard again.'

'Yes, sir. Sorry, sir,' Kevin agreed. Then he quietly excused himself and slipped from the room.

After a brief hesitation Hunter crossed to his desk and flipped open the file marked 'Hampton Homestead.' A white tide of letters, legal documents and several photos spilled across the gleaming ebony surface. Reaching out, he selected two photos of Leah—one identical to the picture he'd studied in the Hampton study, the other a snapshot only a month old.

Examining the more recent of the two, a savage desire clawed through him, unexpected and intense. He still wanted her...wanted to rip her hair free of her braid, feel her silken limbs clinging to him, feel again her softness beneath him.

He dropped the photo to his desk. Soon, he promised himself. Very, very soon.

*   *   *

'We have to talk,' Grandmother Rose announced the next morning, slamming a thick porcelain mug in front of Leah.

Leah closed her eyes, stifling a groan. She hadn't slept a wink last night and could barely face the unrelenting morning sun, let alone a more unrelenting grandmother. 'If this is about Hunter, I don't want to discuss it.'

'It's about Hunter.'

'I don't want to discuss it.'

'Tough toenails. I have a confession to make and you're going to listen to every last word, even if I have to wrestle you to the floor and sit on you.'

The picture of her ninety-pound grandmother putting her in a headlock and forcing her to the tile floor brought a reluctant smile to Leah's mouth. 'Can we at least talk about the weather for five minutes while I drink my coffee?'

'It's sunny and eighty-five in the shade. Hope you swallowed fast. Now. About Hunter.'

Deep purplish-blue eyes held Leah's in a direct, steady gaze. The eye color and a relentless determination were only two of the qualities Leah shared with her grandmother. Unfortunately, Rose's determination included a stubbornness even beyond Leah's. She gave up. She'd never won an argument with her grandmother, a circumstance unlikely to change any time in the near future. 'What about him?' she asked with a sigh.

'What he said yesterday about the sheriff was true,' Rose announced. 'Every word.'

Leah straightened in her chair. 'You heard? You were listening?'

'I did and I was, and I'm not one bit ashamed to

admit it. What I *am* ashamed to admit is that I betrayed your confidence to your father eight years ago.' She twisted her thick gold wedding-band around a knobby finger, the only external sign of her agitation.

'You warned Dad that I planned to run away with Hunter.' It wasn't a question. Leah had already figured out what must have happened. The only person she'd confessed to about that long-ago meeting sat across the table from her. Not that she'd ever expose her grandmother's involvement to Hunter.

'Yes, I told your father,' Rose confirmed. 'I told Ben because, selfishly, I didn't want you to leave.'

'But I promised you I wouldn't go!'

Leah shoved back her chair and stood. Struggling to conceal her distress, she made a production of pouring herself another cup of coffee. She'd told Rose about her meeting for one simple reason: she couldn't leave the woman who'd loved and raised her without a single word of farewell. What she hadn't anticipated was her grandmother's revelation that Leah's father was dying of cancer. Once in possession of the grim news she hadn't had any alternative. She couldn't abandon her father in his time of need, no matter how desperately she yearned to be with Hunter. It just wasn't in her nature.

Leah turned and faced her grandmother. 'I told you I'd meet Hunter and explain about Dad's illness. I planned to ask him to wait…to return after…after…'

Rose shrugged. 'Perhaps he'd have agreed. But I couldn't count on that—on his going away and letting you stay.' She sighed. 'Listen, girl, the reason I'm telling you all this is because I've decided. I want you to marry Hunter.'

Leah stared in shock. 'Come again?'

'What are you, deaf? I said, I want you to marry Hunter.'

'But...why?'

'Because...' Rose lifted her chin and confessed. 'Because I had a call from Conrad Michaels this morning.'

'What did he want?'

'Officially...to announce his retirement. Unofficially...to withdraw his offer of help. No bank loan in any circumstances was the message I got.'

'Hunter!' Leah released his name with a soft sigh.

'That thought occurred to me, too.' Her grandmother's eyes narrowed. 'You suppose his pull is strong enough to force Connie's retirement?'

'Possibly. Though if Hunter is as ruthless as you suspect, I'm surprised you're so anxious to marry me off to him.'

'Ruthless isn't bad...if it's working on your side. And, right now, we could use a whole lot of ruthless on our side.'

'Could we?' Leah questioned. 'I'm not so sure.'

Rose stared into her coffee-cup as though the answers to all their problems lay written in the dregs. Finally she glanced up, her expression as hard and set as Leah had ever seen it. 'You have two choices. You can sell or you can fight to win against Lyon Enterprises. If you want to sell, say the word, and we'll give up and clear out. But if you want to win, Hunter's the man for the job. It took you years to get over him. Fact is, I don't believe you ever did. Marry him or don't. It's your decision. But my vote is to snatch him up fast. Men like that only come along once in a lifetime. You've gotten a lucky break. He's come through your door twice.'

Lucky? Leah had her doubts. He'd loved her with a passion that she'd never forgotten and she'd let him down. He wouldn't give her the chance to hurt him like that again. She simply couldn't read too much into his return. If anything, he'd come back to wreak revenge. And, if that was the case, by placing that ad she had indeed exposed her vulnerability and given him the perfect opportunity to even an old score.

And he'd been swift to take advantage.

One by one he'd cut off every avenue of escape until she faced two tough alternatives. Unfortunately, learning that any possibility of a bank loan had been circumvented left her with no alternatives…if she intended to save the ranch.

Leah returned her mug to the counter, the coffee having gone stone-cold. She looked at her grandmother and saw the hint of desperation lurking in Rose's otherwise impassive expression. No matter what she'd said, losing the ranch would be the death of her. And to be responsible for her demise, when Leah had it within her power to prevent it, just couldn't be borne.

'I'll call Hunter,' she announced quietly.

For the first time in her life, Leah saw tears glitter in her grandmother's eyes. 'Don't accept his first offer, girl,' she advised gruffly. 'Bargain for position and you can still come out of this on top.'

'I'm not your granddaughter for nothing,' Leah said with a teasing smile. 'He won't have it all his own way.'

And he wouldn't. Very soon she'd find out just how badly he wanted the ranch—and just how much ground he'd give up in order to get it.

*   *   *

Not until Leah had completed her list of requests for Hunter—she hesitated to call them demands—did she realize that he hadn't left her a number where he could be reached. Not that it truly presented a problem. Precisely twenty-four hours after their original meeting, Hunter phoned.

'What's your answer?' he asked, dispensing with the preliminaries.

'I want to meet with you and discuss the situation,' Leah temporized.

'You mean discuss terms of surrender?'

'Yes.' She practically choked getting the word out. He must have known, darn him, for a low, intimate laugh sounded in her ear.

'You did that very well,' he approved. 'See? Giving in isn't so bad.'

'Yes, it is,' she assured him. 'You try it some time and you'll know what I mean.'

'No, you handle it much better than I would. All you need is a little more practice.'

Married to him, she didn't doubt she'd get it, either. 'Where are you staying?' she asked, deliberately changing the subject. She knew when to give up on a losing hand. 'Should I meet you there?'

'I'm in Houston. And no, I don't expect you to drive that far. We'll meet tomorrow. Noon. The line-shack.'

She caught her breath in disbelief. 'That's not funny, Hunter!'

'It wasn't meant to be.' All trace of amusement vanished from his voice, his tone acquiring a sharp, cutting edge. 'I'm dead serious. Tomorrow meet me at the line-shack at noon. Just like before. See that you make it this time. There won't be any second chances.'

'There weren't eight years ago. Why should this occasion be any different?'

'It will be different,' he promised. 'You'd be smart to realize that right from the start.'

'Fine. You've made your point and I realize it. Things will be different.'

'Very good, Leah. There's hope for you yet.'

She clamped down on her temper, determined not to be provoked. 'So, let's meet at the ranch-house instead. Okay? Hunter?' But she spoke into a dead phone. So much for not being provoked. She was thoroughly provoked.

Slowly she hung up. This did not bode well for their future together. Not well at all. She reached for her list. She wouldn't have that disaster at the line-shack held over her head like the sword of Damocles for the rest of her life. She'd done all the explaining she intended to do, but apparently he had more to say. Well, this meeting would end it once and for all. She wouldn't spend the rest of her life paying for something that, though her ultimate responsibility, wasn't her fault.

Early the next morning she headed for the south pasture to pay a visit to Dreamseeker, the stallion she'd recently acquired. At the fence she whistled, low and piercing, waiting for the familiar whickered response. From the concealing stand of cottonwoods he came, a coal-black stallion, racing across the grass. He danced to a stop ten yards from the fence, pawing at the ground and shaking his mane.

'You don't fool me,' she called to him. 'You want it. I know you do. All you have to do is come and take it.' She held out her hand so he could see the lumps of sugar she'd brought him.

Without further hesitation he charged the fence, but she didn't flinch. Her hand remained rock-steady. Skidding to a halt beside her, the horse ducked his head into her hand and snatched the sugar from her palm. Then he nipped her fingers—not hard, just enough to establish dominance. With a snort, he spun around and galloped across the pasture.

She cradled her palm, refusing to show her hurt. She wouldn't let herself be hurt. It was an indulgence that she couldn't afford. She'd made her decision—a decision that would protect the stallion, protect her ranch, and protect all the wounded creatures she'd gathered safely beneath her wing.

She also understood why Dreamseeker had bitten her. He'd done it to prove that he was still free—free to choose, free to approach or flee. It saddened her, because she knew he lived a lie. They had that in common. For, no matter how hard they tried, neither was truly free.

Not any more.

Leaving the fence, she saddled a horse and rode to the line-shack. The spring weather had taken a turn for the worse, becoming every bit as hot and humid as that fateful day eight years ago. A sullen mugginess weighted the air, filled it with the threat of a thunderstorm. Leah shuddered. The similarities between then and now were more than she cared to contemplate.

At the line-shack she ground-hitched her gelding. Hunter hadn't arrived yet and she stood outside, reluctant to enter the cabin...reluctant to face any more memories. She'd avoided this place for eight long years. Thanks to Hunter she couldn't avoid it any longer. Setting her chin, she crossed to the door and thrust it open.

She stepped cautiously inside, looking around in disbelief. Everything was spotless. A table, two chairs, a bed—everything in its place. A thin layer of dust was the only visible sign of neglect. Someone had gone to great pains to restore the shack. But who? And why?

'Reliving old memories?'

Leah whirled around. 'Hunter! You startled me.'

He filled the threshold, a blackened silhouette that blocked the sun and caused the walls to close in around them. 'You shouldn't be so easily startled.'

Searching for something to say, she gestured to indicate the cabin. 'It's changed. For some reason I thought the place would have fallen down by now.'

He shrugged. 'You can't run a ranch this size without working line-shacks. The men need someplace to hole up when they're working this far out. Allowing it to fall into ruin would be counterproductive.'

She could feel the tension building between them, despite his air of casual indifference. She wouldn't be able to handle this confrontation for long. Best to get it over with—and fast. She turned and faced him. Unfortunately that only served to heighten her awareness. 'Why did you want to meet here?' she asked, taking the offensive.

'To annoy you.'

Her mouth tightened. 'You succeeded. Was that your only reason?'

'No. I could have had you drive to Houston and negotiate on my turf. But, considering our history...' He shrugged, relaxing against the doorjamb.

He tucked his thumbs into his belt-loops, his jeans hugging his lean hips and clinging to the powerful muscles of his thighs and buttocks. She shouldn't stare, shouldn't remember the times he'd shed his jeans and shirt, exposing his coppery skin to her gaze. But it proved next to impossible to resist the old memories.

He'd had a magnificent physique, something that clearly hadn't changed with time. If anything, his shoulders had broadened, his features had sharpened, becoming more tautly defined. How she wished their circumstances were different, that she didn't fear he'd use her attraction to achieve his goal...to gain his revenge.

Desperately, she forced her attention back to the issue at hand. 'Negotiating here is just as much to your advantage. Dredging up the old memories, playing on my guilt, is supposed to give you added leverage, is that it?'

'Yes. I play to win. You'd be wise to learn that now.'

She ground her teeth in frustration. 'And if I don't?'

He smiled. 'You will. We've come full circle, you and I. We're back where we left off. But nothing's the same as it was. You've changed. I've changed.' He added significantly, 'And our situation has changed.'

'How has it changed?' she asked with sudden curiosity. 'How have you changed? What did you do after you left here?'

He hesitated, and for a minute she thought he wouldn't answer. Then he said, 'I finished my education, for a start. Then I worked twenty-four hours a day building my...fortune.'

'You succeeded, I assume?' she pressed.

'You could say that.'

'That's it? That's all you have to say—you got an education and made your fortune?'

He shrugged. 'That's it.'

She stared at him suspiciously, wondering what he was concealing. Because she didn't doubt for a minute that he hadn't told her everything. What had he left out? And, more importantly, *why*? 'Why so mysterious?' she demanded, voicing her concerns. 'What are you hiding?'

He straightened. 'Still trying to call the shots, Leah? You better get past that, pronto.'

'It's my ranch,' she protested. 'Of course I'm still calling the shots.'

He shook his head. 'It may be your ranch, but I'm the one who'll be in charge. Are we clear on that?'

'No, we're not clear on that!' she asserted vehemently. 'In fact, we're not clear on anything. For one thing, I won't have our past thrown in my face day after day. I won't spend the rest of my life apologizing for what happened.'

'I have no intention of bringing it up again. But I wanted to make it plain, so there's no doubt in your mind. I won't have you claiming later that I didn't warn you.'

She eyed him warily. 'Warn me about what?'

'You've been managing this ranch for over seven years and you've almost run it into the ground. Now I'm supposed to come in and save it. And I will. But you're going to have to understand and accept that I'm in charge. What I say goes. I won't have you questioning me in front of the hired help or second-guessing my decisions. You're going to have to trust me. Implicitly. Without question. And that's going to start here and now.'

'You've been gone a lot of years. It isn't reasonable—'

He grabbed his shirtsleeve and ripped it with one brutal yank, the harsh sound of rending cotton stemming her flow of words. 'You see that scar?' A long, ragged silver line streaked up his forearm.

She swallowed, feeling the blood drain from her face. 'I see it.'

'I got it when the sheriff helped me through that window.' He jerked his head toward the south wall. 'I have another on my inner thigh. One of Lomax's deputies tried to make a point with his spur. He almost succeeded. I broke my collarbone and a couple of ribs on the door here.' He shoved at the casing and it wobbled. 'Still isn't square. Seems I did leave my mark, after all.'

She felt sick. How could her father and Sheriff Lomax have been so cruel? Had Hunter really been such a threat to them? 'Are you doing this for revenge?' she asked in a low voice. 'Trying to get control of the ranch because of how Dad treated you and because I wouldn't go away with you?'

'Believe what you want, but understand this…' He leaned closer, his words cold and harsh. 'I got dragged off this land once. It won't happen again. If you can't accept that, sell out. But if you marry me, don't expect a partnership. I don't work by committee.'

'Those are your conditions? What you say goes? That's it?'

He inclined his head. 'That just about covers it.'

'It doesn't come close to covering it,' she protested. 'I have a few conditions of my own.'

'I didn't doubt it for a minute.'

She pulled the list she'd compiled from her pocket and, ignoring his quiet laugh, asked, 'What about my employees? They've been with me for a long time. What sort of guarantee are you offering that changes won't be made?'

'I'm not making any guarantees. If they can pull their weight, they stay. It's as simple as that.'

She stared in alarm. Pull their weight? Every last one of them pulled his or her own weight…to the best of their ability. But that might not be good enough to suit Hunter's high standards. Patrick had a bad leg and wasn't as fast or strong as another foreman might be.

And what about the Arroyas? Mateo and his wife Inez would have starved if she hadn't taken them in. Inez, as competent a housekeeper as she was, had six children to care for. Leah had always insisted that the children's needs come first, even at the expense of routine chores. Would Hunter feel the same way? And Mateo was a wonder with horses but, having lost his arm in a car accident, certain jobs were difficult for him—tasks she performed in his stead.

'But—'

'Are you already questioning my judgement?' he asked softly.

She stirred uneasily. 'No, not exactly. I'd just appreciate some sort of guarantee that these people won't be fired.' She saw his expression close over. 'I'm responsible for them,' she forced herself to explain. 'They couldn't find work anywhere else. At least, not easily.'

'I'm not an unfair or unreasonable man,' he said in a clipped voice. 'They won't be terminated without due cause.'

It was the best she'd get from him. 'And Grandmother Rose?'

A tiny flicker of anger burned in his eyes. 'Do you think I don't know how much Hampton Homestead means to her? Believe me, I'm well aware of the extent she'd go to to keep the ranch.'

Her fingers tightened on the list. 'You don't expect her to move?'

She could tell from his expression that she'd offended him, and she suspected that it was a slight he wouldn't soon forgive. 'As much as the idea appeals, it isn't my intention to turn her from her home,' he said curtly. 'What's next on your list?'

Taking him at his word, she plunged on. 'I want a prenuptial agreement that states that in the event of a divorce I get to keep the ranch.'

'There won't be a divorce.'

She lifted her chin. 'Then you won't object to the agreement, will you?'

He ran a hand across the back of his neck, clearly impatient with her requests. 'We'll let our lawyers hammer out the finer details. I refuse to start our marriage discussing an imaginary divorce.'

She wouldn't get any more of a concession than that. 'Agreed.'

'Next?'

She took a deep breath. This final item would be the trickiest of all. 'I won't sleep with you.'

His smile was derisive. 'That's an unrealistic request and you damned well know it.'

'It's not. I—'

He cut her off without hesitation. 'This is going to be a real marriage—in every sense of the word. We sleep together, drink, eat and make love together.'

'Not a chance,' she protested, her voice taking on an edge of desperation even she couldn't mistake. 'You wanted control of the ranch and you're getting that. I won't be part of the bargain. I won't barter myself.'

Sardonic amusement touched his expression. 'You will and you'll like it,' he informed her softly. 'I know you too well not to make it good for you.'

'You knew an inexperienced eighteen-year-old girl,' she declared passionately. 'You know nothing about the person I've become. You know nothing of my hopes or dreams or desires. And you never will.'

'Another challenge?' He moved closer. 'Shall we settle that here and now? The bed's a little narrow, but it'll do. I guarantee you won't be disappointed.'

She took a hasty step back, knowing there was nowhere to escape should he decide to put action to words. 'You bastard,' she whispered. 'I won't be forced.'

'I don't use force. I don't have to.' For a horrifying second she thought he'd prove it, that he'd sweep her up without regard and carry her to the bed. That he'd scatter her resistance like so much chaff before the breeze. Then he relaxed, though his gaze remained guarded and watchful. 'What about children?' he asked unexpectedly. 'Or are they off your list, too?'

Events had proceeded so swiftly that she hadn't

given the possibility any thought at all. 'Do you want children?' she asked uncertainly.

He cocked his head to one side, eyeing her with an uncomfortable intensity. 'Do you? Or, should I say, do you want *my* children?'

'Once, that was all I dreamed about,' she confessed in a low voice.

'And now?'

She looked at him, fighting her nervousness. 'Yes, I want children.'

'You won't get them if I agree to your condition. Cross it off your list, Leah. It's not a negotiable point.'

She didn't want to concede defeat, didn't want to agree to give herself to him without love, without commitment. But he'd left her without choice. 'Hunter, please...'

He closed the distance between them. Cupping her head, he tilted her face up to his. 'We'll make love, you and I, and we'll have children. Plenty of them. Though chances are they won't be blue-eyed blondes. Can you live with that?'

'I'm not my father. I know you don't believe it, but it's true. Do you really think I could love my child less because he's dark...' she dared to feather her fingers through his hair '...instead of fair?'

He caught her hand and drew it to his scarred arm, her pale skin standing out starkly against his sun-bronzed tan. 'It matters to some.'

'Not to me. It never mattered to me.'

He nodded, apparently accepting her words at face value. 'Any more conditions?' he asked, flicking her list with a finger.

'No,' she admitted. 'But you'd better know up-front—I can't promise I won't argue with you. I love this ranch. And I'll do all I can to protect the people on it.'

He shook his head. 'That's my job now.'

'That doesn't mean I won't worry.'

'Worrying is also my job,' he informed her gravely.

She nodded. That left only one last decision to be made. 'About the wedding…'

'I want to marry by the end of the week. Tell me where and when and I'll be there. Just make sure it's no later than Saturday.'

'So soon?' she asked in dismay. 'That's less than a week.'

'Are you having second thoughts?'

'Constantly. But it won't change anything. I won't sell and I can't save the ranch unless I marry you. But a wedding… There's a lot to be done and not much time to do it in.'

'Find the time.' He tugged her more fully into his arms. 'I have to go,' he said, and kissed her.

His touch drove out all thought and reason, banishing the ghosts that lingered from that other time and place. And no matter how hard she wanted to oppose him, to keep a small piece of herself safe and protected, he stripped her of all resistance with consummate ease. Deepening the kiss, he cupped her breast, teasing the tender peak through the thin cotton. And she let him…let him touch her as he wished, let him explore where he willed, let him drive her toward that sweet crest she'd once shared exclusively with him.

For a moment Leah was able to pretend that she meant something to him again, that he really cared for her more than he cared for her ranch. But as hard as she tried to lose herself in his embrace, the knowledge that this was in all probability a game of revenge intruded, and finally drove her from his arms.

He released her without protest. 'Call me with the details,' he instructed, and headed for the door. 'We'll need to get the license as soon as possible.'

'There's one last thing,' she suddenly remembered. He paused, waiting for her to continue and, almost stumbling over the words, she said, 'Conrad...Conrad Michaels. He retired.' Hunter didn't say anything, prompting her to state her concerns more openly. 'Are you responsible for his retirement?'

'Yes.'

She'd suspected as much, but it still shocked her to hear him admit it. '*Why?*' He didn't reply. Instead he walked outside, forcing her to give chase. Without breaking stride, he gathered up his buckskin's reins and mounted. She clung to his saddle-skirt, hindering his departure, desperate for an answer. 'Hunter, please. Tell me why. Why did you force Conrad to retire?'

After a momentary hesitation he leaned across the horn, fixing her with hard black eyes. 'Because he put you at risk.'

Alarmed, she took a step back. 'What are you talking about?'

'I'm talking about the ad.'

'But I placed the ad, not Conrad.'

'He knew about it, and not only did he not try and stop it he encouraged you to go ahead with it while in his capacity as your banker.' His face might have been carved from granite. 'You still don't have a clue as to how dangerous that was, do you?'

'We were very selective,' she defended.

'You were a fool,' he stated succinctly. 'You might

as well have painted a bullseye on your backside,
stuck your pinfeathers in the air and proclaimed it
open hunting season. Count yourself lucky that you
and that old harridan of a grandmother weren't mur-
dered in your beds.'

'So you had Conrad fired.'

'I wanted to!' he bit out. 'Believe me, more than
anything I wanted to have him fired for planting such
a criminal suggestion in your head. Considering he's
an old family friend, I let him off easy. I agreed to
an early retirement.'

A sudden thought struck her. 'If you're that powerful—powerful enough to force Conrad's retirement—what do you need with this ranch?' She spoke
urgently. 'It has to be small potatoes to you. Why are
you doing this, Hunter?'

A grim smile touched his mouth and he yanked the
brim of his stetson low over his brow. 'That, my
sweet bride-to-be, is one question I have no intention
of answering.'

And with that he rode off into the approaching
storm, the dark, angry clouds sweeping across the sky
ahead of him, full of flash and fury. A portent of
things to come? Leah wondered uneasily. Or a promise?

CHAPTER FOUR

WITH only five days to prepare for her wedding, Leah realized that the simplest solution would be to hold the ceremony at the ranch. She also decided to make it an evening affair and keep it small, inviting only her closest friends and employees.

Her reasons were twofold. She didn't think she could handle a day-long celebration—the mere thought of celebrating a marriage that was in all actuality a business deal struck her as vulgar. And by holding an evening ceremony they'd entertain the guests for dinner and it would be over quickly. No fuss, no muss.

Her grandmother didn't offer a single word of argument in regard to Leah's wedding-plans. On only one matter did she remain adamant. She insisted that Leah invite Conrad Michaels. 'He's a close friend and should give you away. If that makes Hunter uncomfortable, that's his tough luck.'

'I don't think it's Hunter who will feel uncomfortable,' Leah observed wryly. 'Let me call Conrad and see what he wants to do. If he chooses to decline, I won't pressure him.'

As it turned out, Conrad sounded quite anxious to attend. 'I'd appreciate the opportunity to improve my relationship with Hunter,' he confessed. 'I deserved every harsh word he dished out, and then some.'

'Harsh word?' she repeated in alarm. 'What did he say?'

After a long, awkward silence, Conrad admitted, 'Oh, this and that. Let's just describe the conversation as strained and forget I ever mentioned it. He did make several valid points, though—particularly about your ad.'

So Hunter *had* taken Conrad to task about that. She'd wondered. 'What points?' she questioned.

'I never should have encouraged you to advertise for a husband,' came the prompt reply. 'Looking back, I realize it was foolish in the extreme. It didn't occur to me until Hunter suggested the possibility, but a crazy person could have responded and we wouldn't have known until too late. I never would have forgiven myself if anything had happened to you.'

Unfortunately, something *had* happened. Hunter had answered the ad. To her disgust, she seemed to be the only one to appreciate the irony of that fact. 'It's all worked out for the best,' she lied through her teeth. 'So don't worry about it.' Securing Conrad's agreement to give her away, she ended the conversation and hung up.

The next two days passed in a whirl of confusion. Leah spent her time deciding on caterers and flowers, food and decorations, and obtaining the all-important wedding-license. Finally she threw her hands in the air and dropped the entire mess in the laps of her grandmother and Inez Arroya. 'You decide,' she begged. 'Just keep it simple.'

'But, *señorita, por favor*...' Inez protested. 'The wedding, it should be perfect. What if we make a mistake? You will be very unhappy. Don't you care?'

Didn't she care? Leah turned away. She cared too

much. That was the problem. How could she plan for the wedding of her dreams when the ceremony on Friday would be anything but? 'Whatever you decide will be perfect,' she said flatly. 'Just remember. Keep it simple.'

'What about your dress?' Rose reminded, before Leah could escape. 'You've deliberately ignored that minor detail, haven't you?'

'I thought I could pick something up on Thursday,' Leah said, refusing to acknowledge the truth in her grandmother's words.

But on this one point Rose became surprisingly obstinate. 'Oh, no, you don't, my girl. I have the perfect gown for you. Your mother wore it for her wedding and it's the most unusual dress I've ever laid eyes on. It's packed away in the attic, if memory serves. Find it and see if it fits. Though considering how much you resemble your momma, I'd be surprised if it didn't.'

Reluctantly, Leah obeyed. It took a good bit of searching, but she eventually found a huge, sealed box with her mother's name and the date of her wedding scrawled across one end. Wiping away the dust, she carried it downstairs. She didn't return to the kitchen, needing a moment alone in the privacy of her bedroom to examine her mother's wedding-dress. Closing and locking the door, she settled on the floor and carefully cut open the box.

Lifting off the lid, she sank back on her heels, her breath catching in her throat. Her grandmother had been right. It was the most unusual dress Leah had ever seen. Her mother had been a teacher of medieval history and her dress reflected her obsession, right down to the filmy veil with its accompanying silver circlet. It was beautiful and romantic, the sort of dress young women dreamed of wearing.

And Leah hated it with a passion that left her shaking.

The dress promised joy and happiness, not the businesslike relationship soon to be hers. The dress promised a lifetime of laughter and companionship, not the strife and friction that was all she could expect from an empty marriage. But most of all the dress promised everlasting love, not the bitterness and pain that consumed her husband-to-be. She ached for the future the dress suggested, but knew it could never be hers.

This marriage would be an act of vengeance, and she nothing more than a pawn in Hunter's game. It was a way to even up old scores for the abuse he'd suffered at her father's hands. Soon he would be master of his enemy's castle and she'd be at his mercy. How long would it take before he had it all? How long before he controlled not just the ranch but her heart and soul as well?

How long before he had his final revenge?

Gently she replaced the lid of the box. She couldn't wear her mother's wedding-gown. It wouldn't be right. It would be…sacrilegious. She'd drive into town and find a chic ivory suit that spoke of modern marriages and easy divorces. And instead of a gauzy veil she'd purchase a pert little hat that no one would dream of referring to as 'romantic'.

Not giving herself time to reconsider, she shoved the box beneath her bed. Then she ran outside and whistled for Dreamseeker, needing just for an instant to feel what her stallion felt—free and wild and unfettered. But the horse didn't respond to her call. And in that instant Leah felt more alone than she ever had before in her life.

'What do you mean, I can't wear the suit?' Leah demanded of Inez. 'Why can't I? Where is it?'

'*Arrunina, señorita. Lo siento.*'

'Ruined! How?'

'The iron, it burned your dress.'

'But the dress didn't need ironing.'

The housekeeper looked close to tears. 'I'm sorry. I wanted everything to be perfect for your special day. I was excited and...' She wrung her hands. 'Forgive me.'

'It's all right, Inez,' Leah said with a sigh. 'But I get married in less than an hour. What am I supposed to wear? I can't go down in this.' She indicated the wisps of silk and lace beneath her robe.

'Señora Rose, she suggests the dress of your *madre. Es perfecta, sí*?'

Leah closed her eyes, understanding finally dawning. Of all the conniving, meddling, devious... Before she could gather the courage to yank the first outfit that came to hand from her closet, Inez draped the wedding-dress across the bed. In a swirl of feather-light pleats the silvery-white silk billowed over the quilted spread, the hem trailing to the floor.

In that instant, Leah was lost. She touched the form-fitting bodice—a corset-like affair, decorated with a honeycombed network of tiny seed pearls and silver thread—thinking that it resembled nothing more than a gossamer-fine cobweb. It really was an enchanting gown. And it had been her mother's.

Knowing further arguing would prove fruitless, Leah allowed the housekeeper to help her into the gown. It fit perfectly, as she'd known it would. Thin white ribbons accentuated the puffed sleeves, the deep, flowing points almost brushing the carpet.

'The belt, *señorita*,' Inez said.

The housekeeper lifted the silver linked chain from the bed and wound it twice around Leah's waist and hips, the pearl-studded clasp fastening in front. The ends of the chain, decorated with tiny unicorn charms, fell to her knees, the links whispering like golden-toned chimes with her every movement.

'For purity,' the housekeeper murmured, touching the unicorns.

'Not terribly appropriate,' Leah said in a dry voice. 'I wonder if it's too late to change them.'

'You are pure of heart, which is all that counts,' Inez maintained stoutly. 'I will do your hair now. You wish to wear it loose?'

'I thought I'd braid it.'

'Oh, no, *señorita*. Perhaps a compromise?' Without waiting for a response, she swiftly braided two narrow sections on each side of Leah's face, threading a silver cord into each as she went. Pulling the braids to the back of Leah's head, the housekeeper pinned them into an intricate knot.

'That looks very nice,' Leah admitted.

'We leave the rest loose,' Inez said, brushing the hip-length curls into some semblance of order. Finally she draped the veil over Leah's hair and affixed the circlet to her brow. Stepping back, she clasped her hands and sighed. '*Qué hermosa.* Señor Hunter, he is a lucky man.'

Leah didn't reply. What could she say? That luck had nothing to do with it, unless it was bad luck? Her bad luck. 'How much time is left?' she asked instead.

'A few minutes, no more. Señor Michaels is waiting for you at the bottom of the stairs.'

'I'm ready,' she announced. She picked up her bouquet of freshly picked wild flowers—courtesy of the Arroya children—and kissed Inez's cheek. 'Thank you for all your help. Go on downstairs. I'll follow in a minute.'

The door closed behind the housekeeper and, finally alone, Leah glanced at the stranger in the mirror. What would Hunter think? she wondered. Would he find her gown ridiculous? Attractive? Would her appearance even matter to him? She shut her eyes and whispered an urgent prayer, a prayer that Hunter might some day find happiness and peace in their marriage...that maybe, just maybe, he'd find love. Slightly more relaxed, she turned away from the mirror. She couldn't delay any longer. It was time to go.

As she descended the stairs, the pleated skirt of her dress swirled around her like wisps of silver fog. Conrad waited at the bottom. He looked up at her, and his reaction was all she could have asked. He stared in stunned disbelief, his mouth agape.

'Leah,' he murmured gruffly, his voice rough and choked. 'My dear, you're a vision. You make me wish...'

She traversed the final few steps, a small smile playing about her mouth. 'Wish what?'

'Wish that I hadn't so foolishly encouraged you to place that ad,' he confessed. 'Are you sure this marriage is what you want? It's not too late to change your mind.'

She didn't hesitate for an instant. 'It's much too late and you know it. Not that it matters. I haven't changed my mind.'

He nodded without argument. 'Then this is it.' He offered his elbow. 'Shall we?'

She slipped her hand into the crook of his arm and walked with him to the great room, an area used for entertaining that stretched the full length of the ranch-house. It was her turn to stare in disbelief. Huge urns of flowers filled the room, their delicate perfume heavy in the air. And everywhere was the radiant glow of candlelight, not a single light-bulb disturbing the soft, romantic scene.

Her gaze flew to the far side of the room where Hunter stood, and her heart pounded in her breast. The wrangler she'd always known had disappeared and in his place stood a man who wore a tuxedo with the same ease as he wore jeans. She'd never seen him look so sophisticated, nor so aloof.

His hair reflected the candlelight, gleaming with blue-black highlights, and his eyes glittered like obsidian, burning with the fire of passion held barely in check. Despite that, he remained detached from his surroundings, the high, taut cheekbones and squared chin set in cool, distant lines.

The sudden hush that greeted her arrival drew his attention and his gaze settled on her with piercing intensity. Her hands tightened around her bouquet, sudden fear turning her fingers to ice. With that single glance his air of detachment fell away and his expression came alive, frightening in its ferocity. He looked like a warrior who'd fixed his sights on his next conquest. And she was that prize. It took all her willpower not to gather up her skirts and run.

Conrad started to move and she had no choice but to fall into step beside him. In keeping with the medieval theme, soft stringed instruments played in the

background. She focused on Hunter, barely aware of
her passage down the aisle, even more dimly aware
of Conrad releasing her and stepping back. But every
part of her leapt to life the instant Hunter took possession of her hand.

The minister began the ceremony. She didn't hear
a word he said; she didn't even remember making her
marriage vows. Afterward, she wondered if she'd actually promised to obey her husband or if the minister
had thoughtfully omitted that rather antiquated
phrase. She didn't doubt that Hunter would refresh
her memory at some point.

The ring he eventually slid on her finger felt
strange on her hand, the unaccustomed weight a visible reminder of all the changes soon to come. She
stared at the ring for a long time, studying the simple
scrollwork and wondering why he'd chosen such an
interesting design. Did it have any particular significance or had it been a simple matter of expediency?

'Leah.' Hunter's soft prompt captured her full attention.

She glanced up at him in bewilderment. 'Did I miss
something?' she asked. Quiet laughter broke out
among the guests and brought a flush to her cheeks.
Even Hunter grinned, and she found herself riveted
by that smile, aware that it had been eight long years
since she'd last seen it.

'We've just been pronounced man and wife,' he
told her. 'Which means...' He swung her into his embrace and lowered his head. 'It's time to kiss the
bride.'

And he proceeded to do so with great expertise and
thoroughness. It was her first kiss as his wife and the
warm caress held all the magic she could desire. She

was lost in his embrace, swept up in the moment. Yet, as intensely as she craved his touch, she longed to resist with an equal intensity. She couldn't bear the knowledge that this whole situation was nothing more than Hunter's way of gaining control of her ranch... and of her.

At long last he released her, his look of satisfaction stirring a flash of anger. Fortunately her irritation swiftly disappeared beneath the flurry of congratulations from the press of friends and employees. By the time Inez announced dinner, she'd fully regained her composure.

Like the great room, the dining-room glowed with candlelight, flowers running the length of the oak table and overflowing the side tables and buffet. To her relief she and Hunter were seated at opposite ends, though as dinner progressed she discovered her relief short-lived. Throughout the meal she felt his gaze fixed on her. And as the evening passed her awareness of him grew, along with an unbearable tension.

As the caterers cleared away the final course, Hunter rose, glass in hand. 'A toast,' he announced. Silence descended and all eyes turned in his direction.

'A toast for the bride?' Conrad questioned.

'A toast to my wife.' Hunter lifted the glass. 'To the most beautiful woman I've ever known. May all her dreams come true...and may they be worth the price she pays for them.'

There was a momentary confused silence and then the guests lifted their glasses in tribute, murmuring, 'Hear, hear.'

Slowly Leah stood, well aware of the double edge to Hunter's toast. Lifting her own glass in salute, she said, 'And to my husband. The answer to all my dreams.' And let him make what he wished of that, she thought, drinking deeply.

The party broke up not long after. Rose had arranged to stay with friends for the weekend and all the staff had been given the days off as a paid vacation. Only Patrick would remain, to care for the animals. But, knowing her foreman's sensitivity, he'd make himself scarce. They wouldn't see any sign of him until Monday morning.

Sending the last few guests on their way, Leah stood with Hunter in the front hall. The tension between them threatened to overwhelm her and she twisted her hands together, feeling again the unexpected weight of her wedding-ring.

She glanced at it and asked the question that had troubled her during the ceremony. 'Did you choose it or…?'

'I chose it. Did you really think I'd leave it to my secretary to take care of?'

'I didn't even know you had a secretary,' she confessed. 'What do…did you do?'

He hesitated. 'Mostly I worked as a sort of troubleshooter for a large consortium, taking care of problem situations no one else could handle.'

She drifted toward the great room, snuffing candles as she went. 'I imagine you'd be good at that sort of thing. What made you decide to give it up and return to ranching?'

'What makes you think I've quit?' he asked from directly behind.

Startled, she spun around, her gown flaring out around her. 'Haven't you?'

'They know to call if something urgent comes up. I'll find a way to fit it in.' He drew her away from a low bracket of candles. 'Be careful. I'd hate to see this go up in flames.'

'It was my mother's,' she admitted self-consciously. 'I wasn't sure whether you'd like it.'

His voice deepened. 'I like it.'

She caught her breath, finally managed to say, 'You still haven't answered my question.'

'What question?' A lazy gleam sparked in his eyes and she knew his thoughts were elsewhere. Precisely where, she didn't care to contemplate.

'Why,' she persisted, 'if you had such a good job, did you decide to come back?'

'Let's just call it unfinished business and leave it at that. Do you really want to start an argument to-night?'

She glanced at him in alarm. 'Would it? Start an argument, I mean?'

'Without a doubt.' He pinched out the remaining few candles, leaving them in semi-darkness, the night enclosing them in a cloak of intimacy. 'I have a wed-ding-gift for you.' He picked up a small package tucked among a basket of flowers and handed it to her.

She took it, staring in wonder. 'A wedding-gift?'

'Open it.'

Carefully, she ripped the paper from the jewelry box and removed the lid. Beneath a layer of cotton lay an odd blue stone with a thin gold band wrapped around it, securing it to a delicate herringbone chain. 'It's just like yours!' she exclaimed, tears starting to her eyes.

The only identifying article left with Hunter at the orphanage had been the strange gold-encased stone identical to the one he'd duplicated for a wedding-present. He'd worn it like a talisman all the time she'd known him, though he'd never been able to trace its origin successfully.

'I thought a gold chain a better choice than the leather thong I use.'

'Thank you. It's beautiful.' She handed him the box and turned her back to him. 'Will you put it on?' She lifted her hair and veil out of the way while he fastened the chain around her neck. The stone nestled between her breasts, cool and heavy against her skin.

Before she realized what he intended, Hunter turned her around and swung her into his arms. She clutched at his shoulders, her heart beating frantically, knowing that she couldn't delay the inevitable any longer. He strode across the entrance hall and climbed the stairs, booting open the door to the master bedroom.

She started to protest, but stopped when she saw the candles and flowers that festooned the room. At a guess, it was more of her grandmother's fine handiwork. This time, though, Leah approved. Giving them the master bedroom was Rose's tacit acknowledgement of Hunter's position in the household.

'Where's Rose's room?' he asked, as though reading her mind.

'Downstairs. She had a private wing built when my father married. She said the only smart way for an extended family to cohabit was to live apart.'

A reluctant smile touched his mouth. 'There may be hope for our relationship yet.'

He set her down, his smile fading, a dark, intense expression growing in his eyes. He removed the circlet from her brow and swept the veil from her hair.

It floated to the floor, a gauzy slip of silver against the burgundy carpet.

He stepped back. 'Take off the dress. I don't want to rip it.'

Fumbling awkwardly with the belt links, she unfastened the chain at her waist and placed it among the flowers on the walnut bureau. She slipped off her heels, wondering why removing her shoes always made her feel small and vulnerable. Finally she gathered the hem of her gown and slowly lifted it to her waist.

The next instant she felt Hunter's hands beside her own, easing the dress over her head. He laid it across a chair and turned back to her. She stood in the center of the room, horribly self-conscious in the sheer wisps of silk and lace that were her only covering.

'Hunter,' she whispered. 'I don't think I'm ready for this.'

'Relax,' he murmured. 'There's no rush. We have all the time in the world.' He approached, wrapping her in his embrace. 'Remember how good it was between us?'

She clung to his jacket lapel. 'But we're not the same people any more. Our...our feelings have changed.'

'Some things never change. And this is one of them.' His eyes were so black, full of heat and hunger, his face, tight and drawn, reflecting his desire. He lifted her against him, tracing the length of her jaw with the edge of his thumb.

She shuddered beneath the delicate caress. He'd always been incredibly tender with her, a lover who combined a sensitive awareness of a woman's needs with a forceful passion that had made loving him an

experience she'd never forgotten. It would be so easy
to succumb, to be swept into believing he loved her
still—a fantasy she found all too appealing.

'I can make it so good for you,' he said, his mouth
drifting from her earlobe to the tiny pulse throbbing
in her neck. 'Let me show you.' He found the clasp
of her bra and unhooked it, sliding the silk from her
body.

She closed her eyes, her breathing shallow and
rapid. He didn't lie. She knew from experience that
making love to him would be wonderful. It was the
morning after that concerned her, when she'd have to
face the knowledge that he'd come one step closer to
achieving his goal—of winning both the ranch and
her. His hand closed over her breast and her heart
pounded beneath the warmth of his palm. For an endless instant she hung in the balance between conced-
ing defeat and allowing her emotions free rein, or
fighting for what mattered most. Because if she
couldn't protect *herself* from his determined assault,
how could she ever expect to protect the ranch and
all those who depended on her?

She shifted within his grasp. 'It's too soon,' she
protested in a low voice.

'We'll take it slow.' He traced her curves with a
callused hand, scalding her with his touch. 'We can
always stop.' But we won't want to. The words lay
unvoiced between them, his thoughts as clear to her
as if he'd spoken them aloud, and she shuddered.

Stepping back, he stripped off his jacket and tie.
Ripping open the buttons of his shirt, he swept her
into his arms and carried her to the petal-adorned bed.
Once there he lowered her to the soft mattress and
followed her down.

His fingers sank into her hair, filling his hands with long silvery curls. 'I've wanted to do this ever since I saw that picture of you,' he muttered.

She stirred uneasily. 'What picture?'

He tensed, and for a long moment neither of them moved. Her question had caught him unawares and she struggled to focus on it, to figure out why he'd reacted so strongly. He'd seen a recent picture of her. The knowledge was inescapable and she withdrew slightly, confused, questions hammering at her brain. Where and when had he seen the photo…in the study, perhaps? If so, why the strange reaction?

'The picture on your father's desk,' he explained quietly. 'It shows you with long hair.'

'It was shorter when you worked here.'

'Yeah, well. I like it long.'

But the mood had been broken and she rolled away from him, drawing her knees up against her chest. There was more to his idle comment than she had the strength or energy to analyze. 'Hunter,' she said in a low tone. 'I can't.'

'It's only natural to feel nervous,' he said in a cool voice, making no attempt to touch her.

'It's not just nerves.' She swept up the sheet, wrapping herself in its concealing folds. Shoving her hair back over her shoulders, she met his watchful gaze. 'You've gotten your way, Hunter. We're married and there's no going back. You said yourself that we have all the time in the world. Why rush this part of it and risk damaging our relationship?'

A muscle leapt in his jaw. 'You think making love will damage our relationship?'

She caught her lower lip between her lip and nodded. 'It will if we're not both ready for this. And, in all honesty, I'm not ready.'

'When will you be?' he asked bluntly.

She shrugged uneasily. 'I couldn't say.'

'Give it your best guess. I don't have an infinite amount of patience.'

'That's not what you told me five minutes ago,' she flashed back.

He clasped her shoulders, hauling her close. 'Five minutes ago you were as anxious as I to consummate this marriage. You want me every bit as much as I want you. I know it and you know it.'

'That's lust, not love. And lust isn't enough for me.' Aware of how much she'd inadvertently revealed, she fought free of his hold and scrambled off the bed. 'I...I just need a little bit of time, that's all. Can't you understand? Am I asking so much?'

He laughed harshly, running a hand through his hair. 'What will happen between us is inevitable. Tonight, tomorrow or the next night... What's the difference?'

She peeked at him through long lashes. 'Forty-eight hours,' she said with a hesitant smile. For a minute she didn't think he'd respond. Then he relaxed, his tension dissipating, and he nodded, though she sensed a strong undercurrent of anger just beneath his surface calm.

'Okay, Leah. I'll wait.' His gaze held a warning. 'Just don't push it. My tolerance has limits.'

'I'm well aware of that.' She backed toward the door. 'I'd like to change.'

'Don't be long.'

Striving for as much dignity as possible, considering that she kept tripping over the sheet, she left

Hunter and hurried to her own room. There she stripped off her few remaining clothes. Pawing through her dresser drawers, she pulled out the most modest nightgown she possessed and tugged it on.

Covered from head to toe in yards and yards of baby-fine linen, she sat on the edge of the bed and nibbled on her fingertip. Had she made her situation better or worse? she wondered. She wasn't quite sure. Perhaps it would have been wiser to make love with him and be done with it, regardless of his motivations for marrying her. Only, in her heart of hearts, she knew it wouldn't truly be lovemaking, at least not on his part. It would be sex, pure and not so simple. Or, worse…it would be revenge.

She curled up on the bed, hugging a pillow to her chest. If only he cared. If only he loved her. Her hand closed around his wedding-gift, the talisman he'd so unexpectedly given her. His love would make all the difference in the world. But he no longer felt that way about her. And the sooner she accepted that, the better off she'd be.

But telling herself that didn't prevent a wistful tear from sliding down her cheek.

CHAPTER FIVE

LEAH stirred just as dawn broke the horizon. Confused by the unexpected weight pinning her legs to the mattress, she turned her head and found herself face to face with Hunter—a sleeping Hunter. It brought her fully awake. She risked a quick glance around, confirming her suspicions. So she hadn't dreamed it. She was back in the master bedroom.

Vaguely she remembered Hunter coming to her old room where she'd drifted off on top of the bed, a pillow clutched to her breast. He'd gently pried it free, and at her drowsy protest rasped, 'We sleep together, wife.' With that, he'd lifted her into his arms and carried her from the room. She hadn't fought. Instead, she'd wound her arms around his neck and snuggled against his chest as though she belonged, as though she never wanted to let go.

When he'd put her into his bed she'd been greeted by the sweet aroma of crushed flowers, followed by a stronger, muskier scent as Hunter had joined her on the mattress. All she recalled after that was a delicious warmth and peace invading her, body and soul, as he'd enclosed her in his embrace, wrapping her in a protective cocoon of strong arms and taut, muscular legs.

She glanced at him again, studying his imposing features with an acute curiosity. Even sleep couldn't blunt his tough, masculine edge, a night's growth of beard only serving to intensify the aura of danger and male aggression that clung to him like a second skin. The sheet skimmed his waist, baring his broad chest to her view, and she drank in the clean, powerful lines, wondered if he slept nude. Somehow she suspected that he did, though she didn't have the nerve to peek.

In all their times together, never had they been able to spend a night in each other's arms. Their joining had been passionate and earth-shattering and the most wondrous experience of her life. But it had also consisted of brief, stolen moments away from the suspicious eyes of her father and grandmother and the other ranch employees.

The irony of their current situation didn't escape her. Years ago she'd have given anything to spend a single night with him. To know, just once, the rapture of greeting the dawn safe and secure within his sheltering hold. Finally given her dearest wish, all she felt was apprehension and dismay—and an overwhelming desire to escape before he awoke.

Cautiously she slipped from his loose grasp and eased off the bed. Only then did she realize that some time during the early morning hours her nightgown had become trapped beneath him, and that he'd entwined her hair in his fingers as though, even in his sleep, he couldn't bear to let her go. Precious moments flew by as she untangled her hair and freed her gown. Gathering up the voluminous skirt, she tiptoed from the room.

A quick stop in the kitchen to grab an apple and a handful of sugar cubes, and she was outside and free. She raced across the dew-laden grass to the south pasture fence, the wind catching her hair and sweeping it into the air behind her like long, silver streamers. Whistling for Dreamseeker, she wondered if she'd ever tame such a wild and willful beast.

He came to her then, bursting across the pasture, a streak of jet against a cornflower-blue sky. Forming a deep pocket for the apple and sugar with the excess material of her nightgown, she awkwardly climbed the fence and sat on the top rail, the thin cotton affording little protection from the splintered wood beneath.

Dreamseeker joined her, snatching greedily at the apple she offered. Not satisfied, he butted her shoulder until she relented and gave him the sugar as well. He waited, muscles quivering, head cocked at an arrogant angle, allowing her to scratch and caress his gleaming coat. She crooned in delight, rubbing his withers, thrilled by his show of trust.

'What the *hell* are you doing?'

Leah didn't know who was more startled, she or Dreamseeker. Springing from her grasp, the horse shot away from the fence, leaving her teetering on the rail. With a cry of alarm, she tumbled to the ground at Hunter's feet, the hem of her gown snagging on a protruding nail. She tugged impatiently at it, the sound of ripping cloth making her wince.

She glared up at him, placing the blame where it belonged—square on his broad shoulders. 'Dammit, Hunter! This is all your fault. What do you mean, sneaking around like that?'

He folded his arms across his chest and lifted an eyebrow. 'Sneaking?'

'Yes, sneaking. You scared Dreamseeker and you scared me.' She shook out her nightgown, lifting the dew-soaked hem clear of the grass. Peering over her shoulder, she searched for the source of the ripping sound. Finding it, she muttered in disgust, 'Just look at the size of that hole.'

'I'm looking.'

The hint of amusement in his voice brought her head around with a jerk. His eyes weren't on the tear but on her. Realization came swiftly. With the sun at her back, the thin cotton she wore might as well have been transparent. And Hunter, his thumbs once again thrust in his belt-loops, was enjoying every minute of the show.

'There are times, Hunter Pryde, when I think I hate you,' she declared vehemently. With that, she grabbed a fistful of skirt, lifted her nightgown to her knees and lit off across the pastureland. She didn't get far.

In two swift strides he overtook her, and swept her clean off her feet. 'Hate me all you want, wife. It won't change a damned thing. The sooner you realize that, the better off you'll be.'

She shrieked in fury, lashing out at him, hampered by yards of damp cotton. Her hair, seeming to have acquired a life of its own, further hindered her efforts, wrapping around her arms and torso in a tangle of unruly silver curls. She stopped struggling, battering him with words instead. 'You don't fool me. You may have married me because it was the only way to get your hands on the ranch, but that doesn't mean you've won. I'll never give in.'

'Won't you?' A hint of sardonic amusement touched his aquiline features. 'We'll see.'

She had to convince him. She had to convince herself. 'You won't win, Hunter. I won't let you!'

'So much passion. So much energy,' he murmured,

his arms tightening around her. 'And all of it wasted out here. Why don't we take it inside where we can put it to good use?'

She stiffened, quick to catch his meaning, quicker still to voice her objections. 'You promised. You promised to wait until I was ready. And I'm not ready.'

'No?' His mouth twisted, and a cynical gleam sparked in his jet-black eyes. 'Listen up, wife. It wouldn't take much for me to break that promise. And when I do, count on it, you won't complain for long.'

Without another word he carried her inside. In the front hallway he dumped her on to her feet, forcing her to cling to him while she regained her balance. His biceps were like rock beneath her hands, the breadth of his chest and shoulders an impenetrable wall between her and escape.

'Hunter, let me go,' she whispered, the words an aching plea. She didn't dare look him in the eye, didn't dare see the passion that she knew marked his strong, determined features. If she did, she'd never make it up those steps alone.

'Not a chance.' Then he further destroyed her equilibrium with a single hard, fiery kiss. At last he released her, and she stared at him with wide, anguished eyes. She didn't want him touching her, kissing her, forcing her back to life. She didn't want to feel, to experience anew the pain loving him would bring.

But she suspected that he didn't care what she wanted, or how much he hurt her. He had his own agenda. And she was low on his list of priorities—a minor detail he'd address when he found it convenient.

He snagged the bodice of her nightgown with his finger and tugged her close. 'I warned you last night. I won't wait forever. I catch you running around like this ever again and I won't be responsible for my actions. You hear me?'

She wrenched the gown from his grasp, but all she got for her trouble was a ripped shoulder seam. She gritted her teeth. 'Don't worry,' she muttered, clutching the drooping neckline with one hand and lifting the trailing hem with the other. 'I'm throwing this one out as soon as I get upstairs.'

His mouth curved at the corners, and he plucked a crushed flower petal from her tangled hair. 'Feel free to trash any others while you're at it. They won't be of much use to you…not for long.' Before she could give vent to her outrage, he instructed, 'Hurry up and get dressed. I'm going to inspect the ranch this morning. I leave in five minutes—with you…or without you.'

Leah didn't lose any time changing. Throwing on jeans and a T-shirt, she stuffed her feet into boots. Securing her hair into one long braid, she grabbed a hat from her bedpost and raced downstairs. At some point she'd have to move her things into the bedroom she now shared with Hunter. But there would be plenty of opportunity for that. Weeks. Months. She bit down on her lip. *Years*.

She found Hunter in the barn, saddling the horses. He passed her a paper sack. 'Here. Thought you might be hungry.'

'Thanks. I am.' Peeking inside, she found a half-dozen of Inez's cinnamon and apple muffins. 'I don't suppose you thought to bring coffee.'

'Thermos is in my saddlebag. Help yourself.' He tightened the cinch on his buckskin and glanced at her. 'I moved that Appaloosa mare with the pulled tendon to another stall. There's a leak at that end of the barn. Looks like we'll need a new roof.'

She bit into a muffin. 'I'll have Patrick and a couple of the men patch it,' she said, taking a quick gulp of coffee.

'No.' He yanked the brim of his hat lower on his forehead. 'I said the barn needs a new roof.'

She sighed, capping the Thermos and shoving it and the sack of muffins back into his saddlebag. 'This is one of those marital tests, isn't it?'

'Come again?'

'You know. A test. You say we need a new roof. I say no we don't. You say, I'm the boss and we're getting a new roof. And I say, but we can't afford a roof. And you say, well, we're getting one anyway, even if we have to eat dirt for the next month to pay for it. And if I say anything further you start reminding me that before we married I promised this and I agreed to that, and that you're the boss and what you say goes. Does that about sum up what's happening here?'

He nodded, amusement lightening his expression. 'That about sums it up. Glad to see you catch on so fast.' He tossed her a bright yellow slicker. 'Here. Take this. Forecast calls for rain.'

'Hunter, we really can't afford a new roof.' She rolled the slicker and tied it to the back of her saddle. 'If we could, I'd have stuck one on last spring, or the spring before that, or even the spring before that.'

'We're getting a new roof.' He mounted. 'Though

if it eases your mind any you won't have to eat dirt for the next month to pay for it.'

After a momentary hesitation she followed suit and climbed into the saddle. 'I won't?'

'Nope. Just for the next week.' He clicked his tongue, urging his horse into an easy trot.

They spent the morning investigating the eastern portion of the Hampton spread and Leah began to see the ranch through Hunter's eyes. And what she saw didn't please her. Signs of neglect were everywhere. Fence-lines sagged. Line-shacks had fallen into disrepair. A few of the cattle showed evidence of screwworm and the majority of the calves they came across hadn't been branded or vaccinated.

At the south-eastern tip of the range Hunter stopped by a small stream and dismounted. 'What the hell have your men been doing, Leah?' he asked, disgust heavy in his voice. 'There's no excuse for the condition of this place.'

'Money's been tight,' she protested defensively. 'We don't have a large work crew.'

'I've got news for you. You don't have a work crew, period. Leastwise they don't seem to be working worth a damn.'

'A lot of what we've seen isn't their fault, but mine,' she claimed, evading his searching stare. 'I haven't had the time recently to stay on top of everything.'

Hunter shook his head. 'Not good enough, Leah. Any foreman worth his salt would have caught most of these problems for you.'

'You told me you wouldn't fire anyone until they'd had an opportunity to prove themselves,' she said, taking a different tack. 'I know things look bad, but give us a chance. Tell us what you want done and we'll do it.'

He stripped off his gloves and tucked them in his belt. 'What I want is for you to get off that horse and sit down and discuss the situation with me. One way or another we're going to come to a meeting of the minds, and I can't think of a better time or place than right here and now.'

Still she resisted. 'If we sit under that pecan tree, we'll get ticks.'

He took off his hat and slapped the dust from the brim. 'Did you last time?'

So he did remember this spot. She'd wondered if his stopping here had been coincidental or deliberate. Now she knew. She closed her eyes. How much longer would she have to pay? she wondered in despair. When would it be enough? 'I might have found a tick or two,' she finally admitted.

'Then I'll look you over tonight,' he offered. 'Just to be on the safe side.'

'Thanks all the same,' she said drily. 'But I'll pass.'

He held out a hand. 'Let's go, Leah. I didn't bring you here to go skinny-dipping again. I brought you here to talk. We'll save a return trip down memory lane for another visit.'

Reluctantly, she dismounted. 'What do you want to discuss?'

'The repairs we need to make and your employees,' he stated succinctly.

'I vote we start with the repairs,' she said. 'Have you gotten the loan? Is that why you plan to replace the barn roof?'

'And fix up the line-shacks, and restring fence-line and increase the size of the herd. Yes, the loan's taken care of, and we have enough money to put the ranch back on its feet. But it isn't just lack of repairs that contribute to a ranch going downhill.'

She sank to the grass with a grimace, shifting to one side so he could join her. 'Time to discuss the employees?'

'Time to discuss the employees. I made a point of meeting most of them before we married.'

She gave him a direct look. 'Then you know why I hired them.'

'Leah—'

'Don't say another thing, Hunter! For once you're going to listen and I'm going to talk.' She fought to find the words to convince him, desperate to protect her workers. 'Not a single one of my employees has been able to find jobs anywhere else. The Arroyas were living out of a station wagon when I found them. Lenny's a veteran who doesn't care to sit around collecting government handouts. And Patrick risked his own life to save a child about to be run down by a drunk driver. He shattered his ankle doing it. A week later he got a pink slip because Lyon Enterprises didn't want to be bothered with an employee who might not be able to pull his own weight.'

Hunter shot her a sharp glance. 'He worked for Lyon Enterprises?'

'He used to be foreman of the Circle P. Bull Jones replaced him.'

'And you took Patrick in.'

'I've given them all a home,' she acknowledged. 'I've given them a life. And, as a result, they earn a living. More importantly, they've regained their self-respect. So their work isn't always perfect. I can assure you that it's the best they're capable of doing.

But if you ask for more they'll do everything in their power to give it to you. That's how much working here means to them. They're family. Don't ask me to turn my back on family, because I can't do it.'

He stared out across the pastureland. 'You always were a sucker for an underdog. I often thought that was what attracted you to me.'

'That's not true.' She stopped, afraid of revealing too much. She'd never seen him as an underdog. A champion, a man of drive and determination, someone filled with an intense passion and strength. But not once had she ever seen him as an underdog.

His mouth tightened, as though he'd mistakenly allowed her to get too close—revealed too much of himself. 'That still doesn't change the facts. And the facts are that you can't run a ranch without competent help.'

'Hunter,' she pleaded. 'Give them a fair chance. No more, no less. I swear I won't ask you for anything else.'

His expression turned skeptical. 'Won't you?'

'No. I won't. Because saving the ranch isn't worth it to me if I can't save them as well.'

That caught his attention. 'You'd give up the ranch if it came to a choice between running at a profit or replacing the help?'

She considered his question at length, a frown creasing her brow. 'I suspect I would,' she admitted at last. 'Because otherwise I'd be no better than Lyon Enterprises. And if I wanted to be like them, I'd have sold out long ago.'

'You're that serious about it?'

She nodded. 'I'm that serious.'

It was his turn to consider. Slowly he nodded.

'Okay. We'll do it your way. For now. But I can't make any guarantees about the future. Will that do?'

'I guess it'll have to,' she said with a shrug.

'Why don't we swing south next, and inspect that side of the ranch? Then we'll call it a day.'

'I'm ready,' she claimed, happy to agree now that she'd been granted a reprieve. 'Let's go.'

He shook his head. 'Not yet. There's just one more thing I want before we head out. And I want it from you.'

'What?' she asked warily, his tone warning her that she wouldn't like his request.

'I want you to kiss me.'

'What?' she repeated in a fainter voice.

'You heard me. I want a kiss. I'm willing to wait until you're ready before we go any further, but there's no reason we can't enjoy a preview of coming attractions.' He held her with a searing gaze. 'Come on, Leah. It's not a lot to ask.'

It wasn't, and she knew it. Not giving herself a chance to reconsider, she leaned closer, resting her hands on his chest. She stared up at him, at the features that were almost as familiar as her own. The changes time had wrought were few, more of a strengthening, a fulfillment of what was once a promise. The lines furrowing his brow and radiating from the corners of his eyes reflected a deepening of character that had come with age and experience.

Tenderly she cupped his face, exploring anew the taut, high-boned planes of his cheeks. It had been so long, so very long. Slowly, she allowed her fingers to sink into his thick black hair and, tilting her head just slightly, she feathered a soft, teasing kiss across his mouth. She half expected him to grab her, to crush her in his arms and take what he so clearly wanted. But he didn't. He remained perfectly still, allowing her to set the pace.

She continued to tease, dropping tiny kisses across his jaw and neck before returning to explore his lips. And then she kissed him, really kissed him, the way a woman kissed her man. And for the first time he responded, not with his hands and arms, but with his mouth alone, returning her urgent, eager caresses with a mind-drugging thoroughness that left her shaken and defenseless. He had to know how she felt—had to be aware of how much she gave away with that kiss, how her protective barrier lay in total ruin. At long last his arms closed around her, enfolding her in the sweetest of embraces, and she knew in that moment that she'd willingly give him anything he asked.

How much time passed, Leah wasn't sure. One minute she existed in a sensual haze, secure in his arms, the next Hunter thrust her from him, tumbling her to the ground. In a move so swift that she barely registered it he spun around, crouching protectively in front of her. To her horror, a wickedly curved knife appeared in his hand.

'You're trespassing, Jones. What's your business here?' Hunter demanded.

It wasn't until then that Leah noticed the foreman of the Circle P, mounted on a bay, not more than fifteen feet away. She hadn't heard his approach. But Hunter had.

'Tell your guard-dog to drop the knife, Leah,' Bull Jones called, his gaze riveted to the glinting length of steel in Hunter's hand. 'Or I'll have to get serious with some buckshot.' His hand inched toward his rifle. 'You *comprende* what I'm saying, *hombre*? You have no business threatening me. I'd only be defending myself if I was forced to shoot.'

The expression in Hunter's eyes burned with unmistakable menace. 'You'll feel the hurting end of this blade long before that Remington clears your scabbard. You *comprende* me, *muchacho*? Play it smart. Ride out now.'

For a minute Leah feared that Bull would pull his gun. His hand wavered over the rifle butt for an endless moment, before settling on his thigh. 'Since you're new to the Hampton spread I'll cut you some slack,' he addressed Hunter. 'But nobody threatens me. Ever. Somebody'd better explain that to you pronto, because next time I won't let you off so easy.'

'Last warning.' The blade quivered in Hunter's hand. 'Ride. Now.'

'You'll regret this, Leah,' Bull hollered. Swearing beneath his breath, he sawed at his mount's bit and rode off.

'Oh, God,' Leah moaned, and she began to tremble. In one supple move, Hunter sheathed his knife in his boot and pulled her into his arms.

'It's okay,' he murmured against the top of her head. 'He's gone.'

She clung to him, unable to stop shaking, reaction setting in fast and hard. He didn't release her, just stood silently, enveloping her in a tight, inviolable hold. Yet she'd have had him hold her closer if she thought her ribs would stand the strain. Slowly the warmth of his body and the strength of his arms calmed her, soothing her terror.

'He could have shot you,' she whispered, fighting to hold back her tears.

He tucked a strand of hair behind her ear. 'Not a

chance. I had him dead to rights and he knew it.' His mouth brushed her cheek, her jaw, her lips. 'It's over, Leah. He's gone.'

She melted against him, needing his touch more desperately than she'd ever needed anything before in her life. As though sensing it, he kissed her. But it wasn't like the passionate embrace they'd shared earlier. This caress was so gentle and tender that it nearly broke her heart.

'He frightens me, Hunter,' she confessed in a low voice.

He glanced at the thin cloud of dust disappearing to the south. 'Tell me about him.' It was an order.

She fought to gather her thoughts enough to give him a coherent answer. 'I've told you most of it. Although I can't prove anything, I suspect he's responsible for our fence-lines being cut. We've had a couple of suspicious stampedes and one or two of the wells have been fouled.' She shrugged. 'That sort of thing.'

'He's the reason this place is so neglected.' It wasn't a question. 'You don't ride out here alone, do you? That's why you haven't seen the problems until now.'

She bowed her head. 'I don't let the others come either,' she admitted. 'Unless they're in a group. I've been terrified of something happening.'

'Have you reported any of this to Lyon Enterprises?'

She flashed him a bitter glare. 'Who do you think he's getting his instructions from?'

'Do you know that for a fact?'

She whirled free of his arms, anger replacing her fear. 'I don't know anything for a fact. If I did, Bull

Jones would be in jail and I'd have a nice, fat lawsuit pending against Lyon Enterprises. You married me to get your hands on this ranch, didn't you? If you want to keep it, you're going to have to defend it. Otherwise we both lose.'

Hunter bent down and retrieved his hat. 'Mount up.'

She stared in disbelief. 'Now? Just like that? End of discussion?'

'I want to check the south pasture before dark.'

'That's the direction Bull took. What if we run into him again?' she asked nervously.

The brim of his hat threw Hunter's face into shadow, making his expression unreadable. 'Then I'll make a point of introducing myself.'

She clung to him, checking his move toward his horse. 'Please, Hunter. Can't we go home? We can check the south pasture tomorrow. There's no point in looking for trouble.'

A humorless smile cut across his face. 'You've got it backward. Seems trouble has come looking for us.' For a minute she thought he'd insist they explore the south pasture. But at long last he nodded. 'Okay. I've seen enough. But tomorrow I ride south.' And with that she had to be satisfied.

In the study, Hunter lifted the phone receiver and stared at it for a long minute before punching in a series of numbers. After several clicks the call was connected.

'Kevin Anderson.'

'It's Hunter. Give me an update.' He listened to the lengthy recitation with a frown and jotted down a few notes. 'Okay. Don't do anything for now. We don't want to tip our hand. The rest can wait until I come in.'

'Any problems at your end?' Kevin asked.

'You might say that.' Hunter poured himself a shot of whiskey, and downed it in a single swallow. 'I had another run-in with Bull Jones.'

Alarm sounded in Kevin's voice. 'Does he know who you are yet?'

'Not yet. Our marriage has been kept pretty much under wraps. Not a lot of people know. But Jones could be a problem once he finds out—depending on how much talking he decides to do.'

'What do you want me to do?'

'Send me his file. Overnight it.'

'Will do. Then what? You want him...out of the picture?'

Hunter thought about it, rubbing a weary hand across the back of his neck. 'No. Don't do anything for now. We act too soon and it'll give the whole game away.'

'Whatever you say. You're the boss.'

'Thanks, Kevin.'

Hanging up, Hunter poured a final shot of whiskey and stared at the ceiling. Time to bed down with his beautiful bride. Time to pull that soft, sweet piece of feminine delight into his arms and...sleep. He downed the liquor, praying that it would numb him— at least the parts in dire need of numbing. Patience. He only needed a little more patience. And then that soft, sweet piece of feminine delight would be all his.

CHAPTER SIX

LEAH slipped from Hunter's arms at the crack of dawn the next morning. This time she kept yesterday's warning firmly in mind, and dressed before going to the kitchen for an apple. Running to the south pasture fence, she whistled for her stallion. But instead of the horse all she found was a white-tailed deer and a family of jackrabbits who, startled by her sudden appearance, burst across the grassland and disappeared from view. She climbed on to the top rail and waited for a while, but Dreamseeker proved surprisingly elusive.

Concluding that she'd been stood up in favor of a patch of fresh clover, she bit into the apple. Then she watched as the sun gathered strength, spreading its warm April rays across a nearby field splattered with the vivid purple of bluebonnets and neon-orange of Indian paintbrush. Without question this had to be her favorite time of the day—as well as her favorite season of the year.

A twig snapped behind her. 'Beautiful, isn't it?' she asked in a conversational tone of voice.

'Yes.' Hunter folded his arms across the top rail and glanced at her. 'No accusations of sneaking up on you this morning?'

'You banged the kitchen door.'

'And stomped across the yard.'

A tiny grin touched her mouth. 'I almost turned around to look, but you were being so considerate that I didn't want to spoil it.'

'I appreciate your restraint,' he said, with a touch of wry humor. 'Your horse hasn't shown up yet?'

She frowned, tossing her apple core into the meadow. 'He didn't answer my whistle. But if we're exploring the south pasture we're bound to come across him. Ready to go?' She vaulted off the fence, wanting to get Hunter's inspection tour over and done with. Perhaps if they made an early start they'd avoid Bull Jones.

'No. I'm not ready.' He caught her arm, tugging her to a standstill. 'Not quite yet.'

'Why?' she asked in apprehension. 'Is there something wrong?'

'You might say that.' His hold lightened, though he didn't release her. 'You were gone again this morning.'

She bridled at the hint of censure in his voice. She'd agreed to sleep with him without too much argument; surely he didn't intend to choose which hours that would encompass. If so, he'd soon learn differently. 'Is that a problem?'

'Yes. I don't like it. Tomorrow you start the day in my arms.'

She eased from his grip and a took a quick step back, something in his expression filling her with a discomfiting awareness. 'What difference does it make if I'm there or not?' she asked.

Her question seemed to amuse him. 'If you wake me tomorrow, you'll learn the difference.'

She didn't doubt it for a minute. But that didn't

mean she'd go along. 'I'll consider it,' she conceded. 'But I like having mornings to myself.'

'You'll have other times to yourself,' he informed her. 'I want time alone with you. All marriages need privacy…intimacy.'

Understanding dawned and she fought to breathe normally. So the moment of truth had finally arrived. If she read his request correctly, tomorrow morning she'd fulfill her duties as his wife and make their marriage a real, fully functioning union—no matter how much she wanted to resist. No matter how much that final act alarmed her. That was what she'd committed herself to when they'd exchanged their vows, and that was what she'd soon have to face. If only the thought didn't fill her with dread—dread that she'd couldn't keep a small part of herself safe from his possession; dread that when he took her body he'd take her heart as well.

'All right,' she said at last. 'Mornings can be our time.'

He inclined his head. 'We'll discuss the afternoons and evenings later.'

'Hunter—'

'Time to get to work.' He cut her off, amusement gleaming in his dark eyes. 'Are there any more of those muffins we had yesterday?'

'Plenty,' she admitted grudgingly. 'Inez left us well- stocked. I'll go get them.'

'And a Thermos of coffee, if you would. I'll saddle the horses.'

Fifteen minutes later they rode out, heading south along the fence-line. Hunter's buckskin seemed particularly agitated, fighting the bit and shying at the least little movement. Not that he had any trouble controlling the animal, but Leah could tell that their battle of wills wasn't the norm. As though in response, her mare fidgeted as well.

'Is it something in the air?' she asked uneasily. 'Ladyfinger never acts up like this.'

'Something has them spooked,' he agreed. 'Have your men noticed any sign of cougar recently?'

'None.' She felt a sudden stabbing concern for Dreamseeker. 'It wasn't that hard a winter. There's no reason for one to come this close when the pickings are so easy further out.' But she knew her protests were more to convince herself than to convince him.

'Don't panic. I didn't say it was a cougar. I just thought we should consider the possibility.' He regarded her intently. 'I want you to stay alert, you got me? In the meantime, we have fence-line to inspect. So, let's get to it.'

They didn't converse much after that. Leah kept an eye open for anything out of the ordinary. And, though the animals remained skittish, she couldn't determine what caused their strange behavior.

A short time later Hunter stopped to examine a drooping length of barbed wire. 'This next section abuts Lyon Enterprises' property, doesn't it?' he asked, clearly annoyed with the condition of the fence.

'From here onward,' she confirmed.

'You're just asking for trouble, letting it fall into such a state of disrepair. One good shove and you'll have a week's worth of work combing Circle P hills for your herd. It gets top priority come Monday morning.'

'What about Bull Jones?' she asked uneasily.

A muscle tightened in his jaw. 'You let me worry about him. I don't expect it'll take long to reach an understanding.'

By noon they'd almost finished their inspection. Riding over a low hill, they suddenly discovered the reason for their horses' agitation. The fence between the two ranches lay on the ground. And down a steep grade, on Lyon property, grazed Dreamseeker...with the Circle P mare he'd corralled.

Hunter reined to a stop and shot Leah a sharp look. 'He's a stallion? That horse you were with yesterday morning?'

She glanced at him in surprise. 'Didn't you notice?'

'No, I didn't notice,' came the blunt retort. 'Because it wasn't the damned horse that caught my eye.'

Then what...? Realization swiftly dawned, and color mounted her cheeks. Not what. Who. He'd been distracted by her...and the fact that she'd only been wearing a nightgown. Well, she couldn't help that. Nor did it change anything. 'I don't see what difference it makes whether or not he's a stallion—'

'There's a big difference,' he cut her off. 'Not many geldings I know are going to bust through a fence to get to a mare in heat. But you can count on a stallion doing it every time.' He shoved his hat to the back of his head, apparently debating his options.

Leah didn't show any such hesitation. As far as she was concerned, only one option existed. Without giving thought to the consequences, she charged across the smashed fence and started after her stallion. Or she would have, if Hunter hadn't been quite so quick. He spurred his horse into action and blocked her path.

'What the hell do you think you're doing?' he

shouted, grabbing her horse's bridle and jerking her to a stop.

As much as she wanted to fight his hold, she didn't dare risk injuring Ladyfinger's delicate mouth. 'What does it look like I'm doing?' she flashed back. 'I'm getting my horse. Let go, Hunter. We don't have much time.'

He stared in disbelief. 'You can't be serious.'

'I'm very serious.' Responding to her agitation, Ladyfinger attempted to rear, but a soft word and a gentle hand brought her under control. Leah spoke urgently. 'If Bull Jones finds Dreamseeker on his property, he'll shoot first and ask questions later. I have to get my horse out of there before that happens.' She gathered up the reins, prepared to rip free at the first opportunity.

As though he sensed her intentions, his hold tightened on Ladyfinger's bridle, preventing any sudden movement on her part. 'You try and rope that animal and he'll kill you—which won't matter because I'll have killed you long before he has the chance.'

'Hunter,' she interrupted, prepared to dismount and go after Dreamseeker on foot, 'we're wasting precious time.'

'Tough. You have two choices,' he informed her. 'You can keep fighting me in which case that stallion will stay down there until hell freezes over. Or...'

'Or?' she prompted impatiently.

'Or you can do exactly what I say and we might get him out of there. But I'm telling you, Leah. You ever do anything as stupid as coming between a stallion and his mare and I won't be responsible for my actions.'

'Not responsible...' Anger flared and she made no

attempt to curb it. 'That's what you said about my running around in my nightgown! That's a pretty broad range you've got going there. Maybe you'd better tell me what other actions alleviate you of your responsibilities. Just so there won't be any doubt in my mind.'

'Believe me, the second you commit one, you'll be the first to know.'

She didn't miss the implication. He'd let her know in his own distinctive manner—and chances were excellent that it would involve another of those mind-splintering kisses. She opened her mouth to argue, and was instantly cut off.

'Well? What's it going to be? My way or no way.'

More than anything she wanted to tell him to go to hell. But one quick glance at Dreamseeker and she knew she didn't have any other choice. 'Your way,' she gave in grudgingly. 'How hard will it be to get him back?'

'That depends on how long he's been down there with that mare. With any luck it's been all morning, and he's expended most of his...enthusiasm.'

She eyed the seemingly placid animal. 'By the look of him I'd say he's expended plenty of enthusiasm.'

Hunter didn't appear as certain. 'We'll see. Tie Ladyfinger out of the way and stand by the fence. I'm going to rope the mare and try and bring her across. Dreamseeker will give chase. The second they're both on our property, you get that fence-line back up. If anything goes wrong, stand clear and *don't interfere*.' Serious dark eyes held her with an implacable gaze. 'Got it?'

'Got it.' Following his instructions, she tied her horse out of the way and stuck her fence tool and staples into her utility belt. Pulling on work-gloves, she took up a stance by the downed lines and gave him a nod. 'Ready when you are.'

Jamming his hat low on his brow, he released his rope and slowly rode down the hill. He waited near the bottom. Not wanting to arouse Dreamseeker's territorial instincts, he kept his distance from the mare, and though Leah could barely contain her impatience she knew that Hunter hoped the stallion would make things easy and move off a ways, allowing for a clear shot at the mare. Everything considered, the throw would be a difficult one.

Ten long minutes ticked by before an opportunity presented itself. Gently, he swung the rope overhead and tossed. Leah held her breath as it soared through the air...and landed directly on target. With a swiftness born of both experience and a strong desire to get the deed done before Dreamseeker caught wind of his intentions, Hunter dallied the rope around the horn and began to pull the mare up the hill.

The trapped animal fought him, rearing and pawing the air. Dragging a horse in the exact opposite direction from where she wanted to go was bad enough, but having to do it up a hill made it near impossible. Leah could hear Hunter swearing beneath his breath, the sound of his saddle creaking and his horse blowing carrying to her as they inched their way toward Hampton property.

About halfway up the hill Dreamseeker suddenly realized what they were about. With a shriek of outrage, the stallion gave chase. Hunter's buckskin didn't need any more encouragement than that. The sight of seventeen hundred pounds of rampaging stallion barreling straight for them apparently inspired the gelding to redouble his efforts. Even the mare seemed to lose her reluctance.

All too quickly Dreamseeker reached them. Instead of attacking Hunter, the stallion nipped at the mare, who stopped fighting the rope and abruptly changed direction, charging up the hill, the stallion on her heels. It was all Hunter could do to get out of the way.

'Leah, stand clear!' he shouted.

Intent on regaining his own territory, Dreamseeker drove the frightened mare before him up the hill and on to Hampton property. As the horses stormed past Hunter released the rope and followed close behind.

'Get that fence up fast, before he changes his mind,' Hunter bellowed over his shoulder, positioning himself between Leah and the threatening stallion. An agitated Dreamseeker milled nearby, clearly uncertain whether to challenge the intruders or escape with his prize. Hunter tensed, prepared for either eventuality.

Not wasting a single second, Leah slammed staples into the post, securing the barbed wire. Not that it would stop Dreamseeker if he decided to head back to the Circle P. But maybe now that he'd successfully captured a mare and returned to his own domain he'd be less inclined to break through again. She cast an uneasy glance at her horse. At least, he wouldn't break through unless there were more mares to be had.

With a shrill whinny, Dreamseeker finally chose to retreat. Racing away from them, he hustled the mare toward the far side of the pasture. Assured that the danger had passed, Hunter climbed off his buckskin and tied him to the fence.

'Where's Ladyfinger?' he asked, freeing his fence tool from its holster.

She spared him a quick look. 'Broke the reins and took off. I guess she figured that Dreamseeker meant business and didn't want to get between him and whatever that business might be.'

He made a sound of impatience. 'You'll have to ride with me. Once we're done here, we'll head on in.'

'Right.' She didn't dare say more, not until he'd had a chance to cool off. He joined her at the fence, helping to string wire and reinforce the posts. They worked side by side for several minutes before Leah thought to ask, 'What do we do about that mare?'

'We aren't going to do anything. When she isn't such a bone of contention I'll cut her loose and return her to the Circle P.'

Leah paused in her efforts. 'What about Bull Jones?'

To her surprise a slight smile touched Hunter's mouth. 'I'll send him a bill for stud service.' He strung the final line of wire and glanced at her. 'Is that stallion saddle-broken?'

She shook her head. 'Not yet, but—'

'He's wild?' Hunter didn't wait for her confirmation. 'He goes.'

She straightened, wiping perspiration from her brow. 'You can't be serious!'

'I'm dead serious. He's dangerous and I won't risk your safety on a dangerous animal.'

'Then you'll have to get rid of the bulls, the cows and every other critter around here,' she retorted in exasperation. 'Because in the right circumstances any one of them could be considered dangerous, too.'

'I'm not changing my mind,' he stated unequiv-
ocally, stamping the ground around a listing post.

How could she explain Dreamseeker's importance?
Hunter would never understand. She wasn't sure she
understood. All she knew was that the stallion
touched a need, fulfilled a fantasy of being unfettered
and without responsibilities. Though part of her hoped
some day to tame the wild beast, another part longed
to allow the stallion his freedom—just as she longed
to experience a similar freedom. It was an unrealistic
dream, but she didn't care.

Looking Hunter straight in the eye, Leah said,
'Don't do it. Please don't get rid of him. He means
the world to me.'

His expression turned grim and remote. 'Another
hard luck case?'

'In a way,' she admitted. 'I took him in when others might have put him down. I suspect he's been
abused in the past, which would explain his skittish-
ness.'

Hunter leaned his forearms across the post, his
plaid shirt pulled tight across his broad chest. A fine
sheen of perspiration glinted in the hollow of his
throat, and his thick ebony hair clung to his brow—
a brow furrowed in displeasure. 'You're doing a poor
job persuading me to let him stay. If anything, you've
convinced me he's too dangerous. Besides, you used
up all your favors yesterday, remember?'

'I remember.' Having him give her employees a
chance was still more important to her than any other
consideration—even saving Dreamseeker. 'I'm not
asking for another favor. I promised I wouldn't, and
I won't.' She offered a crooked smile. 'But I'm willing to compromise.'

'You're pushing it.'

She nodded. 'I know. But it's important to me.'

He frowned, and she could sense his struggle between what common sense told him to do and granting her plea. Finally he nodded. 'One month. If I can break him, or at least put some manners on him, he can stay. But you keep clear in the meantime. Agreed?'

Her smile widened. 'Agreed.'

'That's the last time, Leah,' he warned. 'You've pushed me to the limit. Now, mount up.'

'My horse...?' she reminded him.

'I haven't forgotten. We'll ride double.'

He crossed to his buckskin and untied the reins from the fence. Looking from Hunter to the horse, Leah caught her breath in dismay. With her clinging to his back like a limpet, dipping and swaying, rubbing and bumping all the way to the ranch, it would be a long ride home. She shivered.

Real long.

Leah began to ease from the bed the next day, as she had each of the other two mornings, but then remembered her promise to stay. With a tiny sigh she lay down again, and yanked the sheet to her chin. Instantly Hunter caught hold of her, ripped the sheet free and tumbled her into a warm embrace.

'Good morning, wife,' he muttered close to her ear.

'Good morning,' she responded cautiously, waiting for him to pounce, to force himself on her. Considering her forty-eight-hour deadline had expired last night, he'd be well within his rights. Instead he enclosed her hair in a possessive fist and, dropping an arm across her waist, shut his eyes. His breathing deepened and she frowned. 'The sun's up,' she prompted, fighting nervous anticipation.

'Uh-huh.'

He nuzzled her cheek and she drew back. 'This is our time together, remember?'

'I remember.'

'Well?' She could hear the strain in her voice, but couldn't help it. She wanted to get whatever he had planned over and done with. 'You said this time together would make a difference. The only difference I've noticed is that I'm late starting my chores.'

He sighed, opening one eye. 'The chores can wait. Relax. You're stiff as a board.' He slid an arm around her hips and tucked her back against his chest, spoon-fashion. Resting his chin on top of her head, he said, 'Now just relax and talk to me.'

'Talk.' This wasn't quite what she'd expected when he'd made his demand. She'd suspected that he intended to...to do a whole lot more than talk. 'What should I talk about?'

'Anything. Everything. Whatever comes to mind.'

'Okay,' she agreed, knowing she sounded stilted and uncomfortable. 'What are your plans for this morning?'

'I'll start by working with Dreamseeker.'

'And...and the fence-line? The one that runs along-side of the Circle P?'

'It gets fixed today.'

'You'll be careful?' She hesitated to mention her fears, but couldn't help herself. 'I don't trust Bull.'

'I'll take care of it.'

'It's just—' He brushed a length of hair from her brow and she realized that at some point during their conversation she'd rolled over to face him. And with the realization her words died away, and her earlier nervousness returned.

He noticed. She suspected that his sharp, black-eyed gaze noticed everything. Gently, he cupped her cheek, his callused thumb stroking the corner of her mouth. 'I'll take care of it,' he repeated, and kissed her warmly, deeply, sparking an instant response.

She didn't reply—couldn't, in fact. He seemed to sense that, for he pressed his advantage, his kiss becoming more intense, more urgent. Sensing her capitulation, he pressed her into the mattress. Instantly her body reacted, softening as his hardened, moving in concert with his, shifting to accommodate his size and weight.

Her nightgown provided no barrier at all. He unbuttoned the small pearl buttons that ran from neck to waist and swept the cotton from her shoulders. Drawing back, he gazed down at her, the early morning light playing across the taut, drawn lines of his face. Kneeling above her, he seemed like some bold conqueror of old, a bronzed warrior poised to take what he willed, and giving no quarter. Slowly, he reached for her, his black eyes burning like twin flames. His fists closed around her nightgown, and in one swift move he stripped it from her.

Reacting instinctively, she fought to cover herself, the expression on his face frightening her. She shouldn't struggle. She knew she shouldn't, but sudden blind panic overrode all other thought and emotion.

'No!' The tiny urgent whisper escaped before she could prevent it.

'Don't fight me,' he demanded, trapping her beneath him and staring down with intense, passion-filled eyes. 'I won't hurt you. Dammit, Leah! You know how good it was between us, how good it can be again.'

'I know, I know,' she moaned, a sob catching in her throat. 'I can't help it. It's not the same any more. I can't make myself feel what I did before just because we're married now…just because it's what you want.'

'And you don't?' he bit out. His hand swept across the rigid peak of her breast. 'You're only fooling yourself if that's what you think. You can't deny your body's response to me.'

'No, I can't.' The confession, raw and painful, was torn from her. How she wished she could open herself to his embrace and enjoy the momentary pleasure he offered, regardless of the consequences. But something instinctively held her back, making the gesture impossible. He'd taken so much already. She didn't dare allow him to take more. Not yet.

'Give yourself to me, Leah.' His words were raspy, heavy with desire. 'You want to. Stop resisting.'

Urgently, she shook her head. 'I won't be a pawn in your game of revenge. You have the ranch. You can't have me. Not this easily. And not with such casual disregard.'

'You call this casual?' He gripped her hand, drawing it to his body, encouraging the hesitant stroke of her fingers against his heated skin. 'Touch me and then try and call what I feel casual.'

Unable to resist, her hand followed the sinewy contours from chest to abdomen. 'If you feel something, then say the words,' she pleaded. 'Tell me our lovemaking isn't just sex. Tell me honestly that there isn't some deep, secret part of you settling an old score.'

Tears filled her eyes. 'Tell me that, Hunter, so I don't feel used.'

He tensed above her, his hands tightening on her shoulders in automatic reaction. Then his head dropped to her breast, a day's growth of whiskers rasping across her skin, branding her. A tear escaped from the corner of her eye. She had her answer. She'd gambled and lost. His very silence condemned him, told her more clearly than any words that his motivations were far from pure, that his actions weren't inspired by anything as noble as love.

'I could take you by force.' His voice was raw and harsh against her breast.

She prayed that it was only frustration speaking, that his threat was an empty one. 'You once told me force wouldn't be necessary. Have you changed your mind?' She attempted to slip from beneath him, but his hands closed around her shoulders, holding her in place. 'Taking what you want won't help our situation any,' she tried to reason with him.

'The hell it won't! It would help my situation a great deal. And I'd bet my last dollar that it would do a world of good for yours.'

She couldn't deny the truth. She turned her face into the pillow, retreating from the accusation in his eyes. Helpless tears escaped despite her attempts to control them. 'I'm sorry. I wish I could give myself to you and be done with it. But I can't. I can't be that detached about making love.'

'I don't expect you to be detached. I do expect you to resign yourself to the inevitable and face facts.' He threaded his fingers through her hair, forcing her to face him. 'And the fact is, we will be lovers. It will happen whether it's tomorrow or the next day or the one after that. Before long, wife, you'll want my touch. I guarantee it.'

'You're wrong,' she insisted, but they both knew she lied.

With an unexpectedly calming hand he brushed the tears from her cheeks. 'I won't force the issue this time. But understand me; I don't make any promises for the next.'

Then he rolled off her and left the bed…left Leah to her thoughts and to the inescapable knowledge that resisting him would prove futile. Soon her body would betray her and she'd be unable to stop him from completing what he'd started today. And once that happened, he'd have won it all.

Leah headed for the corral a short time later, to observe Hunter work with Dreamseeker. She wasn't alone. The Arroya children and a number of the employees all found excuses to line up along the fence and watch the coming confrontation. But if they had thought that Hunter would simply climb on to the stallion's back and attempt to bust him, they were mistaken. Instead, he lifted a piece of saddle-blanket from the corral fence and, after letting the horse sniff it, ran it over Dreamseeker's shoulders.

'Easy, boy. Easy.' His deep voice carried on the early morning breeze as he calmed the nervous animal.

Leah watched his hands and listened to his low reassurances, uncomfortably aware that his gentling of the nervous animal was remarkably similar to the way he'd soothed her before leaving their bed. She didn't doubt for a minute who would win this battle of wills…any more than she doubted who would ultimately win the age-old battle waged in their bedroom. It was as inevitable as the changing of the seasons; time was the only variable.

Once done with Dreamseeker, he spent until sundown laboring with the men, starting to set the ranch to rights.

As the days winged by, Leah began to relax. He didn't press her to commit to him physically and, contrary to her earlier fears, he also didn't make any sweeping changes. Instead he did just as he'd promised. He gave her employees a chance.

Or so she thought until Inez came tearing up to the corral fence.

'*Señora*, come quick! The men, they are fighting.'

Leah leapt from the horse she'd been training and ducked beneath the fence-rails. 'Where?'

'Behind the barn.'

She ran flat out, skidding to a stop as she came around the corner of the barn. Sprawled in the dust lay one of her more recent hard luck cases; a huge, brawny youngster barely past his teens by the name of Orrie. Above him towered Hunter, his fists cocked, his stance threatening. The rest of the employees stood in a loose circle around the two.

'Hunter!' she called, horrified that he'd actually fight one of her workers, especially one so young.

He spared her a brief glance. 'Stay out of it, Leah,' he warned. 'This doesn't concern you.'

Orrie scrambled to his feet, careful to keep clear of Hunter's reach. 'He fired me, Miz Hampton. He had no call to do that. You have to help me.'

Uncertain, she looked from Orrie to her husband. 'What's this about?'

Hunter's mouth tightened. 'You heard me, Leah. Stay out of it.'

'You have to do something, Miz Hampton,' Orrie insisted, bolting to her side. 'You can't let him get away with it. He's trying to change things.'

'You must be mistaken. He promised to give everyone a fair shot,' she hastened to reassure. 'Do your job and you stay.' She searched the sea of faces for confirmation. 'That was the agreement, right?'

Bitterness filled Orrie's expression. 'Then he strung you along with his lies as well as the rest of us, 'cause he fired me. And that ain't all!' The words were tumbling from him, as though he feared being stopped. Forcibly. 'Lenny's gonna have to leave, too. And he's made Mateo give up the horses.'

She couldn't hide her disbelief. 'Hunter, you can't do that!'

'I can and I have.' He motioned to the men. 'You have your orders. Get to it.' Without a word, they drifted away from the scene.

Orrie stared at her with the saddest, most pathetic eyes she'd ever seen. 'You won't let him fire me, will you, Miz Hampton?'

'Her name is Pryde. *Mrs* Pryde,' Hunter stated coldly. He snagged his hat from the dirt and slapped the dust from the brim. 'And she has no say in this. You have your wages, which is more than you deserve. Pick up your bedroll and clear out.' He started toward them. 'Now.'

Orrie hesitated, shifting so that Leah stood between him and trouble. 'Miz Hampton…Pryde?'

She switched her attention from her employee to Hunter. 'Perhaps if I understood the reason?' she suggested, hoping he'd take the hint and explain himself.

Instead he folded his arms across his chest. 'There's nothing to understand. This is between me and the boy. I suggest you go to the house.'

She stared in shock. 'What?'

'You heard me. You're interfering. So, say goodbye to your friend here and get up to the house. Believe me. I'll be right behind.'

It sounded more like a threat than a promise. For a long minute she stood glaring at him, too furious to speak and too uncertain of the possible consequences to stand her ground. With a muffled exclamation, she turned and walked away, knowing that her cheeks burned with outrage. She could only pray that none of her other employees had been close enough to witness their battle of wills. Especially when she'd been so thoroughly defeated.

'Miz Hampton,' Orrie cried, dogging her retreat. 'Please. You gotta do something.'

She paused, glancing at him apologetically. 'It's out of my hands,' she admitted, risking a quick nervous look over her shoulder.

'That's it? You're going to let him fire me? You're going to give in to that...that half-breed?'

She pulled away in distaste. 'Don't *ever* use that expression around me.'

He'd made a mistake, and apparently knew it. He hastened to correct the situation. 'I...I didn't mean to say that,' he apologized. 'You gotta understand. I'm desperate. I have nowhere else to go.'

It took all her willpower to resist his pleas. 'I'm sorry. There's nothing I can do,' she said, and continued walking.

She didn't turn around again. Once at the house, she stormed into the study and stood helplessly by the

window, watching Orrie's departure. Hunter watched
too, remaining dead center in the middle of the drive
while the youngster packed his things into Patrick's
pick-up and finally left. Then Hunter turned and faced
the house, grim intent marking every line of his body.

Leah didn't even realize that she'd backed from the
window until she found herself up against her father's
desk. Not taking time to analyze her reasons, she put
the width of the oak tabletop between her and the
study door. A minute later it crashed open.

Hunter strode in, slamming the door behind him so
hard that it rocked on its hinges. 'You and I,' he announced in a furious voice, 'have a small matter to
set straight.'

CHAPTER SEVEN

'YOU'RE angry,' she said, stating the obvious... stating the *very* obvious.

He started across the room. 'Good guess.'

'Well, I'm angry too.' She swallowed hard. 'I suggest we discuss this.'

He kept coming.

'Calmly.'

He knocked a mahogany hat rack from his path.

'Rationally.'

He stalked around the desk.

'Like two civilized adults.' She retreated, using her father's swivel chair as a shield. 'Okay?'

In response, he kicked the chair out of the way and trapped her against the wall.

'That's a yes, right?' she said with a gasp.

A muscle jerked in his cheek and he made a small growling sound low in his throat that told her more clearly than anything else just how furious he was. It took every ounce of willpower not to panic and bolt from the room. He grabbed her wrist in one hand and yanked. Bending low, he clipped her across the hips and tossed her over his shoulder.

'*Hunter*! No, don't!' she had time to shriek, before her entire world turned upside-down.

He clamped an arm around her legs just above the knees, effectively immobilizing her. 'We're going to discuss this all right. But not here where everyone and her grandmother can listen in,' he announced.

'Put me down!' She planted her palms in the middle of his back and attempted to wiggle free. Not that it did any good. His grip was as strong as a steel band.

'We could continue this conversation at the line-shack, if you'd prefer.' He shrugged his shoulders, bouncing her like a sack of potatoes. The breath whooshed from her lungs and she stopped bucking.

'No! Why not here? The study is an excellent place for a discussion. You start discussing and you'll see how good a place it is.'

'I say it's not.'

He'd reached the door and Leah began to panic seriously. 'Hunter, please. Put me down.'

He ignored her, stepping into the hallway. Heading for the entrance, he tipped his hat and said, 'After-noon, Rose. Glad you could drop in. Or should I say eavesdrop in? My bride and I are going for a little drive.'

'You don't say.' Rose folded her arms across her chest. 'You're going to have trouble driving like that.'

'It's amazing the things you can accomplish when you set your mind to it. Don't wait dinner for us.' With that, he left the house. Beside his pick-up, he dropped Leah to her feet, and held the truck door open. 'Your choice. You can get in under your own steam, or I can help you.'

She planted her hands on her hips. 'I am perfectly capable of getting into a truck all on my own, thank you very much.'

'Wrong answer.' The next thing she knew, he'd scooped her up and dumped her on the passenger seat. Slamming the door closed, he leaned in the window.

'This conversation may take longer than I thought. Stay here.'

Before she could say a single word, he'd started off toward the barn. He returned several minutes later, carrying two fishing poles and a tackle-box. She stared at the rods in disbelief. 'What's all that for?' she questioned, the second he climbed into the cab.

'Fishing.'

'I know that!' Loath as she was to mention the fact, she forced herself to remind him, 'I meant... I thought we were going to have a discussion.' She gave him a hopeful smile. 'But if you'd rather fish...'

'Believe me,' he said, shooting her a sharp look, 'we'll have that talk. Consider the drive to our... discussion site as a short reprieve.'

She struggled to hide her disappointment. 'And the poles?'

'My reward for not killing you.' He gunned the engine. 'If you were smart, you'd stay real quiet and hope it takes a long time to get there.'

'But—'

'Not another word!' His words exploded with a fury that left her in no doubt as to how tenuous a hold he had on his temper. 'Woman, you are inches away from disaster. I guarantee, you don't want to push me any further.'

Taking his suggestion to heart, she didn't open her mouth the entire length of the ride. She soon realized what destination he had in mind. The rough dirt track that he turned on to led to a small, secluded lake in the far western section of the ranch. It had been one of their favorite meeting-spots eight years ago. It was also about as far from curious eyes and ears as they could get. As much as she dreaded the coming confrontation, she appreciated his determination to keep it as private as possible.

'Hunter,' she began as they neared the lake.

'Not yet,' he bit out. 'I'm still not calm enough to deal with you.'

Pulling the truck to a stop at the end of the track, he climbed from the cab and gathered up the poles, tackle-box and a plastic bucket. 'Let's go,' he called over his shoulder.

Reluctantly Leah left the truck, and rummaged in the back for something to sit on. If they were going to stay a while—and she suspected that they were— she intended to be comfortable. Spreading the colorful Mexican blanket in the grass at the edge of the shore, she removed her boots and socks and rolled her jeans to her knees. Sticking her feet into the cool water, she asked, 'Are we going to talk first or fish?'

He spared her a brief glance. 'Both. You want a rod?'

'Might as well,' she muttered.

She searched the surrounding bermuda grass until she found a good-sized cricket. Carrying it back to the blanket, she knelt beside her pole, closed her eyes, and stuck the insect on the end of the hook. Ready to catch a catfish or two, she cast toward the middle of the lake. A bright yellow and red bobber marked her spot and she settled back on the blanket, wishing she could truly relax and enjoy a lazy afternoon of fishing. But she was all too aware of their coming 'discussion'.

Hunter attached his spinner bait to his line and cast into a marshy, partially shaded section of water known to attract bass. 'I've told you before, you can't bait a hook without looking,' he informed her in a taut voice.

'I just did.'

He yanked on his line. 'One of these times, you're going to set the hook in your finger instead of the cricket. It's going to hurt. It's going to bleed. And I'm going to have to cut the damned thing out.'

'*If* that fine day ever arrives, you can say "I told you so". Until then, I'd rather not see what I'm murdering.' She cupped her chin in her hand and rested her elbow on a bent knee. 'Are we going to fight over fishing, or are we going to fight over the real problem?'

He turned his head and studied her. More than a hint of anger lingered in the depths of his eyes. 'Do you even know what that is?'

'Sure,' she said with a shrug. 'You hit Orrie.'

'You're damned right, I hit him. All things considered, he got off easy.' Hunter slowly reeled in his line. 'But that's not the issue.'

She knew it wasn't, though he'd never get her to admit it. 'Mateo loves working with the horses,' she said instead. 'Did you have to make him give it up? And why fire Lenny? He's a good worker and a wonderful man.'

Hunter cast his line again, his mouth tightening. 'Nor is that the issue.'

'It is so,' she disagreed, her frustration flaring out of control. 'It's why we're arguing.'

'No, it's not. It's why you're annoyed, but it's not why we're arguing,' he corrected harshly. 'You're annoyed because I didn't consult with you before making changes and we're arguing because I won't explain my decision.'

He'd hit the nail on the head, and she focused her attention on that particular aspect of the discussion. 'Why did you do it? Why did you fire Orrie and Lenny and change Mateo's job?' He remained stubbornly silent and she wanted to scream in exasperation. 'You're not going to tell me, are you?'

'No, I'm not.'

'Because it's not the *issue*?' she demanded, tossing her pole to the grass and scrambling to her feet. 'It's my ranch, too. I have a right to know. You promised to give everyone a fair chance. You promised!'

Setting his rod on the blanket, he reached out and swept her feet from under her, catching her before she hit the ground. *'That's* the issue,' he practically snarled. 'I made a promise to you—which I kept. And you made a promise to me—which you didn't keep.'

She fought his hold, with no success. His strength was too great. 'I don't know what you're talking about,' she insisted.

He pushed her back on to the blanket and knelt above her, planting his hands on either side of her head. 'Who's in charge of this ranch?'

'That's not the point.'

'It's precisely the point. Answer me. Who's in charge of this ranch?'

It galled her to say it. 'You are,' she forced herself to admit. She pushed against his chest, struggling to sit up. To her relief, he rocked back on to his heels, allowing her to wriggle out from beneath him.

'So you do remember our conversation at the line-shack,' he said in satisfaction.

She wrapped her arms around her waist. 'Very funny. How could I forget?' It wasn't one of her more pleasant recollections. Every last, painful detail had been burned into her memory.

'And do you also remember the promises we exchanged?'

'Of course.'

'So do I.' He ticked them off on his fingers. 'I promised to give your employees a fair chance. I promised to give your grandmother a home. And I promised to sign a prenuptial agreement. Is that everything?'

She glanced at him uneasily. 'Yes.'

'You promised one thing. What was it?'

She knew where he was headed with this and she didn't like it. 'I seem to remember there being more than one,' she temporized.

'Fine,' he said evenly. 'Name any that you remember.'

Time to face the music. She should be grateful that he wasn't rending her limb from limb. She looked him straight in the eye and said, 'I promised you'd be in charge of the ranch.'

'Which means?'

She sighed. 'That what you say goes. That I'm not to question you in front of the employees or second-guess your decisions. You don't work by committee,' she repeated his demands by rote.

'And did you do that? Did you keep your promise?'

Reluctantly she shook her head. 'No.' Nor had she kept her agreement to make their marriage a fully functioning one. She should be grateful that he hadn't pointed that out as well.

'*That's* why I'm angry. One of these days you'll trust me to do what's right for you and for the ranch. You'll trust me without question.'

'You mean blindly.'

'Okay. That's what I mean.'

She bit down on her lip. How could she do what he asked when it might all be part of an elaborate game of revenge, an attempt to even the score for old wrongs? 'I don't think I can do that, Hunter. You're asking me to risk everything.'

'Yes. I am.'

'It's too much,' she whispered, staring down at the blanket, running the wool fringe through her fingers. 'I can't give it to you. Not yet.'

A long minute ticked by before he inclined his head. 'All right. I'll answer your questions—this time.'

She glanced up in surprise. 'You'll tell me why you fired Orrie and Lenny? Why you made Mateo give up the horses?'

'Yes. This once I'll explain myself. Next time you either trust me or you don't; I don't care which. But don't expect me to defend my actions again. You understand?' At her nod, he said, 'I put Mateo in charge of the haying operation. It meant an increase in wages—something he and his family need. Plus he knows more about mechanics than he does about horses.'

'But...he knows everything about horses.'

'He knows more about repairing our equipment. As for Lenny... He wasn't happy working on a ranch. But employment meant more to him than his dislike of ranching, which says a lot about the man's character, so I recommended him for a job as a security-guard at your godfather's bank. Lenny jumped at the opportunity.'

She could hardly take it in. 'And Orrie?'

He frowned. 'Orrie was a thief,' he told her reluctantly.

'A thief! I don't believe it. What did he steal?' An obstinate look appeared in his eyes, a look she didn't doubt he'd find reflected in her own. 'Hunter?' she prompted, refusing to let it drop.

'He took your silver circlet.'

She stared in shock. 'From my wedding-gown? But that was in our...'

'Bedroom,' he finished for her.

The full implication gradually sank in. Without a word she turned away and reached for her pole. It felt as if she'd been stabbed in the back by a family member. Her betrayal went so deep that she couldn't even find the words to express it. Slowly, she brought in the line, blinking hard. The cricket was long-gone and she didn't have the stomach to kill another. At some point during their conversation she'd lost her enthusiasm for fishing.

As though sensing her distress, Hunter caught her braid and used it to reel her in. She didn't resist. Right now she needed all the comfort she could get. He folded his arms around her and she snuggled into his embrace. 'You okay?' he asked.

'No,' she replied, her voice muffled against his shirt. 'See what happens when you trust people?'

'Yes, I see. But I'm not Orrie.'

She sighed. 'No, you're not. I'm sorry, Hunter. I should have trusted you to do the right thing for the ranch.'

'Yes, you should have.'

'And I shouldn't have questioned your judgement in front of the men.'

'No, you shouldn't have. Apology accepted.' Without warning he released her, and stripped off his shirt and boots. Then, snatching her high in his arms, he walked into the lake, holding her above the water.

She clung to him, laughing. 'Don't! Don't drop me.'

'Do you trust me?'

'Blindly?'

'Is there any other way?'

She bit her lower lip. 'Okay. I trust you. Blindly.'

'Close your eyes.'

'They're closed.'

'And take a deep breath.'

'Hunter, no!' she yelped. He tossed her into the air and she tumbled, shrieking, landing in the water with a huge splash. An instant later Hunter dived in beside her, kicking with her to the surface. She gasped for air. 'I thought you said I could trust you.'

A slow grin drifted across his lean face and he caught her close. 'I never said what you could trust me to do.'

And therein lay the real crux of the matter. She knew he'd do what he thought best—but would it be right for her? As much as she wanted to believe, she couldn't. Not yet.

As they drifted toward shore her hair floated free of its braid, wrapping them in a net of long silvery tendrils. He beached them in the grass and gazed down at her, his attention snared by the wet shirt clinging to her breasts. His palm settled on the taut, supple lines of her midriff, where her shirt had parted company with her jeans. As though unable to resist he lowered his head, and gently bit the rigid peak of her breast through the wet cotton.

Her breath stopped in her throat and her nails bit

into his shoulders, marking him with tiny crescent scars of passion. 'Hunter!' His name escaped her as though ripped from her throat, filled with an undeniable urgency.

He responded instantly, releasing her breast and plundering her mouth, parting her lips in search of the sweet warmth within. She couldn't seem to get enough of him. Her hands swept down his back, stroking him, needing to absorb him into her very pores, the seductive brush of cloth against skin an almost painful stimulation. His taste filled her mouth, his unique musky scent her lungs. She felt him tug at the fastening of his jeans... And then he hesitated.

Slowly he lifted his head, his angled features stark with want, dark with intent. She knew that expression, knew how close to the edge he must be. She stared at him uncertainly, caught between completing the intimacy he so clearly craved and she so desperately needed, and retreating from an act that would enable him to wrest the final bit of control from her possession. And she waited, waited for him to give in to his desire, to strip away the wet clothes and make her his wife in fact as well as name. But instead he drew away, and she could only imagine the amount of willpower it must have taken him.

He kissed her again, the caress hard and swift. 'Not here. Not like this. But soon,' he warned in a determined voice. 'Very soon. When there are no more doubts in your mind...when there's no chance of turning back, we will finish this and you will be mine.'

She didn't argue. How could she? He was right. Soon they would be lovers, and if she wasn't very, very careful she'd lose her heart as surely as she was losing control of the ranch. And, when that happened, Hunter would finally have his revenge.

The next few days passed with a comfortable ease that gave Leah hope for the future. Hunter continued to work with Dreamseeker, though whether or not he'd made any headway with the stallion was a topic of hot debate. Still, she didn't doubt who would eventually win their battle of wills.

To her relief, the employees seemed quite content working under Hunter's management. Losing two wranglers left ample work for everyone, and she suspected that the fear of being laid off had finally dissipated. Mateo was far happier than she'd ever seen him. And dropping in on Lenny in his new position as security-guard proved that Hunter had been right about that change as well.

Returning from the bank late one cloudy afternoon, she was surprised to discover Hunter Rototilling the ground around the porch. The powerful blades bit into the dark soil, grinding up the crushed remains of Grandmother Rose's begonias.

'What are you doing?' she called. He didn't answer, merely lifted a hand in greeting and resumed his work. Inez stood on the porch and Leah joined her. 'What's he doing?' she asked the housekeeper. 'Or perhaps I should ask why. Why is he plowing the garden under?'

'*No sé,*' Inez replied with a shrug. 'Abuela Rosa, she took one look, said a nasty word, and stomped off to the kitchen. I don't think she is happy that Señor Pryde has decided to ruin her garden.'

Leah frowned. 'Hunter isn't ruining her garden;

Bull Jones took care of that already. Hunter's just finishing the job.'

Rose appeared in the doorway, carrying a tray with a pitcher of iced tea and glasses. 'If we're going to stand around and watch all my hard work being ground into mulch, we might as well be comfortable.'

Leah hastened to take the tray, setting it on a low wrought-iron table. 'There wasn't much left to mulch,' she reassured, pouring drinks and handing them around. 'Our neighboring foreman made sure of that.'

With a noisy humph, Rose sat in a rocker. 'If Hunter thinks I'm starting over again, he's got another think coming. That garden can grow rocks and weeds for all I care.' She took a sip of tea. 'What's he doing over there? What's in those bags?'

'*Es abono, sí*?' Inez suggested.

'Fertilizer, huh?' Rose slowly rocked in her chair. 'Yes, sir. That'll give him a fine crop of weeds. A truly fine crop.' She craned her neck. 'Where's he going now?'

Leah shrugged, frowning as Hunter walked toward the rear of the house. 'I don't know. Maybe he's through for the day.'

'Through!' Rose rocked a little faster. 'With everything such a mess? He'd better not leave my garden like that, or I'll have a thing or two to say about it. See if I don't.'

Leah jumped to her feet and leaned over the rail. 'False alarm. Here he comes. He was just pulling the pick-up around.' He climbed out of the cab and crossed to the back of the truck. Lowering the tailgate, he removed an assortment of bedding plants. She glanced over her shoulder at Rose. 'He bought jasmine for the trellis. I adore jasmine.'

Inez joined her at the railing, beaming in delight. '*Y mira!*'

Slowly Rose stood. 'Well, I'll be. He bought some roses.'

Leah began to laugh. 'How appropriate. They're peace roses.'

Hunter lined the plants around the perimeter of the house, then approached, carrying a shovel. He stood at the bottom of the porch steps and looked directly at Rose. 'Well? You going to play lady of the manor, or do you want to get your hands dirty and help?'

Rose lifted her chin. 'Whose garden is it?' she demanded.

Hunter shrugged. 'I'm no gardener. Just thought I'd get it started.'

'In that case, I'll fetch my gloves,' she agreed. At the door she paused, and with a crotchety glare demanded, 'Don't you break ground without me. Hear?'

Leah waited until Rose was out of earshot before approaching Hunter, offering him a glass of iced tea. 'This is very thoughtful of you. When Bull destroyed her last flowerbed, she gave in to the inevitable and didn't try again.'

He drank the tea and handed her the empty glass. 'He won't destroy another.'

She didn't doubt it for a minute. 'Peace roses?' she asked, raising an eyebrow.

He tipped his hat to the back of his head with a gloved finger, and in that moment, Leah didn't think she'd ever seen him look more attractive. 'Yeah, well. I figured it was past time we came to terms. We'll stick in a few rose bushes and talk. Before we're done we'll have worked out our differences.'

Leah smiled. 'I'm sure you will,' she said softly. 'It's just difficult for her to adjust to all the changes.'

'I'm not done making them, you know,' he warned.

She nodded. 'I know.'

He'd never promised not to make changes. But they were for the better. And more and more she realized how important he'd become—to her employees, to the ranch...even to her grandmother, loath as Rose might be to admit it.

But most of all, he'd become important to her, perhaps even vital. And before much longer she'd have to deal with that knowledge.

Leah watched in concern the next morning as Hunter and his men drove one of the ranch bulls into a pen in preparation for transporting him to his new owner. She'd nicknamed the animal 'Red' because of his tendency to charge anything or anyone foolish enough to wear that color. After nearly being gored by the bull, Hunter had decided to sell the animal.

He'd also flatly refused to allow her to help move Red to the pen, saying it was 'much too dangerous'. She'd heard that phrase used more than once and had rapidly grown to hate it. But she didn't dare argue, especially in front of the employees and especially when—in this particular case—he was right. The bull was very dangerous.

She climbed to the top rail of the corral fence and looked on from a safe distance. With Red secure and peaceful in the holding-pen, the men only awaited the arrival of the truck to move the bull to his new home.

'Señora Leah!' came a childish shout from behind her. 'Silkie! Get Silkie.'

She turned in time to see all six Arroya children chasing after their new sheepdog puppy. The tiny animal, yapping for all she was worth, streaked beneath the rail of the corral, barreling straight toward the holding-pen...and the bull. And around her neck, bouncing in the dust, hung a huge, red floppy bow.

'Stay there!' she called over her shoulder, hopping off the rail. 'Don't you dare come into the corral. You understand?'

The children obediently skidded to a halt and nodded as one. Six pairs of huge dark eyes stared at her, wide with mingled fear and hope. Wincing at their trusting expressions, Leah hotfooted it after the wayward puppy.

Across the corral the dog ran, and Leah realized that she'd have only one chance to catch the animal before it was too late. At the last possible second, just as they reached the holding-pen, she flung herself at Silkie. Belly-flopping to a dusty halt, inches from the bottom rail, her hand closed around the furry, struggling puppy. For a brief second she held the animal safely in her grasp. Then, with a frantic wiggle, Silkie scrambled free and scooted beneath the rail.

'Silkie, no!' she yelled.

Set on a course of total annihilation, the puppy darted toward the bull. Taking a deep breath and whispering a fervent prayer, Leah ducked beneath the rail, hoping she could snag the animal and escape unscathed. A hard, relentless hand landed on her arm and jerked her back, spinning her around. She stared up into Hunter's furious face.

'Are you nuts?' he practically roared.

'The puppy!' she cried, fighting his hold. 'I've got to save the puppy!'

He glanced from Leah to the Arroya children. 'Open the gates!' he shouted to his men. 'Get the bull out of there!'

Yelling and whistling, the wranglers unlatched the gate between the holding-pen and the pasture. But the bull didn't notice. Focused entirely on Silkie, he lowered his head, pawing at the ground and bellowing in fury. He scored the ground with his horns, just missing the dog.

Swearing beneath his breath, Hunter tossed his hat to the ground and ripped off his shirt. Before anyone could stop him, he climbed beneath the rail and entered the holding-pen.

'Hunter, don't do it!' Leah started to follow, but the look on his face stopped her. If she moved another step, she'd divert his attention and the bull would kill him. It was that simple. She clasped her trembling hands together, hardly daring to breathe. With a fervor bordering on hysteria, she began to pray.

Waving his shirt in the air, Hunter caught the bull's attention. Distracted by this new, more accessible target, the huge animal instantly charged. At the last possible second Hunter threw his shirt at the bull's head and, diving to one side, rolled clear of the vicious hooves and horns. Red pounded by and Hunter leapt to his feet. Snagging the puppy by the scruff of her neck, he vaulted over the fence to safety.

Blinded, Red crashed into the fence between the holding-pen and the corral, the rails splintering beneath the impact. Keeping Silkie tucked safely under his arm, Hunter grabbed Leah by the wrist and ran flat out for the far side of the corral. The bull stood close to the splintered rails, blowing hard. With several shakes of his head he reduced the shirt covering him to rags. Then he looked around for his next victim. At long last, he spied the open gate and, to Leah's eternal relief, he barreled through it, racing into the pasture.

Leaving her side, Hunter carried the dog over to the Arroya children and dropped to one knee in the dirt in front of them. Leah watched anxiously, wondering what he intended to say to them, hoping he wouldn't be too rough.

'Is this your puppy?' he asked the children.

'Yes, sir.' The oldest, Ernesto, stepped forward, swallowing hard. 'She sort of got away from us. We're sorry.'

'You know what could have happened?'

Every last one of them nodded. The youngest, Tina, clung to Ernesto, tears streaking her cheeks. 'We'll be more careful next time,' the boy said solemnly. 'I promise.'

'Promise,' Tina repeated. After a brief hesitation, she held her arms out for Silkie.

Hunter handed over the dog. 'Tie her up until she's old enough to mind. Okay?'

Tina wrapped her arms around the puppy, burying her face in the dog's fluffy coat. With a playful yip, Silkie washed the dirt and tears from the little girl's face. Satisfied that her pet was indeed safe, she peeked up at Hunter from beneath long, dark lashes. 'Promise,' she repeated and offered a gap-toothed smile.

Hunter ruffled her hair and stood. He glanced at Leah and lifted an eyebrow. Without a word, she ran to his side and threw her arms around him, blinking back the tears that threatened to fall. His skin felt warm and hard beneath her hands, and she drew in a ragged breath, picturing what he might have looked like had he not been quite so agile. She clung to him, not wanting ever to let go.

In that instant she realized that she loved him...had always loved him and always would. If he'd died beneath the bull's horns, a part of her would have died as well. For weeks now she'd held him at a distance, reluctant to commit herself fully, because deep in her heart of hearts she knew that, once she did, he'd own her body and soul.

Held in the safe harbor of his arms, she surrendered to the inevitable.

'You do anything that stupid again and *I* won't be responsible for *my* actions,' she whispered fiercely, repeating the words he'd so often used when taking her to task. 'You hear me, Hunter Pryde?'

He held her tight against him. 'I didn't have a choice. You and the children were counting on me to save that damned dog.'

And suddenly she realized he was right. As frightened as she'd been, she hadn't doubted for a minute that he'd save Silkie. Nor had the children. She glanced over Hunter's shoulder, seeing the men laughing and slapping each other on the back. The men hadn't doubted either. They all trusted him, all believed in him. Every last one.

'And you did save her. But then, I...I knew you would,' she confessed.

He stiffened. 'Blind trust, Leah? You?'

She lifted a shaky hand to swipe at an escaped tear. 'A temporary aberration, I'm sure.'

A laugh rumbled deep in his chest. 'Of course.

Come on. Let's get that fence fixed. We've got a bull to bring in.'

Reluctantly, she slid her arms from around his neck and stepped back. 'I'll be right there.' She watched him return to the corral and snag his hat from the dirt. She did trust him, she realized. She trusted him every bit as much as she loved him. Blindly. Totally. Completely.

And she'd never been more frightened in her life. For Hunter had it all now...the ranch and her heart. The only question was...what would he do when he found out?

CHAPTER EIGHT

EARLY the next morning Lyon Enterprises' latest offer arrived by special messenger. Gazing in fury at the papers, Leah knocked back the kitchen chair and went in search of Hunter. Eventually she tracked him down in the barn, running a curry-comb over his buckskin.

'Look at this,' she said, holding out the white embossed envelope.

He set aside his equipment and took the papers, scanning them. His mouth tightened briefly, then he shrugged. 'So? Either write your acceptance or trash it.'

She stared in disbelief as he guided his gelding from the grooming-box and returned the horse to his stall. 'That's it? That's all you're going to say?' she demanded, trailing behind.

He shouldered past her and crossed the barn aisle to a stack of hay bales. Using two large hooks, he lifted a bale and carried it to the stall. 'What do you want me to say?'

She regarded him with frustration. 'Something more than what you have. I'm tired of their pestering me. I'd think you would be, too. Or don't you care if I sell out to them?'

He released a gusty sigh and glanced over his shoulder at her. 'Is that what you want? To sell? I thought the whole point of marrying was to prevent Lyon from getting their hands on your ranch.'

'It was, but you seem so...' She shrugged. 'I don't know. Detached.'

'I am. It's not my ranch.'

She wasn't sure why she kept pushing it. But something about his careless indifference didn't quite ring true. After all, he'd also married in order to secure the ranch. She didn't believe for one minute that he was as unconcerned about her accepting Lyon's offer as he claimed. 'So you wouldn't object if I sold to them.'

'No.' He paused in his labors. 'Though legally you can't without offering me first refusal.'

She blinked, momentarily sidetracked. 'Come again?'

He rolled up his sleeves and leaned his arms on the stall door, exposing the powerful muscles of his forearms. 'The prenup, remember? You retain title of the ranch in the event of a divorce. But if you choose to sell, I have right of first refusal.' He frowned at her, tilting his hat to the back of his head. 'You're the one who insisted we sign the damned thing. Didn't you even bother to read it?'

'Yes.' No. She'd just signed where her lawyer had told her in order to get it over and done with.

'Yeah, right,' he said, clearly not believing her. 'You should have read it, Leah. There are one or two other important clauses in there that you should be familiar with. If that's the way you conduct all your business, it's a wonder you weren't bankrupt years ago.'

She hadn't come to argue. She'd come to vent her anger over Lyon Enterprises' non-stop harassment—

an anger that had finally reached the boiling point.
'That's not what's at issue,' she said, determined to
get the conversation back on track. 'I'd like to discuss
this offer.'

'So discuss it. I'm listening.'

She took a deep breath. 'I plan to drive to Houston
this week and talk to them.'

That stopped him. 'You *what*?'

'I want to have it out once and for all—tell them I
won't sell.'

He stared at her as though she'd lost her mind. 'If
you don't want to sell, just trash the thing. You don't
need to drive all the way to Houston to do that. Last
time I looked you kept a wastebasket in the study.
Use that one.'

'Very funny. I have to go to Houston.'

'Why?'

'So I can address the Lyon Enterprises board.'

He froze for a split-second, the check in his movements so brief she almost missed it. Leaving the stall,
he slung the remains of the bale on to the stack and
crossed to her side. His hat brim threw his face into
shadow, but she could see the dark glitter of his eyes
and the taut line of his jaw. Was he angry? She
couldn't quite tell.

'And why,' he asked softly, 'would you want to
address the board of Lyon Enterprises?'

Her voice sharpened. 'I've had it with these people.
As far as I'm concerned this latest offer is the final
straw. I'm not putting up with it any more. I'm going
to make it clear that I won't be entertaining any future
offers and that I won't sell to them. Ever. If necessary
I'll even tell them what you said—that our prenuptial
agreement gives you first right of refusal.'

He shook his head. 'Over my dead body. That's nobody's business but ours.'

'Okay,' she conceded, uncertain of his temperament. Any time his voice dropped to such a low, husky note she tended to tread warily. 'But I still want to go to Houston and talk to them. And I want you to go with me.'

'Why?' he said again.

She glanced at him uncertainly. 'To support me, if you're willing.'

He turned away, resting a booted foot on the haystack. She could tell from the tense set of his shoulders that she'd thrown him, and she studied his expressionless profile in concern. Perhaps she'd pushed it by requesting his support. If only she could read his thoughts, she'd know. But he'd always been exceptionally successful at keeping them hidden from her.

Finally he nodded. 'Okay. I'll go. We'll leave Friday and spend the weekend at my apartment.'

'You have an apartment in Houston?' she asked in astonishment.

'You can see for yourself when we get there.' His brows drew together. 'Leah, I need you to agree to something.'

She eyed him warily. 'What?'

He stripped off his gloves and tucked them into his belt. 'Once you've confronted the board, I want to handle the situation from then on.'

'But it's not your problem.'

'Yes, it is. Anything that affects this ranch is my problem. And dealing with companies like Lyon Enterprises is my area of expertise—my former area of expertise.'

'Do you think you can get them to leave me alone?'

'No. But I can do a good job of holding them at bay. I'm better equipped than you to wage this war.'

Suddenly she recalled her need for a knight on a white charger, battling the nasty dragon in order to save the damsel in distress. When Hunter had shown up she'd been sure he was the dragon, and that she'd have to fight her own battles. Now she wondered. Perhaps they'd fight those battles together, and Lyon Enterprises would be vanquished once and for all.

'Let me have my say, and then it's your problem,' she promised.

'Fine.' He dropped an arm across her shoulders. 'I'm starved. How about you?'

She grinned. It felt as though the weight of the world had been lifted from her shoulders. 'I think I could eat a horse,' she confessed, and walked with him to the house.

Late that night Hunter lifted the phone receiver and punched in a series of numbers. A minute later Kevin answered.

'It's me,' Hunter said. 'I'm coming in. Call the board together.'

'What's wrong?' Kevin demanded. 'What happened?'

'Leah received Lyon's latest offer and wants to meet with them.'

'She *what*?'

'You heard me.'

'What the hell are you going to do?'

'Introduce her to the board of Lyon Enterprises, what else?'

'I mean...what are *you* going to do? What if...what if she finds out?'

'She won't.' Hunter spoke with absolute confidence.

'Why not?'

'Because no one would dare tell her anything.'

'If they think it'll help with the sale—'

'Once they meet her, they'll see that she trusts me,' Hunter cut in briskly. 'And they'll realize it's to their advantage to keep quiet. Telling her who I am won't help their cause any, and they're smart enough to know it.'

A long moment of silence followed while Kevin mulled over Hunter's words. 'You could be right. You usually are. I'll tell everyone you're coming.'

'And open up the apartment. We'll be spending the weekend there.'

'Won't she be suspicious? It's not precisely a poor man's pad.'

'She'll have other things on her mind by that time.'

Kevin gave a knowing chuckle. 'Understood. See you Friday.'

'Right.'

Hunter hung up and leaned back in the chair. Matters were rapidly coming to a head. More than anything he'd like to get this situation over and done with, but some things just couldn't be rushed. And this, though he'd prefer it otherwise, was one of them.

He heard a soft knock and Leah opened the door. 'Busy?' she asked.

'No. Come on in.'

She stepped into the room, standing just outside the spill of lamplight and wearing a knee-length cotton nightshirt. Unfortunately, this one wasn't the least transparent. His mouth tightened. As much as he enjoyed seeing his wife in next to nothing, he couldn't have her running around half-dressed. One of these days he'd need to make a serious effort to break her of the habit.

'Who were you talking to?' she asked.

'A business associate.'

She came closer. Her hair, cascading past her waist, caught the light from the desk lamp and gleamed like fallen moonbeams. 'Is there a problem?'

He shook his head. 'Just thought I'd tell him I'd be in town at the end of the week.'

'Oh.' She stood a little uncertainly in the middle of the room. 'Are you coming to bed soon?'

He shoved back the chair and walked toward her. 'Is now soon enough?'

'Yes.' She couldn't quite meet his eyes and he felt her sudden tension.

He reached her side and stared down into her face. He'd never seen such perfection. Her eyes glowed like amethysts, her heart-shaped face full of strength and character and determination. 'I want to make love to you,' he told her bluntly, thrusting his fingers into the silken fall of her hair. 'I've been patient long enough.'

She twisted her hands together. 'I know. But...'

'Friday,' he stated, catching her chin with his knuckle and forcing her to look at him. 'I want a decision by Friday, Leah. You have to commit at some point.'

Slowly she nodded. 'Okay. Friday. We'll meet with the Lyon board and then have the rest of the weekend to ourselves.'

He smiled in satisfaction. 'Done. And now, wife,

it's time for bed.' He slid an arm around her and lifted her close. She trembled in his arms, which told him more than anything his effect on her.

'Hunter—'

He sensed that her nervousness had gotten the better of her, that given the opportunity she'd rescind her agreement. He stopped her words with a swift, rough kiss, then took her mouth again in a second, slower, more thorough kiss—a precursory taste of the pleasure he intended to share with her over the weekend.

They left early on Friday, arranging to meet with the Lyon personnel after lunch. Leah had dressed carefully, choosing a pearl-gray suit, matching pumps and a white silk blouse. To add a touch of sophistication, she'd looped her hair into a businesslike chignon, and as a morale booster displayed the necklace Hunter had given her as a wedding-gift.

To her surprise, Hunter dressed casually, exchanging his jeans for cotton trousers, his plaid shirt no different from the ones he wore when working. The boa tie he'd strung around his neck was his only concession to the occasion.

'Relax,' he said, driving toward the Post Oak section of Houston. 'They won't eat you.'

Her expression felt stiff and unnatural. 'I'm more concerned about them slitting my throat,' she attempted to joke. 'Especially after I tell them not to contact me ever again.'

'Too obvious. They'll just sell you off to white slavers.' He looked at her and sighed. 'I'm kidding, honey.'

'Oh.' She grinned weakly and her hand closed over the pendant; she was hoping it would give her even a minuscule amount of Hunter's strength and perseverance. 'I'm beginning to think this isn't such a great idea.'

He spared her another brief glance. 'You want to turn back?'

'No. Maybe if I do this they'll finally leave me alone.' She shifted in her seat and studied Hunter's profile. 'Do you think they will? Leave me alone, I mean?'

He shrugged. 'They might. But don't count on it. They're businessmen. All they care about is the bottom line on the balance sheet. If buying your ranch means a substantial profit, then no. They won't leave you alone.'

A small frown knit her brow. 'I'll have to think of a way to convince them I mean business.'

'Short of a stick of dynamite between their ears, I don't know how.'

His comment gave her an idea and a secretive smile crept across her mouth. 'I'm not so sure about the dynamite, although the idea has merit. Perhaps a slightly less drastic demonstration would be in order.' Opening the glove compartment, she rummaged around until she found what she sought. Without a word, she pocketed the item, hoping Hunter hadn't noticed the furtive act.

A few minutes later he pointed out a tall, modern glass building with smoked windows. 'That's where we're headed,' he told her, pulling into an underground parking-lot.

Leaving the car, they took the garage elevator to the lobby. 'Which floor is Lyon Enterprises?' Leah asked.

'All of them.'

She stopped dead in her tracks. 'They own the *building*?'

'They're a large company. Lots of companies own entire buildings.' He cupped her elbow and ushered her along. 'Come on. We want the executive level.'

She clutched her purse and the large white envelope with Lyon's offer to her chest. She hadn't realized. She'd had no idea they were such an immense concern. Suddenly she felt very small and vulnerable. How could she ever hope to defeat this Goliath of a company? She was no David. She glanced at Hunter. But he was. He'd protect her. All she had to do was trust him.

Filled with renewed confidence, she walked with him to the security desk. After presenting their credentials, they were escorted to a private bank of elevators that carried them directly to the executive level. Inside the car, she tucked back an escaped wisp of hair and straightened her skirt.

Hunter caught her hand, stilling her nervous exertions. 'Listen to me, Leah. These corporate types eat people like you for a midnight snack. So, don't fidget. Keep your arms relaxed at your side unless you're handing them something. Look them straight in the eye. Think before you speak. Don't answer any question you don't want to. And above all don't lose your temper. Got it?'

Her tension eased. 'Got it.'

His mouth curled to one side and she realized in amazement that he actually relished the coming confrontation. 'Remember, I'll support you every step of the way. The instant you get in too deep, I'll bail you out. Otherwise, it's your show.'

'Hunter?'

He lifted an eyebrow. 'What?'

She squeezed his hand. 'Thanks.'

'Don't thank me, Leah,' he said, and the serious-
ness of his tone gave his words an ominous weight.
'Not yet.'

The doors slid open and she released her death grip
on him. It wouldn't do for the Lyon board to think
that she needed his assistance, even if she did. Stepping from the car, they found a secretary awaiting
their arrival.

'Welcome to Lyon Enterprises,' she said. 'You're
expected, of course. If you'd follow me?'

She led the way to a pair of wide, double doors.
Pushing them open, she gestured for Hunter and Leah
to enter. As though in a calculated gesture, the doors
banged closed behind, barring their exit. A huge glass
table dominated the conference room, and around the
table sat a dozen men and women. The man at the
far end rose to his feet.

'Miss Hampton,' he said. 'A pleasure to finally
meet you. I'm Buddy Peterson. Our chairman requested that I conduct these proceedings, if you have
no objections.'

She did object. She wanted to speak directly to the
head honcho. 'He's not here?'

'He preferred that I negotiate in his place.' It didn't
quite answer her question, but from long experience
with Hunter she knew she wouldn't get a more direct
response. 'Pryde,' Peterson said, switching his attention to Hunter. 'We were somewhat surprised to hear
you'd be attending this meeting—with Miss
Hampton, that is.'

'Were you?' Hunter replied. 'I don't know why,
considering Leah's my wife.'

'Your *wife*!' The board members exchanged quick glances and Peterson slowly sank back into his seat. 'This puts a slightly different complexion on matters.'

Hunter inclined his head. 'Yes, it does, doesn't it?'

Peterson laughed, a cynical expression gleaming in his eyes. 'Congratulations… I'm impressed. I couldn't have done better myself.'

Leah looked up at Hunter in confusion. 'They know you?' she murmured.

'We're acquainted.'

'You didn't tell me.'

'It wasn't important.' His dark, unfathomable gaze captured hers. 'Do you have something to say to these people?'

She nodded. 'Yes.'

'Then get to it.'

She felt like a pawn in a game without rules. She glanced at Hunter, sudden doubts assailing her, acutely aware that she'd missed a vital piece of information, a clue that would help explain the mysterious undercurrents shifting through the room. She also suspected that what had to be said already had been, though in a language she couldn't hope to decipher. What she chose to contribute would be considered, at best, an empty gesture. Still, she wouldn't have this opportunity ever again. She wanted to say something they'd remember…do something they'd remember. She wanted them to know that Leah Hampton Pryde had been here and made a statement.

Taking a deep breath, she stepped to the table and held out the envelope. 'This arrived the other day.'

'Yes, our offer,' Peterson said with an impatient edge. 'Don't tell me you plan to accept?' He glanced

at Hunter. 'It would certainly save much of this
board's time and energy if you would.'

'Not only do I not accept, I don't want to hear from
you ever again. You people have harassed me for the
last time. I'm not the vulnerable woman struggling on
my own any more.' She spared Hunter a quick,
searching look. At his brief nod, she added, 'I have
help now. We won't allow Bull Jones to foul our
wells or stampede our herd. We won't be intimidated
by you any longer.'

'Yes, yes,' Buddy Peterson interrupted, 'you've
made your point.'

'Not yet, I haven't.'

She reached into her suit jacket pocket and pulled
out the lighter she'd taken from the glove compartment. With a flick of her thumb she spun the wheel,
and a small flame leapt to life. Stepping closer, she
held the flame beneath the corner of the envelope and
waited until it caught fire. Then she tossed the burning
packet into the center of the glass table. Flames and
smoke billowed. Frantic executives scrambled from
their seats, shouting and cursing.

Beside her, Hunter sighed. 'You really shouldn't
have done that.'

She lifted her chin. 'Yes, I should have. *Now* I've
made my point.'

'That…and more.'

'Good. Are you ready to leave?'

To her bewilderment, he shot a chary glance at the
ceiling, pulled his hat lower over his brow and raised
the collar of his shirt. 'In a minute. Go to the car. I'll
be right behind.'

The instant the door closed behind her an alarm
bell began to scream and the overhead sprinklers burst

to life. In a mad dash the executives scurried from the room, like rats deserting a sinking ship.

'Get these sprinklers turned off!' Buddy Peterson bellowed. He continued to sit at the table, his arms folded across his chest, ignoring the drenching spray. 'That was damned clever, Hunter,' he called above the screeching siren.

'She does have a certain...flair, doesn't she?' Hunter said, impervious to the water funneling in a small waterfall from his hat brim.

Peterson stood and approached. 'That's not what I meant, and you know it. How long are you going to keep her in the dark—not tell her who you really are?'

'As long as it takes.'

'You're playing a dangerous game. You could lose everything,' Peterson advised.

'I don't lose.' Hunter's voice dropped, a hard, threatening note coloring his words. 'Fair warning. One leak from anyone at this table and you'll all suffer the consequences. I'll be in touch soon.' He didn't wait for a response. Turning, he left.

'I still don't understand how you got so wet.'

'I told you. A freak shower.'

'Where? There isn't a cloud in the sky.' Sarcasm crept into her voice. 'Or perhaps it rained somewhere between the executive floor and the garage.'

He released a soft laugh. 'Something like that.'

She gave up. Hunter could be incredibly close-mouthed when he chose. If he'd decided that he wouldn't tell her, then he wouldn't. It was that simple. 'What did you say to the board after I left?'

He swung into another parking garage, this one beneath a brand-new, high-rise apartment complex. 'Not much. They didn't hang around for long.'

'Hunter!' she exclaimed in exasperation. 'Why won't you give me a straight answer? What did you say? How do you know them? For that matter, how did you know your way around their building? And why all the secrecy?'

He pulled into a wide parking space with H. Pryde stenciled on to the wall above it. Switching off the engine, he rested his arms on the steering-wheel and turned and looked at her. 'I know the Lyon board through work, which is also how I knew my way around their complex. I told Peterson that I'd be in touch soon. And I'm not being in the least secretive—just selective in what I tell you.'

'Why?'

'Because Lyon is my problem now, and I'll handle it.'

She could accept that. Having to deal all these years with the constant stream of difficulties on the ranch, it was a welcome change to have a second set of shoulders to help carry the burden. 'Why did you tell Buddy Peterson you'd be in touch?'

'To make certain he doesn't bother you again.'

'And he'll agree to that?' she asked in amazement.

'I won't give him any choice.' He opened his door. 'Coming?'

After unloading their overnight bags, Hunter led the way to the bank of elevators. Once there, he keyed the security lock for the penthouse and Leah stiffened. 'The penthouse?'

He paused before answering, and for some reason his momentary hesitation made her think of his advice about addressing the board members of Lyon

Enterprises. 'Think before you speak,' he'd told her. 'Don't answer any question you don't want to.' Perhaps that advice didn't apply solely to board members. Perhaps it applied to recalcitrant wives as well.

'They paid me well in my previous job,' he finally said.

'I guess so. I'm surprised you left.' The car glided rapidly upward and she peeked at him from beneath her lashes. 'But that's right... You said you'd still do occasional jobs for them if they called. Troubleshooting, isn't that your speciality?'

'Yes.'

'What did you say the name of the company was?'

'I didn't.' He leaned back against the wall and folded his arms across his chest. 'Why all the questions, Leah?'

'You can't expect me not to have questions.' Her grip on her purse tightened. 'I'm...surprised.'

'Because I'm not the dirt-poor ranch-hand I once was?'

She shot him a sharp look. 'We've been over this before. That's not the problem and you know it. You ask me to trust you. To trust you blindly. But you tell me nothing about yourself, which means *you* don't trust *me*.'

'Point taken,' he conceded.

The doors slid silently apart, opening on to a huge entrance hall. Swallowing nervously, she stepped out of the car. 'Good heavens, Hunter, look at this place!'

'I've seen it before, remember?' he said gently. 'Make yourself at home.'

Her heels clicked on the oak parquet flooring as she crossed to the sunken living-room. 'Why didn't you tell me?' she asked quietly. 'Why the games?'

His hat sailed past her, skimming the coffee-table and landing dead-center in the middle of the *chaise longue*. 'All right. I admit I may have omitted a detail or two about my life these past eight years.'

'A detail or two?' she questioned with irony.

'Or three. What difference does it make? I have money. And I have an apartment in Houston. So what?'

'It's a penthouse apartment,' she was quick to remind him.

He shrugged irritably. 'Fine. It's a penthouse apartment. It doesn't change a damned thing. We're still married. I still work the ranch. And you're still my wife.'

'Am I?'

He thrust a hand through his hair. 'What the hell is that supposed to mean?'

'Why did you marry me, Hunter?'

'You know why.'

She nodded. 'For the ranch. Perhaps also for a bit of revenge. But what I don't understand is…why? Why would you care about such a small concern when you have all this?' He didn't respond, and she realized that she could stand there until doomsday and he wouldn't answer her questions. She picked up her overnight bag. 'I'd like to freshen up. Where do I go?'

'Down the hallway. Third door on the right.'

She didn't look back. Walking away, she fought an unease—an unease she couldn't express and chose not to analyze fully. The door he'd indicated was to the master bedroom. She closed herself in the adjoining bathroom and stripped off her clothes, indulging in a quick, refreshing shower. Slipping on a bathrobe, she returned to the bedroom.

She stood beside the bed for several minutes before giving into temptation. Climbing on top of the down coverlet, she curled up in the center and shut her eyes. A short catnap would do her a world of good. But, despite the best of intentions, her thoughts kept returning to Hunter and their conversation.

The situation between them grew more and more confusing with each passing day. Standing in the middle of the penthouse living-room, seeing the visual proof of the wealth and power she'd long suspected, had forced her to face facts. Hunter Pryde had returned to the ranch for a reason...a reason he'd chosen not to share with her.

And no matter how hard she tried to fight it, the same question drummed incessantly in the back of her mind. Having so much, what in heaven's name did he want with her and Hampton Homestead...if not revenge?

CHAPTER NINE

'LEAH? Wake up, sweetheart.'

She stirred, pulled from the most delicious dream of laughter and peace roses and babies with ebony hair and eyes. She looked up to find Hunter sitting beside her on the bed. He must have showered recently; his hair was damp and slicked back from his brow, drawing attention to his angled bone-structure. He'd also discarded his shirt and wore faded jeans that rode low on his hips and emphasized his lean, muscular build. He bent closer, smoothing her hair from her eyes, and his amulet caught the light, glowing a rich blue against his deeply bronzed chest.

'What time is it?' she murmured, stretching.

'Time for dinner. You've been sleeping for two hours.'

'That long?' She sat up, adjusting the gaping robe. 'I should get dressed.'

'Don't bother on my account,' he said with a slow grin. 'I thought we'd go casual tonight.'

She wrinkled her nose. 'I suspect this might be considered a little too casual.'

'Only one person will see.' He held out his hand. 'Let me show you.'

Curious, she slipped her fingers into his and clambered off the bed. He returned to the living-room and gestured toward a spiral staircase she'd failed to notice earlier. 'Follow me.' At the top he blocked her path. 'Close your eyes and hold on,' he instructed.

'Why?'

'You'll see.'

'Okay. Don't let me fall.'

Before she knew what he intended, he scooped her up into his arms. 'Trust, remember?' he murmured against her ear. A few minutes later he set her on her feet. 'You can look now.'

She opened her eyes and gasped in disbelief. They stood on the roof of the apartment building, but it was unlike any rooftop she'd ever seen. If she hadn't known better, she'd have sworn they stood in the middle of a park. Grass grew beneath her feet and everywhere she glanced were flowers—barrels of petunias, pansies and impatiens. Even irises and tulips bloomed in profusion.

'I thought you said you weren't a gardener,' she accused.

'I lied,' he said with a careless shrug. He indicated a greenhouse occupying one end of the roof. 'Some of the more delicate flowers are grown there. But I've had an outside concern take over since I moved to the ranch. They prepared everything for our visit.'

'It's...it's incredible.'

'Hungry?'

Suddenly she realized that she was. 'Starving,' she admitted.

'I thought we'd eat here. You can change if you want, but it isn't necessary.'

She caught the underlying message. She could dine in nothing but a robe, just as he dined in nothing but jeans, or she could dress and use her clothes as a shield, a subtle way of distancing herself.

'This is fine,' she said casually. 'Satisfy my curiosity, though. What sort of meal goes with scruffiness and bare feet?'

'A picnic, of course.'

He pointed to a secluded corner where a blanket had already been spread on the grass. All around the sheltered nook were pots and pots of azaleas, heavy with blossoms in every conceivable shade. A bucket anchored one corner of the blanket, the top of a champagne bottle thrusting out of the ice. Next to the champagne she saw a huge wicker basket covered with a red-checked square of linen.

She chuckled at the cliché. 'Fried chicken?' she guessed.

'Coleslaw and potato salad,' he confirmed.

'Fast food?'

He looked insulted. 'Catered.' Crossing to their picnic spot, he knelt beside the basket and unloaded the goodies on to china.

'You're kidding,' she said in disbelief, joining him on the blanket. 'China? For a picnic?'

He gave her a bland smile. 'Isn't that what you use?'

'Not likely.' She examined the champagne. 'Perrier Jouet flower bottle? Lalique flutes? Hunter, I'm almost afraid to touch anything.' She stared at him helplessly. 'Why are you doing this?'

'It seemed…appropriate.'

She bowed her head, her emotions threatening to shatter her self-control. 'Thank you,' she whispered. 'It's beautiful.'

'You're hungry,' he said, and she wondered if she just imagined the tenderness in his voice. 'Try this.'

He held out a succulent sliver of chicken that he'd

stripped from the bone. She took it from him and almost groaned aloud. He was right. This didn't come close to fast food. She'd never tasted chicken with such a light, delicate flavor. Drawing her knees up against her chest, she tucked into the next piece he offered.

'Don't you trust me with the china?' she teased.

He extended a forkful of potato salad. 'Not when I'm seducing you.'

'With potatoes and fried chicken?' She nibbled the potato salad and this time did groan aloud. 'Ignore that question. This is delicious.'

'Want more?' At her eager nod, he patted the spot next to him. 'Then come closer.'

With a laugh she scrambled across the blanket to his side, and before long they shared a plate between them, exchanging finger food and dispensing with silverware whenever possible. Finally replete, she didn't resist when he drew her down so her head rested in his lap.

'Look at the sunset,' she said, gesturing at the vivid colors streaking across the sky above them.

'That's one of the reasons we're eating out here.' He filled a flute with champagne. Impaling a strawberry on the rim, he handed it to her. 'There's dessert.'

'No, thanks.' She sipped the champagne. 'This is all I need.' His fingers slipped into her hair and she closed her eyes beneath the delicate stroke of his hand, his abdomen warm against her cheek.

'Leah, watch,' he murmured.

She glanced up at the sky. As the last touch of purple faded into black, tiny pinpricks of light flickered to life around the rooftop. It was as though the stars had fallen from the heavens and been scattered like glittering dewdrops among the flowers. She raised a trembling hand to her mouth.

'Hunter, why?' She couldn't phrase the question any clearer, but he seemed to understand what she asked.

'I wanted tonight to be perfect.'

She released a shaky laugh. 'You succeeded.'

'Good. Because I'm going to make love to you and I want it to be special. Very special.' He made no move to carry out his promise. Instead he sat motionless, apparently enjoying the serenity of the evening. 'Eight years ago you told your grandmother about our meeting at the line-shack, didn't you?' he asked unexpectedly.

It was the last question she had ever envisioned him broaching. She didn't even consider lying to protect Rose. 'Yes.'

'You came to the line-shack and waited for me.'

'Yes,' she admitted again.

'When did you find out I'd been arrested?'

'When you told me.'

'I was afraid of that.' He released a long sigh. 'I owe you an apology, Leah. I didn't believe you. I thought you were lying about what happened back then.'

'Did Grandmother Rose tell you the truth?'

'Yes. She told me.'

'I'm glad.' Leah hesitated, then said, 'There's also an explanation for why I wouldn't leave with you— if you're willing to listen.'

The muscles in his jaw tightened, but he nodded. 'I'm listening.'

'I told my grandmother about our meeting because

I couldn't leave without saying goodbye to her. That was when I learned about Dad. He was dying of cancer, Hunter. I had to stay and help take care of him. That's why I wouldn't have gone with you. But I would have asked you to come back...afterward.' She stared at him with nervous dread. 'I hope you believe me, because it's the truth.'

For a long time he remained silent. Then he spoke in a low, rough voice, the words sounding as though they were torn from him. 'Growing up in an orphanage, honesty came in short supply. So did trust. No one cared much about the truth, just about finding a culprit.'

'And were you usually the culprit?' she asked compassionately.

'Not always. But often enough.'

'Didn't you try and explain?'

'Why?' he asked simply. 'No one would have believed me. I was a mongrel. Not that I was innocent, you understand. I provoked my share of trouble.'

She could believe he had, though she suspected that the trouble he'd provoked had never been undeserved. 'And then one day...' she prompted.

'How did you know there was a "one day"?'

She shrugged. 'It makes sense.' She felt his laugh rumble beneath her ear.

'You're right. Okay. One day—on my fifteenth birthday, as a matter of fact—they accused me of doing something I didn't. It was the last time that happened.'

'What did they accuse you of?'

'Breaking a snow crystal—remember, those globes you shake and the little flakes swirl around inside? This one had a knight fighting a dragon.'

She stilled. 'A knight and a dragon?'

'Yes. I'd always been fascinated by the crystal, but it belonged to one of the live-in workers and was off-limits. When it broke, I took the rap.'

'But you didn't break it.'

'No.'

'Why was that the last time they accused you?'

'I left. For good.'

'Blind trust,' she whispered.

'Blind trust,' he confirmed. 'I've never had anyone give me unconditional trust before—never had anyone stand by me in the face of overwhelming odds. I guess it's a futile dream. Still...it's my dream.'

She sat up and slipped her arms around his neck. 'If I could wrap my trust in a box, I'd give it to you as my wedding-gift,' she told him. 'But all I have is words.'

'Don't make promises you can't keep,' he warned.

Her brows drew together and she nodded. 'Then I'll promise to try. That's the best I can offer right now.'

'It's a start.'

He cupped her face and, after what seemed an endless moment, he lowered his mouth to hers. It was as though she'd been waiting an eternity for his possession. There'd be no further reprieve, no postponing the inevitable. After tonight she'd belong to him, joined with bonds more permanent than his ring on her finger.

Champagne and strawberries flavored his kiss, a kiss he ended all too soon, leaving her desperately hungry for more. 'Hunter,' she pleaded.

'Easy,' he answered, his lips drifting the length of her jaw. 'Slow and easy, love.'

And he did take it slow, seducing her with long, deep kisses, igniting the fires that burned so hotly between them. Slipping her robe from her shoulders, he cupped the pendant that had become a permanent fixture about her neck and in silent homage his mouth found the spot between her breasts where it so often nestled.

She gripped his shoulders, her eyes falling shut, blocking out the pagan sight of his dark head against her white skin. All she could do after that was feel…feel the touch of his tongue and teeth on her breasts, feel the hard, possessive sweep of his hands as he stripped off her robe, baring her to his gaze.

'You're even more beautiful than I remember,' he told her.

'Make love to me, Hunter. Now.' She shifted in his grasp, wanting to be closer, trembling with the strength of her need.

He lowered her to the blanket and she opened her eyes, staring up at him. He held himself above her, the embodiment of lean, masculine grace and raw power—a power muted only by the tenderness reflected in the black depths of his gaze. Then he came to her, joined with her, his body a welcome weight, hard and angled and taut beneath her hands.

And there, sequestered within their tiny slice of heaven, he showed her anew the true meaning of ecstasy. She didn't hold back. She couldn't. For, if she gave him nothing else, she'd give him all the love she possessed.

They spent the entire weekend at the apartment, relearning their roles as lovers. For Leah it deepened a love that had never truly died. Unfortunately,

Hunter's reaction proved more difficult to read. He wanted her; she didn't doubt that for a minute. She could inflame him with the simplest of touches—his dark eyes burning with a hunger that stole her breath. Nor could she complain of his treatment, his gentleness revealing a certain level of caring. But love? If he experienced such an emotion, he kept it well-hidden.

To Leah's dismay, leaving the seclusion of the apartment and returning to the ranch proved to be the hardest thing she'd ever done.

Worse, the morning after their return Hunter rode Dreamseeker, the stallion at long last surrendering to the stronger, more determined force. Leah couldn't help drawing a comparison, feeling as though she, too, had surrendered to Hunter's perseverance, giving everything while he remained aloof and independent and in control. Never had she felt so defenseless, so aware of her own vulnerability—nor had she ever felt so afraid. As much as she'd have liked to protect herself, she suspected it was far too late.

The morning after Hunter broke the stallion, her fears took a new direction. Dreamseeker was missing from the pasture.

'Saddle Ladyfinger,' Hunter directed. 'And grab your slicker. It looks like more rain.'

Struggling to hide her concern, she did as he'd ordered, lashing the yellow oilskin to the back of her saddle. 'Could he have smashed down the fence again?' she asked apprehensively.

Hunter shook his head. 'Not a chance.'

He mounted his buckskin and they started out, riding toward the area the horse had broken through before. They'd almost reached the southernmost point of Hampton land when the first scream reverberated across the pasture.

Leah had heard that sound only twice before in her life, and it was one she'd never forget. It turned her blood to ice. Throwing a panicked glance in Hunter's direction, she dug her heels into Ladyfinger's flanks and charged toward the sound, Hunter at her side. Throughout the tense moments of that mad dash to the Circle P she prayed she'd be wrong. Prayed that Dream-seeker was safe.

Arriving at the property line, they paused briefly. The fence separating the two ranches had indeed been knocked down again, and Leah's heart sank. There was no doubt now as to what had happened...nor what was about to happen. Another scream echoed from over the next ridge, answered by an equally infuriated trumpeting. Crossing on to Circle P land, they sprinted to the top of the hill and discovered Bull Jones sitting on his mount, watching the scene below unfold.

Dreamseeker stood at one end of a small, tree-enclosed meadow, circling a chestnut thoroughbred stallion. Off to one side milled a nervous herd of mares, undoubtedly the motivation for the fight. Dreamseeker reared on to his hind legs, gnashing his teeth and striking out with his hooves. The chestnut joined in the ritualistic dance, copying each threatening move.

'You did this, Leah,' Bull growled, gimlet-eyed. 'I told you to secure your fence-line. Now it's too late. If that stallion of yours injures our thoroughbred, you'll pay big. Real big. Baby Blue's worth a fortune. If he goes down, it'll cost you your ranch.'

Leah glared at the foreman. 'You deliberately

moved Baby Blue and those mares to this pasture in order to rile up our stallion. As to the fence…we reinforced it just last week. The only way Dreamseeker could have broken through is if you cut the wire.'

He laughed. 'Knowing something's one thing. Proving it is a whole different story.'

'She won't have to,' Hunter said in a clipped voice. 'I will.'

With a shrill roar, Dreamseeker reared back, then dropped to the ground with a bone-jarring thud and charged. Baby Blue, his eyes rolling back in his head, raced to meet his challenger.

'No!' Leah shrieked. Without thought or consideration of the danger, she slammed her heels into her horse's flanks, slipping and sliding down the hill.

'Leah!' she heard Hunter shout.

She ignored him, fighting to stay in the saddle while forcing her mare toward the heat of battle. Halfway down the hill, she realized that the terrified animal would go no further. Leah reined to a stop and flung herself out of the saddle. In two seconds flat she'd ripped her rain-slicker free. Screaming at the top of her lungs, she ran straight at the stallions, slapping the bright yellow oilskin in the air as hard as she could.

Just as she reached them the thoroughbred went down, and a sudden image of Hunter distracting the bull with his shirt flashed through her mind. Before Dreamseeker could move in for the kill she threw the slicker directly into her horse's face. He shied wildly, dropping his head and shaking it in an attempt to rid himself of the entrapping coat.

'Leah, move!' Hunter yelled, sprinting to her side. Clamping an arm around her waist, he threw her clear

of the danger. Without a moment's hesitation he
planted himself between her and imminent peril, nothing at hand with which to protect himself but his rope.

Dreamseeker bucked madly and finally succeeded
in flinging the slicker off his head. He froze for an
instant, as though trying to decide whether to charge
the man or the downed stallion. It was all the opportunity Hunter needed. In one swift move his rope
ripped through the air, snagging the stallion's forefeet.
Throwing every ounce of mass and muscle behind the
effort, Hunter wrenched the rope taut, dropping the
horse in his tracks.

Spinning around, he ran flat out toward Leah.
Snatching her to her feet with one hand, he hurled
the rope around the nearest tree with the other. With
more speed than artistry he secured the rope, effectively hobbling the horse.

Breathing hard, he slowly turned to face Leah.
'Woman, you and I are going to have a serious conversation. And, when it's done, your sit-down may be
a little the worse for wear.'

'Are you threatening me with physical violence?'
Leah asked in disbelief.

His wrath shredded his rigid control. 'You're
damned right I'm threatening you with physical violence!' he bit out. 'After what you pulled you'll be
lucky if that's all I threaten you with.'

'I couldn't just wait while one of those stallions
killed the other!'

He towered over her, his hands clenched, a muscle
leaping in his jaw. 'Oh, yes, you could have, and you
damned well should have. Before this day is through
I intend to explain it to you in terms you won't soon

forget. For now, you have a more pressing matter to take care of.'

'What's that?'

He gestured. 'Your horse,' he said flatly.

She couldn't believe she'd been so easily side-tracked. To her relief, she saw that Baby Blue had regained his feet and abandoned the field of battle, driving his harem of mares before him. She ran toward Dreamseeker, careful to keep a safe distance. Slowly she circled the downed animal, searching for any serious damage. He lay on his side, blowing hard and trembling, but without apparent injury. Before she could decide how to handle the stallion's safe return to his pasture, Bull Jones rode up.

'Move out of the way, Leah,' he ordered furiously. She looked up, horrified to discover Bull's Remington free of his scabbard and aimed at her stallion. 'I'm gonna shoot that bronco right between the eyes. If you don't want to get hurt, you'll stand clear.'

Leah never saw Hunter move. One minute Bull sat astride his horse, the next minute he lay flat on his back, his gun thrown out of reach and Hunter's foot planted in the center of his chest.

'We never had the chance to introduce ourselves,' Hunter said in a soft, menacing voice. 'It's time to correct that oversight.'

'I don't care who you are, *hombre*. Get the hell off me and get the hell off my land.' He squirmed in the dirt, attempting to worm his way out of his predicament. Not that it did him any good. Leah could tell he'd remain where he was until Hunter decided otherwise.

'First, it's not your land.' The boot pressed a little harder. 'And second, the name's Pryde. Hunter Pryde.

You call me *hombre* once more and you won't be talking—or chewing—any time soon.'

'*Pryde*!' Bull's eyes bulged. 'I know you! You're—'

'Leah's husband,' Hunter interrupted smoothly.

'Aw, shoot. I didn't know *you* were Pryde...' Bull protested. 'You shoulda said something.'

'Being a fair and reasonable man, I'm going to give you two choices. You can get up, climb on your horse, and ride out of here, nice and friendly-like, or you can stay and we'll discuss the situation further. Well, *muchacho*? What's it going to be?'

'Let me up. I'll leave.'

Hunter removed his foot and stepped back. And though he seemed relaxed—his hands at his sides, his legs slightly spread—Leah knew that he stood poised for action should Bull offer any further threat. The foreman slowly gained his feet and reached for his rifle.

'Don't bother. You won't be needing it,' Hunter said, an unmistakable warning in his voice. 'And one more thing.'

'What's that?' Bull asked warily.

'As you ride out of here, take a final, long look around.'

Understanding dawned and a heavy flush crept up Bull's neck. 'You can't do that. I have pull, you know.'

Hunter's chilly smile was empty of humor. 'I have more.'

'You haven't heard the last of this,' Bull growled, mounting up.

'Any time you want to finish the discussion, feel free to drop by. I'll be happy to accommodate you.'

Hunter waited until the foreman had ridden out of earshot before switching his attention to Leah. 'Your turn.'

'How can you do that?' she demanded, gesturing toward Bull's rapidly retreating back. 'How can *you* fire him?'

Hunter's gaze became enigmatic. 'Let's just say that Buddy Peterson will find it in his best interest to follow through with my…suggestion.'

A tiny frown creased her brow. After a moment's consideration she nodded. 'Let's hope you're right.'

'I am.'

He took a step in her direction and she froze. As much as she'd have liked to run for the hills, she refused to back down. 'I know. I know. It's my turn. Well, go ahead. Yell at me some more. Stomp around and cuss if you want. Just get it over with.'

'This isn't some sort of joke, Leah.' He snatched her close, practically shaking her. 'You could have been killed. And there wouldn't have been a damned thing I could have done to prevent it. I'd never have reached you in time.'

'I had to save Dreamseeker,' she protested.

He thrust her away, as though afraid of what he might do if he continued to touch her. 'You don't get it, do you? That horse is nothing compared to your safety. I should have let Jones shoot the damned animal and be done with it.'

She caught her breath in disbelief. 'You can't be serious.'

His eyes burned with barely suppressed rage, his features set in stark, remote lines. 'I'm dead serious. You promise me here and now that you won't ever, for any reason, risk your life for that horse again, or he goes.'

He wasn't kidding. She could tell when a man had reached the end of his rope and, without question, Hunter had reached it. Slowly she nodded. 'I promise.'

'I intend to hold you to that promise,' he warned.

She twisted her hands together. 'But you won't sell Dreamseeker?'

His voice turned dry, the rage slowly dying from his eyes. 'Don't worry, Leah. Your horse is safe for now, even if you aren't. Mount up. Let's get this bronco home. And when we get there, and my temper has had a chance to cool, you and I will finish this conversation.'

'That'll be some time next week, right?' she dared to suggest.

He yanked the brim of his stetson low over his brow. 'Try next month.' And with that he headed for his horse.

Hunter placed a call to Kevin Anderson, not bothering to waste time on preliminaries. 'I fired Bull Jones today.'

Kevin swore softly. 'What do you want me to do?'

'Take care of it. Make sure there aren't any... complications.'

'Is it Leah? Has she found out?'

'No. I don't think so. But considering I gave Jones his walking papers in front of her, it'll be a miracle if she doesn't at least suspect.'

'If she does—'

'Don't worry,' Hunter interrupted sharply. 'I'll handle my wife.'

A small sound brought his head around. Leah stood at the door, looking nervous and uncertain. Had she heard? he wondered, keeping his expression impassive. He gestured for her to come in.

'Listen, I have to go, Kevin. I'll be in touch.'

He hung up, not waiting for an answer. He stood up and walked around the desk, leaning against the edge. There he stayed, silent and watchful, as she approached. Catching her braid, he tugged her close. He wanted her. God, he wanted her. And he knew without a doubt that she wanted him as well. He could see it in her eyes, in the faint trembling of her lips and the rapid pounding of her heart.

Not bothering to conceal the strength of his desire, he pulled her roughly between his legs. Her eyes widened, the color almost violet with emotion. Her breath came swiftly between her parted lips, a delicate flush tinting her cheeks. It took only a minute to unbraid her hair, spreading the silvery curls around them like a silken cloak.

Unable to resist, he kissed her, taking her softness with a desire fast flaring out of control. 'Don't fight me,' he muttered against her mouth. 'Not now. Not any more.'

'Fight you?' she said, her voice wavering between laughter and passion. 'I wish I could.'

'Then kiss me, Leah. Kiss me like you mean it.'

She seemed to melt into him. 'I've always meant it. Haven't you realized that by now?' she whispered. And, wrapping her arms around his neck, she gave herself to him.

Leah stared at the ceiling, the moon throwing a shadowed pattern of branches across the smooth surface. What had he meant? she wondered uneasily.

She turned her head and studied Hunter as he slept. His passion tonight had exceeded anything that had ever gone before. More than once she'd nearly said the words, almost told him how much she loved him. But something had held her back. His conversation with 'Kevin', perhaps?

She frowned up at the ceiling again. So what had Hunter meant? What, precisely, did 'I'll handle my wife' signify? And why did it fill her with such an overwhelming dread?

CHAPTER TEN

LEAH awoke the next morning and for the first time found herself alone in bed. She sat up in a panic, not liking the sensation of having been deserted. Hunter was right. Waking in his arms made a difference to her entire day and she didn't appreciate the abrupt change.

She got up and went in search of him, only to discover that he'd left a brief note explaining he'd been unexpectedly called to Houston. The knowledge filled her with a vague alarm. She'd hoped to talk to him, to be held by him, to be reassured that his conversation with this…Kevin had nothing to do with their marriage—or the ranch.

So much for blind trust, she thought with a guilty pang. Let one small incident a little out of the ordinary happen and her trust evaporated like mist before the morning sun.

'I think I'll go into town and do some shopping,' she told her grandmother, needing an outlet for her restlessness.

'Stop by the jewelers and see if my watch is fixed,' Rose requested. 'They've had it a full week and my wrist feels naked.'

'Sure thing,' Leah agreed.

Not long after, she climbed into the ranch pick-up and drove the thirty minutes to the small town of

Crossroads. She spent a full hour window-shopping and indulging in an éclair at Cindy's Sinful Pastries before coming upon a new antiques store. Intrigued, she went in, and after much diligent poking around unearthed a small statue that she knew she'd purchase regardless of the price.

Made of pewter, a dull silver knight rode a rearing charger. In one hand he clasped a lance, holding a fierce, ruby-eyed dragon at bay. With his other he pulled a veiled damsel to safety. The damsel's flowing gown reminded Leah of her own wedding-dress and she grinned. Considering the snow crystal story he'd told her, it was perfect. She'd put it in the study and see how long it took Hunter to notice—and whether he caught the significance of the gesture. After paying for the statue she crossed the street to the jewelers.

'Morning, Leah.' Clyde, the owner, greeted her, with a familiar smile. 'I just finished Rose's repair job last night.' He punched the charge into his register and handed her the boxed watch. Eyeing the imprinted shopping bag she carried, he said, 'I see you visited our new antiques store. Find something you liked?'

'Sure did. Want to see?' At his interested nod she carefully unwrapped her purchase, and proudly displayed it for the jeweler.

'My, that's a fine piece.' He peered at it over his wire-rimmed spectacles. 'A belated wedding-gift?' he asked, with the presumptuousness of a lifelong friendship. At her shy acknowledgement he beamed. 'I'm glad. Hunter's a good man.'

A sudden idea occurred to her and she pulled

Hunter's pendant from beneath her blouse. 'Clyde... Can you make a miniature of this?'

'To go around the knight's neck?' he guessed. His mouth puckered in a thoughtful frown. 'Shouldn't be too difficult. Actually, I have a stone that would be ideal.'

'How long would it take?' she asked anxiously.

His eyes twinkled with amusement. 'I think Mrs Whitehaven's ring adjustment can wait. How does an hour sound?'

She sighed in relief. 'It sounds ideal.'

'And if I can make one small suggestion?' He crossed to a display of pewter charms and removed one of the larger pieces—a cowboy hat. It fit the knight as though made for him. 'I could snip off the link and smooth it down, fix it to the knight's head so it won't come off. What do you think?'

It was perfect. 'Do it,' she directed. 'I'll be back in an hour. And Clyde?' He glanced up from the statue and she grinned. 'Thanks.'

'Any time, Leah. Any time.'

Precisely sixty minutes later she left the jewelers for the second time, her statue—complete with cowboy hat and pendant—gift-wrapped and safely tucked away in her handbag. To her dismay, the first person she ran into was Bull Jones. Before she could evade him, he blocked her path.

'Why, if it isn't Miz Hampton.' He removed his cigar from between his teeth. 'Oh, excuse me. That's Mrs Pryde, isn't it?'

'Yes, it is,' she retorted sharply. 'If you were smart, you'd remember that and stay clear, before Hunter hears you've been bothering me again.'

'I'm not worried. Your husband isn't here. And by the time he returns, I'll be long gone.'

Her blood ran cold and she glanced around, reassured to see that their confrontation had witnesses. She glared at Bull. 'You have something to say to me? Then say it. Otherwise, move out of my way before I bring the whole town down around your ears.'

'You always were a feisty little shrew. Okay. Why beat around the bush? Your husband's in Houston, isn't he?' He laughed at her expression. 'What, nothing to say? Aren't you even going to ask how I know?'

'I couldn't care less.' She refused to play into this man's hands. Not that it stopped him.

'I'll tell you anyway,' he offered with mock generosity. 'He's there because he's called the Lyon Enterprises' board together.'

She shrugged indifferently. 'He knows the board. That's not news to me,' she claimed.

But Bull shook his head. 'He doesn't just know the board. He *runs* the board.'

She jerked as though slapped. 'What are you talking about?' she demanded.

'That got your attention, didn't it?' He laughed, the sound hard-edged and rough. 'Hunter Pryde *is* Lyon Enterprises. Course I didn't find that out until he had me fired.'

'I don't believe you.'

'Suit yourself. But think about it.' His cigar jabbed the air, making small smoky punctuation marks. 'Lyon…Pryde…the Circle *P*. It all fits. And if you wanted to confirm it, it'd be easy enough to check out.'

'How?' The question was dragged from her.

'Call Lyon Enterprises. Ask for Pryde's office. If he has one there, you'll have your answer. You'll know he married you to get his hands on your ranch.'

'All I'll know is that he has an office,' she said scornfully. 'That doesn't mean he owns Lyon Enterprises. Nor does it mean he married me to get the ranch.' She wondered if he heard the edge of desperation in her voice. Probably.

'He owns it,' Bull said with absolute confidence. 'And when he realized he couldn't buy you out or force you out, he married you.'

She had to leave. She wouldn't stand here and be poisoned by any more of this man's filth. 'Get away from me, Jones. I'm not listening to you.' She attempted to push past him, but he grabbed her arm and jerked her to a stop.

He spoke fast, his words striking with a deadly accuracy. 'You were all set to marry some joe so that you wouldn't lose your spread. If you had, Lyon would have been permanently blocked. The second Pryde heard about it, he shows up, and marries you himself. Pretty shrewd move. He gets the girl and the land without paying one red cent.'

'I still own the ranch, not Hunter.'

'Do you?' He leaned closer and she turned her head away in revulsion. 'Maybe you do now. But for how much longer? Those business types will find a way around that little problem. They always do. And then you and your granny will be out on your collective backsides.'

With that he released her and, clamping his cigar between his teeth, walked away. She stood in the middle of the sidewalk for an endless moment. Then she practically ran to the truck. Sitting safely in the cab, she gripped the steering-wheel as though her life depended on it, struggling for a measure of calm.

Putting the conversation into perspective, she knew Bull had an ax to grind and so she needed to weigh his comments accordingly. But what horrified her so was that every word he had uttered made perfect sense, playing on her most intrinsic fears. Hunter *had* wanted the ranch above all else. And never once had he been willing to tell her why.

Because he knew she'd never marry him if he did?

She stared blindly out the front windshield for several minutes. She had to think, had to keep a clear head. Either Bull spoke the truth or he lied. It was that simple. All she had to do was figure out which.

Conrad Michaels. The name came to her from nowhere and she seized it with relief. Of course! He had contacts. He could do some digging...off the record. Without giving it further consideration, she started the engine and pointed the truck in the direction of home. She'd call Conrad. He'd help her.

So much for blind trust, she thought in anguish. But how could she be expected to trust when her knight had suddenly turned back into the dragon?

Leah took a deep breath and spoke brightly into the phone, 'Conrad? It's Leah. I'm fine, thanks. And you?' She listened for several minutes while he told her, then admitted, 'Yes, I did call for a reason. I was curious about something and thought you could help.'

'Of course, Leah,' Conrad said agreeably enough. 'What can I do for you?'

She tapped her pencil against the desk blotter. 'It's...it's about our loan. The ranch loan. Did Hunter arrange for it with your bank? I mean… You had the old one and I thought…'

'It's not with our bank,' Conrad informed her bluntly. 'Not any more. Your lawyer insisted that Hunter initially place it with us as part of your prenuptial agreement. But I heard that shortly after your marriage it was bought out by an independent concern. All perfectly legal, you understand.'

'But it was with you originally?'

'Yes.'

Now for the hard part. After a brief pause, she asked, 'Do you know who bought it out?'

'What's this about, Leah? Why aren't you asking Hunter these questions?'

She heard the tension in his voice and regretted putting him in such an uncomfortable position. Unfortunately, she had to know. 'I'm asking you, Connie,' she said evenly, deliberately used the family nickname. 'I need to make sure the payments are current, that I'm not in arrears.'

'I see.' He sounded old and tired.

She closed her eyes, hating herself for involving him. But there'd been no one else she could turn to. 'I realize you're retired and out of the loop. Still, I'd hoped you'd have contacts who could give you the information. I'm sorry to ask for such a big favor. I wouldn't, unless it was important,' she apologized.

'Of course. I'll look into it.'

'You'll be discreet?'

'Don't worry. I'll be discreet.'

She thanked him and hung up, checking his name off the list she'd composed. One down. Studying the piece of paper in front of her, she eyed the second name and number. This next would take even more nerve. She forced herself to reach for the phone again and dial the number. An operator answered almost immediately.

'Lyon Enterprises. How may I direct your call?'

'Hunter Pryde, please.'

'One moment.'

After a brief delay a secretary answered. 'Felicia Carter speaking. May I help you?'

Leah frowned. 'I'm sorry. I asked for Hunter Pryde's office.'

'I can help you,' the secretary hastened to assure. 'May I ask who's calling?'

'Is he in?' Leah persisted.

'He's tied up with the board all day. I can give him a message if you'd like.'

Leah closed her eyes. 'No message.' She started to hang up, then froze. 'Wait! His title. Could you tell me his title with the company?'

'I'm afraid you'll have to discuss that with Mr Pryde.' A hint of suspicion tinged Felicia's voice. 'Could I have your name, please?'

Without another word, Leah cradled the receiver. So. Part of Bull's story checked out. Hunter could be reached at Lyon Enterprises. But that didn't mean he had an office there; it didn't even mean he worked there. And it was far from indisputable evidence that he owned the company. There's no need to panic, she told herself, breathing a little easier. She'd managed to glean two facts. He had business in Houston with Lyon and their meeting was ongoing.

Beneath her hand the phone rang and she lifted it. 'Yes? Hello?'

'It's Conrad.'

From the reluctance in his voice she could tell that

she wouldn't appreciate the information he'd gathered. 'Get it over with. I can take it,' she told him.

'It's not anything definitive,' he was quick to explain, 'so don't jump to any conclusions. The company that bought out your note is named HP, Inc.'

'HP, Inc? As in…Hunter Pryde, Incorporated?'

'It's…possible, I suppose. I couldn't get the status of the loan itself. But I have their number in Houston, if you want it.'

'I want it.' She jotted down the information and thanked him.

'Let me know if you need me,' Conrad said. 'I had hoped…' He didn't finish his sentence. He didn't have to.

'Me, too,' she said in a soft voice.

This time she didn't delay placing the call. Asking for Hunter's office, the operator once again put her through, and once again a secretary offered to take a message.

'This is Felicia Carter at Lyon Enterprises,' Leah said. 'I'm trying to track down Mr Pryde.'

'Why… I believe he's working over there today, Ms Carter.'

Leah managed a careless laugh. 'How silly of me. I must have gotten my days mixed up.' Then on impulse she said, 'I don't know how he keeps it straight. It must be difficult owning two such large companies.'

'Yes, it is. But Mr Pryde's an unusual man. And he only hires the best. Delegation. It makes his life much easier. One minute, please.' Leah could hear a brief, muffled conversation before the secretary came back on the line. 'Mr Pryde's assistant just came in. Would you like to speak to him?'

'Kevin?' she asked casually.

'Oh, you know him?'

She ducked the question. 'That won't be necessary. I'll get the information I need at this end.' To her horror, her voice broke. 'Thank you for your help,' she managed to say, and hung up.

The tears, once started, couldn't be stopped. She despised herself for being so weak. It wasn't the end of all her dreams. She still had her grandmother and the ranch. She still had her employees and Dreamseeker. But somehow it wasn't enough. She wanted Hunter. Most of all, she wanted Hunter's love.

Too bad all Hunter wanted was her ranch.

'What's going on, Leah?'

Leah looked up, distressed to see her grandmother standing in the doorway. Silently she shook her head, swiping at her damp cheeks and struggling to bring her emotions under control.

'Is it Hunter?' Rose asked, stepping into the room. 'Has something happened to him?'

'No! Yes!' Leah covered her face with her hands, fighting to maintain control. She couldn't afford to break down again. 'His health is fine, if that's what you mean.'

Rose crossed to the desk. 'Then, what's wrong?'

'Hunter owns Lyon Enterprises, that's what's wrong.' She slumped in the chair. 'I'm…I'm sorry. I didn't mean to blurt it out like that.'

'Hunter owns Lyon Enterprises,' Rose repeated. 'You're joking.'

'It's true,' Leah said in a tired voice. 'I just got off the phone with his office. Dammit! What am I going to do?'

'You're going to talk to him, of course.'

'*Talk*?' She stared at her grandmother in disbelief. 'What's to say? ''Oh, by the way, did you really marry me just to get your hands on my ranch?'' That's why he proposed. He never made any secret of the fact.'

Rose planted her hands on her hips. 'Then why act so betrayed?' she snapped. 'What's the difference if he wanted the ranch for himself or for his business? If you married the owner of Lyon Enterprises it sounds to me like you were the one to get the better end of that deal.'

That brought her up short. 'Excuse me?'

'You heard me. Think about it. Hunter's gotten one thing out of this so-called bargain—a lot of hard work and darned little thanks. But if he's Lyon, you get the ranch, the Circle P, and anything else he cares to throw into the hat...' She cackled. 'Best of all, you get Hunter. Yessir. Sounds like a damned good trade to me.'

'Until he manages to obtain title to the ranch and forecloses on us. Next comes the divorce and then we're begging on the streets.'

Rose snorted. 'You really are a ninny. Get your butt out of that chair, climb into the pick-up and drive to Houston. Talk to the man. Ask him why he married you. Flat out.'

'I already know—'

'He actually told you he married you for the ranch?' Rose asked with raised eyebrows. 'Or did you assume it?'

Leah shook her head in bewilderment. 'I don't remember. I...I don't think he said. Every time I asked, he'd just stand there.'

'Looking insulted, maybe? I would have.'

'Why?' she demanded. 'That's the reason we married. It's not a secret. No matter how much you try to wrap it up in pretty ribbons and bows, I married for business, not love. And so did Hunter.'

'I'm sure you're right. A man as rich as Croesus, as smart as a whip and as handsome as ever came down the pike is going to sacrifice himself in marriage in order to get his hands on one little old Texas ranch.' She heaved a sigh. 'Sounds reasonable to me.'

Leah bit down on her lip. 'Stop making so much sense! You're confusing me.'

'Good. Now for the punchline. Do you love him?'

There was only one possible answer to that question. 'Yes,' she said without a moment's hesitation. 'More than anything.'

Her grandmother grinned. 'That's all you need to remember. Here's your purse. Here's the keys to the pick-up. Go to Houston. I'll see you tomorrow. Or the next day. Or the one after that. Go hide out in that apartment of Hunter's and make some babies. I want to be a great-grandma. Soon. You hear me, girl?'

'I hear you. Judging by how loud you're shouting I'm sure Inez, her children and at least two-thirds of our wranglers heard you, too.'

But she obeyed. Without another word of argument, Leah took the keys and her purse and walked out of the study. Not giving herself a chance to reconsider and chicken out, she climbed into the pickup and started the engine. Pulling a Bull Jones, she spun the wheel and stomped on the gas, kicking up an impressive rooster tail of dirt and gravel as she headed down the drive.

Half a dozen times she almost turned back. But

something kept her going. One way or another she'd have her answers—whether she liked them or not. And maybe—just maybe—she could convince Hunter to give their marriage a chance. A real chance. She loved him. And she intended to fight for that love.

She only got lost twice, but the delay added to her growing tension. Finally she found the Lyon Enterprises building and pulled into the underground garage. She didn't know how she'd talk her way into the board meeting, but somehow she'd do it. Stopping at the security desk, she showed her credentials.

'Leah Pryde,' she told the guard. 'Mrs Hunter Pryde. I'm supposed to meet my husband.'

'Certainly, Mrs Pryde. I'll ring upstairs and let him know you're here.'

'I'd rather you didn't,' she said, offering her most persuasive smile. 'I'd like to surprise him.'

He looked momentarily uncertain, then nodded. 'Sure. I suppose that would be all right.'

'Thanks.'

With a calm that she was far from feeling she walked to the bank of elevators, and all too soon arrived on the executive floor. This time no secretary waited to greet her. She glanced down at her clothes and wished she'd thought to change before leaving home. Jeans and a cotton blouse didn't seem quite appropriate. Did they have dress codes on executive floors? At the very least she should have brushed her hair. Her braid was almost nonexistent, loose curls drifting into her face.

She peeked up and down the deserted hallway, aware that it wouldn't be wise to delay much longer. Someone would soon stop her and she didn't doubt for a minute that they'd call security or, worse…Hunter. Looking neither right nor left, she started for the boardroom. If she was going to get thrown out of the place, she'd rather have done something to earn it.

Five yards from the huge double doors, the first roadblock appeared. 'Excuse me,' the tall, perfectly groomed woman said. 'May I help you?'

'No,' Leah replied and kept walking.

The persistent woman scooted ahead, planting herself square in front of the boardroom doors. 'I'm Felicia Carter,' she tried again, offering her hand. 'And you are?'

'Late. Excuse me.' Leah brushed past the secretary and reached for the door, but Felicia proved too quick. The woman grasped Leah's hand and shook it.

'It's a pleasure, Miss…?'

'Leah.'

'Leah.' The handshake turned to an iron-like clasp. 'If you'd come this way, we can find out what your situation is and we can get it taken care of right away.'

'*We* appreciate your help,' Leah said with an amiable smile, and turned in the direction Felicia indicated. The second the woman moved from the door Leah broke free, and lunged for the knob. An instant later she scooted inside the boardroom and slammed the huge door in Felicia's face, locking it.

'Take care of that,' she muttered beneath her breath, and turned to face the board members.

To her horror there were about twice the number there'd been on her last visit. And every last one of them stared at her as though she'd just pulled up in a flying saucer. At the far end, where Buddy Peterson had last been, sat Hunter, his chair pushed back, his feet propped on the glass table. Buddy now sat to Hunter's right.

'Don't be shy.' Hunter's words, gentle and yet oddly menacing, dropped into the deafening silence. 'Come on in.'

'Okay.' She took a single step forward. 'I think that's far enough.'

For an endless minute their gazes met and held— and if his was implacably black and remote, she didn't doubt for an instant that hers was filled with a mixture of defiance and fear.

The phone at Hunter's elbow emitted a muted beep and he picked it up. 'Yes, Felicia, she's here. Relax. I'll take care of it.' He hung up and addressed the board members. 'Ladies. Gentlemen. My wife.' Cautious murmurs of greeting drifted around the room and after a long, tense moment, he asked, 'What can we do for you, Leah?'

She swallowed hard. Maybe she should have rehearsed this part at some point during the drive. She glanced at him uncertainly. 'I wondered...' She took a deep breath. 'I wondered if there was something you have to tell me.'

His eyes narrowed and he removed his feet from the table and straightened in his chair. 'No. Is there something you have to tell me?'

So, he wasn't going to admit who he really was. He'd warned her that he'd never explain himself again. Still, he had to know that she wouldn't be here if she didn't at least suspect the truth. He had to know that the cards were stacked against him. And yet he expected her to trust him...or not. It was that simple. And suddenly she realized that despite everything she'd been told, despite all the facts that proved his duplicity, she did trust him. And she loved him.

'No,' she whispered. 'I don't have anything to tell you.'

His mouth tightened. 'Then if you'd excuse us?'

With a passion that brought tears to her eyes she wished she'd never come, that she'd never listened to Bull Jones, that she'd never given an ounce of weight to any of the despicable suggestions he'd made. Did she believe Jones more than Hunter? Never. Now she'd failed. She'd failed her husband, and she'd failed herself. When it came to a choice, she'd chosen to doubt him. And he'd never forgive her for that.

Her shoulders sagged in defeat and she started to turn away. Then she froze. What had he said that night at his apartment? 'I've never had anyone give me unconditional trust before—never had anyone stand by me in the face of overwhelming odds. I guess it's a futile dream. Still…it's my dream.'

She set her jaw. No. She wouldn't walk away. She wouldn't give up. She loved him. She loved him more than anything in her life. More than Dreamseeker, more than her employees, even more than the damned ranch. He wanted blind trust? Fine. She'd give it to him.

'Yes,' she said, turning around again. 'I do have something to say. In private, if you don't mind.'

'Ladies, gentlemen. Sign the papers,' Hunter ordered, snapping his briefcase closed and lifting it from the table. 'If you'll excuse us. My wife and I have a few matters to discuss in private.' He stood and walked to a door that opened on to a small office off the conference-room. Shutting them in the restrictive confines, he tossed his briefcase on to the desk and turned to her. 'What the hell is this about, Leah?'

She gathered her nerve to speak, to say the words that were long, long overdue. 'The whole time we've been married you've asked for only one thing from me. You told me that it's more precious to you than anything else. I offered to box it up for a wedding-gift if I could. Well... Here it is. My gift to you. It's up to you what you do with it.' She opened her purse and pulled out the gift-box from the jewelers.

He stared at it, making no move to take what she offered. 'What is it?'

'Open it and find out.'

He took the box then, and ripped it apart, removing the statue. She heard the swift intake of his breath, saw the lines of his jaw tighten. And then he looked at her, his black eyes aflame with a fierce, raw joy. 'Do you mean this?' he demanded. 'You trust me?'

She nodded, biting down on her lip. 'With all my heart.'

A brief knock sounded at the door and Buddy Peterson stuck his head in the office. 'Papers are signed and the boardroom's all yours. By the way, that was a gutsy move. Some might call it chivalrous. You could have lost everything you own.'

Hunter inclined his head in acknowledgement. 'Instead I won.' He glanced at Leah. 'Everything.'

Buddy grinned. 'I guess things will change now that you own the whole shooting-match.'

'Count on it,' Hunter agreed.

The door closed behind the executive and they were alone again. 'I don't understand,' she whispered. 'I thought you already owned Lyon Enterprises.'

He shook his head. 'Not until two minutes ago.'

'And before that?'

'I was their chief rival…and their worst nightmare.'

She could hardly take it in. 'Why didn't you tell me?'

'Because until the papers were signed there was nothing to tell. Like the man said, I could have failed in my takeover bid and lost everything.'

'Not everything,' she suddenly realized, tears starting to her eyes. 'Not the ranch.'

'No,' he conceded. 'I made sure that was protected by our prenuptial agreement.'

'You told me to read it. I guess I should have.' She gazed up at him a little uncertainly. 'Hunter?'

His eyes glittered with amusement. 'Yes, Leah? Could it be there's something you forgot to tell me after all?' He reached for her braid, releasing the strands and draping the curls across her shoulders.

'I believe there is.' A slow smile crept across her mouth and she tilted her head to one side. 'Yes, now that I think about it, I'm positive there is.' She stepped into his arms and rested her cheek against his chest. 'Have I told you yet how much I love you?'

He dragged the air into his lungs, releasing his breath in a long, gusty sigh. 'No. I believe you forgot to mention that part.'

'I have another question, and this time you have to answer,' she said, pulling back to look up at him. 'Why did you marry me?'

He didn't hesitate. 'Because you were going to marry the next man who walked through your door. And I couldn't let you do that unless I was that next man.' His tone reflected his determination. 'Fact is, I planned to be the only man to walk through your door.'

'But you wanted to buy the ranch.' It wasn't a question.

'True. At first, I wanted it in order to block Lyon and force them into a vulnerable position. Later it was so that I could protect you from them.'

'That's what Buddy Peterson meant when he said that the takeover attempt was a chivalrous move?'

Hunter shook his head. 'It wasn't. Buying the ranch would have facilitated my takeover. Marrying you...'

'Was riskier?' she guessed.

'A little. But worth it.' He reached behind her and removed a file folder from his briefcase, handing it to her.

'What's this?'

'Open it and find out,' he said, throwing her own words back at her.

She flipped open the file. Inside she found the deed to Hampton Homestead—free and clear, and in her name. The date on the title was the day before their wedding. 'Hunter...' she whispered.

'I love you, Leah. I've always loved you. How could I not? You've given me my dream.'

She managed a wobbly smile, tears clinging to her lashes. 'I think it's time for some new dreams, don't you?'

He enfolded her in his arms. 'Only if they're made with you,' he said.

And he kissed her. He kissed her with a love and passion that she couldn't mistake. And wrapped in his embrace she knew she'd found her life, her heart and her soul. She'd found her knight in shining armor.

At long last her dragon had been vanquished.

EPILOGUE

LEAH took a sip of coffee as she leafed through the morning paper. And then she saw it—the ad practically jumping off the page at her.

WIFE WANTED!

Male rancher in immediate and desperate need of his woman! Interested applicant should:

1. Be 27 today and have eyes the color of Texas bluebonnets—a feisty and ornery personality is a plus!
2. Have extensive ranching background—and the good sense to know when *not* to use it!
3. Have solid business know-how—particularly the ability to dampen the tempers of bullheaded board members.
4. Be pregnant. Did I mention the doctor called?

I am a thirty-four-year-old man and can offer you a comfortable bed and an occasional rooftop picnic with all the stars a Texas sky can hold. (Details of a more intimate nature are open to negotiation as soon as you hightail it upstairs). Your husband awaits. Impatiently!

Tossing the ad to one side, Leah leapt from her chair and ran...ran to her husband, the love of her life...but, most important of all, to the father of her baby.

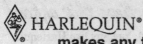

You're not going to believe this offer!

In October and November 2000, buy any two Harlequin or Silhouette books and save $10.00 off future purchases, or buy any three and save $20.00 off future purchases!

Just fill out this form and attach 2 proofs of purchase (cash register receipts) from October and November 2000 books and Harlequin will send you a coupon booklet worth a total savings of $10.00 off future purchases of Harlequin and Silhouette books in 2001. Send us 3 proofs of purchase and we will send you a coupon booklet worth a total savings of $20.00 off future purchases.

Saving money has never been this easy.

I accept your offer! Please send me a coupon booklet:

Name: _____

Address: _____ City: _____

State/Prov.: _____ Zip/Postal Code: _____